Henry James OM (15 April 1843 – 28 February 1916) was an American-British author regarded as a key transitional figure between literary realism and literary modernism, and is considered by many to be among the greatest novelists in the English language. He was the son of Henry James Sr. and the brother of renowned philosopher and psychologist William James and diarist Alice James.

He is best known for a number of novels dealing with the social and marital interplay between émigré Americans, English people, and continental Europeans. Examples of such novels include The Portrait of a Lady, The Ambassadors, and The Wings of the Dove. His later works were increasingly experimental. In describing the internal states of mind and social dynamics of his characters, James often made use of a style in which ambiguous or contradictory motives and impressions were overlaid or juxtaposed in the discussion of a character's psyche.(Source: Wikipedia)

Literary works:
Watch and Ward (1871)
Roderick Hudson (1875)
The American (1877)
The Europeans (1878)
Confidence (1879)
Washington Square (1880)
The Portrait of a Lady (1881)
The Bostonians (1886)
The Princess Casamassima (1886)
The Reverberator (1888)
The Tragic Muse (1890)
The Other House (1896)
The Spoils of Poynton (1897)
What Maisie Knew (1897)

A London Life;
The Patagonia;
The Liar;
Mrs. Temperly

HENRY JAMES

PRINCE CLASSICS

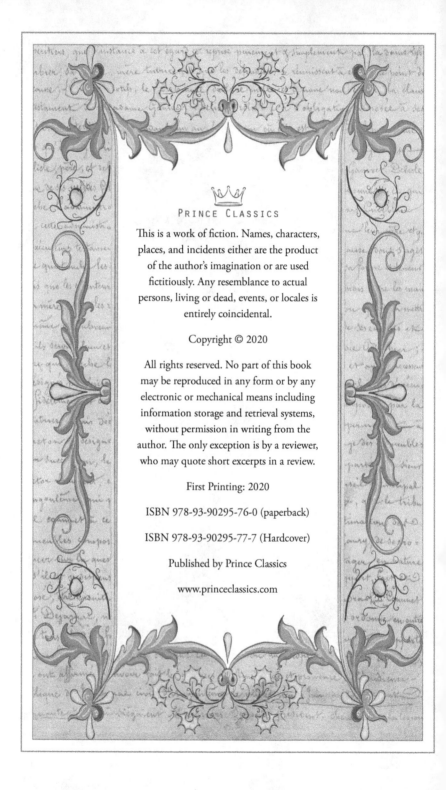

PRINCE CLASSICS

First Printing: 2020

ISBN 978-93-90295-76-0 (paperback)

ISBN 978-93-90295-77-7 (Hardcover)

Published by Prince Classics

www.princeclassics.com

Contents

A LONDON LIFE;
THE PATAGONIA;
THE LIAR;
MRS. TEMPERLY

NOTE

The last of the following four Tales originally appeared under a different name.

A LONDON LIFE

I

It was raining, apparently, but she didn't mind—she would put on stout shoes and walk over to Plash. She was restless and so fidgety that it was a pain; there were strange voices that frightened her—they threw out the ugliest intimations—in the empty rooms at home. She would see old Mrs. Berrington, whom she liked because she was so simple, and old Lady Davenant, who was staying with her and who was interesting for reasons with which simplicity had nothing to do. Then she would come back to the children's tea—she liked even better the last half-hour in the schoolroom, with the bread and butter, the candles and the red fire, the little spasms of confidence of Miss Steet the nursery-governess, and the society of Scratch and Parson (their nicknames would have made you think they were dogs) her small, magnificent nephews, whose flesh was so firm yet so soft and their eyes so charming when they listened to stories. Plash was the dower-house and about a mile and a half, through the park, from Mellows. It was not raining after all, though it had been; there was only a grayness in the air, covering all the strong, rich green, and a pleasant damp, earthy smell, and the walks were smooth and hard, so that the expedition was not arduous.

The girl had been in England more than a year, but there were some satisfactions she had not got used to yet nor ceased to enjoy, and one of these was the accessibility, the convenience of the country. Within the lodge-gates or without them it seemed all alike a park—it was all so intensely 'property.' The very name of Plash, which was quaint and old, had not lost its effect upon her, nor had it become indifferent to her that the place was a dower-house— the little red walled, ivied asylum to which old Mrs. Berrington had retired when, on his father's death, her son came into the estates. Laura Wing thought very ill of the custom of the expropriation of the widow in the evening of her days, when honour and abundance should attend her more than ever; but her condemnation of this wrong forgot itself when so many of the consequences looked right—barring a little dampness: which was the fate sooner or later of most of her unfavourable judgments of English institutions. Iniquities in such a country somehow always made pictures; and there had been dower-houses in the novels, mainly of fashionable life, on which her later childhood was fed. The iniquity did not as a general thing prevent these retreats from being occupied by old ladies with wonderful reminiscences and rare voices, whose reverses had not deprived them of a great deal of becoming hereditary lace. In the park, half-way, suddenly, Laura stopped, with a pain—a moral pang—that almost took away her breath; she looked at the misty glades and the dear old beeches (so familiar they were now and loved as much as if she owned them); they seemed in their unlighted December bareness conscious of all the trouble, and they made her conscious of all the change. A year ago she knew nothing, and now she knew almost everything; and the worst of her knowledge (or at least the worst of the fears she had raised upon it) had come to her in that beautiful place, where everything was so full of peace and purity, of the air of happy submission to immemorial law. The place was the same but her eyes were different: they had seen such sad, bad things in so short a time. Yes, the time was short and everything was strange. Laura Wing was too uneasy even to sigh, and as she walked on she lightened her tread almost as if she were going on tiptoe.

At Plash the house seemed to shine in the wet air—the tone of the mottled red walls and the limited but perfect lawn to be the work of an artist's brush. Lady Davenant was in the drawing-room, in a low chair by one of the windows, reading the second volume of a novel. There was the same look of crisp chintz, of fresh flowers wherever flowers could be put, of a wall-paper that was in the bad taste of years before, but had been kept so that no more money should be spent, and was almost covered over with amateurish drawings and superior engravings, framed in narrow gilt with large margins. The room had its bright, durable, sociable air, the air that Laura Wing liked in so many English things—that of being meant for daily life, for long periods, for uses of high decency. But more than ever to-day was it incongruous that such an habitation, with its chintzes and its British poets, its well-worn carpets and domestic art—the whole aspect so unmeretricious and sincere—should have to do with lives that were not right. Of course however it had to do only indirectly, and the wrong life was not old Mrs. Berrington's nor yet Lady Davenant's. If Selina and Selina's doings were not an implication of such an interior any more than it was for them an explication, this was because she had come from so far off, was a foreign element altogether. Yet it was there she had found her occasion, all the influences that had altered her so (her sister had a theory that she was metamorphosed, that when she was young she seemed born for innocence) if not at Plash at least at Mellows, for the two places after all had ever so much in common, and there were rooms at the great house that looked remarkably like Mrs. Berrington's parlour.

Lady Davenant always had a head-dress of a peculiar style, original and appropriate—a sort of white veil or cape which came in a point to the place on her forehead where her smooth hair began to show and then covered her shoulders. It was always exquisitely fresh and was partly the reason why she struck the girl rather as a fine portrait than as a living person. And yet she was full of life, old as she was, and had been made finer, sharper and more delicate, by nearly eighty years of it. It was the hand of a master that Laura seemed to see in her face, the witty expression of which shone like a lamp through the ground-glass of her good breeding; nature was always an artist, but not so much of an artist as that. Infinite knowledge the girl attributed to her, and that was why she liked her a little fearfully. Lady Davenant was not as a general thing fond of the young or of invalids; but she made an exception as regards youth for the little girl from America, the sister of the daughter-in-law of her dearest friend. She took an interest in Laura partly perhaps to make up for the tepidity with which she regarded Selina. At all events she had assumed the general responsibility of providing her with a husband. She pretended to care equally little for persons suffering from other forms of misfortune, but she was capable of finding excuses for them when they had been sufficiently to blame. She expected a great deal of attention, always wore gloves in the house and never had anything in her hand but a book. She neither embroidered nor wrote—only read and talked. She had no special conversation for girls but generally addressed them in the same manner that she found effective with her contemporaries. Laura Wing regarded this as an honour, but very often

13

she didn't know what the old lady meant and was ashamed to ask her. Once in a while Lady Davenant was ashamed to tell. Mrs. Berrington had gone to a cottage to see an old woman who was ill—an old woman who had been in her service for years, in the old days. Unlike her friend she was fond of young people and invalids, but she was less interesting to Laura, except that it was a sort of fascination to wonder how she could have such abysses of placidity. She had long cheeks and kind eyes and was devoted to birds; somehow she always made Laura think secretly of a tablet of fine white soap—nothing else was so smooth and clean.

'And what's going on *chez vous*—who is there and what are they doing?' Lady Davenant asked, after the first greetings.

'There isn't any one but me—and the children—and the governess.'

'What, no party—no private theatricals? How do you live?'

'Oh, it doesn't take so much to keep me going,' said Laura. 'I believe there were some people coming on Saturday, but they have been put off, or they can't come. Selina has gone to London.'

'And what has she gone to London for?'

'Oh, I don't know—she has so many things to do.'

'And where is Mr. Berrington?'

'He has been away somewhere; but I believe he is coming back to-morrow—or next day.'

'Or the day after?' said Lady Davenant. 'And do they never go away together?' she continued after a pause.

'Yes, sometimes—but they don't come back together.'

'Do you mean they quarrel on the way?'

'I don't know what they do, Lady Davenant—I don't understand,' Laura Wing replied, with an unguarded tremor in her voice. 'I don't think they are very happy.'

'Then they ought to be ashamed of themselves. They have got everything so comfortable—what more do they want?'

'Yes, and the children are such dears!'

'Certainly—charming. And is she a good person, the present governess? Does she look after them properly?'

'Yes—she seems very good—it's a blessing. But I think she's unhappy too.'

'Bless us, what a house! Does she want some one to make love to her?'

'No, but she wants Selina to see—to appreciate,' said the young girl.

'And doesn't she appreciate—when she leaves them that way quite to the young woman?'

'Miss Steet thinks she doesn't notice how they come on—she is never there.'

'And has she wept and told you so? You know they are always crying, governesses—whatever line you take. You shouldn't draw them out too much—they are always looking for a chance. She ought to be thankful to be let alone. You mustn't be too sympathetic—it's mostly wasted,' the old lady went on.

'Oh, I'm not—I assure you I'm not,' said Laura Wing. 'On the contrary, I see so much about me that I don't sympathise with.'

'Well, you mustn't be an impertinent little American either!' her interlocutress exclaimed. Laura sat with her for half an hour and the conversation took a turn through the affairs of Plash and through Lady Davenant's own, which were visits in prospect and ideas suggested more or less directly by them as well as by the books she had been reading, a heterogeneous pile on a table near her, all of them new and clean, from a circulating library in London. The old woman had ideas and Laura liked them, though they often struck her as very sharp and hard, because at Mellows she had no diet of that sort. There had never been an idea in the house, since she came at least, and there was wonderfully little reading. Lady Davenant still went from country-house to country-house all winter, as she had done all her life, and when Laura asked her she told her the places and the people she probably should find at each of them. Such an enumeration was much less interesting to the girl than it would have been a year before: she herself had now seen a great many places and people and the freshness of her curiosity was gone. But she still cared for Lady Davenant's descriptions and judgments, because they were the thing in her life which (when she met the old woman from time to time) most represented talk—the rare sort of talk that was not mere chaff. That was what she had dreamed of before she came to England, but in Selina's set the dream had not come true. In Selina's set people only harried each other from morning till night with extravagant accusations—it was all a kind of horse-play of false charges. When Lady Davenant was accusatory it was within the limits of perfect verisimilitude.

Laura waited for Mrs. Berrington to come in but she failed to appear, so that the girl gathered her waterproof together with an intention of departure. But she was secretly reluctant, because she had walked over to Plash with a vague hope that some soothing hand would be laid upon her pain. If there was no comfort at the dower-house she knew not where to look for it, for there was certainly none at home—not even with Miss Steet and the children. It was not Lady Davenant's leading characteristic that she was comforting, and Laura had not aspired to be coaxed or coddled into forgetfulness: she wanted rather to be taught a certain fortitude—how to live and hold up one's head even while knowing that things were very bad. A brazen indifference—it was not exactly that that she wished to acquire; but were there not some sorts of indifference that were philosophic and noble? Could Lady Davenant not teach them, if she should take the trouble? The girl remembered to have heard that there had been years before some disagreeable occurrences in *her* family; it was not a race in which the ladies inveterately turned out well. Yet who to-day had the stamp of honour and credit—of a past which was either no one's business or was part and parcel of a fair public record—and carried it so much as a matter of course? She herself had been a good woman and that was the only thing that told in the long run. It was Laura's own idea to be a good woman and that this would make it an advantage for Lady Davenant to show her how not to feel too much. As regards feeling enough, that was a branch in which she had no need to take lessons.

The old woman liked cutting new books, a task she never remitted to her maid, and while her young visitor sat there she went through the greater part of a volume with the paper-knife. She didn't proceed very fast—there was a kind of patient, awkward fumbling of her aged hands; but as she passed her knife into the last leaf she said abruptly—'And how is your sister going on? She's very light!' Lady Davenant added before Laura had time to reply.

'Oh, Lady Davenant!' the girl exclaimed, vaguely, slowly, vexed with herself as soon as she had spoken for having uttered the words as a protest, whereas she wished to draw her companion out. To correct this impression she threw back her waterproof.

'Have you ever spoken to her?' the old woman asked.

'Spoken to her?'

'About her behaviour. I daresay you haven't—you Americans have such a lot of false delicacy. I daresay Selina wouldn't speak to you if you were in her place (excuse the supposition!) and yet she is capable——' But Lady Davenant paused, preferring not to say of what young Mrs. Berrington was capable. 'It's a bad house for a girl.'

'It only gives me a horror,' said Laura, pausing in turn.

'A horror of your sister? That's not what one should aim at. You ought to get married—and the sooner the better. My dear child, I have neglected you dreadfully.'

'I am much obliged to you, but if you think marriage looks to me happy!' the girl exclaimed, laughing without hilarity.

'Make it happy for some one else and you will be happy enough yourself. You ought to get out of your situation.'

Laura Wing was silent a moment, though this was not a new reflection to her. 'Do you mean that I should leave Selina altogether? I feel as if I should abandon her—as if I should be a coward.'

'Oh, my dear, it isn't the business of little girls to serve as parachutes to fly-away wives! That's why if you haven't spoken to her you needn't take the trouble at this time of day. Let her go—let her go!'

'Let her go?' Laura repeated, staring.

Her companion gave her a sharper glance. 'Let her stay, then! Only get out of the house. You can come to me, you know, whenever you like. I don't know another girl I would say that to.'

'Oh, Lady Davenant,' Laura began again, but she only got as far as this; in a moment she had covered her face with her hands—she had burst into tears.

'Ah my dear, don't cry or I shall take back my invitation! It would never do if you were to *larmoyer*. If I have offended you by the way I have spoken of Selina I think you are too sensitive. We shouldn't feel more for people than they feel for themselves. She has no tears, I'm sure.'

'Oh, she has, she has!' cried the girl, sobbing with an odd effect as she put forth this pretension for her sister.

'Then she's worse than I thought. I don't mind them so much when they are merry but I hate them when they are sentimental.'

'She's so changed—so changed!' Laura Wing went on.

'Never, never, my dear: *c'est de naissance*.'

'You never knew my mother,' returned the girl; 'when I think of mother——' The words failed her while she sobbed.

'I daresay she was very nice,' said Lady Davenant gently. 'It would take that to account for you: such women as Selina are always easily enough accounted for. I didn't mean it was inherited—for that sort of thing skips about. I daresay there was some improper ancestress—except that you Americans don't seem to have ancestresses.'

Laura gave no sign of having heard these observations; she was occupied in brushing away her tears. 'Everything is so changed—you don't know,' she remarked in a moment. 'Nothing could have been happier—nothing could have been sweeter. And now to be so dependent—so helpless—so poor!'

'Have you nothing at all?' asked Lady Davenant, with simplicity.

'Only enough to pay for my clothes.'

'That's a good deal, for a girl. You are uncommonly dressy, you know.'

'I'm sorry I seem so. That's just the way I don't want to look.'

'You Americans can't help it; you "wear" your very features and your eyes look as if they had just been sent home. But I confess you are not so smart as Selina.'

'Yes, isn't she splendid?' Laura exclaimed, with proud inconsequence. 'And the worse she is the better she looks.'

'Oh my child, if the bad women looked as bad as they are——! It's only the good ones who can afford that,' the old lady murmured.

'It was the last thing I ever thought of—that I should be ashamed,' said Laura.

'Oh, keep your shame till you have more to do with it. It's like lending your umbrella—when you have only one.'

'If anything were to happen—publicly—I should die, I should die!' the girl exclaimed passionately and with a motion that carried her to her feet. This time she settled herself for departure. Lady Davenant's admonition rather frightened than sustained her.

The old woman leaned back in her chair, looking up at her. 'It would be very bad, I daresay. But it wouldn't prevent me from taking you in.'

Laura Wing returned her look, with eyes slightly distended, musing. 'Think of having to come to that!'

Lady Davenant burst out laughing. 'Yes, yes, you must come; you are so original!'

'I don't mean that I don't feel your kindness,' the girl broke out, blushing. 'But to be only protected—always protected: is that a life?'

'Most women are only too thankful and I am bound to say I think you are *difficile.*' Lady Davenant used a good many French words, in the old-fashioned manner and with a pronunciation not perfectly pure: when she did so she reminded Laura Wing of Mrs. Gore's novels. 'But you shall be better protected than even by me. *Nous verrons cela.* Only you must stop crying—this isn't a crying country.'

'No, one must have courage here. It takes courage to marry for such a reason.'

'Any reason is good enough that keeps a woman from being an old maid. Besides, you will like him.'

'He must like me first,' said the girl, with a sad smile.

'There's the American again! It isn't necessary. You are too proud—you expect too much.'

'I'm proud for what I am—that's very certain. But I don't expect anything,' Laura Wing declared. 'That's the only form my pride takes. Please give my love to Mrs. Berrington. I am so sorry—so sorry,' she went on, to change the talk from the subject of her marrying. She wanted to marry but she wanted also not to want it and, above all, not to appear to. She lingered in the room, moving about a little; the place was always so pleasant to her that to go away—to return to her own barren home—had the effect of forfeiting a sort of privilege of sanctuary. The afternoon had faded but the lamps had been brought in, the smell of flowers was in the air and the old house of Plash seemed to recognise the hour that suited it best. The quiet old lady in the firelight, encompassed with the symbolic security of chintz and water-colour, gave her a sudden vision of how blessed it would be to jump all the middle dangers of life and have arrived at the end, safely, sensibly, with a cap and gloves and consideration and memories. 'And, Lady Davenant, what does *she* think?' she asked abruptly, stopping short and referring to Mrs. Berrington.

'Think? Bless your soul, she doesn't do that! If she did, the things she says would be unpardonable.'

'The things she says?'

'That's what makes them so beautiful—that they are not spoiled by preparation. You could never think of them *for* her.' The girl smiled at this description of the dearest friend of her interlocutress, but she wondered a little what Lady Davenant would say to visitors about *her* if she should accept a refuge under her roof. Her speech was after all a flattering proof of confidence. 'She wishes it had been you—I happen to know that,' said the old woman.

'It had been me?'

'That Lionel had taken a fancy to.'

'I wouldn't have married him,' Laura rejoined, after a moment.

'Don't say that or you will make me think it won't be easy to help you. I shall depend upon you not to refuse anything so good.'

'I don't call him good. If he were good his wife would be better.'

'Very likely; and if you had married him *he* would be better, and that's more to the purpose. Lionel is as idiotic as a comic song, but you have cleverness for two.'

'And you have it for fifty, dear Lady Davenant. Never, never—I shall never marry a man I can't respect!' Laura Wing exclaimed.

She had come a little nearer her old friend and taken her hand; her companion held her a moment and with the other hand pushed aside one of the flaps of the waterproof. 'And what is it your clothing costs you?' asked Lady Davenant, looking at the dress underneath and not giving any heed to this declaration.

'I don't exactly know: it takes almost everything that is sent me from America. But that is dreadfully little—only a few pounds. I am a wonderful manager. Besides,' the girl added, 'Selina wants one to be dressed.'

21

'And doesn't she pay any of your bills?'

'Why, she gives me everything—food, shelter, carriages.'

'Does she never give you money?'

'I wouldn't take it,' said the girl. 'They need everything they have—their life is tremendously expensive.'

'That I'll warrant!' cried the old woman. 'It was a most beautiful property, but I don't know what has become of it now. *Ce n'est pas pour vous blesser*, but the hole you Americans *can* make——'

Laura interrupted immediately, holding up her head; Lady Davenant had dropped her hand and she had receded a step. 'Selina brought Lionel a very considerable fortune and every penny of it was paid.'

'Yes, I know it was; Mrs. Berrington told me it was most satisfactory. That's not always the case with the fortunes you young ladies are supposed to bring!' the old lady added, smiling.

The girl looked over her head a moment. 'Why do your men marry for money?'

'Why indeed, my dear? And before your troubles what used your father to give you for your personal expenses?'

'He gave us everything we asked—we had no particular allowance.'

'And I daresay you asked for everything?' said Lady Davenant.

'No doubt we were very dressy, as you say.'

'No wonder he went bankrupt—for he did, didn't he?'

'He had dreadful reverses but he only sacrificed himself—he protected others.'

'Well, I know nothing about these things and I only ask *pour me renseigner*,' Mrs. Berrington's guest went on. 'And after their reverses your father and mother lived I think only a short time?'

Laura Wing had covered herself again with her mantle; her eyes were now bent upon the ground and, standing there before her companion with her umbrella and her air of momentary submission and self-control, she might very well have been a young person in reduced circumstances applying for a place. 'It was short enough but it seemed—some parts of it—terribly long and painful. My poor father—my dear father,' the girl went on. But her voice trembled and she checked herself.

'I feel as if I were cross-questioning you, which God forbid!' said Lady Davenant. 'But there is one thing I should really like to know. Did Lionel and his wife, when you were poor, come freely to your assistance?'

'They sent us money repeatedly—it was *her* money of course. It was almost all we had.'

'And if you have been poor and know what poverty is tell me this: has it made you afraid to marry a poor man?'

It seemed to Lady Davenant that in answer to this her young friend looked at her strangely; and then the old woman heard her say something that had not quite the heroic ring she expected. 'I am afraid of so many things to-day that I don't know where my fears end.'

'I have no patience with the highstrung way you take things. But I have to know, you know.'

'Oh, don't try to know any more shames—any more horrors!' the girl wailed with sudden passion, turning away.

Her companion got up, drew her round again and kissed her. 'I think you would fidget me,' she remarked as she released her. Then, as if this were too cheerless a leave-taking, she added in a gayer tone, as Laura had her hand on the door: 'Mind what I tell you, my dear; let her go!' It was to this that the girl's lesson in philosophy reduced itself, she reflected, as she walked back to Mellows in the rain, which had now come on, through the darkening park.

II

The children were still at tea and poor Miss Steet sat between them, consoling herself with strong cups, crunching melancholy morsels of toast and dropping an absent gaze on her little companions as they exchanged small, loud remarks. She always sighed when Laura came in—it was her way of expressing appreciation of the visit—and she was the one person whom the girl frequently saw who seemed to her more unhappy than herself. But Laura envied her—she thought her position had more dignity than that of her employer's dependent sister. Miss Steet had related her life to the children's pretty young aunt and this personage knew that though it had had painful elements nothing so disagreeable had ever befallen her or was likely to befall her as the odious possibility of her sister's making a scandal. She had two sisters (Laura knew all about them) and one of them was married to a clergyman in Staffordshire (a very ugly part) and had seven children and four hundred a year; while the other, the eldest, was enormously stout and filled (it was a good deal of a squeeze) a position as matron in an orphanage at Liverpool. Neither of them seemed destined to go into the English divorce-court, and such a circumstance on the part of one's near relations struck Laura as in itself almost sufficient to constitute happiness. Miss Steet never lived in a state of nervous anxiety—everything about her was respectable. She made the girl almost angry sometimes, by her drooping, martyr-like air: Laura was near breaking out at her with, 'Dear me, what have you got to complain of? Don't you earn your living like an honest girl and are you obliged to see things going on about you that you hate?'

But she could not say things like that to her, because she had promised Selina, who made a great point of this, that she would never be too familiar with her. Selina was not without her ideas of decorum—very far from it indeed; only she erected them in such queer places. She was not familiar with her children's governess; she was not even familiar with the children themselves. That was why after all it was impossible to address much of a remonstrance to Miss Steet when she sat as if she were tied to the stake and the fagots were being lighted. If martyrs in this situation had tea and cold meat served them they would strikingly have resembled the provoking young woman in the schoolroom at Mellows. Laura could not have denied that it was natural she should have liked it better if Mrs. Berrington would *sometimes* just look in and give a sign that she was pleased with her system; but poor Miss Steet only knew by the servants or by Laura whether Mrs. Berrington were at home or not: she was for the most part not, and the governess had a way of silently intimating (it was the manner she put her head on one side when she looked at Scratch and Parson—of course *she* called them Geordie and Ferdy) that she was immensely handicapped and even that they were. Perhaps they were, though they certainly showed it little in their appearance and manner, and Laura was at least sure that if Selina had been perpetually dropping in Miss Steet would have taken that discomfort even more tragically. The sight of this young woman's either real or fancied wrongs did not diminish her conviction that she herself would have found courage to become a governess. She would have had to teach very young children, for she believed she was too ignorant for higher flights. But Selina would never have consented to that—she would have considered it a disgrace or even worse—a *pose*. Laura had proposed to her six months before that she should dispense with a paid governess and suffer *her* to take charge of the little boys: in that way she should not feel so completely dependent—she should be doing something in return. 'And pray what would happen when you came to dinner? Who would look after them then?' Mrs. Berrington had demanded, with a very shocked air. Laura had replied that perhaps it was not absolutely necessary that she should come to dinner—she could dine early, with the children; and that if her presence in the drawing-room should be required the children had their nurse—and what did they have their nurse for? Selina looked at her as if she was deplorably superficial and told her that they had their nurse to dress them and look after their clothes—did she wish the poor little ducks to go in rags? She had her own ideas of thoroughness and when Laura hinted that after all at that hour the children were in bed she declared that even when they were asleep she desired the governess to be at hand—that was the way a mother felt who really took an interest. Selina was wonderfully thorough; she said something about the evening hours in the quiet schoolroom being the proper time for the governess to 'get up' the children's lessons for the next day. Laura Wing was conscious of her own ignorance; nevertheless she presumed to believe that she could have taught Geordie and Ferdy the alphabet without anticipatory nocturnal researches. She wondered what her sister supposed Miss Steet taught them—whether she had a cheap theory that they were in Latin and algebra.

The governess's evening hours in the quiet schoolroom would have suited Laura well—so at least she believed; by touches of her own she would make the place even prettier than it was already, and in the winter nights, near the bright fire, she would get through a delightful course of reading. There was the question of a new piano (the old one was pretty bad—Miss Steet had a finger!) and perhaps she should have to ask Selina for that—but it would be all. The schoolroom at Mellows was not a charmless place and the girl often wished that she might have spent her own early years in so dear a scene. It was a sort of panelled parlour, in a wing, and looked out on the great cushiony lawns and a part of the terrace where the peacocks used most to spread their tails. There were quaint old maps on the wall, and 'collections'—birds and shells—under glass cases, and there was a wonderful pictured screen which old Mrs. Berrington had made when Lionel was young out of primitive woodcuts illustrative of nursery-tales. The place was a setting for rosy childhood, and Laura believed her sister never knew how delightful Scratch and Parson looked there. Old Mrs. Berrington had known in the case of Lionel—it had all been arranged for him. That was the story told by ever so many other things in the house, which betrayed the full perception of a comfortable, liberal, deeply domestic effect, addressed to eternities of possession, characteristic thirty years before of the unquestioned and unquestioning old lady whose sofas and 'corners' (she had perhaps been the first person in England to have corners) demonstrated the most of her cleverness.

Laura Wing envied English children, the boys at least, and even her own chubby nephews, in spite of the cloud that hung over them; but she had already noted the incongruity that appeared to-day between Lionel Berrington at thirty-five and the influences that had surrounded his younger years. She did not dislike her brother-in-law, though she admired him scantily,

26

and she pitied him; but she marvelled at the waste involved in some human institutions (the English country gentry for instance) when she perceived that it had taken so much to produce so little. The sweet old wainscoted parlour, the view of the garden that reminded her of scenes in Shakespeare's comedies, all that was exquisite in the home of his forefathers—what visible reference was there to these fine things in poor Lionel's stable-stamped composition? When she came in this evening and saw his small sons making competitive noises in their mugs (Miss Steet checked this impropriety on her entrance) she asked herself what *they* would have to show twenty years later for the frame that made them just then a picture. Would they be wonderfully ripe and noble, the perfection of human culture? The contrast was before her again, the sense of the same curious duplicity (in the literal meaning of the word) that she had felt at Plash—the way the genius of such an old house was all peace and decorum and the spirit that prevailed there, outside of the schoolroom, was contentious and impure. She had often been struck with it before—with that perfection of machinery which can still at certain times make English life go on of itself with a stately rhythm long after there is corruption within it.

She had half a purpose of asking Miss Steet to dine with her that evening downstairs, so absurd did it seem to her that two young women who had so much in common (enough at least for that) should sit feeding alone at opposite ends of the big empty house, melancholy on such a night. She would not have cared just now whether Selina did think such a course familiar: she indulged sometimes in a kind of angry humility, placing herself near to those who were laborious and sordid. But when she observed how much cold meat the governess had already consumed she felt that it would be a vain form to propose to her another repast. She sat down with her and presently, in the firelight, the two children had placed themselves in position for a story. They were dressed like the mariners of England and they smelt of the ablutions to which they had been condemned before tea and the odour of which was but partly overlaid by that of bread and butter. Scratch wanted an old story and Parson a new, and they exchanged from side to side a good many powerful arguments. While they were so engaged Miss Steet narrated at her visitor's invitation the walk she had taken with them and revealed that

27

she had been thinking for a long time of asking Mrs. Berrington—if she only had an opportunity—whether she should approve of her giving them a few elementary notions of botany. But the opportunity had not come—she had had the idea for a long time past. She was rather fond of the study herself; she had gone into it a little—she seemed to intimate that there had been times when she extracted a needed comfort from it. Laura suggested that botany might be a little dry for such young children in winter, from text-books—that the better way would be perhaps to wait till the spring and show them out of doors, in the garden, some of the peculiarities of plants. To this Miss Steet rejoined that her idea had been to teach some of the general facts slowly—it would take a long time—and then they would be all ready for the spring. She spoke of the spring as if it would not arrive for a terribly long time. She had hoped to lay the question before Mrs. Berrington that week—but was it not already Thursday? Laura said, 'Oh yes, you had better do anything with the children that will keep them profitably occupied;' she came very near saying anything that would occupy the governess herself.

She had rather a dread of new stories—it took the little boys so long to get initiated and the first steps were so terribly bestrewn with questions. Receptive silence, broken only by an occasional rectification on the part of the listener, never descended until after the tale had been told a dozen times. The matter was settled for 'Riquet with the Tuft,' but on this occasion the girl's heart was not much in the entertainment. The children stood on either side of her, leaning against her, and she had an arm round each; their little bodies were thick and strong and their voices had the quality of silver bells. Their mother had certainly gone too far; but there was nevertheless a limit to the tenderness one could feel for the neglected, compromised bairns. It was difficult to take a sentimental view of them—they would never take such a view of themselves. Geordie would grow up to be a master-hand at polo and care more for that pastime than for anything in life, and Ferdy perhaps would develop into 'the best shot in England.' Laura felt these possibilities stirring within them; they were in the things they said to her, in the things they said to each other. At any rate they would never reflect upon anything in the world. They contradicted each other on a question of ancestral history to which their attention apparently had been drawn by their nurse, whose people had been tenants for generations. Their grandfather had had the hounds for fifteen years—Ferdy maintained that he had always had them. Geordie ridiculed this idea, like a man of the world; he had had them till he went into volunteering—then he had got up a magnificent regiment, he had spent thousands of pounds on it. Ferdy was of the opinion that this was wasted money—he himself intended to have a real regiment, to be a colonel in the Guards. Geordie looked as if he thought that a superficial ambition and could see beyond it; his own most definite view was that he would have back the hounds. He didn't see why papa didn't have them—unless it was because he wouldn't take the trouble.

'I know—it's because mamma is an American!' Ferdy announced, with confidence.

'And what has that to do with it?' asked Laura.

'Mamma spends so much money—there isn't any more for anything!'

This startling speech elicited an alarmed protest from Miss Steet; she blushed and assured Laura that she couldn't imagine where the child could have picked up such an extraordinary idea. 'I'll look into it—you may be sure I'll look into it,' she said; while Laura told Ferdy that he must never, never, never, under any circumstances, either utter or listen to a word that should be wanting in respect to his mother.

'If any one should say anything against any of my people I would give him a good one!' Geordie shouted, with his hands in his little blue pockets.

'I'd hit him in the eye!' cried Ferdy, with cheerful inconsequence.

'Perhaps you don't care to come to dinner at half-past seven,' the girl said to Miss Steet; 'but I should be very glad—I'm all alone.'

'Thank you so much. All alone, really?' murmured the governess.

'Why don't you get married? then you wouldn't be alone,' Geordie interposed, with ingenuity.

'Children, you are really too dreadful this evening!' Miss Steet exclaimed.

'I shan't get married—I want to have the hounds,' proclaimed Geordie, who had apparently been much struck with his brother's explanation.

'I will come down afterwards, about half-past eight, if you will allow me,' said Miss Steet, looking conscious and responsible.

'Very well—perhaps we can have some music; we will try something together.'

'Oh, music—*we* don't go in for music!' said Geordie, with clear superiority; and while he spoke Laura saw Miss Steet get up suddenly, looking even less alleviated than usual. The door of the room had been pushed open and Lionel Berrington stood there. He had his hat on and a cigar in his mouth and his face was red, which was its common condition. He took off his hat as he came into the room, but he did not stop smoking and he turned a little redder than before. There were several ways in which his sister-in-law often wished he had been very different, but she had never disliked him for a certain boyish shyness that was in him, which came out in his dealings with almost all women. The governess of his children made him uncomfortable and Laura had already noticed that he had the same effect upon Miss Steet. He was fond of his children, but he saw them hardly more frequently than their mother and they never knew whether he were at home or away. Indeed his goings and comings were so frequent that Laura herself scarcely knew: it was an accident that on this occasion his absence had been marked for her. Selina had had her reasons for wishing not to go up to town while her husband was still at Mellows, and she cherished the irritating belief that he stayed at home on purpose to watch her—to keep her from going away. It was her theory that she herself was perpetually at home—that few women were more domestic, more glued to the fireside and absorbed in the duties belonging to it; and unreasonable as she was she recognised the fact that for her to establish this theory she must make her husband sometimes see her at Mellows. It was not enough for her to maintain that he would see her if he were sometimes there himself. Therefore she disliked to be caught in the crude fact of absence—to go away under his nose; what she preferred was to take the next train after his own and return an hour or two before him. She managed this often with great ability, in spite of her not being able to be sure when he *would* return. Of late however she had ceased to take so much trouble, and Laura, by no desire of the girl's own, was enough in the confidence of her impatiences and perversities to know that for her to have wished (four days before the moment I write of) to put him on a wrong scent—or to keep him at least off the right one—she must have had something more dreadful than usual in her head. This was why the girl had been so nervous and why the sense of an impending catastrophe, which had lately gathered strength in her mind, was at present almost intolerably pressing: she knew how little Selina could afford to be more dreadful than usual.

Lionel startled her by turning up in that unexpected way, though she could not have told herself when it would have been natural to expect him. This attitude, at Mellows, was left to the servants, most of them inscrutable and incommunicative and erect in a wisdom that was founded upon telegrams—you couldn't speak to the butler but he pulled one out of his pocket. It was a house of telegrams; they crossed each other a dozen times an hour, coming and going, and Selina in particular lived in a cloud of them. Laura had but vague ideas as to what they were all about; once in a while, when they fell under her eyes, she either failed to understand them or judged them to be about horses. There were an immense number of horses, in one way and another, in Mrs. Berrington's life. Then she had so many friends, who were always rushing about like herself and making appointments and putting them off and wanting to know if she were going to certain places or whether she would go if they did or whether she would come up to town and dine and 'do a theatre.' There were also a good many theatres in the existence of this busy lady. Laura remembered how fond their poor father had been of telegraphing, but it was never about the theatre: at all events she tried to give her sister the benefit or the excuse of heredity. Selina had her own opinions, which were superior to this—she once remarked to Laura that it was idiotic for a woman to write to telegraph was the only way not to get into trouble. If doing so sufficed to keep a lady out of it Mrs. Berrington's life should have flowed like the rivers of Eden.

III

Laura, as soon as her brother-in-law had been in the room a moment, had a particular fear; she had seen him twice noticeably under the influence of liquor; she had not liked it at all and now there were some of the same signs. She was afraid the children would discover them, or at any rate Miss Steet, and she felt the importance of not letting him stay in the room. She thought it almost a sign that he should have come there at all—he was so rare an apparition. He looked at her very hard, smiling as if to say, 'No, no, I'm not—not if you think it!' She perceived with relief in a moment that he was not very bad, and liquor disposed him apparently to tenderness, for he indulged in an interminable kissing of Geordie and Ferdy, during which Miss Steet turned away delicately, looking out of the window. The little boys asked him no questions to celebrate his return—they only announced that they were going to learn botany, to which he replied: 'Are you, really? Why, I never did,' and looked askance at the governess, blushing as if to express the hope that she would let him off from carrying that subject further. To Laura and to Miss Steet he was amiably explanatory, though his explanations were not quite coherent. He had come back an hour before—he was going to spend the night—he had driven over from Churton—he was thinking of taking the last train up to town. Was Laura dining at home? Was any one coming? He should enjoy a quiet dinner awfully.

'Certainly I'm alone,' said the girl. 'I suppose you know Selina is away.'

'Oh yes—I know where Selina is!' And Lionel Berrington looked round, smiling at every one present, including Scratch and Parson. He stopped while he continued to smile and Laura wondered what he was so much pleased at. She preferred not to ask—she was sure it was something that wouldn't give *her* pleasure; but after waiting a moment her brother-in-law went on: 'Selina's in Paris, my dear; that's where Selina is!'

'In Paris?' Laura repeated.

'Yes, in Paris, my dear—God bless her! Where else do you suppose? Geordie my boy, where should *you* think your mummy would naturally be?'

'Oh, I don't know,' said Geordie, who had no reply ready that would express affectingly the desolation of the nursery. 'If I were mummy I'd travel.'

'Well now that's your mummy's idea—she has gone to travel,' returned the father. 'Were you ever in Paris, Miss Steet?'

Miss Steet gave a nervous laugh and said No, but she had been to Boulogne; while to her added confusion Ferdy announced that he knew where Paris was—it was in America. 'No, it ain't—it's in Scotland!' cried Geordie; and Laura asked Lionel how he knew—whether his wife had written to him.

'Written to me? when did she ever write to me? No, I saw a fellow in town this morning who saw her there—at breakfast yesterday. He came over last night. That's how I know my wife's in Paris. You can't have better proof than that!'

'I suppose it's a very pleasant season there,' the governess murmured, as if from a sense of duty, in a distant, discomfortable tone.

'I daresay it's very pleasant indeed—I daresay it's awfully amusing!' laughed Mr. Berrington. 'Shouldn't you like to run over with me for a few days, Laura—just to have a go at the theatres? I don't see why we should always be moping at home. We'll take Miss Steet and the children and give mummy a pleasant surprise. Now who do you suppose she was with, in Paris—who do you suppose she was seen with?'

Laura had turned pale, she looked at him hard, imploringly, in the eyes: there was a name she was terribly afraid he would mention. 'Oh sir, in that case we had better go and get ready!' Miss Steet quavered, betwixt a laugh and a groan, in a spasm of discretion; and before Laura knew it she had gathered Geordie and Ferdy together and swept them out of the room. The door closed behind her with a very quick softness and Lionel remained a moment staring at it.

'I say, what does she mean?—ain't that damned impertinent?' he stammered. 'What did she think I was going to say? Does she suppose I would say any harm before—before *her*? Dash it, does she suppose I would give away my wife to the servants?' Then he added, 'And I wouldn't say any harm before you, Laura. You are too good and too nice and I like you too much!'

'Won't you come downstairs? won't you have some tea?' the girl asked, uneasily.

'No, no, I want to stay here—I like this place,' he replied, very gently and reasoningly. 'It's a deuced nice place—it's an awfully jolly room. It used to be this way—always—when I was a little chap. I was a rough one, my dear; I wasn't a pretty little lamb like that pair. I think it's because you look after them—that's what makes 'em so sweet. The one in my time—what was her name? I think it was Bald or Bold—I rather think she found me a handful. I used to kick her shins—I was decidedly vicious. And do *you* see it's kept so well, Laura?' he went on, looking round him. ''Pon my soul, it's the prettiest room in the house. What does she want to go to Paris for when she has got such a charming house? Now can you answer me that, Laura?'

'I suppose she has gone to get some clothes: her dressmaker lives in Paris, you know.'

'Dressmaker? Clothes? Why, she has got whole rooms full of them. Hasn't she got whole rooms full of them?'

'Speaking of clothes I must go and change mine,' said Laura. 'I have been out in the rain—I have been to Plash—I'm decidedly damp.'

'Oh, you have been to Plash? You have seen my mother? I hope she's in very good health.' But before the girl could reply to this he went on: 'Now, I want you to guess who she's in Paris with. Motcomb saw them together—at that place, what's his name? close to the Madeleine.' And as Laura was silent, not wishing at all to guess, he continued—'It's the ruin of any woman, you know; I can't think what she has got in her head.' Still Laura said nothing, and as he had hold of her arm, she having turned away, she led him this time out of the room. She had a horror of the name, the name that was in her mind and that was apparently on his lips, though his tone was so singular, so contemplative. 'My dear girl, she's with Lady Ringrose—what do you say to that?' he exclaimed, as they passed along the corridor to the staircase.

'With Lady Ringrose?'

'They went over on Tuesday—they are knocking about there alone.'

'I don't know Lady Ringrose,' Laura said, infinitely relieved that the name was not the one she had feared. Lionel leaned on her arm as they went downstairs.

'I rather hope not—I promise you she has never put her foot in this house! If Selina expects to bring her here I should like half an hour's notice; yes, half an hour would do. She might as well be seen with——' And Lionel Berrington checked himself. 'She has had at least fifty——' And again he stopped short. 'You must pull me up, you know, if I say anything you don't like!'

'I don't understand you—let me alone, please!' the girl broke out, disengaging herself with an effort from his arm. She hurried down the rest of the steps and left him there looking after her, and as she went she heard him give an irrelevant laugh.

IV

She determined not to go to dinner—she wished for that day not to meet him again. He would drink more—he would be worse—she didn't know what he might say. Besides she was too angry—not with him but with Selina—and in addition to being angry she was sick. She knew who Lady Ringrose was; she knew so many things to-day that when she was younger—and only a little—she had not expected ever to know. Her eyes had been opened very wide in England and certainly they had been opened to Lady Ringrose. She had heard what she had done and perhaps a good deal more, and it was not very different from what she had heard of other women. She knew Selina had been to her house; she had an impression that her ladyship had been to Selina's, in London, though she herself had not seen her there. But she had not known they were so intimate as that—that Selina would rush over to Paris with her. What they had gone to Paris for was not necessarily criminal; there were a hundred reasons, familiar to ladies who were fond of change, of movement, of the theatres and of new bonnets; but nevertheless it was the fact of this little excursion quite as much as the companion that excited Laura's disgust.

She was not ready to say that the companion was any worse, though Lionel appeared to think so, than twenty other women who were her sister's intimates and whom she herself had seen in London, in Grosvenor Place, and even under the motherly old beeches at Mellows. But she thought it unpleasant and base in Selina to go abroad that way, like a commercial traveller, capriciously, clandestinely, without giving notice, when she had left her to understand that she was simply spending three or four days in town. It was bad taste and bad form, it was *cabotin* and had the mark of Selina's complete, irremediable frivolity—the worst accusation (Laura tried to cling to that opinion) that she laid herself open to. Of course frivolity that was never ashamed of itself was like a neglected cold—you could die of it morally as well as of anything else. Laura knew this and it was why she was inexpressibly vexed with her sister. She hoped she should get a letter from

Selina the next morning (Mrs. Berrington would show at least that remnant of propriety) which would give her a chance to despatch her an answer that was already writing itself in her brain. It scarcely diminished Laura's eagerness for such an opportunity that she had a vision of Selina's showing her letter, laughing, across the table, at the place near the Madeleine, to Lady Ringrose (who would be painted—Selina herself, to do her justice, was not yet) while the French waiters, in white aprons, contemplated *ces dames*. It was new work for our young lady to judge of these shades—the gradations, the probabilities of license, and of the side of the line on which, or rather how far on the wrong side, Lady Ringrose was situated.

A quarter of an hour before dinner Lionel sent word to her room that she was to sit down without him—he had a headache and wouldn't appear. This was an unexpected grace and it simplified the position for Laura; so that, smoothing her ruffles, she betook herself to the table. Before doing this however she went back to the schoolroom and told Miss Steet she must contribute her company. She took the governess (the little boys were in bed) downstairs with her and made her sit opposite, thinking she would be a safeguard if Lionel were to change his mind. Miss Steet was more frightened than herself—she was a very shrinking bulwark. The dinner was dull and the conversation rare; the governess ate three olives and looked at the figures on the spoons. Laura had more than ever her sense of impending calamity; a draught of misfortune seemed to blow through the house; it chilled her feet under her chair. The letter she had in her head went out like a flame in the wind and her only thought now was to telegraph to Selina the first thing in the morning, in quite different words. She scarcely spoke to Miss Steet and there was very little the governess could say to her: she had already related her history so often. After dinner she carried her companion into the drawing-room, by the arm, and they sat down to the piano together. They played duets for an hour, mechanically, violently; Laura had no idea what the music was—she only knew that their playing was execrable. In spite of this   'That's a very nice thing, that last,' she heard a vague voice say, behind her, at the end; and she became aware that her brother-in-law had joined them again.

Miss Steet was pusillanimous—she retreated on the spot, though Lionel had already forgotten that he was angry at the scandalous way she had carried off the children from the schoolroom. Laura would have gone too if Lionel had not told her that he had something very particular to say to her. That made her want to go more, but she had to listen to him when he expressed the hope that she hadn't taken offence at anything he had said before. He didn't strike her as tipsy now; he had slept it off or got rid of it and she saw no traces of his headache. He was still conspicuously cheerful, as if he had got some good news and were very much encouraged. She knew the news he had got and she might have thought, in view of his manner, that it could not really have seemed to him so bad as he had pretended to think it. It was not the first time however that she had seen him pleased that he had a case against his wife, and she was to learn on this occasion how extreme a satisfaction he could take in his wrongs. She would not sit down again; she only lingered by the fire, pretending to warm her feet, and he walked to and fro in the long room, where the lamp-light to-night was limited, stepping on certain figures of the carpet as if his triumph were alloyed with hesitation.

'I never know how to talk to you—you are so beastly clever,' he said. 'I can't treat you like a little girl in a pinafore—and yet of course you are only a young lady. You're so deuced good—that makes it worse,' he went on, stopping in front of her with his hands in his pockets and the air he himself had of being a good-natured but dissipated boy; with his small stature, his smooth, fat, suffused face, his round, watery, light-coloured eyes and his hair growing in curious infantile rings. He had lost one of his front teeth and always wore a stiff white scarf, with a pin representing some symbol of the turf or the chase. 'I don't see why *she* couldn't have been a little more like you. If I could have had a shot at you first!'

'I don't care for any compliments at my sister's expense,' Laura said, with some majesty.

'Oh I say, Laura, don't put on so many frills, as Selina says. You know what your sister is as well as I do!' They stood looking at each other a moment and he appeared to see something in her face which led him to add—'You know, at any rate, how little we hit it off.'

'I know you don't love each other—it's too dreadful.'

'Love each other? she hates me as she'd hate a hump on her back. She'd do me any devilish turn she could. There isn't a feeling of loathing that she doesn't have for me! She'd like to stamp on me and hear me crack, like a black beetle, and she never opens her mouth but she insults me.' Lionel Berrington delivered himself of these assertions without violence, without passion or the sting of a new discovery; there was a familiar gaiety in his trivial little tone and he had the air of being so sure of what he said that he did not need to exaggerate in order to prove enough.

'Oh, Lionel!' the girl murmured, turning pale. 'Is that the particular thing you wished to say to me?'

'And you can't say it's my fault—you won't pretend to do that, will you?' he went on. 'Ain't I quiet, ain't I kind, don't I go steady? Haven't I given her every blessed thing she has ever asked for?'

'You haven't given her an example!' Laura replied, with spirit. 'You don't care for anything in the wide world but to amuse yourself, from the beginning of the year to the end. No more does she—and perhaps it's even worse in a woman. You are both as selfish as you can live, with nothing in your head or your heart but your vulgar pleasure, incapable of a concession, incapable of a sacrifice!' She at least spoke with passion; something that had been pent up in her soul broke out and it gave her relief, almost a momentary joy.

It made Lionel Berrington stare; he coloured, but after a moment he threw back his head with laughter. 'Don't you call me kind when I stand here and take all that? If I'm so keen for my pleasure what pleasure do *you* give me? Look at the way I take it, Laura. You ought to do me justice. Haven't I sacrificed my home? and what more can a man do?'

'I don't think you care any more for your home than Selina does. And it's so sacred and so beautiful, God forgive you! You are all blind and senseless and heartless and I don't know what poison is in your veins. There is a curse on you and there will be a judgment!' the girl went on, glowing like a young prophetess.

'What do you want me to do? Do you want me to stay at home and read the Bible?' her companion demanded with an effect of profanity, confronted with her deep seriousness.

'It wouldn't do you any harm, once in a while.'

'There will be a judgment on *her*—that's very sure, and I know where it will be delivered,' said Lionel Berrington, indulging in a visible approach to a wink. 'Have I done the half to her she has done to me? I won't say the half but the hundredth part? Answer me truly, my dear!'

'I don't know what she has done to you,' said Laura, impatiently.

'That's exactly what I want to tell you. But it's difficult. I'll bet you five pounds she's doing it now!'

'You are too unable to make yourself respected,' the girl remarked, not shrinking now from the enjoyment of an advantage—that of feeling herself superior and taking her opportunity.

Her brother-in-law seemed to feel for the moment the prick of this observation. 'What has such a piece of nasty boldness as that to do with respect? She's the first that ever defied me!' exclaimed the young man, whose aspect somehow scarcely confirmed this pretension. 'You know all about her—don't make believe you don't,' he continued in another tone. 'You see everything—you're one of the sharp ones. There's no use beating about the bush, Laura—you've lived in this precious house and you're not so green as that comes to. Besides, you're so good yourself that you needn't give a shriek if one is obliged to say what one means. Why didn't you grow up a little sooner? Then, over there in New York, it would certainly have been you I would have made up to. *You* would have respected me—eh? now don't say you wouldn't.' He rambled on, turning about the room again, partly like a person whose sequences were naturally slow but also a little as if, though he knew what he had in mind, there were still a scruple attached to it that he was trying to rub off.

'I take it that isn't what I must sit up to listen to, Lionel, is it?' Laura said, wearily.

'Why, you don't want to go to bed at nine o'clock, do you? That's all rot, of course. But I want you to help me.'

'To help you—how?'

'I'll tell you—but you must give me my head. I don't know what I said to you before dinner—I had had too many brandy and sodas. Perhaps I was too free; if I was I beg your pardon. I made the governess bolt—very proper in the superintendent of one's children. Do you suppose they saw anything? I shouldn't care for that. I did take half a dozen or so; I was thirsty and I was awfully gratified.'

'You have little enough to gratify you.'

'Now that's just where you are wrong. I don't know when I've fancied anything so much as what I told you.'

'What you told me?'

'About her being in Paris. I hope she'll stay a month!'

'I don't understand you,' Laura said.

'Are you very sure, Laura? My dear, it suits my book! Now you know yourself he's not the first.'

Laura was silent; his round eyes were fixed on her face and she saw something she had not seen before—a little shining point which on Lionel's part might represent an idea, but which made his expression conscious as well as eager. 'He?' she presently asked. 'Whom are you speaking of?'

'Why, of Charley Crispin, G——' And Lionel Berrington accompanied this name with a startling imprecation.

'What has he to do——?'

'He has everything to do. Isn't he with her there?'

'How should I know? You said Lady Ringrose.'

'Lady Ringrose is a mere blind—and a devilish poor one at that. I'm sorry to have to say it to you, but he's her lover. I mean Selina's. And he ain't the first.'

There was another short silence while they stood opposed, and then Laura asked—and the question was unexpected—'Why do you call him Charley?'

'Doesn't he call me Lion, like all the rest?' said her brother-in-law, staring.

'You're the most extraordinary people. I suppose you have a certain amount of proof before you say such things to me?'

'Proof, I've oceans of proof! And not only about Crispin, but about Deepmere.'

'And pray who is Deepmere?'

'Did you never hear of Lord Deepmere? He has gone to India. That was before you came. I don't say all this for my pleasure, Laura,' Mr. Berrington added.

'Don't you, indeed?' asked the girl with a singular laugh. 'I thought you were so glad.'

'I'm glad to know it but I'm not glad to tell it. When I say I'm glad to know it I mean I'm glad to be fixed at last. Oh, I've got the tip! It's all open country now and I know just how to go. I've gone into it most extensively; there's nothing you can't find out to-day—if you go to the right place. I've—I've——' He hesitated a moment, then went on: 'Well, it's no matter what I've done. I know where I am and it's a great comfort. She's up a tree, if ever a woman was. Now we'll see who's a beetle and who's a toad!' Lionel Berrington concluded, gaily, with some incongruity of metaphor.

'It's not true—it's not true—it's not true,' Laura said, slowly.

'That's just what she'll say—though that's not the way she'll say it. Oh, if she could get off by your saying it for her!—for you, my dear, would be believed.'

'Get off—what do you mean?' the girl demanded, with a coldness she failed to feel, for she was tingling all over with shame and rage.

'Why, what do you suppose I'm talking about? I'm going to haul her up and to have it out.'

'You're going to make a scandal?'

'*Make* it? Bless my soul, it isn't me! And I should think it was made enough. I'm going to appeal to the laws of my country—that's what I'm going to do. She pretends I'm stopped, whatever she does. But that's all gammon—I ain't!'

'I understand—but you won't do anything so horrible,' said Laura, very gently.

'Horrible as you please, but less so than going on in this way; I haven't told you the fiftieth part—you will easily understand that I can't. They are not nice things to say to a girl like you—especially about Deepmere, if you didn't know it. But when they happen you've got to look at them, haven't you? That's the way I look at it.'

'It's not true—it's not true—it's not true,' Laura Wing repeated, in the same way, slowly shaking her head.

'Of course you stand up for your sister—but that's just what I wanted to say to you, that you ought to have some pity for *me* and some sense of justice. Haven't I always been nice to you? Have you ever had so much as a nasty word from me?'

This appeal touched the girl; she had eaten her brother-in-law's bread for months, she had had the use of all the luxuries with which he was surrounded, and to herself personally she had never known him anything but good-natured. She made no direct response however; she only said—'Be quiet, be quiet and leave her to me. I will answer for her.'

'Answer for her—what do you mean?'

'She shall be better—she shall be reasonable—there shall be no more talk of these horrors. Leave her to me—let me go away with her somewhere.'

43

'Go away with her? I wouldn't let you come within a mile of her, if you were *my* sister!'

'Oh, shame, shame!' cried Laura Wing, turning away from him.

She hurried to the door of the room, but he stopped her before she reached it. He got his back to it, he barred her way and she had to stand there and hear him. 'I haven't said what I wanted—for I told you that I wanted you to help me. I ain't cruel—I ain't insulting—you can't make out that against me; I'm sure you know in your heart that I've swallowed what would sicken most men. Therefore I will say that you ought to be fair. You're too clever not to be; *you* can't pretend to swallow——' He paused a moment and went on, and she saw it was his idea—an idea very simple and bold. He wanted her to side with him—to watch for him—to help him to get his divorce. He forbore to say that she owed him as much for the hospitality and protection she had in her poverty enjoyed, but she was sure that was in his heart. 'Of course she's your sister, but when one's sister's a perfect bad 'un there's no law to force one to jump into the mud to save her. It *is* mud, my dear, and mud up to your neck. You had much better think of her children—you had much better stop in *my* boat.'

'Do you ask me to help you with evidence against her?' the girl murmured. She had stood there passive, waiting while he talked, covering her face with her hands, which she parted a little, looking at him.

He hesitated a moment. 'I ask you not to deny what you have seen—what you feel to be true.'

'Then of the abominations of which you say you have proof, you haven't proof.'

'Why haven't I proof?'

'If you want *me* to come forward!'

'I shall go into court with a strong case. You may do what you like. But I give you notice and I expect you not to forget that I have given it. Don't forget—because you'll be asked—that I have told you to-night where she is and with whom she is and what measures I intend to take.'

'Be asked—be asked?' the girl repeated.

'Why, of course you'll be cross-examined.'

'Oh, mother, mother!' cried Laura Wing. Her hands were over her face again and as Lionel Berrington, opening the door, let her pass, she burst into tears. He looked after her, distressed, compunctious, half-ashamed, and he exclaimed to himself—'The bloody brute, the bloody brute!' But the words had reference to his wife.

V

'And are you telling me the perfect truth when you say that Captain Crispin was not there?'

'The perfect truth?' Mrs. Berrington straightened herself to her height, threw back her head and measured her interlocutress up and down; it is to be surmised that this was one of the many ways in which she knew she looked very handsome indeed. Her interlocutress was her sister, and even in a discussion with a person long since initiated she was not incapable of feeling that her beauty was a new advantage. On this occasion she had at first the air of depending upon it mainly to produce an effect upon Laura; then, after an instant's reflection, she determined to arrive at her result in another way. She exchanged her expression of scorn (of resentment at her veracity's being impugned) for a look of gentle amusement; she smiled patiently, as if she remembered that of course Laura couldn't understand of what an impertinence she had been guilty. There was a quickness of perception and lightness of hand which, to her sense, her American sister had never acquired: the girl's earnest, almost barbarous probity blinded her to the importance of certain pleasant little forms. 'My poor child, the things you do say! One doesn't put a question about the perfect truth in a manner that implies that a person is telling a perfect lie. However, as it's only you, I don't mind satisfying your clumsy curiosity. I haven't the least idea whether Captain Crispin was there or not. I know nothing of his movements and he doesn't keep me informed—why should he, poor man?—of his whereabouts. He was not there for me—isn't that all that need interest you? As far as I was concerned he might have been at the North Pole. I neither saw him nor heard of him. I didn't see the end of his nose!' Selina continued, still with her wiser, tolerant brightness, looking straight into her sister's eyes. Her own were clear and lovely and she was but little less handsome than if she had been proud and freezing. Laura wondered at her more and more; stupefied suspense was now almost the girl's constant state of mind.

Mrs. Berrington had come back from Paris the day before but had not proceeded to Mellows the same night, though there was more than one train she might have taken. Neither had she gone to the house in Grosvenor Place but had spent the night at an hotel. Her husband was absent again; he was supposed to be in Grosvenor Place, so that they had not yet met. Little as she was a woman to admit that she had been in the wrong she was known to have granted later that at this moment she had made a mistake in not going straight to her own house. It had given Lionel a degree of advantage, made it appear perhaps a little that she had a bad conscience and was afraid to face him. But she had had her reasons for putting up at an hotel, and she thought it unnecessary to express them very definitely. She came home by a morning train, the second day, and arrived before luncheon, of which meal she partook in the company of her sister and in that of Miss Steet and the children, sent for in honour of the occasion. After luncheon she let the governess go but kept Scratch and Parson—kept them on ever so long in the morning-room where she remained; longer than she had ever kept them before. Laura was conscious that she ought to have been pleased at this, but there was a perversity even in Selina's manner of doing right; for she wished immensely now to see her alone—she had something so serious to say to her. Selina hugged her children repeatedly, encouraging their sallies; she laughed extravagantly at the artlessness of their remarks, so that at table Miss Steet was quite abashed by her unusual high spirits. Laura was unable to question her about Captain Crispin and Lady Ringrose while Geordie and Ferdy were there: they would not understand, of course, but names were always reflected in their limpid little minds and they gave forth the image later—often in the most extraordinary connections. It was as if Selina knew what she was waiting for and were determined to make her wait. The girl wished her to go to her room, that she might follow her there. But Selina showed no disposition to retire, and one could never entertain the idea for her, on any occasion, that it would be suitable that she should change her dress. The dress she wore—whatever it was—was too becoming to her, and to the moment, for that. Laura noticed how the very folds of her garment told that she had been to Paris; she had spent only a week there but the mark of her *couturière* was all over her: it was simply to confer with this great artist that, from her own account, she had crossed the Channel. The signs of the conference were so conspicuous that it was as if she had said, 'Don't you see the proof that it was for nothing but *chiffons?*' She walked up and down the room with Geordie in her arms, in an access of maternal tenderness; he was much too big to nestle gracefully in her bosom, but that only made her seem younger, more flexible, fairer in her tall, strong slimness. Her distinguished figure bent itself hither and thither, but always in perfect freedom, as she romped with her children; and there was another moment, when she came slowly down the room, holding one of them in each hand and singing to them while they looked up at her beauty, charmed and listening and a little surprised at such new ways—a moment when she might have passed for some grave, antique statue of a young matron, or even for a picture of Saint Cecilia. This morning, more than ever, Laura was struck with her air of youth, the inextinguishable freshness that would have made any one exclaim at her being the mother of such bouncing little boys. Laura had always admired her, thought her the prettiest woman in London, the beauty with the finest points; and now these points were so vivid (especially her finished slenderness and the grace, the natural elegance of every turn—the fall of her shoulders had never looked so perfect) that the girl almost detested them: they appeared to her a kind of advertisement of danger and even of shame.

Miss Steet at last came back for the children, and as soon as she had taken them away Selina observed that she would go over to Plash—just as she was: she rang for her hat and jacket and for the carriage. Laura could see that she would not give her just yet the advantage of a retreat to her room. The hat and jacket were quickly brought, but after they were put on Selina kept her maid in the drawing-room, talking to her a long time, telling her elaborately what she wished done with the things she had brought from Paris. Before the maid departed the carriage was announced, and the servant, leaving the door of the room open, hovered within earshot. Laura then, losing patience, turned out the maid and closed the door; she stood before her sister, who was prepared for her drive. Then she asked her abruptly, fiercely, but colouring with her question, whether Captain Crispin had been in Paris. We have heard Mrs. Berrington's answer, with which her strenuous sister was imperfectly satisfied; a fact the perception of which it doubtless was that led

Selina to break out, with a greater show of indignation: 'I never heard of such extraordinary ideas for a girl to have, and such extraordinary things for a girl to talk about! My dear, you have acquired a freedom—you have emancipated yourself from conventionality—and I suppose I must congratulate you.' Laura only stood there, with her eyes fixed, without answering the sally, and Selina went on, with another change of tone: 'And pray if he *was* there, what is there so monstrous? Hasn't it happened that he is in London when I am there? Why is it then so awful that he should be in Paris?'

'Awful, awful, too awful,' murmured Laura, with intense gravity, still looking at her—looking all the more fixedly that she knew how little Selina liked it.

'My dear, you do indulge in a style of innuendo, for a respectable young woman!' Mrs. Berrington exclaimed, with an angry laugh. 'You have ideas that when I was a girl——' She paused, and her sister saw that she had not the assurance to finish her sentence on that particular note.

'Don't talk about my innuendoes and my ideas—you might remember those in which I have heard you indulge! Ideas? what ideas did I ever have before I came here?' Laura Wing asked, with a trembling voice. 'Don't pretend to be shocked, Selina; that's too cheap a defence. You have said things to me—if you choose to talk of freedom! What is the talk of your house and what does one hear if one lives with you? I don't care what I hear now (it's all odious and there's little choice and my sweet sensibility has gone God knows where!) and I'm very glad if you understand that I don't care what I say. If one talks about your affairs, my dear, one mustn't be too particular!' the girl continued, with a flash of passion.

Mrs. Berrington buried her face in her hands. 'Merciful powers, to be insulted, to be covered with outrage, by one's wretched little sister!' she moaned.

'I think you should be thankful there is one human being—however wretched—who cares enough for you to care about the truth in what concerns you,' Laura said. 'Selina, Selina—are you hideously deceiving us?'

'Us?' Selina repeated, with a singular laugh. 'Whom do you mean by us?'

Laura Wing hesitated; she had asked herself whether it would be best she should let her sister know the dreadful scene she had had with Lionel; but she had not, in her mind, settled that point. However, it was settled now in an instant. 'I don't mean your friends—those of them that I have seen. I don't think *they* care a straw—I have never seen such people. But last week Lionel spoke to me—he told me he *knew* it, as a certainty.'

'Lionel spoke to you?' said Mrs. Berrington, holding up her head with a stare. 'And what is it that he knows?'

'That Captain Crispin was in Paris and that you were with him. He believes you went there to meet him.'

'He said this to *you*?'

'Yes, and much more—I don't know why I should make a secret of it.'

'The disgusting beast!' Selina exclaimed slowly, solemnly. 'He enjoys the right—the legal right—to pour forth his vileness upon *me*; but when he is so lost to every feeling as to begin to talk to you in such a way——!' And Mrs. Berrington paused, in the extremity of her reprobation.

'Oh, it was not his talk that shocked me—it was his believing it,' the girl replied. 'That, I confess, made an impression on me.'

'Did it indeed? I'm infinitely obliged to you! You are a tender, loving little sister.'

'Yes, I am, if it's tender to have cried about you—all these days—till I'm blind and sick!' Laura replied. 'I hope you are prepared to meet him. His mind is quite made up to apply for a divorce.'

Laura's voice almost failed her as she said this—it was the first time that in talking with Selina she had uttered that horrible word. She had heard it however, often enough on the lips of others; it had been bandied lightly enough in her presence under those somewhat austere ceilings of Mellows, of which the admired decorations and mouldings, in the taste of the middle of the last century, all in delicate plaster and reminding her of Wedgewood pottery, consisted of slim festoons, urns and trophies and knotted ribbons, so many symbols of domestic affection and irrevocable union. Selina herself had flashed it at her with light superiority, as if it were some precious jewel kept in reserve, which she could convert at any moment into specie, so that it would constitute a happy provision for her future. The idea—associated with her own point of view—was apparently too familiar to Mrs. Berrington to be the cause of her changing colour; it struck her indeed, as presented by Laura, in a ludicrous light, for her pretty eyes expanded a moment and she smiled pityingly. 'Well, you are a poor dear innocent, after all. Lionel would be about as able to divorce me—even if I were the most abandoned of my sex—as he would be to write a leader in the *Times*.'

'I know nothing about that,' said Laura.

'So I perceive—as I also perceive that you must have shut your eyes very tight. Should you like to know a few of the reasons—heaven forbid I should attempt to go over them all; there are millions!—why his hands are tied?'

'Not in the least.'

'Should you like to know that his own life is too base for words and that his impudence in talking about me would be sickening if it weren't grotesque?' Selina went on, with increasing emotion. 'Should you like me to tell you to what he has stooped—to the very gutter—and the charming history of his relations with——'

'No, I don't want you to tell me anything of the sort,' Laura interrupted. 'Especially as you were just now so pained by the license of my own allusions.'

'You listen to him then—but it suits your purpose not to listen to me!'

'Oh, Selina, Selina!' the girl almost shrieked, turning away.

'Where have your eyes been, or your senses, or your powers of observation? You can be clever enough when it suits you!' Mrs. Berrington continued, throwing off another ripple of derision. 'And now perhaps, as the carriage is waiting, you will let me go about my duties.'

51

Laura turned again and stopped her, holding her arm as she passed toward the door. 'Will you swear—will you swear by everything that is most sacred?'

'Will I swear what?' And now she thought Selina visibly blanched.

'That you didn't lay eyes on Captain Crispin in Paris.'

Mrs. Berrington hesitated, but only for an instant. 'You are really too odious, but as you are pinching me to death I will swear, to get away from you. I never laid eyes on him.'

The organs of vision which Mrs. Berrington was ready solemnly to declare that she had not misapplied were, as her sister looked into them, an abyss of indefinite prettiness. The girl had sounded them before without discovering a conscience at the bottom of them, and they had never helped any one to find out anything about their possessor except that she was one of the beauties of London. Even while Selina spoke Laura had a cold, horrible sense of not believing her, and at the same time a desire, colder still, to extract a reiteration of the pledge. Was it the asseveration of her innocence that she wished her to repeat, or only the attestation of her falsity? One way or the other it seemed to her that this would settle something, and she went on inexorably—'By our dear mother's memory—by our poor father's?'

'By my mother's, by my father's,' said Mrs. Berrington, 'and by that of any other member of the family you like!' Laura let her go; she had not been pinching her, as Selina described the pressure, but had clung to her with insistent hands. As she opened the door Selina said, in a changed voice: 'I suppose it's no use to ask you if you care to drive to Plash.'

'No, thank you, I don't care—I shall take a walk.'

'I suppose, from that, that your friend Lady Davenant has gone.'

'No, I think she is still there.'

'That's a bore!' Selina exclaimed, as she went off.

<u>VI</u>

Laura Wing hastened to her room to prepare herself for her walk; but when she reached it she simply fell on her knees, shuddering, beside her bed. She buried her face in the soft counterpane of wadded silk; she remained there a long time, with a kind of aversion to lifting it again to the day. It burned with horror and there was coolness in the smooth glaze of the silk. It seemed to her that she had been concerned in a hideous transaction, and her uppermost feeling was, strangely enough, that she was ashamed—not of her sister but of herself. She did not believe her—that was at the bottom of everything, and she had made her lie, she had brought out her perjury, she had associated it with the sacred images of the dead. She took no walk, she remained in her room, and quite late, towards six o'clock, she heard on the gravel, outside of her windows, the wheels of the carriage bringing back Mrs. Berrington. She had evidently been elsewhere as well as to Plash; no doubt she had been to the vicarage—she was capable even of that. She could pay 'duty-visits,' like that (she called at the vicarage about three times a year), and she could go and be nice to her mother-in-law with her fresh lips still fresher for the lie she had just told. For it was as definite as an aching nerve to Laura that she did not believe her, and if she did not believe her the words she had spoken were a lie. It was the lie, the lie to *her* and which she had dragged out of her that seemed to the girl the ugliest thing. If she had admitted her folly, if she had explained, attenuated, sophisticated, there would have been a difference in her favour; but now she was bad because she was hard. She had a surface of polished metal. And she could make plans and calculate, she could act and do things for a particular effect. She could go straight to old Mrs. Berrington and to the parson's wife and his many daughters (just as she had kept the children after luncheon, on purpose, so long) because that looked innocent and domestic and denoted a mind without a feather's weight upon it.

A servant came to the young lady's door to tell her that tea was ready; and on her asking who else was below (for she had heard the wheels of a second vehicle just after Selina's return), she learned that Lionel had come back. At this news she requested that some tea should be brought to her room—she determined not to go to dinner. When the dinner-hour came she sent down word that she had a headache, that she was going to bed. She wondered whether Selina would come to her (she could forget disagreeable scenes amazingly); but her fervent hope that she would stay away was gratified. Indeed she would have another call upon her attention if her meeting with her husband was half as much of a concussion as was to have been expected. Laura had found herself listening hard, after knowing that her brother-in-law was in the house: she half expected to hear indications of violence—loud cries or the sound of a scuffle. It was a matter of course to her that some dreadful scene had not been slow to take place, something that discretion should keep her out of even if she had not been too sick. She did not go to bed—partly because she didn't know what might happen in the house. But she was restless also for herself: things had reached a point when it seemed to her that she must make up her mind. She left her candles unlighted—she sat up till the small hours, in the glow of the fire. What had been settled by her scene with Selina was that worse things were to come (looking into her fire, as the night went on, she had a rare prevision of the catastrophe that hung over the house), and she considered, or tried to consider, what it would be best for her, in anticipation, to do. The first thing was to take flight.

It may be related without delay that Laura Wing did not take flight and that though the circumstance detracts from the interest that should be felt in her character she did not even make up her mind. That was not so easy when action had to ensue. At the same time she had not the excuse of a conviction that by not acting—that is by not withdrawing from her brother-in-law's roof—she should be able to hold Selina up to her duty, to drag her back into the straight path. The hopes connected with that project were now a phase that she had left behind her; she had not to-day an illusion about her sister large enough to cover a sixpence. She had passed through the period of superstition, which had lasted the longest—the time when it seemed to her, as at first, a kind of profanity to doubt of Selina and judge her, the elder sister whose beauty and success she had ever been proud of and who carried herself, though with the most good-natured fraternisings, as one native to an upper

54

air. She had called herself in moments of early penitence for irrepressible suspicion a little presumptuous prig: so strange did it seem to her at first, the impulse of criticism in regard to her bright protectress. But the revolution was over and she had a desolate, lonely freedom which struck her as not the most cynical thing in the world only because Selina's behaviour was more so. She supposed she should learn, though she was afraid of the knowledge, what had passed between that lady and her husband while her vigil ached itself away. But it appeared to her the next day, to her surprise, that nothing was changed in the situation save that Selina knew at present how much more she was suspected. As this had not a chastening effect upon Mrs. Berrington nothing had been gained by Laura's appeal to her. Whatever Lionel had said to his wife he said nothing to Laura: he left her at perfect liberty to forget the subject he had opened up to her so luminously. This was very characteristic of his good-nature; it had come over him that after all she wouldn't like it, and if the free use of the gray ponies could make up to her for the shock she might order them every day in the week and banish the unpleasant episode from her mind.

Laura ordered the gray ponies very often: she drove herself all over the country. She visited not only the neighbouring but the distant poor, and she never went out without stopping for one of the vicar's fresh daughters. Mellows was now half the time full of visitors and when it was not its master and mistress were staying with their friends either together or singly. Sometimes (almost always when she was asked) Laura Wing accompanied her sister and on two or three occasions she paid an independent visit. Selina had often told her that she wished her to have her own friends, so that the girl now felt a great desire to show her that she had them. She had arrived at no decision whatever; she had embraced in intention no particular course. She drifted on, shutting her eyes, averting her head and, as it seemed to herself, hardening her heart. This admission will doubtless suggest to the reader that she was a weak, inconsequent, spasmodic young person, with a standard not really, or at any rate not continuously, high; and I have no desire that she shall appear anything but what she was. It must even be related of her that since she could not escape and live in lodgings and paint fans (there were reasons why this combination was impossible) she determined to try and be happy in the given circumstances—to float in shallow, turbid water. She gave up the attempt to understand the cynical *modus vivendi* at which her companions seemed to have arrived; she knew it was not final but it served them sufficiently for the time; and if it served them why should it not serve her, the dependent, impecunious, tolerated little sister, representative of the class whom it behoved above all to mind their own business? The time was coming round when they would all move up to town, and there, in the crowd, with the added movement, the strain would be less and indifference easier.

Whatever Lionel had said to his wife that evening she had found something to say to him: that Laura could see, though not so much from any change in the simple expression of his little red face and in the vain bustle of his existence as from the grand manner in which Selina now carried herself. She was 'smarter' than ever and her waist was smaller and her back straighter and the fall of her shoulders finer; her long eyes were more oddly charming and the extreme detachment of her elbows from her sides conduced still more to the exhibition of her beautiful arms. So she floated, with a serenity not disturbed by a general tardiness, through the interminable succession of her engagements. Her photographs were not to be purchased in the Burlington Arcade—she had kept out of that; but she looked more than ever as they would have represented her if they had been obtainable there. There were times when Laura thought her brother-in-law's formless desistence too frivolous for nature: it even gave her a sense of deeper dangers. It was as if he had been digging away in the dark and they would all tumble into the hole. It happened to her to ask herself whether the things he had said to her the afternoon he fell upon her in the schoolroom had not all been a clumsy practical joke, a crude desire to scare, that of a schoolboy playing with a sheet in the dark; or else brandy and soda, which came to the same thing. However this might be she was obliged to recognise that the impression of brandy and soda had not again been given her. More striking still however was Selina's capacity to recover from shocks and condone imputations; she kissed again—kissed Laura—without tears, and proposed problems connected with the rearrangement of trimmings and of the flowers at dinner, as candidly—as earnestly—as if there had never been an intenser question between them. Captain Crispin was not mentioned; much less of course, so far as Laura was concerned, was he seen. But Lady Ringrose appeared; she came down for two days, during an absence of Lionel's. Laura, to her surprise, found her no such Jezebel but a clever little woman with a single eye-glass and short hair who had read Lecky and could give her useful hints about water-colours: a reconciliation that encouraged the girl, for this was the direction in which it now seemed to her best that she herself should grow.

VII

In Grosvenor Place, on Sunday afternoon, during the first weeks of the season, Mrs. Berrington was usually at home: this indeed was the only time when a visitor who had not made an appointment could hope to be admitted to her presence. Very few hours in the twenty-four did she spend in her own house. Gentlemen calling on these occasions rarely found her sister: Mrs. Berrington had the field to herself. It was understood between the pair that Laura should take this time for going to see her old women: it was in that manner that Selina qualified the girl's independent social resources. The old women however were not a dozen in number; they consisted mainly of Lady Davenant and the elder Mrs. Berrington, who had a house in Portman Street. Lady Davenant lived at Queen's Gate and also was usually at home of a Sunday afternoon: her visitors were not all men, like Selina Berrington's, and Laura's maidenly bonnet was not a false note in her drawing-room. Selina liked her sister, naturally enough, to make herself useful, but of late, somehow, they had grown rarer, the occasions that depended in any degree upon her aid, and she had never been much appealed to—though it would have seemed natural she should be—on behalf of the weekly chorus of gentlemen. It came to be recognised on Selina's part that nature had dedicated her more to the relief of old women than to that of young men. Laura had a distinct sense of interfering with the free interchange of anecdote and pleasantry that went on at her sister's fireside: the anecdotes were mostly such an immense secret that they could not be told fairly if she were there, and she had their privacy on her conscience. There was an exception however; when Selina expected Americans she naturally asked her to stay at home: not apparently so much because their conversation would be good for her as because hers would be good for them.

One Sunday, about the middle of May, Laura Wing prepared herself to go and see Lady Davenant, who had made a long absence from town at Easter but would now have returned. The weather was charming, she had from the first established her right to tread the London streets alone (if she was a poor girl she could have the detachment as well as the helplessness of it) and she promised herself the pleasure of a walk along the park, where the new grass was bright. A moment before she quitted the house her sister sent for her to the drawing-room; the servant gave her a note scrawled in pencil: 'That man from New York is here—Mr. Wendover, who brought me the introduction the other day from the Schoolings. He's rather a dose—you must positively come down and talk to him. Take him out with you if you can.' The description was not alluring, but Selina had never made a request of her to which the girl had not instantly responded: it seemed to her she was there for that. She joined the circle in the drawing-room and found that it consisted of five persons, one of whom was Lady Ringrose. Lady Ringrose was at all times and in all places a fitful apparition; she had described herself to Laura during her visit at Mellows as 'a bird on the branch.' She had no fixed habit of receiving on Sunday, she was in and out as she liked, and she was one of the few specimens of her sex who, in Grosvenor Place, ever turned up, as she said, on the occasions to which I allude. Of the three gentlemen two were known to Laura; she could have told you at least that the big one with the red hair was in the Guards and the other in the Rifles; the latter looked like a rosy child and as if he ought to be sent up to play with Geordie and Ferdy: his social nickname indeed was the Baby. Selina's admirers were of all ages—they ranged from infants to octogenarians.

She introduced the third gentleman to her sister; a tall, fair, slender young man who suggested that he had made a mistake in the shade of his tight, perpendicular coat, ordering it of too heavenly a blue. This added however to the candour of his appearance, and if he was a dose, as Selina had described him, he could only operate beneficently. There were moments when Laura's heart rather yearned towards her countrymen, and now, though she was preoccupied and a little disappointed at having been detained, she tried to like Mr. Wendover, whom her sister had compared invidiously, as it seemed to her, with her other companions. It struck her that his surface at least was as glossy as theirs. The Baby, whom she remembered to have heard spoken of as a dangerous flirt, was in conversation with Lady Ringrose and the guardsman with Mrs. Berrington; so she did her best to entertain the American visitor, as to whom any one could easily see (she thought) that he had brought a letter of introduction—he wished so to maintain the credit of those who had given it to him. Laura scarcely knew these people, American friends of her sister who had spent a period of festivity in London and gone back across the sea before her own advent; but Mr. Wendover gave her all possible information about them. He lingered upon them, returned to them, corrected statements he had made at first, discoursed upon them earnestly and exhaustively. He seemed to fear to leave them, lest he should find nothing again so good, and he indulged in a parallel that was almost elaborate between Miss Fanny and Miss Katie. Selina told her sister afterwards that she had overheard him—that he talked of them as if he had been a nursemaid; upon which Laura defended the young man even to extravagance. She reminded her sister that people in London were always saying Lady Mary and Lady Susan: why then shouldn't Americans use the Christian name, with the humbler prefix with which they had to content themselves? There had been a time when Mrs. Berrington had been happy enough to be Miss Lina, even though she was the elder sister; and the girl liked to think there were still old friends—friends of the family, at home, for whom, even should she live to sixty years of spinsterhood, she would never be anything but Miss Laura. This was as good as Donna Anna or Donna Elvira: English people could never call people as other people did, for fear of resembling the servants.

Mr. Wendover was very attentive, as well as communicative; however his letter might be regarded in Grosvenor Place he evidently took it very seriously himself; but his eyes wandered considerably, none the less, to the other side of the room, and Laura felt that though he had often seen persons like her before (not that he betrayed this too crudely) he had never seen any one like Lady Ringrose. His glance rested also on Mrs. Berrington, who, to do her justice, abstained from showing, by the way she returned it, that she wished her sister to get him out of the room. Her smile was particularly pretty on Sunday afternoons and he was welcome to enjoy it as a part of the decoration of the place. Whether or no the young man should prove interesting he was at any rate interested; indeed she afterwards learned that what Selina deprecated in him was the fact that he would eventually display a fatiguing intensity of observation. He would be one of the sort who noticed all kinds of little things—things she never saw or heard of—in the newspapers or in society, and would call upon her (a dreadful prospect) to explain or even to defend them. She had not come there to explain England to the Americans; the more particularly as her life had been a burden to her during the first years of her marriage through her having to explain America to the English. As for defending England to her countrymen she had much rather defend it *from* them: there were too many—too many for those who were already there. This was the class she wished to spare—she didn't care about the English. They could obtain an eye for an eye and a cutlet for a cutlet by going over there; which she had no desire to do—not for all the cutlets in Christendom!

When Mr. Wendover and Laura had at last cut loose from the Schoolings he let her know confidentially that he had come over really to see London; he had time, that year; he didn't know when he should have it again (if ever, as he said) and he had made up his mind that this was about the best use he could make of four months and a half. He had heard so much of it; it was talked of so much to-day; a man felt as if he ought to know something about it. Laura wished the others could hear this—that England was coming up, was making her way at last to a place among the topics of societies more universal. She thought Mr. Wendover after all remarkably like an Englishman, in spite of his saying that he believed she had resided in London quite a time. He talked a great deal about things being characteristic, and wanted to know, lowering his voice to make the inquiry, whether Lady Ringrose were not particularly so. He had heard of her very often, he said; and he observed that it was very interesting to see her: he could not have used a different tone if he had been speaking of the prime minister or the laureate. Laura was ignorant of what he had heard of Lady Ringrose; she doubted whether it could be the same as what she had heard from her brother-in-law: if this had been the case he never would have mentioned it. She foresaw that his friends in London would have a good deal to do in the way of telling him whether this or that were characteristic or not; he would go about in much the same way that English travellers did in America, fixing his attention mainly on society (he let Laura know that this was especially what he wished to go into) and neglecting the antiquities and sights, quite as if he failed to believe in their importance. He would ask questions it was impossible to answer; as to

61

whether for instance society were very different in the two countries. If you said yes you gave a wrong impression and if you said no you didn't give a right one: that was the kind of thing that Selina had suffered from. Laura found her new acquaintance, on the present occasion and later, more philosophically analytic of his impressions than those of her countrymen she had hitherto encountered in her new home: the latter, in regard to such impressions, usually exhibited either a profane levity or a tendency to mawkish idealism.

Mrs. Berrington called out at last to Laura that she must not stay if she had prepared herself to go out: whereupon the girl, having nodded and smiled good-bye at the other members of the circle, took a more formal leave of Mr. Wendover—expressed the hope, as an American girl does in such a case, that they should see him again. Selina asked him to come and dine three days later; which was as much as to say that relations might be suspended till then. Mr. Wendover took it so, and having accepted the invitation he departed at the same time as Laura. He passed out of the house with her and in the street she asked him which way he was going. He was too tender, but she liked him; he appeared not to deal in chaff and that was a change that relieved her—she had so often had to pay out that coin when she felt wretchedly poor. She hoped he would ask her leave to go with her the way she was going— and this not on particular but on general grounds. It would be American, it would remind her of her old times; she should like him to be as American as that. There was no reason for her taking so quick an interest in his nature, inasmuch as she had not fallen under his spell; but there were moments when she felt a whimsical desire to be reminded of the way people felt and acted at home. Mr. Wendover did not disappoint her, and the bright chocolate-coloured vista of the Fifth Avenue seemed to surge before her as he said, 'May I have the pleasure of making my direction the same as yours?' and moved round, systematically, to take his place between her and the curbstone. She had never walked much with young men in America (she had been brought up in the new school, the school of attendant maids and the avoidance of certain streets) and she had very often done so in England, in the country; yet, as at the top of Grosvenor Place she crossed over to the park, proposing they should take that way, the breath of her native land was in her nostrils. It was certainly only an American who could have the tension of Mr. Wendover;

his solemnity almost made her laugh, just as her eyes grew dull when people 'slanged' each other hilariously in her sister's house; but at the same time he gave her a feeling of high respectability. It would be respectable still if she were to go on with him indefinitely—if she never were to come home at all. He asked her after a while, as they went, whether he had violated the custom of the English in offering her his company; whether in that country a gentleman might walk with a young lady—the first time he saw her—not because their roads lay together but for the sake of the walk.

'Why should it matter to me whether it is the custom of the English? I am not English,' said Laura Wing. Then her companion explained that he only wanted a general guidance—that with her (she was so kind) he had not the sense of having taken a liberty. The point was simply—and rather comprehensively and strenuously he began to set forth the point. Laura interrupted him; she said she didn't care about it and he almost irritated her by telling her she was kind. She was, but she was not pleased at its being recognised so soon; and he was still too importunate when he asked her whether she continued to go by American usage, didn't find that if one lived there one had to conform in a great many ways to the English. She was weary of the perpetual comparison, for she not only heard it from others—she heard it a great deal from herself. She held that there were certain differences you felt, if you belonged to one or the other nation, and that was the end of it: there was no use trying to express them. Those you *could* express were not real or not important ones and were not worth talking about. Mr. Wendover asked her if she liked English society and if it were superior to American; also if the tone were very high in London. She thought his questions 'academic'—the term she used to see applied in the *Times* to certain speeches in Parliament. Bending his long leanness over her (she had never seen a man whose material presence was so insubstantial, so unoppressive) and walking almost sidewise, to give her a proper attention, he struck her as innocent, as incapable of guessing that she had had a certain observation of life. They were talking about totally different things: English society, as he asked her judgment upon it and she had happened to see it, was an affair that he didn't suspect. If she were to give him that judgment it would be more than he doubtless bargained for; but she would do it not to make him open his eyes—only to relieve

63

herself. She had thought of that before in regard to two or three persons she had met—of the satisfaction of breaking out with some of her feelings. It would make little difference whether the person understood her or not; the one who should do so best would be far from understanding everything. 'I want to get out of it, please—out of the set I live in, the one I have tumbled into through my sister, the people you saw just now. There are thousands of people in London who are different from that and ever so much nicer; but I don't see them, I don't know how to get at them; and after all, poor dear man, what power have you to help me?' That was in the last analysis the gist of what she had to say.

Mr. Wendover asked her about Selina in the tone of a person who thought Mrs. Berrington a very important phenomenon, and that by itself was irritating to Laura Wing. Important—gracious goodness, no! She might have to live with her, to hold her tongue about her; but at least she was not bound to exaggerate her significance. The young man forbore decorously to make use of the expression, but she could see that he supposed Selina to be a professional beauty and she guessed that as this product had not yet been domesticated in the western world the desire to behold it, after having read so much about it, had been one of the motives of Mr. Wendover's pilgrimage. Mrs. Schooling, who must have been a goose, had told him that Mrs. Berrington, though transplanted, was the finest flower of a rich, ripe society and as clever and virtuous as she was beautiful. Meanwhile Laura knew what Selina thought of Fanny Schooling and her incurable provinciality. 'Now was that a good example of London talk—what I heard (I only heard a little of it, but the conversation was more general before you came in) in your sister's drawing-room? I don't mean literary, intellectual talk—I suppose there are special places to hear that; I mean—I mean——' Mr. Wendover went on with a deliberation which gave his companion an opportunity to interrupt him. They had arrived at Lady Davenant's door and she cut his meaning short. A fancy had taken her, on the spot, and the fact that it was whimsical seemed only to recommend it.

'If you want to hear London talk there will be some very good going on in here,' she said. 'If you would like to come in with me——?'

Henry James

'Oh, you are very kind—I should be delighted,' replied Mr. Wendover, endeavouring to emulate her own more rapid processes. They stepped into the porch and the young man, anticipating his companion, lifted the knocker and gave a postman's rap. She laughed at him for this and he looked bewildered; the idea of taking him in with her had become agreeably exhilarating. Their acquaintance, in that moment, took a long jump. She explained to him who Lady Davenant was and that if he was in search of the characteristic it would be a pity he shouldn't know her; and then she added, before he could put the question:

'And what I am doing is *not* in the least usual. No, it is not the custom for young ladies here to take strange gentlemen off to call on their friends the first time they see them.'

'So that Lady Davenant will think it rather extraordinary?' Mr. Wendover eagerly inquired; not as if that idea frightened him, but so that his observation on this point should also be well founded. He had entered into Laura's proposal with complete serenity.

'Oh, most extraordinary!' said Laura, as they went in. The old lady however concealed such surprise as she may have felt, and greeted Mr. Wendover as if he were any one of fifty familiars. She took him altogether for granted and asked him no questions about his arrival, his departure, his hotel or his business in England. He noticed, as he afterwards confided to Laura, her omission of these forms; but he was not wounded by it—he only made a mark against it as an illustration of the difference between English and American manners: in New York people always asked the arriving stranger the first thing about the steamer and the hotel. Mr. Wendover appeared greatly impressed with Lady Davenant's antiquity, though he confessed to his companion on a subsequent occasion that he thought her a little flippant, a little frivolous even for her years. 'Oh yes,' said the girl, on that occasion, 'I have no doubt that you considered she talked too much, for one so old. In America old ladies sit silent and listen to the young.' Mr. Wendover stared a little and replied to this that with her—with Laura Wing—it was impossible to tell which side she was on, the American or the English: sometimes she seemed to take one, sometimes the other. At any rate, he added, smiling,

65

with regard to the other great division it was easy to see—she was on the side of the old. 'Of course I am,' she said; 'when one *is* old!' And then he inquired, according to his wont, if she were thought so in England; to which she answered that it was England that had made her so.

Lady Davenant's bright drawing-room was filled with mementoes and especially with a collection of portraits of distinguished people, mainly fine old prints with signatures, an array of precious autographs. 'Oh, it's a cemetery,' she said, when the young man asked her some question about one of the pictures; 'they are my contemporaries, they are all dead and those things are the tombstones, with the inscriptions. I'm the grave-digger, I look after the place and try to keep it a little tidy. I have dug my own little hole,' she went on, to Laura, 'and when you are sent for you must come and put me in.' This evocation of mortality led Mr. Wendover to ask her if she had known Charles Lamb; at which she stared for an instant, replying: 'Dear me, no—one didn't meet him.'

'Oh, I meant to say Lord Byron,' said Mr. Wendover.

'Bless me, yes; I was in love with him. But he didn't notice me, fortunately—we were so many. He was very nice-looking but he was very vulgar.' Lady Davenant talked to Laura as if Mr. Wendover had not been there; or rather as if his interests and knowledge were identical with hers. Before they went away the young man asked her if she had known Garrick and she replied: 'Oh, dear, no, we didn't have them in our houses, in those days.'

'He must have been dead long before you were born!' Laura exclaimed.

'I daresay; but one used to hear of him.'

'I think I meant Edmund Kean,' said Mr. Wendover.

'You make little mistakes of a century or two,' Laura Wing remarked, laughing. She felt now as if she had known Mr. Wendover a long time.

'Oh, he was very clever,' said Lady Davenant.

'Very magnetic, I suppose,' Mr. Wendover went on.

'What's that? I believe he used to get tipsy.'

'Perhaps you don't use that expression in England?' Laura's companion inquired.

'Oh, I daresay we do, if it's American; we talk American now. You seem very good-natured people, but such a jargon as you *do* speak!'

'I like *your* way, Lady Davenant,' said Mr. Wendover, benevolently, smiling.

'You might do worse,' cried the old woman; and then she added: 'Please go out!' They were taking leave of her but she kept Laura's hand and, for the young man, nodded with decision at the open door. 'Now, wouldn't *he* do?' she asked, after Mr. Wendover had passed into the hall.

'Do for what?'

'For a husband, of course.'

'For a husband—for whom?'

'Why—for me,' said Lady Davenant.

'I don't know—I think he might tire you.'

'Oh—if he's tiresome!' the old lady continued, smiling at the girl.

'I think he is very good,' said Laura.

'Well then, he'll do.'

'Ah, perhaps *you* won't!' Laura exclaimed, smiling back at her and turning away.

VIII

She was of a serious turn by nature and unlike many serious people she made no particular study of the art of being gay. Had her circumstances been different she might have done so, but she lived in a merry house (heaven save the mark! as she used to say) and therefore was not driven to amuse herself for conscience sake. The diversions she sought were of a serious cast and she liked those best which showed most the note of difference from Selina's interests and Lionel's. She felt that she was most divergent when she attempted to cultivate her mind, and it was a branch of such cultivation to visit the curiosities, the antiquities, the monuments of London. She was fond of the Abbey and the British Museum—she had extended her researches as far as the Tower. She read the works of Mr. John Timbs and made notes of the old corners of history that had not yet been abolished—the houses in which great men had lived and died. She planned a general tour of inspection of the ancient churches of the City and a pilgrimage to the queer places commemorated by Dickens. It must be added that though her intentions were great her adventures had as yet been small. She had wanted for opportunity and independence; people had other things to do than to go with her, so that it was not till she had been some time in the country and till a good while after she had begun to go out alone that she entered upon the privilege of visiting public institutions by herself. There were some aspects of London that frightened her, but there were certain spots, such as the Poets' Corner in the Abbey or the room of the Elgin marbles, where she liked better to be alone than not to have the right companion. At the time Mr. Wendover presented himself in Grosvenor Place she had begun to put in, as they said, a museum or something of that sort whenever she had a chance. Besides her idea that such places were sources of knowledge (it is to be feared that the poor girl's notions of knowledge were at once conventional and crude) they were also occasions for detachment, an escape from worrying thoughts. She forgot Selina and she 'qualified' herself a little—though for what she hardly knew.

The day Mr. Wendover dined in Grosvenor Place they talked about St. Paul's, which he expressed a desire to see, wishing to get some idea of the great past, as he said, in England as well as of the present. Laura mentioned that she had spent half an hour the summer before in the big black temple on Ludgate Hill; whereupon he asked her if he might entertain the hope that—if it were not disagreeable to her to go again—she would serve as his guide there. She had taken him to see Lady Davenant, who was so remarkable and worth a long journey, and now he should like to pay her back—to show *her* something. The difficulty would be that there was probably nothing she had not seen; but if she could think of anything he was completely at her service. They sat together at dinner and she told him she would think of something before the repast was over. A little while later she let him know that a charming place had occurred to her—a place to which she was afraid to go alone and where she should be grateful for a protector: she would tell him more about it afterwards. It was then settled between them that on a certain afternoon of the same week they would go to St. Paul's together, extending their ramble as much further as they had time. Laura lowered her voice for this discussion, as if the range of allusion had had a kind of impropriety. She was now still more of the mind that Mr. Wendover was a good young man—he had such worthy eyes. His principal defect was that he treated all subjects as if they were equally important; but that was perhaps better than treating them with equal levity. If one took an interest in him one might not despair of teaching him to discriminate.

Laura said nothing at first to her sister about her appointment with him: the feelings with which she regarded Selina were not such as to make it easy for her to talk over matters of conduct, as it were, with this votary of pleasure at any price, or at any rate to report her arrangements to her as one would do to a person of fine judgment. All the same, as she had a horror of positively hiding anything (Selina herself did that enough for two) it was her purpose to mention at luncheon on the day of the event that she had agreed to accompany Mr. Wendover to St. Paul's. It so happened however that Mrs. Berrington was not at home at this repast; Laura partook of it in the company of Miss Steet and her young charges. It very often happened now that the sisters failed to meet in the morning, for Selina remained very late in her room and there had been a considerable intermission of the girl's earlier custom of visiting her there. It was Selina's habit to send forth from this fragrant sanctuary little hieroglyphic notes in which she expressed her wishes or gave her directions for the day. On the morning I speak of her maid put into Laura's hand one of these communications, which contained the words: 'Please be sure and replace me with the children at lunch—I meant to give them that hour to-day. But I have a frantic appeal from Lady Watermouth; she is worse and beseeches me to come to her, so I rush for the 12.30 train.' These lines required no answer and Laura had no questions to ask about Lady Watermouth. She knew she was tiresomely ill, in exile, condemned to forego the diversions of the season and calling out to her friends, in a house she had taken for three months at Weybridge (for a certain particular air) where Selina had already been to see her. Selina's devotion to her appeared commendable— she had her so much on her mind. Laura had observed in her sister in relation to other persons and objects these sudden intensities of charity, and she had said to herself, watching them—'Is it because she is bad?—does she want to make up for it somehow and to buy herself off from the penalties?'

Mr. Wendover called for his *cicerone* and they agreed to go in a romantic, Bohemian manner (the young man was very docile and appreciative about this), walking the short distance to the Victoria station and taking the mysterious underground railway. In the carriage she anticipated the inquiry that she figured to herself he presently would make and said, laughing: 'No, no, this is very exceptional; if we were both English—and both what we are, otherwise—we wouldn't do this.'

'And if only one of us were English?'

'It would depend upon which one.'

'Well, say me.'

'Oh, in that case I certainly—on so short an acquaintance—would not go sight-seeing with you.'

'Well, I am glad I'm American,' said Mr. Wendover, sitting opposite to her.

'Yes, you may thank your fate. It's much simpler,' Laura added.

'Oh, you spoil it!' the young man exclaimed—a speech of which she took no notice but which made her think him brighter, as they used to say at home. He was brighter still after they had descended from the train at the Temple station (they had meant to go on to Blackfriars, but they jumped out on seeing the sign of the Temple, fired with the thought of visiting that institution too) and got admission to the old garden of the Benchers, which lies beside the foggy, crowded river, and looked at the tombs of the crusaders in the low Romanesque church, with the cross-legged figures sleeping so close to the eternal uproar, and lingered in the flagged, homely courts of brick, with their much-lettered door-posts, their dull old windows and atmosphere of consultation—lingered to talk of Johnson and Goldsmith and to remark how London opened one's eyes to Dickens; and he was brightest of all when they stood in the high, bare cathedral, which suggested a dirty whiteness, saying it was fine but wondering why it was not finer and letting a glance as cold as the dusty, colourless glass fall upon epitaphs that seemed to make most of the defunct bores even in death. Mr. Wendover was decorous but he was increasingly gay, and these qualities appeared in him in spite of the fact that St. Paul's was rather a disappointment. Then they felt the advantage of having the other place—the one Laura had had in mind at dinner—to fall back upon: that perhaps would prove a compensation. They entered a hansom now (they had to come to that, though they had walked also from the Temple to St. Paul's) and drove to Lincoln's Inn Fields, Laura making the reflection as they went that it was really a charm to roam about London under valid protection—such a mixture of freedom and safety—and that perhaps she had been unjust, ungenerous to her sister. A good-natured, positively charitable doubt came into her mind—a doubt that Selina might have the benefit of. What she liked in her present undertaking was the element of the *imprévu* that it contained, and perhaps it was simply the same happy sense of getting the laws of London—once in a way—off her back that had led Selina to go over to Paris to ramble about with Captain Crispin. Possibly they had done nothing worse than go together to the Invalides and Notre Dame; and if any one were to meet *her* driving that way, so far from home, with Mr. Wendover—Laura, mentally, did not finish her sentence, overtaken as she was by the reflection that she had fallen again into her old assumption (she

71

had been in and out of it a hundred times), that Mrs. Berrington *had* met Captain Crispin—the idea she so passionately repudiated. She at least would never deny that she had spent the afternoon with Mr. Wendover: she would simply say that he was an American and had brought a letter of introduction.

The cab stopped at the Soane Museum, which Laura Wing had always wanted to see, a compatriot having once told her that it was one of the most curious things in London and one of the least known. While Mr. Wendover was discharging the vehicle she looked over the important old-fashioned square (which led her to say to herself that London was endlessly big and one would never know all the places that made it up) and saw a great bank of cloud hanging above it—a definite portent of a summer storm. 'We are going to have thunder; you had better keep the cab,' she said; upon which her companion told the man to wait, so that they should not afterwards, in the wet, have to walk for another conveyance. The heterogeneous objects collected by the late Sir John Soane are arranged in a fine old dwelling-house, and the place gives one the impression of a sort of Saturday afternoon of one's youth—a long, rummaging visit, under indulgent care, to some eccentric and rather alarming old travelled person. Our young friends wandered from room to room and thought everything queer and some few objects interesting; Mr. Wendover said it would be a very good place to find a thing you couldn't find anywhere else—it illustrated the prudent virtue of keeping. They took note of the sarcophagi and pagodas, the artless old maps and medals. They admired the fine Hogarths; there were uncanny, unexpected objects that Laura edged away from, that she would have preferred not to be in the room with. They had been there half an hour—it had grown much darker—when they heard a tremendous peal of thunder and became aware that the storm had broken. They watched it a while from the upper windows—a violent June shower, with quick sheets of lightning and a rainfall that danced on the pavements. They took it sociably, they lingered at the window, inhaling the odour of the fresh wet that splashed over the sultry town. They would have to wait till it had passed, and they resigned themselves serenely to this idea, repeating very often that it would pass very soon. One of the keepers told them that there were other rooms to see—that there were very interesting things in the basement. They made their way down—it grew much darker and they heard a great deal of thunder—and entered a part of the house which presented itself to Laura as a series of dim, irregular vaults—passages and little narrow avenues—encumbered with strange vague things, obscured for the time but some of which had a wicked, startling look, so that she wondered how the keepers could stay there. 'It's very fearful—it looks like a cave of idols!' she said to her companion; and then she added—'Just look there—is that a person or a thing?' As she spoke they drew nearer to the object of her reference—a figure in the middle of a small vista of curiosities, a figure which answered her question by uttering a short shriek as they approached. The immediate cause of this cry was apparently a vivid flash of lightning, which penetrated into the room and illuminated both Laura's face and that of the mysterious person. Our young lady recognised her sister, as Mrs. Berrington had evidently recognised her. 'Why, Selina!' broke from her lips before she had time to check the words. At the same moment the figure turned quickly away, and then Laura saw that it was accompanied by another, that of a tall gentleman with a light beard which shone in the dusk. The two persons retreated together—dodged out of sight, as it were, disappearing in the gloom or in the labyrinth of the objects exhibited. The whole encounter was but the business of an instant.

'Was it Mrs. Berrington?' Mr. Wendover asked with interest while Laura stood staring.

'Oh no, I only thought it was at first,' she managed to reply, very quickly. She had recognised the gentleman—he had the fine fair beard of Captain Crispin—and her heart seemed to her to jump up and down. She was glad her companion could not see her face, and yet she wanted to get out, to rush up the stairs, where he would see it again, to escape from the place. She wished not to be there with *them*—she was overwhelmed with a sudden horror. 'She has lied—she has lied again—she has lied!'—that was the rhythm to which her thought began to dance. She took a few steps one way and then another: she was afraid of running against the dreadful pair again. She remarked to her companion that it was time they should go off, and then when he showed her the way back to the staircase she pleaded that she had not half seen the things. She pretended suddenly to a deep interest in them, and lingered there roaming and prying about. She was flurried still more by the thought that he would have seen her flurry, and she wondered whether he believed the woman who had shrieked and rushed away was *not* Selina. If she was not Selina why had she shrieked? and if she was Selina what would Mr. Wendover think of her behaviour, and of her own, and of the strange accident of their meeting? What must she herself think of that? so astonishing it was that in the immensity of London so infinitesimally small a chance should have got itself enacted. What a queer place to come to—for people like them! They would get away as soon as possible, of that she could be sure; and she would wait a little to give them time.

Mr. Wendover made no further remark—that was a relief; though his silence itself seemed to show that he was mystified. They went upstairs again and on reaching the door found to their surprise that their cab had disappeared—a circumstance the more singular as the man had not been paid. The rain was still coming down, though with less violence, and the square had been cleared of vehicles by the sudden storm. The doorkeeper, perceiving the dismay of our friends, explained that the cab had been taken up by another lady and another gentleman who had gone out a few minutes before; and when they inquired how he had been induced to depart without the money they owed him the reply was that there evidently had been a discussion (he hadn't heard it, but the lady seemed in a fearful hurry) and the gentleman had told him that they would make it all up to him and give him a lot more into the bargain. The doorkeeper hazarded the candid surmise that the cabby would make ten shillings by the job. But there were plenty more cabs; there would be one up in a minute and the rain moreover was going to stop. 'Well, that *is* sharp practice!' said Mr. Wendover. He made no further allusion to the identity of the lady.

IX

The rain did stop while they stood there, and a brace of hansoms was not slow to appear. Laura told her companion that he must put her into one—she could go home alone: she had taken up enough of his time. He deprecated this course very respectfully; urged that he had it on his conscience to deliver her at her own door; but she sprang into the cab and closed the apron with a movement that was a sharp prohibition. She wanted to get away from him—it would be too awkward, the long, pottering drive back. Her hansom started off while Mr. Wendover, smiling sadly, lifted his hat. It was not very comfortable, even without him; especially as before she had gone a quarter of a mile she felt that her action had been too marked—she wished she had let him come. His puzzled, innocent air of wondering what was the matter annoyed her; and she was in the absurd situation of being angry at a desistence which she would have been still angrier if he had been guiltless of. It would have comforted her (because it would seem to share her burden) and yet it would have covered her with shame if he had guessed that what she saw was wrong. It would not occur to him that there was a scandal so near her, because he thought with no great promptitude of such things; and yet, since there was—but since there was after all Laura scarcely knew what attitude would sit upon him most gracefully. As to what he might be prepared to suspect by having heard what Selina's reputation was in London, of that Laura was unable to judge, not knowing what was said, because of course it was not said to *her*. Lionel would undertake to give her the benefit of this any moment she would allow him, but how in the world could *he* know either, for how could things be said to him? Then, in the rattle of the hansom, passing through streets for which the girl had no eyes, 'She has lied, she has lied, she has lied!' kept repeating itself. Why had she written and signed that wanton falsehood about her going down to Lady Watermouth? How could she have gone to Lady Watermouth's when she was making so very different and so extraordinary a use of the hours she had announced her intention of spending there? What had been the need of that misrepresentation and why did she lie before she was driven to it?

It was because she was false altogether and deception came out of her with her breath; she was so depraved that it was easier to her to fabricate than to let it alone. Laura would not have asked her to give an account of her day, but she would ask her now. She shuddered at one moment, as she found herself saying—even in silence—such things of her sister, and the next she sat staring out of the front of the cab at the stiff problem presented by Selina's turning up with the partner of her guilt at the Soane Museum, of all places in the world. The girl shifted this fact about in various ways, to account for it—not unconscious as she did so that it was a pretty exercise of ingenuity for a nice girl. Plainly, it was a rare accident: if it had been their plan to spend the day together the Soane Museum had not been in the original programme. They had been near it, they had been on foot and they had rushed in to take refuge from the rain. But how did they come to be near it and above all to be on foot? How could Selina do anything so reckless from her own point of view as to walk about the town—even an out-of-the-way part of it—with her suspected lover? Laura Wing felt the want of proper knowledge to explain such anomalies. It was too little clear to her where ladies went and how they proceeded when they consorted with gentlemen in regard to their meetings with whom they had to lie. She knew nothing of where Captain Crispin lived; very possibly—for she vaguely remembered having heard Selina say of him that he was very poor—he had chambers in that part of the town, and they were either going to them or coming from them. If Selina had neglected to take her way in a four-wheeler with the glasses up it was through some chance that would not seem natural till it was explained, like that of their having darted into a public institution. Then no doubt it would hang together with the rest only too well. The explanation most exact would probably be that the pair had snatched a walk together (in the course of a day of many edifying episodes) for the 'lark' of it, and for the sake of the walk had taken the risk, which in that part of London, so detached from all gentility, had appeared to them small. The last thing Selina could have expected was to meet her sister in such a strange corner—her sister with a young man of her own!

She was dining out that night with both Selina and Lionel—a conjunction that was rather rare. She was by no means always invited with them, and Selina constantly went without her husband. Appearances, however, sometimes got a sop thrown them; three or four times a month Lionel and she entered the brougham together like people who still had forms, who still said 'my dear.' This was to be one of those occasions, and Mrs. Berrington's young unmarried sister was included in the invitation. When Laura reached home she learned, on inquiry, that Selina had not yet come in, and she went straight to her own room. If her sister had been there she would have gone to hers instead—she would have cried out to her as soon as she had closed the door: 'Oh, stop, stop—in God's name, stop before you go any further, before exposure and ruin and shame come down and bury us!' That was what was in the air—the vulgarest disgrace, and the girl, harder now than ever about her sister, was conscious of a more passionate desire to save herself. But Selina's absence made the difference that during the next hour a certain chill fell upon this impulse from other feelings: she found suddenly that she was late and she began to dress. They were to go together after dinner to a couple of balls; a diversion which struck her as ghastly for people who carried such horrors in their breasts. Ghastly was the idea of the drive of husband, wife and sister in pursuit of pleasure, with falsity and detection and hate between them. Selina's maid came to her door to tell her that she was in the carriage—an extraordinary piece of punctuality, which made her wonder, as Selina was always dreadfully late for everything. Laura went down as quickly as she could, passed through the open door, where the servants were grouped in the foolish majesty of their superfluous attendance, and through the file of dingy gazers who had paused at the sight of the carpet across the pavement and the waiting carriage, in which Selina sat in pure white splendour. Mrs. Berrington had a tiara on her head and a proud patience in her face, as if her sister were really a sore trial. As soon as the girl had taken her place she said to the footman: 'Is Mr. Berrington there?'—to which the man replied: 'No ma'am, not yet.' It was not new to Laura that if there was any one later as a general thing than Selina it was Selina's husband. 'Then he must take a hansom. Go on.' The footman mounted and they rolled away.

There were several different things that had been present to Laura's mind during the last couple of hours as destined to mark—one or the other—this present encounter with her sister; but the words Selina spoke the moment the brougham began to move were of course exactly those she had not foreseen.

She had considered that she might take this tone or that tone or even no tone at all; she was quite prepared for her presenting a face of blankness to any form of interrogation and saying, 'What on earth are you talking about?' It was in short conceivable to her that Selina would deny absolutely that she had been in the museum, that they had stood face to face and that she had fled in confusion. She was capable of explaining the incident by an idiotic error on Laura's part, by her having seized on another person, by her seeing Captain Crispin in every bush; though doubtless she would be taxed (of course she would say *that* was the woman's own affair) to supply a reason for the embarrassment of the other lady. But she was not prepared for Selina's breaking out with: 'Will you be so good as to inform me if you are engaged to be married to Mr. Wendover?'

'Engaged to him? I have seen him but three times.'

'And is that what you usually do with gentlemen you have seen three times?'

'Are you talking about my having gone with him to see some sights? I see nothing wrong in that. To begin with you see what he is. One might go with him anywhere. Then he brought us an introduction—we have to do something for him. Moreover you threw him upon me the moment he came—you asked me to take charge of him.'

'I didn't ask you to be indecent! If Lionel were to know it he wouldn't tolerate it, so long as you live with us.'

Laura was silent a moment. 'I shall not live with you long.' The sisters, side by side, with their heads turned, looked at each other, a deep crimson leaping into Laura's face. 'I wouldn't have believed it—that you are so bad,' she said. 'You are horrible!' She saw that Selina had not taken up the idea of denying—she judged that would be hopeless: the recognition on either side had been too sharp. She looked radiantly handsome, especially with the strange new expression that Laura's last word brought into her eyes. This expression seemed to the girl to show her more of Selina morally than she had ever yet seen—something of the full extent and the miserable limit.

'It's different for a married woman, especially when she's married to a cad. It's in a girl that such things are odious—scouring London with strange men. I am not bound to explain to you—there would be too many things to say. I have my reasons—I have my conscience. It was the oddest of all things, our meeting in that place—I know that as well as you,' Selina went on, with her wonderful affected clearness; 'but it was not your finding me that was out of the way; it was my finding you—with your remarkable escort! That was incredible. I pretended not to recognise you, so that the gentleman who was with me shouldn't see you, shouldn't know you. He questioned me and I repudiated you. You may thank me for saving you! You had better wear a veil next time—one never knows what may happen. I met an acquaintance at Lady Watermouth's and he came up to town with me. He happened to talk about old prints; I told him how I have collected them and we spoke of the bother one has about the frames. He insisted on my going with him to that place—from Waterloo—to see such an excellent model.'

Laura had turned her face to the window of the carriage again; they were spinning along Park Lane, passing in the quick flash of other vehicles an endless succession of ladies with 'dressed' heads, of gentlemen in white neckties. 'Why, I thought your frames were all so pretty!' Laura murmured. Then she added: 'I suppose it was your eagerness to save your companion the shock of seeing me—in my dishonour—that led you to steal our cab.'

'Your cab?'

'Your delicacy was expensive for you!'

'You don't mean you were knocking about in *cabs* with him!' Selina cried.

'Of course I know that you don't really think a word of what you say about me,' Laura went on; 'though I don't know that that makes your saying it a bit less unspeakably base.'

The brougham pulled up in Park Lane and Mrs. Berrington bent herself to have a view through the front glass. 'We are there, but there are two other carriages,' she remarked, for all answer. 'Ah, there are the Collingwoods.'

'Where are you going—where are you going—where are you going?' Laura broke out.

The carriage moved on, to set them down, and while the footman was getting off the box Selina said: 'I don't pretend to be better than other women, but you do!' And being on the side of the house she quickly stepped out and carried her crowned brilliancy through the long-lingering daylight and into the open portals.

X

'What do you intend to do? You will grant that I have a right to ask you that.'

'To do? I shall do as I have always done—not so badly, as it seems to me.'

This colloquy took place in Mrs. Berrington's room, in the early morning hours, after Selina's return from the entertainment to which reference was last made. Her sister came home before her—she found herself incapable of 'going on' when Selina quitted the house in Park Lane at which they had dined. Mrs. Berrington had the night still before her, and she stepped into her carriage with her usual air of graceful resignation to a brilliant lot. She had taken the precaution, however, to provide herself with a defence, against a little sister bristling with righteousness, in the person of Mrs. Collingwood, to whom she offered a lift, as they were bent upon the same business and Mr. Collingwood had a use of his own for his brougham. The Collingwoods were a happy pair who could discuss such a divergence before their friends candidly, amicably, with a great many 'My loves' and 'Not for the worlds.' Lionel Berrington disappeared after dinner, without holding any communication with his wife, and Laura expected to find that he had taken the carriage, to repay her in kind for her having driven off from Grosvenor Place without him. But it was not new to the girl that he really spared his wife more than she spared him; not so much perhaps because he wouldn't do the 'nastiest' thing as because he couldn't. Selina could always be nastier. There was ever a whimsicality in her actions: if two or three hours before it had been her fancy to keep a third person out of the carriage she had now her reasons for bringing such a person in. Laura knew that she would not only pretend, but would really believe, that her vindication of her conduct on their way to dinner had been powerful and that she had won a brilliant victory. What need, therefore, to thresh out further a subject that she had chopped into atoms? Laura Wing, however, had needs of her own, and her remaining in the carriage when the footman next opened the door was intimately connected with them.

'I don't care to go in,' she said to her sister. 'If you will allow me to be driven home and send back the carriage for you, that's what I shall like best.'

Selina stared and Laura knew what she would have said if she could have spoken her thought. 'Oh, you are furious that I haven't given you a chance to fly at me again, and you must take it out in sulks!' These were the ideas—ideas of 'fury' and sulks—into which Selina could translate feelings that sprang from the pure depths of one's conscience. Mrs. Collingwood protested—she said it was a shame that Laura shouldn't go in and enjoy herself when she looked so lovely. 'Doesn't she look lovely?' She appealed to Mrs. Berrington. 'Bless us, what's the use of being pretty? Now, if she had *my* face!'

'I think she looks rather cross,' said Selina, getting out with her friend and leaving her sister to her own inventions. Laura had a vision, as the carriage drove away again, of what her situation would have been, or her peace of mind, if Selina and Lionel had been good, attached people like the Collingwoods, and at the same time of the singularity of a good woman's being ready to accept favours from a person as to whose behaviour she had the lights that must have come to the lady in question in regard to Selina. She accepted favours herself and she only wanted to be good: that was oppressively true; but if she had not been Selina's sister she would never drive in her carriage. That conviction was strong in the girl as this vehicle conveyed her to Grosvenor Place; but it was not in its nature consoling. The prevision of disgrace was now so vivid to her that it seemed to her that if it had not already overtaken them she had only to thank the loose, mysterious, rather ignoble tolerance of people like Mrs. Collingwood. There were plenty of that species, even among the good; perhaps indeed exposure and dishonour would begin only when the bad had got hold of the facts. Would the bad be most horrified and do most to spread the scandal? There were, in any event, plenty of them too.

Laura sat up for her sister that night, with that nice question to help her to torment herself—whether if she was hard and merciless in judging Selina it would be with the bad too that she would associate herself. Was she all wrong after all—was she cruel by being too rigid? Was Mrs. Collingwood's attitude the right one and ought she only to propose to herself to 'allow' more and more, and to allow ever, and to smooth things down by gentleness, by sympathy, by not looking at them too hard? It was not the first time that the just measure of things seemed to slip from her hands as she became conscious of possible, or rather of very actual, differences of standard and usage. On this occasion Geordie and Ferdy asserted themselves, by the mere force of lying asleep upstairs in their little cribs, as on the whole the proper measure. Laura went into the nursery to look at them when she came home—it was her habit almost any night—and yearned over them as mothers and maids do alike over the pillow of rosy childhood. They were an antidote to all casuistry; for Selina to forget *them*—that was the beginning and the end of shame. She came back to the library, where she should best hear the sound of her sister's return; the hours passed as she sat there, without bringing round this event. Carriages came and went all night; the soft shock of swift hoofs was on the wooden roadway long after the summer dawn grew fair—till it was merged in the rumble of the awakening day. Lionel had not come in when she returned, and he continued absent, to Laura's satisfaction; for if she wanted not to miss Selina she had no desire at present to have to tell her brother-in-law why she was sitting up. She prayed Selina might arrive first: then she would have more time to think of something that harassed her particularly— the question of whether she ought to tell Lionel that she had seen her in a far-away corner of the town with Captain Crispin. Almost impossible as she found it now to feel any tenderness for her, she yet detested the idea of bearing witness against her: notwithstanding which it appeared to her that she could make up her mind to do this if there were a chance of its preventing the last scandal—a catastrophe to which she saw her sister rushing straight. That Selina was capable at a given moment of going off with her lover, and capable of it precisely because it was the greatest ineptitude as well as the greatest wickedness—there was a voice of prophecy, of warning, to this effect in the silent, empty house. If repeating to Lionel what she had seen would contribute to prevent anything, or to stave off the danger, was it not her duty to denounce his wife, flesh and blood of her own as she was, to his further reprobation? This point was not intolerably difficult to determine, as she sat there waiting, only because even what was righteous in that reprobation could not present itself to her as fruitful or efficient. What could Lionel frustrate, after all, and what intelligent or authoritative step was he capable of taking? Mixed with all that now haunted her was her consciousness of what his own absence at such an hour represented in the way of the unedifying. He might be at some sporting club or he might be anywhere else; at any rate he was not where he ought to be at three o'clock in the morning. Such the husband such the wife, she said to herself; and she felt that Selina would have a kind of advantage, which she grudged her, if she should come in and say: 'And where is *he*, please—where is he, the exalted being on whose behalf you have undertaken to preach so much better than he himself practises?'

But still Selina failed to come in—even to take that advantage; yet in proportion as her waiting was useless did the girl find it impossible to go to bed. A new fear had seized her, the fear that she would never come back at all—that they were already in the presence of the dreaded catastrophe. This made her so nervous that she paced about the lower rooms, listening to every sound, roaming till she was tired. She knew it was absurd, the image of Selina taking flight in a ball-dress; but she said to herself that she might very well have sent other clothes away, in advance, somewhere (Laura had her own ripe views about the maid); and at any rate, for herself, that was the fate she had to expect, if not that night then some other one soon, and it was all the same: to sit counting the hours till a hope was given up and a hideous certainty remained. She had fallen into such a state of apprehension that when at last she heard a carriage stop at the door she was almost happy, in spite of her prevision of how disgusted her sister would be to find her. They met in the hall—Laura went out as she heard the opening of the door, Selina stopped short, seeing her, but said nothing—on account apparently of the presence of the sleepy footman. Then she moved straight to the stairs, where she paused again, asking the footman if Mr. Berrington had come in.

'Not yet, ma'am,' the footman answered.

'Ah!' said Mrs. Berrington, dramatically, and ascended the stairs.

'I have sat up on purpose—I want particularly to speak to you,' Laura remarked, following her.

'Ah!' Selina repeated, more superior still. She went fast, almost as if she wished to get to her room before her sister could overtake her. But the girl was close behind her, she passed into the room with her. Laura closed the door; then she told her that she had found it impossible to go to bed without asking her what she intended to do.

'Your behaviour is too monstrous!' Selina flashed out. 'What on earth do you wish to make the servants suppose?'

'Oh, the servants—in *this* house; as if one could put any idea into their heads that is not there already!' Laura thought. But she said nothing of this—she only repeated her question: aware that she was exasperating to her sister but also aware that she could not be anything else. Mrs. Berrington, whose maid, having outlived surprises, had gone to rest, began to divest herself of some of her ornaments, and it was not till after a moment, during which she stood before the glass, that she made that answer about doing as she had always done. To this Laura rejoined that she ought to put herself in her place enough to feel how important it was to *her* to know what was likely to happen, so that she might take time by the forelock and think of her own situation. If anything should happen she would infinitely rather be out of it—be as far away as possible. Therefore she must take her measures.

It was in the mirror that they looked at each other—in the strange, candle-lighted duplication of the scene that their eyes met. Selina drew the diamonds out of her hair, and in this occupation, for a minute, she was silent. Presently she asked: 'What are you talking about—what do you allude to as happening?'

'Why, it seems to me that there is nothing left for you but to go away with him. If there is a prospect of that insanity——' But here Laura stopped; something so unexpected was taking place in Selina's countenance—the movement that precedes a sudden gush of tears. Mrs. Berrington dashed down the glittering pins she had detached from her tresses, and the next moment she had flung herself into an armchair and was weeping profusely, extravagantly. Laura forbore to go to her; she made no motion to soothe or reassure her, she only stood and watched her tears and wondered what they signified. Somehow even the slight refreshment she felt at having affected her in that particular and, as it had lately come to seem, improbable way did not suggest to her that they were precious symptoms. Since she had come to disbelieve her word so completely there was nothing precious about Selina any more. But she continued for some moments to cry passionately, and while this lasted Laura remained silent. At last from the midst of her sobs Selina broke out, 'Go away, go away—leave me alone!'

'Of course I infuriate you,' said the girl; 'but how can I see you rush to your ruin—to that of all of us—without holding on to you and dragging you back?'

'Oh, you don't understand anything about anything!' Selina wailed, with her beautiful hair tumbling all over her.

'I certainly don't understand how you can give such a tremendous handle to Lionel.'

At the mention of her husband's name Selina always gave a bound, and she sprang up now, shaking back her dense braids. 'I give him no handle and you don't know what you are talking about! I know what I am doing and what becomes me, and I don't care if I do. He is welcome to all the handles in the world, for all that he can do with them!'

'In the name of common pity think of your children!' said Laura.

'Have I ever thought of anything else? Have you sat up all night to have the pleasure of accusing me of cruelty? Are there sweeter or more delightful children in the world, and isn't that a little my merit, pray?' Selina went on, sweeping away her tears. 'Who has made them what they are, pray?—is it their lovely father? Perhaps you'll say it's you! Certainly you have been nice to them, but you must remember that you only came here the other day. Isn't it only for them that I am trying to keep myself alive?'

This formula struck Laura Wing as grotesque, so that she replied with a laugh which betrayed too much her impression, 'Die for them—that would be better!'

Her sister, at this, looked at her with an extraordinary cold gravity. 'Don't interfere between me and my children. And for God's sake cease to harry me!'

Laura turned away: she said to herself that, given that intensity of silliness, of course the worst would come. She felt sick and helpless, and, practically, she had got the certitude she both wanted and dreaded. 'I don't know what has become of your mind,' she murmured; and she went to the door. But before she reached it Selina had flung herself upon her in one of her strange but, as she felt, really not encouraging revulsions. Her arms were about her, she clung to her, she covered Laura with the tears that had again begun to flow. She besought her to save her, to stay with her, to help her against herself, against *him*, against Lionel, against everything—to forgive her also all the horrid things she had said to her. Mrs. Berrington melted, liquefied, and the room was deluged with her repentance, her desolation, her confession, her promises and the articles of apparel which were detached from her by the high tide of her agitation. Laura remained with her for an hour, and before they separated the culpable woman had taken a tremendous vow—kneeling before her sister with her head in her lap—never again, as long as she lived, to consent to see Captain Crispin or to address a word to him, spoken or written. The girl went terribly tired to bed.

A month afterwards she lunched with Lady Davenant, whom she had not seen since the day she took Mr. Wendover to call upon her. The old woman had found herself obliged to entertain a small company, and as she disliked set parties she sent Laura a request for sympathy and assistance. She had disencumbered herself, at the end of so many years, of the burden of hospitality; but every now and then she invited people, in order to prove that she was not too old. Laura suspected her of choosing stupid ones on purpose to prove it better—to show that she could submit not only to the extraordinary but, what was much more difficult, to the usual. But when they had been properly fed she encouraged them to disperse; on this occasion as the party broke up Laura was the only person she asked to stay. She wished to know in the first place why she had not been to see her for so long, and in the second how that young man had behaved—the one she had brought that Sunday. Lady Davenant didn't remember his name, though he had been so

87

good-natured, as she said, since then, as to leave a card. If he had behaved well that was a very good reason for the girl's neglect and Laura need give no other. Laura herself would not have behaved well if at such a time she had been running after old women. There was nothing, in general, that the girl liked less than being spoken of, off-hand, as a marriageable article—being planned and arranged for in this particular. It made too light of her independence, and though in general such inventions passed for benevolence they had always seemed to her to contain at bottom an impertinence—as if people could be moved about like a game of chequers. There was a liberty in the way Lady Davenant's imagination disposed of her (with such an *insouciance* of her own preferences), but she forgave that, because after all this old friend was not obliged to think of her at all.

'I knew that you were almost always out of town now, on Sundays— and so have we been,' Laura said. 'And then I have been a great deal with my sister—more than before.'

'More than before what?'

'Well, a kind of estrangement we had, about a certain matter.'

'And now you have made it all up?'

'Well, we have been able to talk of it (we couldn't before—without painful scenes), and that has cleared the air. We have gone about together a good deal,' Laura went on. 'She has wanted me constantly with her.'

'That's very nice. And where has she taken you?' asked the old lady.

'Oh, it's I who have taken her, rather.' And Laura hesitated.

'Where do you mean?—to say her prayers?'

'Well, to some concerts—and to the National Gallery.'

Lady Davenant laughed, disrespectfully, at this, and the girl watched her with a mournful face. 'My dear child, you are too delightful! You are trying to reform her? by Beethoven and Bach, by Rubens and Titian?'

'She is very intelligent, about music and pictures—she has excellent ideas,' said Laura.

'And you have been trying to draw them out? that is very commendable.'

'I think you are laughing at me, but I don't care,' the girl declared, smiling faintly.

'Because you have a consciousness of success?—in what do they call it?—the attempt to raise her tone? You have been trying to wind her up, and you *have* raised her tone?'

'Oh, Lady Davenant, I don't know and I don't understand!' Laura broke out. 'I don't understand anything any more—I have given up trying.'

'That's what I recommended you to do last winter. Don't you remember that day at Plash?'

'You told me to let her go,' said Laura.

'And evidently you haven't taken my advice.'

'How can I—how can I?'

'Of course, how can you? And meanwhile if she doesn't go it's so much gained. But even if she should, won't that nice young man remain?' Lady Davenant inquired. 'I hope very much Selina hasn't taken you altogether away from him.'

Laura was silent a moment; then she returned: 'What nice young man would ever look at me, if anything bad should happen?'

'I would never look at *him* if he should let that prevent him!' the old woman cried. 'It isn't for your sister he loves you, I suppose; is it?'

'He doesn't love me at all.'

'Ah, then he does?' Lady Davenant demanded, with some eagerness, laying her hand on the girl's arm. Laura sat near her on her sofa and looked at her, for all answer to this, with an expression of which the sadness appeared to strike the old woman freshly. 'Doesn't he come to the house—doesn't he say anything?' she continued, with a voice of kindness.

'He comes to the house—very often.'

'And don't you like him?'

'Yes, very much—more than I did at first.'

'Well, as you liked him at first well enough to bring him straight to see me, I suppose that means that now you are immensely pleased with him.'

'He's a gentleman,' said Laura.

'So he seems to me. But why then doesn't he speak out?'

'Perhaps that's the very reason! Seriously,' the girl added, 'I don't know what he comes to the house for.'

'Is he in love with your sister?'

'I sometimes think so.'

'And does she encourage him?'

'She detests him.'

'Oh, then, I like him! I shall immediately write to him to come and see me: I shall appoint an hour and give him a piece of my mind.'

'If I believed that, I should kill myself,' said Laura.

'You may believe what you like; but I wish you didn't show your feelings so in your eyes. They might be those of a poor widow with fifteen children. When I was young I managed to be happy, whatever occurred; and I am sure I looked so.'

'Oh yes, Lady Davenant—for you it was different. You were safe, in so many ways,' Laura said. 'And you were surrounded with consideration.'

'I don't know; some of us were very wild, and exceedingly ill thought of, and I didn't cry about it. However, there are natures and natures. If you will come and stay with me to-morrow I will take you in.'

'You know how kind I think you, but I have promised Selina not to leave her.'

'Well, then, if she keeps you she must at least go straight!' cried the old woman, with some asperity. Laura made no answer to this and Lady Davenant asked, after a moment: 'And what is Lionel doing?'

'I don't know—he is very quiet.'

'Doesn't it please him—his wife's improvement?' The girl got up; apparently she was made uncomfortable by the ironical effect, if not by the ironical intention, of this question. Her old friend was kind but she was penetrating; her very next words pierced further. 'Of course if you are really protecting her I can't count upon you': a remark not adapted to enliven Laura, who would have liked immensely to transfer herself to Queen's Gate and had her very private ideas as to the efficacy of her protection. Lady Davenant kissed her and then suddenly said—'Oh, by the way, his address; you must tell me that.'

'His address?'

'The young man's whom you brought here. But it's no matter,' the old woman added; 'the butler will have entered it—from his card.'

'Lady Davenant, you won't do anything so loathsome!' the girl cried, seizing her hand.

'Why is it loathsome, if he comes so often? It's rubbish, his caring for Selina—a married woman—when you are there.'

'Why is it rubbish—when so many other people do?'

'Oh, well, he is different—I could see that; or if he isn't he ought to be!'

'He likes to observe—he came here to take notes,' said the girl. 'And he thinks Selina a very interesting London specimen.'

'In spite of her dislike of him?'

'Oh, he doesn't know that!' Laura exclaimed.

'Why not? he isn't a fool.'

'Oh, I have made it seem——' But here Laura stopped; her colour had risen.

Lady Davenant stared an instant. 'Made it seem that she inclines to him? Mercy, to do that how fond of him you must be!' An observation which had the effect of driving the girl straight out of the house.

XI

On one of the last days of June Mrs. Berrington showed her sister a note she had received from 'your dear friend,' as she called him, Mr. Wendover. This was the manner in which she usually designated him, but she had naturally, in the present phase of her relations with Laura, never indulged in any renewal of the eminently perverse insinuations by means of which she had attempted, after the incident at the Soane Museum, to throw dust in her eyes. Mr. Wendover proposed to Mrs. Berrington that she and her sister should honour with their presence a box he had obtained for the opera three nights later—an occasion of high curiosity, the first appearance of a young American singer of whom considerable things were expected. Laura left it to Selina to decide whether they should accept this invitation, and Selina proved to be of two or three differing minds. First she said it wouldn't be convenient to her to go, and she wrote to the young man to this effect. Then, on second thoughts, she considered she might very well go, and telegraphed an acceptance. Later she saw reason to regret her acceptance and communicated this circumstance to her sister, who remarked that it was still not too late to change. Selina left her in ignorance till the next day as to whether she had retracted; then she told her that she had let the matter stand—they would go. To this Laura replied that she was glad—for Mr. Wendover. 'And for yourself,' Selina said, leaving the girl to wonder why every one (this universality was represented by Mrs. Lionel Berrington and Lady Davenant) had taken up the idea that she entertained a passion for her compatriot. She was clearly conscious that this was not the case; though she was glad her esteem for him had not yet suffered the disturbance of her seeing reason to believe that Lady Davenant had already meddled, according to her terrible threat. Laura was surprised to learn afterwards that Selina had, in London parlance, 'thrown over' a dinner in order to make the evening at the opera fit in. The dinner would have made her too late, and she didn't care about it: she wanted to hear the whole opera.

The sisters dined together alone, without any question of Lionel, and on alighting at Covent Garden found Mr. Wendover awaiting them in the portico.

His box proved commodious and comfortable, and Selina was gracious to him: she thanked him for his consideration in not stuffing it full of people. He assured her that he expected but one other inmate—a gentleman of a shrinking disposition, who would take up no room. The gentleman came in after the first act; he was introduced to the ladies as Mr. Booker, of Baltimore. He knew a great deal about the young lady they had come to listen to, and he was not so shrinking but that he attempted to impart a portion of his knowledge even while she was singing. Before the second act was over Laura perceived Lady Ringrose in a box on the other side of the house, accompanied by a lady unknown to her. There was apparently another person in the box, behind the two ladies, whom they turned round from time to time to talk with. Laura made no observation about Lady Ringrose to her sister, and she noticed that Selina never resorted to the glass to look at her. That Mrs. Berrington had not failed to see her, however, was proved by the fact that at the end of the second act (the opera was Meyerbeer's *Huguenots*) she suddenly said, turning to Mr. Wendover: 'I hope you won't mind very much if I go for a short time to sit with a friend on the other side of the house.' She smiled with all her sweetness as she announced this intention, and had the benefit of the fact that an apologetic expression is highly becoming to a pretty woman. But she abstained from looking at her sister, and the latter, after a wondering glance at her, looked at Mr. Wendover. She saw that he was disappointed—even slightly wounded: he had taken some trouble to get his box and it had been no small pleasure to him to see it graced by the presence of a celebrated beauty. Now his situation collapsed if the celebrated beauty were going to transfer her light to another quarter. Laura was unable to imagine what had come into her sister's head—to make her so inconsiderate, so rude. Selina tried to perform her act of defection in a soothing, conciliating way, so far as appealing eyebeams went; but she gave no particular reason for her escapade, withheld the name of the friends in question and betrayed no consciousness that it was not usual for ladies to roam about the lobbies. Laura asked her no question, but she said to her, after an hesitation: 'You won't be long, surely. You know you oughtn't to leave me here.' Selina took no notice of this—excused herself in no way to the girl. Mr. Wendover only exclaimed, smiling in reference to Laura's last remark: 'Oh, so far as leaving you here goes——!' In spite of his great defect (and it was his only one, that she could see) of having only an ascending scale of seriousness, she judged him interestedly enough to feel a real pleasure in noticing that though he was annoyed at Selina's going away and not saying that she would come back soon, he conducted himself as a gentleman should, submitted respectfully, gallantly, to her wish. He suggested that her friends might perhaps, instead, be induced to come to his box, but when she had objected, 'Oh, you see, there are too many,' he put her shawl on her shoulders, opened the box, offered her his arm. While this was going on Laura saw Lady Ringrose studying them with her glass. Selina refused Mr. Wendover's arm; she said, 'Oh no, you stay with *her*—I daresay *he'll* take me:' and she gazed inspiringly at Mr. Booker. Selina never mentioned a name when the pronoun would do. Mr. Booker of course sprang to the service required and led her away, with an injunction from his friend to bring her back promptly. As they went off Laura heard Selina say to her companion—and she knew Mr. Wendover could also hear it—'Nothing would have induced me to leave her alone with *you*!' She thought this a very extraordinary speech—she thought it even vulgar; especially considering that she had never seen the young man till half an hour before and since then had not exchanged twenty words with him. It came to their ears so distinctly that Laura was moved to notice it by exclaiming, with a laugh: 'Poor Mr. Booker, what does she suppose I would do to him?'

'Oh, it's for you she's afraid,' said Mr. Wendover.

Laura went on, after a moment: 'She oughtn't to have left me alone with you, either.'

'Oh yes, she ought—after all!' the young man returned.

The girl had uttered these words from no desire to say something flirtatious, but because they simply expressed a part of the judgment she passed, mentally, on Selina's behaviour. She had a sense of wrong—of being made light of; for Mrs. Berrington certainly knew that honourable women didn't (for the appearance of the thing) arrange to leave their unmarried sister sitting alone, publicly, at the playhouse, with a couple of young men—the couple that there would be as soon as Mr. Booker should come back. It displeased her that the people in the opposite box, the people Selina had joined, should see her exhibited in this light. She drew the curtain of the box a little, she moved a little more behind it, and she heard her companion utter a vague appealing, protecting sigh, which seemed to express his sense (her own corresponded with it) that the glory of the occasion had somehow suddenly departed. At the end of some minutes she perceived among Lady Ringrose and her companions a movement which appeared to denote that Selina had come in. The two ladies in front turned round—something went on at the back of the box. 'She's there,' Laura said, indicating the place; but Mrs. Berrington did not show herself—she remained masked by the others. Neither was Mr. Booker visible; he had not, seemingly, been persuaded to remain, and indeed Laura could see that there would not have been room for him. Mr. Wendover observed, ruefully, that as Mrs. Berrington evidently could see nothing at all from where she had gone she had exchanged a very good place for a very bad one. 'I can't imagine—I can't imagine——' said the girl; but she paused, losing herself in reflections and wonderments, in conjectures that soon became anxieties. Suspicion of Selina was now so rooted in her heart that it could make her unhappy even when it pointed nowhere, and by the end of half an hour she felt how little her fears had really been lulled since that scene of dishevelment and contrition in the early dawn.

The opera resumed its course, but Mr. Booker did not come back. The American singer trilled and warbled, executed remarkable flights, and there was much applause, every symptom of success; but Laura became more and more unaware of the music—she had no eyes but for Lady Ringrose and her friend. She watched them earnestly—she tried to sound with her glass the curtained dimness behind them. Their attention was all for the stage and they gave no present sign of having any fellow-listeners. These others had either gone away or were leaving them very much to themselves. Laura was unable to guess any particular motive on her sister's part, but the conviction grew within her that she had not put such an affront on Mr. Wendover simply in order to have a little chat with Lady Ringrose. There was something else, there was some one else, in the affair; and when once the girl's idea had become as definite as that it took but little longer to associate itself with the image of Captain Crispin. This image made her draw back further behind her curtain, because it brought the blood to her face; and if she coloured for shame she coloured also for anger. Captain Crispin was there, in the opposite box; those horrible women concealed him (she forgot how harmless and well-read Lady Ringrose had appeared to her that time at Mellows); they had lent themselves to this abominable proceeding. Selina was nestling there in safety with him, by their favour, and she had had the baseness to lay an honest girl, the most loyal, the most unselfish of sisters, under contribution to the same end. Laura crimsoned with the sense that she had been, unsuspectingly, part of a scheme, that she was being used as the two women opposite were used, but that she had been outraged into the bargain, inasmuch as she was not, like them, a conscious accomplice and not a person to be given away in that manner before hundreds of people. It came back to her how bad Selina had been the day of the business in Lincoln's Inn Fields, and how in spite of intervening comedies the woman who had then found such words of injury would be sure to break out in a new spot with a new weapon. Accordingly, while the pure music filled the place and the rich picture of the stage glowed beneath it, Laura found herself face to face with the strange inference that the evil of Selina's nature made her wish—since she had given herself to it—to bring her sister to her own colour by putting an appearance of 'fastness' upon her. The girl said to herself that she would have succeeded, in the cynical view of London; and to her troubled spirit the immense theatre had a myriad eyes, eyes that she knew, eyes that would know her, that would see her sitting there with a strange young man. She had recognised many faces already and her imagination quickly multiplied them. However, after she had burned a while with this particular revolt she ceased to think of herself and of what, as regarded herself, Selina had intended: all her thought went to the mere calculation of Mrs. Berrington's return. As she did not return, and still did not, Laura felt a sharp constriction of the heart. She knew not what she feared—she knew not what she supposed. She was so nervous (as she had been the night she waited, till morning, for her sister to re-enter the house in Grosvenor Place) that when Mr. Wendover occasionally made a remark to her she failed to understand him, was unable to answer him. Fortunately he made very few; he was preoccupied—either wondering also what Selina was 'up to' or, more probably, simply absorbed in the music. What she *had* comprehended, however, was that when at three different moments she had said, restlessly, 'Why doesn't Mr. Booker come back?' he replied, 'Oh, there's plenty of time—we are very comfortable.' These words she was conscious of; she particularly noted them and they interwove themselves with her restlessness. She also noted, in her tension, that after her third inquiry Mr. Wendover said something about looking up his friend, if she didn't mind being left alone a moment. He quitted the box and during this interval Laura tried more than ever to see with her glass what had become of her sister. But it was as if the ladies opposite had arranged themselves, had arranged their curtains, on purpose to frustrate such an attempt: it was impossible to her even to assure herself of what she had begun to suspect, that Selina was now not with them. If she was not with them where in the world had she gone? As the moments elapsed, before Mr. Wendover's return, she went to the door of the box and stood watching the lobby, for the chance that he would bring back the absentee. Presently she saw him coming alone, and something in the expression of his face made her step out into the lobby to meet him. He was smiling, but he looked embarrassed and strange, especially when he saw her standing there as if she wished to leave the place.

'I hope you don't want to go,' he said, holding the door for her to pass back into the box.

'Where are they—where are they?' she demanded, remaining in the corridor.

'I saw our friend—he has found a place in the stalls, near the door by which you go into them—just here under us.'

'And does he like that better?'

Mr. Wendover's smile became perfunctory as he looked down at her. 'Mrs. Berrington has made such an amusing request of him.'

'An amusing request?'

'She made him promise not to come back.'

'Made him promise——?' Laura stared.

'She asked him—as a particular favour to her—not to join us again. And he said he wouldn't.'

'Ah, the monster!' Laura exclaimed, blushing crimson.

'Do you mean poor Mr. Booker?' Mr. Wendover asked. 'Of course he had to assure her that the wish of so lovely a lady was law. But he doesn't understand!' laughed the young man.

'No more do I. And where is the lovely lady?' said Laura, trying to recover herself.

'He hasn't the least idea.'

'Isn't she with Lady Ringrose?'

'If you like I will go and see.'

Laura hesitated, looking down the curved lobby, where there was nothing to see but the little numbered doors of the boxes. They were alone in the lamplit bareness; the *finale* of the act was ringing and booming behind them. In a moment she said: 'I'm afraid I must trouble you to put me into a cab.'

'Ah, you won't see the rest? *Do* stay—what difference does it make?' And her companion still held open the door of the box. Her eyes met his, in which it seemed to her that as well as in his voice there was conscious sympathy, entreaty, vindication, tenderness. Then she gazed into the vulgar corridor again; something said to her that if she should return she would be taking the most important step of her life. She considered this, and while she did so a great burst of applause filled the place as the curtain fell. 'See what we are losing! And the last act is so fine,' said Mr. Wendover. She returned to her seat and he closed the door of the box behind them.

Then, in this little upholstered receptacle which was so public and yet so private, Laura Wing passed through the strangest moments she had known. An indication of their strangeness is that when she presently perceived that while she was in the lobby Lady Ringrose and her companion had quite disappeared, she observed the circumstance without an exclamation, holding herself silent. Their box was empty, but Laura looked at it without in the least feeling this to be a sign that Selina would now come round. She would never come round again, nor would she have gone home from the opera. That was by this time absolutely definite to the girl, who had first been hot and now was cold with the sense of what Selina's injunction to poor Mr. Booker exactly meant. It was worthy of her, for it was simply a vicious little kick as she took her flight. Grosvenor Place would not shelter her that night and would never shelter her more: that was the reason she tried to spatter her sister with the mud into which she herself had jumped. She would not have dared to treat her in such a fashion if they had had a prospect of meeting again. The strangest part of this remarkable juncture was that what ministered most to our young lady's suppressed emotion was not the tremendous reflection that this time Selina had really 'bolted' and that on the morrow all London would know it: all that had taken the glare of certainty (and a very hideous hue it was), whereas the chill that had fallen upon the girl now was that of a mystery which waited to be cleared up. Her heart was full of suspense—suspense of which she returned the pressure, trying to twist it into expectation. There was a certain chance in life that sat there beside her, but it would go for ever if it should not move nearer that night; and she listened, she watched, for it to move. I need not inform the reader that this chance presented itself in the person of Mr. Wendover, who more than any one she knew had it in his hand to transmute her detestable position. To-morrow he would know, and would think sufficiently little of a young person of *that* breed: therefore it could only be a question of his speaking on the spot. That was what she had come back into the box for—to give him his opportunity. It was open to her to think he had asked for it—adding everything together.

The poor girl added, added, deep in her heart, while she said nothing. The music was not there now, to keep them silent; yet he remained quiet, even as she did, and that for some minutes was a part of her addition. She felt as if she were running a race with failure and shame; she would get in first if she should get in before the degradation of the morrow. But this was not very far off, and every minute brought it nearer. It would be there in fact, virtually, that night, if Mr. Wendover should begin to realise the brutality of Selina's not turning up at all. The comfort had been, hitherto, that he didn't realise brutalities. There were certain violins that emitted tentative sounds in the orchestra; they shortened the time and made her uneasier—fixed her idea that he could lift her out of her mire if he would. It didn't appear to prove that he would, his also observing Lady Ringrose's empty box without making an encouraging comment upon it. Laura waited for him to remark that her sister obviously would turn up now; but no such words fell from his lips. He must either like Selina's being away or judge it damningly, and in either case why didn't he speak? If he had nothing to say, why *had* he said, why had he done, what did he mean——? But the girl's inward challenge to him lost itself in a mist of faintness; she was screwing herself up to a purpose of her own, and it hurt almost to anguish, and the whole place, around her, was a blur and swim, through which she heard the tuning of fiddles. Before she knew it she had said to him, 'Why have you come so often?'

'So often? To see you, do you mean?'

'To see *me*—it was for that? Why have you come?' she went on. He was evidently surprised, and his surprise gave her a point of anger, a desire almost that her words should hurt him, lash him. She spoke low, but she heard herself, and she thought that if what she said sounded to *him* in the same way——! 'You have come very often—too often, too often!'

He coloured, he looked frightened, he was, clearly, extremely startled. 'Why, you have been so kind, so delightful,' he stammered.

'Yes, of course, and so have you! Did you come for Selina? She is married, you know, and devoted to her husband.' A single minute had sufficed to show the girl that her companion was quite unprepared for her question, that he was distinctly not in love with her and was face to face with a situation entirely new. The effect of this perception was to make her say wilder things.

'Why, what is more natural, when one likes people, than to come often? Perhaps I have bored you—with our American way,' said Mr. Wendover.

'And is it because you like me that you have kept me here?' Laura asked. She got up, leaning against the side of the box; she had pulled the curtain far forward and was out of sight of the house.

101

He rose, but more slowly; he had got over his first confusion. He smiled at her, but his smile was dreadful. 'Can you have any doubt as to what I have come for? It's a pleasure to me that you have liked me well enough to ask.'

For an instant she thought he was coming nearer to her, but he didn't: he stood there twirling his gloves. Then an unspeakable shame and horror—horror of herself, of him, of everything—came over her, and she sank into a chair at the back of the box, with averted eyes, trying to get further into her corner. 'Leave me, leave me, go away!' she said, in the lowest tone that he could hear. The whole house seemed to her to be listening to her, pressing into the box.

'Leave you alone—in this place—when I love you? I can't do that—indeed I can't.'

'You don't love me—and you torture me by staying!' Laura went on, in a convulsed voice. 'For God's sake go away and don't speak to me, don't let me see you or hear of you again!'

Mr. Wendover still stood there, exceedingly agitated, as well he might be, by this inconceivable scene. Unaccustomed feelings possessed him and they moved him in different directions. Her command that he should take himself off was passionate, yet he attempted to resist, to speak. How would she get home—would she see him to-morrow—would she let him wait for her outside? To this Laura only replied: 'Oh dear, oh dear, if you would only go!' and at the same instant she sprang up, gathering her cloak around her as if to escape from him, to rush away herself. He checked this movement, however, clapping on his hat and holding the door. One moment more he looked at her—her own eyes were closed; then he exclaimed, pitifully, 'Oh Miss Wing, oh Miss Wing!' and stepped out of the box.

When he had gone she collapsed into one of the chairs again and sat there with her face buried in a fold of her mantle. For many minutes she was perfectly still—she was ashamed even to move. The one thing that could have justified her, blown away the dishonour of her monstrous overture, would have been, on his side, the quick response of unmistakable passion. It had not come, and she had nothing left but to loathe herself. She did so, violently, for a long time, in the dark corner of the box, and she felt that he loathed her too. 'I love you!'—how pitifully the poor little make-believe words had quavered out and how much disgust they must have represented! 'Poor man—poor man!' Laura Wing suddenly found herself murmuring: compassion filled her mind at the sense of the way she had used him. At the same moment a flare of music broke out: the last act of the opera had begun and she had sprung up and quitted the box.

The passages were empty and she made her way without trouble. She descended to the vestibule; there was no one to stare at her and her only fear was that Mr. Wendover would be there. But he was not, apparently, and she saw that she should be able to go away quickly. Selina would have taken the carriage—she could be sure of that; or if she hadn't it wouldn't have come back yet; besides, she couldn't possibly wait there so long as while it was called. She was in the act of asking one of the attendants, in the portico, to get her a cab, when some one hurried up to her from behind, overtaking her—a gentleman in whom, turning round, she recognised Mr. Booker. He looked almost as bewildered as Mr. Wendover, and his appearance disconcerted her almost as much as that of his friend would have done. 'Oh, are you going away, alone? What must you think of me?' this young man exclaimed; and he began to tell her something about her sister and to ask her at the same time if he might not go with her—help her in some way. He made no inquiry about Mr. Wendover, and she afterwards judged that that distracted gentleman had sought him out and sent him to her assistance; also that he himself was at that moment watching them from behind some column. He would have been hateful if he had shown himself; yet (in this later meditation) there was a voice in her heart which commended his delicacy. He effaced himself to look after her—he provided for her departure by proxy.

'A cab, a cab—that's all I want!' she said to Mr. Booker; and she almost pushed him out of the place with the wave of the hand with which she indicated her need. He rushed off to call one, and a minute afterwards the messenger whom she had already despatched rattled up in a hansom. She quickly got into it, and as she rolled away she saw Mr. Booker returning in all haste with another. She gave a passionate moan—this common confusion seemed to add a grotesqueness to her predicament.

XII

The next day, at five o'clock, she drove to Queen's Gate, turning to Lady Davenant in her distress in order to turn somewhere. Her old friend was at home and by extreme good fortune alone; looking up from her book, in her place by the window, she gave the girl as she came in a sharp glance over her glasses. This glance was acquisitive; she said nothing, but laying down her book stretched out her two gloved hands. Laura took them and she drew her down toward her, so that the girl sunk on her knees and in a moment hid her face, sobbing, in the old woman's lap. There was nothing said for some time: Lady Davenant only pressed her tenderly—stroked her with her hands. 'Is it very bad?' she asked at last. Then Laura got up, saying as she took a seat, 'Have you heard of it and do people know it?'

'I haven't heard anything. Is it very bad?' Lady Davenant repeated.

'We don't know where Selina is—and her maid's gone.'

Lady Davenant looked at her visitor a moment. 'Lord, what an ass!' she then ejaculated, putting the paper-knife into her book to keep her place. 'And whom has she persuaded to take her—Charles Crispin?' she added.

'We suppose—we suppose——' said Laura.

'And he's another,' interrupted the old woman. 'And who supposes—Geordie and Ferdy?'

'I don't know; it's all black darkness!'

'My dear, it's a blessing, and now you can live in peace.'

'In peace!' cried Laura; 'with my wretched sister leading such a life?'

'Oh, my dear, I daresay it will be very comfortable; I am sorry to say anything in favour of such doings, but it very often is. Don't worry; you take her too hard. Has she gone abroad?' the old lady continued. 'I daresay she has gone to some pretty, amusing place.'

'I don't know anything about it. I only know she is gone. I was with her last evening and she left me without a word.'

'Well, that was better. I hate 'em when they make parting scenes: it's too mawkish!'

'Lionel has people watching them,' said the girl; 'agents, detectives, I don't know what. He has had them for a long time; I didn't know it.'

'Do you mean you would have told her if you had? What is the use of detectives now? Isn't he rid of her?'

'Oh, I don't know, he's as bad as she; he talks too horribly—he wants every one to know it,' Laura groaned.

'And has he told his mother?'

'I suppose so: he rushed off to see her at noon. She'll be overwhelmed.'

'Overwhelmed? Not a bit of it!' cried Lady Davenant, almost gaily. 'When did anything in the world overwhelm her and what do you take her for? She'll only make some delightful odd speech. As for people knowing it,' she added, 'they'll know it whether he wants them or not. My poor child, how long do you expect to make believe?'

'Lionel expects some news to-night,' Laura said. 'As soon as I know where she is I shall start.'

'Start for where?'

'To go to her—to do something.'

'Something preposterous, my dear. Do you expect to bring her back?'

'He won't take her in,' said Laura, with her dried, dismal eyes. 'He wants his divorce—it's too hideous!'

'Well, as she wants hers what is simpler?'

'Yes, she wants hers. Lionel swears by all the gods she can't get it.'

'Bless me, won't one do?' Lady Davenant asked. 'We shall have some pretty reading.'

105

'It's awful, awful, awful!' murmured Laura.

'Yes, they oughtn't to be allowed to publish them. I wonder if we couldn't stop that. At any rate he had better be quiet: tell him to come and see me.'

'You won't influence him; he's dreadful against her. Such a house as it is to-day!'

'Well, my dear, naturally.'

'Yes, but it's terrible for me: it's all more sickening than I can bear.'

'My dear child, come and stay with me,' said the old woman, gently.

'Oh, I can't desert her; I can't abandon her!'

'Desert—abandon? What a way to put it! Hasn't she abandoned you?'

'She has no heart—she's too base!' said the girl. Her face was white and the tears now began to rise to her eyes again.

Lady Davenant got up and came and sat on the sofa beside her: she put her arms round her and the two women embraced. 'Your room is all ready,' the old lady remarked. And then she said, 'When did she leave you? When did you see her last?'

'Oh, in the strangest, maddest, crudest way, the way most insulting to me. We went to the opera together and she left me there with a gentleman. We know nothing about her since.'

'With a gentleman?'

'With Mr. Wendover—that American, and something too dreadful happened.'

'Dear me, did he kiss you?' asked Lady Davenant.

Laura got up quickly, turning away. 'Good-bye, I'm going, I'm going!' And in reply to an irritated, protesting exclamation from her companion she went on, 'Anywhere—anywhere to get away!'

'To get away from your American?'

'I asked him to marry me!' The girl turned round with her tragic face.

'He oughtn't to have left that to you.'

'I knew this horror was coming and it took possession of me, there in the box, from one moment to the other—the idea of making sure of some other life, some protection, some respectability. First I thought he liked me, he had behaved as if he did. And I like him, he is a very good man. So I asked him, I couldn't help it, it was too hideous—I offered myself!' Laura spoke as if she were telling that she had stabbed him, standing there with dilated eyes.

Lady Davenant got up again and went to her; drawing off her glove she felt her cheek with the back of her hand. 'You are ill, you are in a fever. I'm sure that whatever you said it was very charming.'

'Yes, I am ill,' said Laura.

'Upon my honour you shan't go home, you shall go straight to bed. And what did he say to you?'

'Oh, it was too miserable!' cried the girl, pressing her face again into her companion's kerchief. 'I was all, all mistaken; he had never thought!'

'Why the deuce then did he run about that way after you? He was a brute to say it!'

'He didn't say it and he never ran about. He behaved like a perfect gentleman.'

'I've no patience—I wish I had seen him that time!' Lady Davenant declared.

'Yes, that would have been nice! You'll never see him; if he *is* a gentleman he'll rush away.'

'Bless me, what a rushing away!' murmured the old woman. Then passing her arm round Laura she added, 'You'll please to come upstairs with me.'

Half an hour later she had some conversation with her butler which led to his consulting a little register into which it was his law to transcribe with great neatness, from their cards, the addresses of new visitors. This volume, kept in the drawer of the hall table, revealed the fact that Mr. Wendover was staying in George Street, Hanover Square. 'Get into a cab immediately and tell him to come and see me this evening,' Lady Davenant said. 'Make him understand that it interests him very nearly, so that no matter what his engagements may be he must give them up. Go quickly and you'll just find him: he'll be sure to be at home to dress for dinner.' She had calculated justly, for a few minutes before ten o'clock the door of her drawing-room was thrown open and Mr. Wendover was announced.

'Sit there,' said the old lady; 'no, not that one, nearer to me. We must talk low. My dear sir, I won't bite you!'

'Oh, this is very comfortable,' Mr. Wendover replied vaguely, smiling through his visible anxiety. It was no more than natural that he should wonder what Laura Wing's peremptory friend wanted of him at that hour of the night; but nothing could exceed the gallantry of his attempt to conceal the symptoms of alarm.

'You ought to have come before, you know,' Lady Davenant went on. 'I have wanted to see you more than once.'

'I have been dining out—I hurried away. This was the first possible moment, I assure you.'

'I too was dining out and I stopped at home on purpose to see you. But I didn't mean to-night, for you have done very well. I was quite intending to send for you—the other day. But something put it out of my head. Besides, I knew she wouldn't like it.'

'Why, Lady Davenant, I made a point of calling, ever so long ago—after that day!' the young man exclaimed, not reassured, or at any rate not enlightened.

'I daresay you did—but you mustn't justify yourself; that's just what I don't want; it isn't what I sent for you for. I have something very particular to say to you, but it's very difficult. Voyons un peu!'

The old woman reflected a little, with her eyes on his face, which had grown more grave as she went on; its expression intimated that he failed as yet to understand her and that he at least was not exactly trifling. Lady Davenant's musings apparently helped her little, if she was looking for an artful approach; for they ended in her saying abruptly, 'I wonder if you know what a capital girl she is.'

'Do you mean—do you mean——?' stammered Mr. Wendover, pausing as if he had given her no right not to allow him to conceive alternatives.

'Yes, I do mean. She's upstairs, in bed.'

'Upstairs in bed!' The young man stared.

'Don't be afraid—I'm not going to send for her!' laughed his hostess; 'her being here, after all, has nothing to do with it, except that she *did* come—yes, certainly, she did come. But my keeping her—that was my doing. My maid has gone to Grosvenor Place to get her things and let them know that she will stay here for the present. Now am I clear?'

'Not in the least,' said Mr. Wendover, almost sternly.

Lady Davenant, however, was not of a composition to suspect him of sternness or to care very much if she did, and she went on, with her quick discursiveness: 'Well, we must be patient; we shall work it out together. I was afraid you would go away, that's why I lost no time. Above all I want you to understand that she has not the least idea that I have sent for you, and you must promise me never, never, never to let her know. She would be monstrous angry. It is quite my own idea—I have taken the responsibility. I know very little about you of course, but she has spoken to me well of you. Besides, I am very clever about people, and I liked you that day, though you seemed to think I was a hundred and eighty.'

'You do me great honour,' Mr. Wendover rejoined.

'I'm glad you're pleased! You must be if I tell you that I like you now even better. I see what you are, except for the question of fortune. It doesn't perhaps matter much, but have you any money? I mean have you a fine income?'

'No, indeed I haven't!' And the young man laughed in his bewilderment. 'I have very little money indeed.'

'Well, I daresay you have as much as I. Besides, that would be a proof she is not mercenary.'

'You haven't in the least made it plain whom you are talking about,' said Mr. Wendover. 'I have no right to assume anything.'

'Are you afraid of betraying her? I am more devoted to her even than I want you to be. She has told me what happened between you last night—what she said to you at the opera. That's what I want to talk to you about.'

'She was very strange,' the young man remarked.

'I am not so sure that she was strange. However, you are welcome to think it, for goodness knows she says so herself. She is overwhelmed with horror at her own words; she is absolutely distracted and prostrate.'

Mr. Wendover was silent a moment. 'I assured her that I admire her—beyond every one. I was most kind to her.'

'Did you say it in that tone? You should have thrown yourself at her feet! From the moment you didn't—surely you understand women well enough to know.'

'You must remember where we were—in a public place, with very little room for throwing!' Mr. Wendover exclaimed.

'Ah, so far from blaming you she says your behaviour was perfect. It's only I who want to have it out with you,' Lady Davenant pursued. 'She's so clever, so charming, so good and so unhappy.'

'When I said just now she was strange, I meant only in the way she turned against me.'

'She turned against you?'

'She told me she hoped she should never see me again.'

'And you, should you like to see her?'

'Not now—not now!' Mr. Wendover exclaimed, eagerly.

'I don't mean now, I'm not such a fool as that. I mean some day or other, when she has stopped accusing herself, if she ever does.'

'Ah, Lady Davenant, you must leave that to me,' the young man returned, after a moment's hesitation.

'Don't be afraid to tell me I'm meddling with what doesn't concern me,' said his hostess. 'Of course I know I'm meddling; I sent for you here to meddle. Who wouldn't, for that creature? She makes one melt.'

'I'm exceedingly sorry for her. I don't know what she thinks she said.'

'Well, that she asked you why you came so often to Grosvenor Place. I don't see anything so awful in that, if you did go.'

'Yes, I went very often. I liked to go.'

'Now, that's exactly where I wish to prevent a misconception,' said Lady Davenant. 'If you liked to go you had a reason for liking, and Laura Wing was the reason, wasn't she?'

'I thought her charming, and I think her so now more than ever.'

'Then you are a dear good man. Vous faisiez votre cour, in short.'

Mr. Wendover made no immediate response: the two sat looking at each other. 'It isn't easy for me to talk of these things,' he said at last; 'but if you mean that I wished to ask her to be my wife I am bound to tell you that I had no such intention.'

'Ah, then I'm at sea. You thought her charming and you went to see her every day. What then did you wish?'

'I didn't go every day. Moreover I think you have a very different idea in this country of what constitutes—well, what constitutes making love. A man commits himself much sooner.'

'Oh, I don't know what *your* odd ways may be!' Lady Davenant exclaimed, with a shade of irritation.

111

'Yes, but I was justified in supposing that those ladies did: they at least are American.'

'"They," my dear sir! For heaven's sake don't mix up that nasty Selina with it!'

'Why not, if I admired her too? I do extremely, and I thought the house most interesting.'

'Mercy on us, if that's your idea of a nice house! But I don't know—I have always kept out of it,' Lady Davenant added, checking herself. Then she went on, 'If you are so fond of Mrs. Berrington I am sorry to inform you that she is absolutely good-for-nothing.'

'Good-for-nothing?'

'Nothing to speak of! I have been thinking whether I would tell you, and I have decided to do so because I take it that your learning it for yourself would be a matter of but a very short time. Selina has bolted, as they say.'

'Bolted?' Mr. Wendover repeated.

'I don't know what you call it in America.'

'In America we don't do it.'

'Ah, well, if they stay, as they do usually abroad, that's better. I suppose you didn't think her capable of behaving herself, did you?'

'Do you mean she has left her husband—with some one else?'

'Neither more nor less; with a fellow named Crispin. It appears it all came off last evening, and she had her own reasons for doing it in the most offensive way—publicly, clumsily, with the vulgarest bravado. Laura has told me what took place, and you must permit me to express my surprise at your not having divined the miserable business.'

'I saw something was wrong, but I didn't understand. I'm afraid I'm not very quick at these things.'

'Your state is the more gracious; but certainly you are not quick if you could call there so often and not see through Selina.'

'Mr. Crispin, whoever he is, was never there,' said the young man.

'Oh, she was a clever hussy!' his companion rejoined.

'I knew she was fond of amusement, but that's what I liked to see. I wanted to see a house of that sort.'

'Fond of amusement is a very pretty phrase!' said Lady Davenant, laughing at the simplicity with which her visitor accounted for his assiduity. 'And did Laura Wing seem to you in her place in a house of that sort?'

'Why, it was natural she should be with her sister, and she always struck me as very gay.'

'That was your enlivening effect! And did she strike you as very gay last night, with this scandal hanging over her?'

'She didn't talk much,' said Mr. Wendover.

'She knew it was coming—she felt it, she saw it, and that's what makes her sick now, that at *such* a time she should have challenged you, when she felt herself about to be associated (in people's minds, of course) with such a vile business. In people's minds and in yours—when you should know what had happened.'

'Ah, Miss Wing isn't associated——' said Mr. Wendover. He spoke slowly, but he rose to his feet with a nervous movement that was not lost upon his companion: she noted it indeed with a certain inward sense of triumph. She was very deep, but she had never been so deep as when she made up her mind to mention the scandal of the house of Berrington to her visitor and intimated to him that Laura Wing regarded herself as near enough to it to receive from it a personal stain. 'I'm extremely sorry to hear of Mrs. Berrington's misconduct,' he continued gravely, standing before her. 'And I am no less obliged to you for your interest.'

'Don't mention it,' she said, getting up too and smiling. 'I mean my interest. As for the other matter, it will all come out. Lionel will haul her up.'

'Dear me, how dreadful!'

113

'Yes, dreadful enough. But don't betray me.'

'Betray you?' he repeated, as if his thoughts had gone astray a moment.

'I mean to the girl. Think of her shame!'

'Her shame?' Mr. Wendover said, in the same way.

'It seemed to her, with what was becoming so clear to her, that an honest man might save her from it, might give her his name and his faith and help her to traverse the bad place. She exaggerates the badness of it, the stigma of her relationship. Good heavens, at that rate where would some of us be? But those are her ideas, they are absolutely sincere, and they had possession of her at the opera. She had a sense of being lost and was in a real agony to be rescued. She saw before her a kind gentleman who had seemed—who had certainly seemed——' And Lady Davenant, with her fine old face lighted by her bright sagacity and her eyes on Mr. Wendover's, paused, lingering on this word. 'Of course she must have been in a state of nerves.'

'I am very sorry for her,' said Mr. Wendover, with his gravity that committed him to nothing.

'So am I! And of course if you were not in love with her you weren't, were you?'

'I must bid you good-bye, I am leaving London.' That was the only answer Lady Davenant got to her inquiry.

'Good-bye then. She is the nicest girl I know. But once more, mind you don't let her suspect!'

'How can I let her suspect anything when I shall never see her again?'

'Oh, don't say that,' said Lady Davenant, very gently.

'She drove me away from her with a kind of ferocity.'

'Oh, gammon!' cried the old woman.

'I'm going home,' he said, looking at her with his hand on the door.

'Well, it's the best place for you. And for her too!' she added as he went out. She was not sure that the last words reached him.

XIII

Laura Wing was sharply ill for three days, but on the fourth she made up her mind she was better, though this was not the opinion of Lady Davenant, who would not hear of her getting up. The remedy she urged was lying still and yet lying still; but this specific the girl found well-nigh intolerable—it was a form of relief that only ministered to fever. She assured her friend that it killed her to do nothing: to which her friend replied by asking her what she had a fancy to do. Laura had her idea and held it tight, but there was no use in producing it before Lady Davenant, who would have knocked it to pieces. On the afternoon of the first day Lionel Berrington came, and though his intention was honest he brought no healing. Hearing she was ill he wanted to look after her—he wanted to take her back to Grosvenor Place and make her comfortable: he spoke as if he had every convenience for producing that condition, though he confessed there was a little bar to it in his own case. This impediment was the 'cheeky' aspect of Miss Steet, who went sniffing about as if she knew a lot, if she should only condescend to tell it. He saw more of the children now; 'I'm going to have 'em in every day, poor little devils,' he said; and he spoke as if the discipline of suffering had already begun for him and a kind of holy change had taken place in his life. Nothing had been said yet in the house, of course, as Laura knew, about Selina's disappearance, in the way of treating it as irregular; but the servants pretended so hard not to be aware of anything in particular that they were like pickpockets looking with unnatural interest the other way after they have cribbed a fellow's watch. To a certainty, in a day or two, the governess would give him warning: she would come and tell him she couldn't stay in such a place, and he would tell her, in return, that she was a little donkey for not knowing that the place was much more respectable now than it had ever been.

This information Selina's husband imparted to Lady Davenant, to whom he discoursed with infinite candour and humour, taking a highly philosophical view of his position and declaring that it suited him down to the ground. His wife couldn't have pleased him better if she had done it on purpose; he knew where she had been every hour since she quitted Laura at the opera—he knew where she was at that moment and he was expecting to find another telegram on his return to Grosvenor Place. So if it suited *her* it was all right, wasn't it? and the whole thing would go as straight as a shot. Lady Davenant took him up to see Laura, though she viewed their meeting with extreme disfavour, the girl being in no state for talking. In general Laura had little enough mind for it, but she insisted on seeing Lionel: she declared that if this were not allowed her she would go after him, ill as she was—she would dress herself and drive to his house. She dressed herself now, after a fashion; she got upon a sofa to receive him. Lady Davenant left him alone with her for twenty minutes, at the end of which she returned to take him away. This interview was not fortifying to the girl, whose idea—the idea of which I have said that she was tenacious—was to go after her sister, to take possession of her, cling to her and bring her back. Lionel, of course, wouldn't hear of taking her back, nor would Selina presumably hear of coming; but this made no difference in Laura's heroic plan. She would work it, she would compass it, she would go down on her knees, she would find the eloquence of angels, she would achieve miracles. At any rate it made her frantic not to try, especially as even in fruitless action she should escape from herself—an object of which her horror was not yet extinguished.

As she lay there through inexorably conscious hours the picture of that hideous moment in the box alternated with the vision of her sister's guilty flight. She wanted to fly, herself—to go off and keep going for ever. Lionel was fussily kind to her and he didn't abuse Selina—he didn't tell her again how that lady's behaviour suited his book. He simply resisted, with a little exasperating, dogged grin, her pitiful appeal for knowledge of her sister's whereabouts. He knew what she wanted it for and he wouldn't help her in any such game. If she would promise, solemnly, to be quiet, he would tell her when she got better, but he wouldn't lend her a hand to make a fool of herself. Her work was cut out for her—she was to stay and mind the children: if she was so keen to do her duty she needn't go further than that for it. He talked a great deal about the children and figured himself as pressing the little deserted darlings to his bosom. He was not a comedian, and she could see that he really believed he was going to be better and purer now. Laura said she was sure Selina would make an attempt to get them—or at least one of them; and he replied, grimly, 'Yes, my dear, she had better try.' The girl was so angry with him, in her hot, tossing weakness, for refusing to tell her even whether the desperate pair had crossed the Channel, that she was guilty of the immorality of regretting that the difference in badness between husband and wife was so distinct (for it was distinct, she could see that) as he made his dry little remark about Selina's trying. He told her he had already seen his solicitor, the clever Mr. Smallshaw, and she said she didn't care.

On the fourth day of her absence from Grosvenor Place she got up, at an hour when she was alone (in the afternoon, rather late), and prepared herself to go out. Lady Davenant had admitted in the morning that she was better, and fortunately she had not the complication of being subject to a medical opinion, having absolutely refused to see a doctor. Her old friend had been obliged to go out—she had scarcely quitted her before—and Laura had requested the hovering, rustling lady's-maid to leave her alone: she assured her she was doing beautifully. Laura had no plan except to leave London that night; she had a moral certainty that Selina had gone to the Continent. She had always done so whenever she had a chance, and what chance had ever been larger than the present? The Continent was fearfully vague, but she would deal sharply with Lionel—she would show him she had a right to knowledge. He would certainly be in town; he would be in a complacent bustle with his lawyers. She had told him that she didn't believe he had yet gone to them, but in her heart she believed it perfectly. If he didn't satisfy her she would go to Lady Ringrose, odious as it would be to her to ask a favour of this depraved creature: unless indeed Lady Ringrose had joined the little party to France, as on the occasion of Selina's last journey thither. On her way downstairs she met one of the footmen, of whom she made the request that he would call her a cab as quickly as possible—she was obliged to go out for half an hour. He expressed the respectful hope that she was better and she replied that she was perfectly well—he would please tell her ladyship when she came in. To this the footman rejoined that her ladyship *had* come in—she had returned five minutes before and had gone to her room. 'Miss Frothingham told her you were asleep, Miss,' said the man, 'and her ladyship said it was a blessing and you were not to be disturbed.'

117

'Very good, I will see her,' Laura remarked, with dissimulation: 'only please let me have my cab.'

The footman went downstairs and she stood there listening; presently she heard the house-door close—he had gone out on his errand. Then she descended very softly—she prayed he might not be long. The door of the drawing-room stood open as she passed it, and she paused before it, thinking she heard sounds in the lower hall. They appeared to subside and then she found herself faint—she was terribly impatient for her cab. Partly to sit down till it came (there was a seat on the landing, but another servant might come up or down and see her), and partly to look, at the front window, whether it were not coming, she went for a moment into the drawing-room. She stood at the window, but the footman was slow; then she sank upon a chair—she felt very weak. Just after she had done so she became aware of steps on the stairs and she got up quickly, supposing that her messenger had returned, though she had not heard wheels. What she saw was not the footman she had sent out, but the expansive person of the butler, followed apparently by a visitor. This functionary ushered the visitor in with the remark that he would call her ladyship, and before she knew it she was face to face with Mr. Wendover. At the same moment she heard a cab drive up, while Mr. Wendover instantly closed the door.

'Don't turn me away; do see me—do see me!' he said. 'I asked for Lady Davenant—they told me she was at home. But it was you I wanted, and I wanted her to help me. I was going away—but I couldn't. You look very ill—do listen to me! You don't understand—I will explain everything. Ah, how ill you look!' the young man cried, as the climax of this sudden, soft, distressed appeal. Laura, for all answer, tried to push past him, but the result of this movement was that she found herself enclosed in his arms. He stopped her, but she disengaged herself, she got her hand upon the door. He was leaning against it, so she couldn't open it, and as she stood there panting she shut her eyes, so as not to see him. 'If you would let me tell you what I think—I would do anything in the world for you!' he went on.

'Let me go—you persecute me!' the girl cried, pulling at the handle.

'You don't do me justice—you are too cruel!' Mr. Wendover persisted.

'Let me go—let me go!' she only repeated, with her high, quavering, distracted note; and as he moved a little she got the door open. But he followed her out: would she see him that night? Where was she going? might he not go with her? would she see him to-morrow?

'Never, never, never!' she flung at him as she hurried away. The butler was on the stairs, descending from above; so he checked himself, letting her go. Laura passed out of the house and flew into her cab with extraordinary speed, for Mr. Wendover heard the wheels bear her away while the servant was saying to him in measured accents that her ladyship would come down immediately.

Lionel was at home, in Grosvenor Place: she burst into the library and found him playing papa. Geordie and Ferdy were sporting around him, the presence of Miss Steet had been dispensed with, and he was holding his younger son by the stomach, horizontally, between his legs, while the child made little sprawling movements which were apparently intended to represent the act of swimming. Geordie stood impatient on the brink of the imaginary stream, protesting that it was his turn now, and as soon as he saw his aunt he rushed at her with the request that she would take him up in the same fashion. She was struck with the superficiality of their childhood; they appeared to have no sense that she had been away and no care that she had been ill. But Lionel made up for this; he greeted her with affectionate jollity, said it was a good job she had come back, and remarked to the children that they would have great larks now that auntie was home again. Ferdy asked if she had been with mummy, but didn't wait for an answer, and she observed that they put no question about their mother and made no further allusion to her while they remained in the room. She wondered whether their father had enjoined upon them not to mention her, and reflected that even if he had such a command would not have been efficacious. It added to the ugliness of Selina's flight that even her children didn't miss her, and to the dreariness, somehow, to Laura's sense, of the whole situation that one could neither spend tears on the mother and wife, because she was not worth it, nor sentimentalise about the little boys, because they didn't inspire it. 'Well, you do look seedy—I'm bound to say that!' Lionel exclaimed; and he recommended strongly a glass of port, while Ferdy, not seizing this reference, suggested that daddy should take her by the waistband and teach her to 'strike out.' He represented himself in the act of drowning, but Laura interrupted this entertainment, when the servant answered the bell (Lionel having rung for the port), by requesting that the children should be conveyed to Miss Steet. 'Tell her she must never go away again,' Lionel said to Geordie, as the butler took him by the hand; but the only touching consequence of this injunction was that the child piped back to his father, over his shoulder, 'Well, you mustn't either, you know!'

'You must tell me or I'll kill myself—I give you my word!' Laura said to her brother-in-law, with unnecessary violence, as soon as they had left the room.

'I say, I say,' he rejoined, 'you *are* a wilful one! What do you want to threaten me for? Don't you know me well enough to know that ain't the way? That's the tone Selina used to take. Surely you don't want to begin and imitate her!' She only sat there, looking at him, while he leaned against the chimney-piece smoking a short cigar. There was a silence, during which she felt the heat of a certain irrational anger at the thought that a little ignorant, red-faced jockey should have the luck to be in the right as against her flesh and blood. She considered him helplessly, with something in her eyes that had never been there before—something that, apparently, after a moment, made an impression on him. Afterwards, however, she saw very well that it was not her threat that had moved him, and even at the moment she had a sense, from the way he looked back at her, that this was in no manner the first time a baffled woman had told him that she would kill herself. He had always accepted his kinship with her, but even in her trouble it was part of her consciousness that he now lumped her with a mixed group of female figures, a little wavering and dim, who were associated in his memory with 'scenes,' with importunities and bothers. It is apt to be the disadvantage of women, on occasions of measuring their strength with men, that they may perceive that the man has a larger experience and that they themselves are a part of it. It is doubtless as a provision against such emergencies that nature has opened to them operations of the mind that are independent of experience.

Laura felt the dishonour of her race the more that her brother-in-law seemed so gay and bright about it: he had an air of positive prosperity, as if his misfortune had turned into that. It came to her that he really liked the idea of the public *éclaircissement*—the fresh occupation, the bustle and importance and celebrity of it. That was sufficiently incredible, but as she was on the wrong side it was also humiliating. Besides, higher spirits always suggest finer wisdom, and such an attribute on Lionel's part was most humiliating of all. 'I haven't the least objection at present to telling you what you want to know. I shall have made my little arrangements very soon and you will be subpœnaed.'

'Subpœnaed?' the girl repeated, mechanically.

'You will be called as a witness on my side.'

'On your side.'

'Of course you're on my side, ain't you?'

'Can they force me to come?' asked Laura, in answer to this.

'No, they can't force you, if you leave the country.'

'That's exactly what I want to do.'

'That will be idiotic,' said Lionel, 'and very bad for your sister. If you don't help me you ought at least to help her.'

She sat a moment with her eyes on the ground. 'Where is she—where is she?' she then asked.

'They are at Brussels, at the Hôtel de Flandres. They appear to like it very much.'

'Are you telling me the truth?'

'Lord, my dear child, *I* don't lie!' Lionel exclaimed. 'You'll make a jolly mistake if you go to her,' he added. 'If you have seen her with him how can you speak for her?'

'I won't see her with him.'

'That's all very well, but he'll take care of that. Of course if you're ready for perjury——!' Lionel exclaimed.

'I'm ready for anything.'

'Well, I've been kind to you, my dear,' he continued, smoking, with his chin in the air.

'Certainly you have been kind to me.'

'If you want to defend her you had better keep away from her,' said Lionel. 'Besides for yourself, it won't be the best thing in the world—to be known to have been in it.'

'I don't care about myself,' the girl returned, musingly.

'Don't you care about the children, that you are so ready to throw them over? For you would, my dear, you know. If you go to Brussels you never come back here—you never cross this threshold—you never touch them again!'

Laura appeared to listen to this last declaration, but she made no reply to it; she only exclaimed after a moment, with a certain impatience, 'Oh, the children will do anyway!' Then she added passionately, 'You *won't*, Lionel; in mercy's name tell me that you won't!'

'I won't what?'

'Do the awful thing you say.'

'Divorce her? The devil I won't!'

'Then why do you speak of the children—if you have no pity for them?'

Lionel stared an instant. 'I thought you said yourself that they would do anyway!'

Laura bent her head, resting it on the back of her hand, on the leathern arm of the sofa. So she remained, while Lionel stood smoking; but at last, to leave the room, she got up with an effort that was a physical pain. He came to her, to detain her, with a little good intention that had no felicity for her, trying to take her hand persuasively. 'Dear old girl, don't try and behave just

122

as *she* did! If you'll stay quietly here I won't call you, I give you my honour I won't; there! You want to see the doctor—that's the fellow you want to see. And what good will it do you, even if you bring her home in pink paper? Do you candidly suppose I'll ever look at her—except across the court-room?'

'I must, I must, I must!' Laura cried, jerking herself away from him and reaching the door.

'Well then, good-bye,' he said, in the sternest tone she had ever heard him use.

She made no answer, she only escaped. She locked herself in her room; she remained there an hour. At the end of this time she came out and went to the door of the schoolroom, where she asked Miss Steet to be so good as to come and speak to her. The governess followed her to her apartment and there Laura took her partly into her confidence. There were things she wanted to do before going, and she was too weak to act without assistance. She didn't want it from the servants, if only Miss Steet would learn from them whether Mr. Berrington were dining at home. Laura told her that her sister was ill and she was hurrying to join her abroad. It had to be mentioned, that way, that Mrs. Berrington had left the country, though of course there was no spoken recognition between the two women of the reasons for which she had done so. There was only a tacit hypocritical assumption that she was on a visit to friends and that there had been nothing queer about her departure. Laura knew that Miss Steet knew the truth, and the governess knew that she knew it. This young woman lent a hand, very confusedly, to the girl's preparations; she ventured not to be sympathetic, as that would point too much to badness, but she succeeded perfectly in being dismal. She suggested that Laura was ill herself, but Laura replied that this was no matter when her sister was so much worse. She elicited the fact that Mr. Berrington was dining out—the butler believed with his mother—but she was of no use when it came to finding in the 'Bradshaw' which she brought up from the hall the hour of the night-boat to Ostend. Laura found it herself; it was conveniently late, and it was a gain to her that she was very near the Victoria station, where she would take the train for Dover. The governess wanted to go to the station with her, but the girl would not listen to this—she would only allow her to see that she had a cab. Laura let her help her still further; she sent her down to talk to Lady Davenant's maid when that personage arrived in Grosvenor Place to inquire, from her mistress, what in the world had become of poor Miss Wing. The maid intimated, Miss Steet said on her return, that her ladyship would have come herself, only she was too angry. She was very bad indeed. It was an indication of this that she had sent back her young friend's dressing-case and her clothes. Laura also borrowed money from the governess—she had too little in her pocket. The latter brightened up as the preparations advanced; she had never before been concerned in a flurried night-episode, with an unavowed clandestine side; the very imprudence of it (for a sick girl alone) was romantic, and before Laura had gone down to the cab she began to say that foreign life must be fascinating and to make wistful reflections. She saw that the coast was clear, in the nursery—that the children were asleep, for their aunt to come in. She kissed Ferdy while her companion pressed her lips upon Geordie, and Geordie while Laura hung for a moment over Ferdy. At the door of the cab she tried to make her take more money, and our heroine had an odd sense that if the vehicle had not rolled away she would have thrust into her hand a keepsake for Captain Crispin.

A quarter of an hour later Laura sat in the corner of a railway-carriage, muffled in her cloak (the July evening was fresh, as it so often is in London— fresh enough to add to her sombre thoughts the suggestion of the wind in the Channel), waiting in a vain torment of nervousness for the train to set itself in motion. Her nervousness itself had led her to come too early to the station, and it seemed to her that she had already waited long. A lady and a gentleman had taken their place in the carriage (it was not yet the moment for the outward crowd of tourists) and had left their appurtenances there while they strolled up and down the platform. The long English twilight was still in the air, but there was dusk under the grimy arch of the station and Laura flattered herself that the off-corner of the carriage she had chosen was in shadow. This, however, apparently did not prevent her from being recognised by a gentleman who stopped at the door, looking in, with the movement of a person who was going from carriage to carriage. As soon as he saw her he stepped quickly in, and the next moment Mr. Wendover was seated on the edge of the place beside her, leaning toward her, speaking to her low, with clasped hands. She fell back in her seat, closing her eyes again. He barred the way out of the compartment.

'I have followed you here—I saw Miss Steet—I want to implore you not to go! Don't, don't! I know what you're doing. Don't go, I beseech you. I saw Lady Davenant, I wanted to ask her to help me, I could bear it no longer. I have thought of you, night and day, these four days. Lady Davenant has told me things, and I entreat you not to go!'

Laura opened her eyes (there was something in his voice, in his pressing nearness), and looked at him a moment: it was the first time she had done so since the first of those detestable moments in the box at Covent Garden. She had never spoken to him of Selina in any but an honourable sense. Now she said, 'I'm going to my sister.'

'I know it, and I wish unspeakably you would give it up—it isn't good—it's a great mistake. Stay here and let me talk to you.'

The girl raised herself, she stood up in the carriage. Mr. Wendover did the same; Laura saw that the lady and gentleman outside were now standing near the door. 'What have you to say? It's my own business!' she returned, between her teeth. 'Go out, go out, go out!'

'Do you suppose I would speak if I didn't care—do you suppose I would care if I didn't love you?' the young man murmured, close to her face.

'What is there to care about? Because people will know it and talk? If it's bad it's the right thing for me! If I don't go to her where else shall I go?'

'Come to me, dearest, dearest!' Mr. Wendover went on. 'You are ill, you are mad! I love you—I assure you I do!'

She pushed him away with her hands. 'If you follow me I will jump off the boat!'

'Take your places, take your places!' cried the guard, on the platform. Mr. Wendover had to slip out, the lady and gentleman were coming in. Laura huddled herself into her corner again and presently the train drew away.

Mr. Wendover did not get into another compartment; he went back that evening to Queen's Gate. He knew how interested his old friend there, as he now considered her, would be to hear what Laura had undertaken (though, as he learned, on entering her drawing-room again, she had already heard of it from her maid), and he felt the necessity to tell her once more how her words of four days before had fructified in his heart, what a strange, ineffaceable impression she had made upon him: to tell her in short and to repeat it over and over, that he had taken the most extraordinary fancy———! Lady Davenant was tremendously vexed at the girl's perversity, but she counselled him patience, a long, persistent patience. A week later she heard from Laura Wing, from Antwerp, that she was sailing to America from that port—a letter containing no mention whatever of Selina or of the reception she had found at Brussels. To America Mr. Wendover followed his young compatriot (that at least she had no right to forbid), and there, for the moment, he has had a chance to practise the humble virtue recommended by Lady Davenant. He knows she has no money and that she is staying with some distant relatives in Virginia; a situation that he—perhaps too superficially—figures as unspeakably dreary. He knows further that Lady Davenant has sent her fifty pounds, and he himself has ideas of transmitting funds, not directly to Virginia but by the roundabout road of Queen's Gate. Now, however, that Lionel Berrington's deplorable suit is coming on he reflects with some satisfaction that the Court of Probate and Divorce is far from the banks of the Rappahannock. 'Berrington *versus* Berrington and Others' is coming on— but these are matters of the present hour.

THE PATAGONIA

I

The houses were dark in the August night and the perspective of Beacon Street, with its double chain of lamps, was a foreshortened desert. The club on the hill alone, from its semi-cylindrical front, projected a glow upon the dusky vagueness of the Common, and as I passed it I heard in the hot stillness the click of a pair of billiard balls. As 'every one' was out of town perhaps the servants, in the extravagance of their leisure, were profaning the tables. The heat was insufferable and I thought with joy of the morrow, of the deck of the steamer, the freshening breeze, the sense of getting out to sea. I was even glad of what I had learned in the afternoon at the office of the company—that at the eleventh hour an old ship with a lower standard of speed had been put on in place of the vessel in which I had taken my passage. America was roasting, England might very well be stuffy, and a slow passage (which at that season of the year would probably also be a fine one) was a guarantee of ten or twelve days of fresh air.

I strolled down the hill without meeting a creature, though I could see through the palings of the Common that that recreative expanse was peopled with dim forms. I remembered Mrs. Nettlepoint's house—she lived in those days (they are not so distant, but there have been changes) on the water-side, a little way beyond the spot at which the Public Garden terminates; and I reflected that like myself she would be spending the night in Boston if it were true that, as had been mentioned to me a few days before at Mount Desert, she was to embark on the morrow for Liverpool. I presently saw this appearance confirmed by a light above her door and in two or three of her windows, and I determined to ask for her, having nothing to do till bedtime. I had come out simply to pass an hour, leaving my hotel to the blaze of its gas and the perspiration of its porters; but it occurred to me that my old friend might very well not know of the substitution of the *Patagonia* for the *Scandinavia*, so that it would be an act of consideration to prepare her mind. Besides, I could offer to help her, to look after her in the morning: lone women are grateful for support in taking ship for far countries.

As I stood on her doorstep I remembered that as she had a son she might not after all be so lone; yet at the same time it was present to me that Jasper Nettlepoint was not quite a young man to lean upon, having (as I at least supposed) a life of his own and tastes and habits which had long since drawn him away from the maternal side. If he did happen just now to be at home my solicitude would of course seem officious; for in his many wanderings—I believed he had roamed all over the globe—he would certainly have learned how to manage. None the less I was very glad to show Mrs. Nettlepoint I thought of her. With my long absence I had lost sight of her; but I had liked her of old; she had been a close friend of my sisters; and I had in regard to her that sense which is pleasant to those who, in general, have grown strange or detached—the feeling that she at least knew all about me. I could trust her at any time to tell people what a respectable person I was. Perhaps I was conscious of how little I deserved this indulgence when it came over me that for years I had not communicated with her. The measure of this neglect was given by my vagueness of mind about her son. However, I really belonged nowadays to a different generation: I was more the old lady's contemporary than Jasper's.

Mrs. Nettlepoint was at home: I found her in her back drawing-room, where the wide windows opened upon the water. The room was dusky—it was too hot for lamps—and she sat slowly moving her fan and looking out on the little arm of the sea which is so pretty at night, reflecting the lights of Cambridgeport and Charlestown. I supposed she was musing upon the loved ones she was to leave behind, her married daughters, her grandchildren; but she struck a note more specifically Bostonian as she said to me, pointing with her fan to the Back Bay—'I shall see nothing more charming than that over there, you know!' She made me very welcome, but her son had told her about the *Patagonia*, for which she was sorry, as this would mean a longer voyage. She was a poor creature on shipboard and mainly confined to her cabin, even in weather extravagantly termed fine—as if any weather could be fine at sea.

'Ah, then your son's going with you?' I asked.

'Here he comes, he will tell you for himself much better than I am able to do.'

Jasper Nettlepoint came into the room at that moment, dressed in white flannel and carrying a large fan.

'Well, my dear, have you decided?' his mother continued, with some irony in her tone. 'He hasn't yet made up his mind, and we sail at ten o'clock!'

'What does it matter, when my things are put up?' said the young man. 'There is no crowd at this moment; there will be cabins to spare. I'm waiting for a telegram—that will settle it. I just walked up to the club to see if it was come—they'll send it there because they think the house is closed. Not yet, but I shall go back in twenty minutes.'

'Mercy, how you rush about in this temperature!' his mother exclaimed, while I reflected that it was perhaps *his* billiard-balls I had heard ten minutes before. I was sure he was fond of billiards.

'Rush? not in the least. I take it uncommonly easy.'

'Ah, I'm bound to say you do,' Mrs. Nettlepoint exclaimed, inconsequently. I divined that there was a certain tension between the pair and a want of consideration on the young man's part, arising perhaps from selfishness. His mother was nervous, in suspense, wanting to be at rest as to whether she should have his company on the voyage or be obliged to make it alone. But as he stood there smiling and slowly moving his fan he struck me somehow as a person on whom this fact would not sit very heavily. He was of the type of those whom other people worry about, not of those who worry about other people. Tall and strong, he had a handsome face, with a round head and close-curling hair; the whites of his eyes and the enamel of his teeth, under his brown moustache, gleamed vaguely in the lights of the Back Bay. I made out that he was sunburnt, as if he lived much in the open air, and that he looked intelligent but also slightly brutal, though not in a morose way. His brutality, if he had any, was bright and finished. I had to tell him who I was, but even then I saw that he failed to place me and that my explanations gave me in his mind no great identity or at any rate no great importance. I foresaw that he would in intercourse make me feel sometimes very young and sometimes very old. He mentioned, as if to show his mother that he might safely be left to his own devices, that he had once started from London to Bombay at three-quarters of an hour's notice.

'Yes, and it must have been pleasant for the people you were with!'

'Oh, the people I was with——!' he rejoined; and his tone appeared to signify that such people would always have to come off as they could. He asked if there were no cold drinks in the house, no lemonade, no iced syrups; in such weather something of that sort ought always to be kept going. When his mother remarked that surely at the club they *were* going he went on, 'Oh, yes, I had various things there; but you know I have walked down the hill since. One should have something at either end. May I ring and see?' He rang while Mrs. Nettlepoint observed that with the people they had in the house—an establishment reduced naturally at such a moment to its simplest expression (they were burning-up candle-ends and there were no luxuries) she would not answer for the service. The matter ended in the old lady's going out of the room in quest of syrup with the female domestic who had appeared in response to the bell and in whom Jasper's appeal aroused no visible intelligence.

She remained away some time and I talked with her son, who was sociable but desultory and kept moving about the room, always with his fan, as if he were impatient. Sometimes he seated himself for an instant on the window-sill, and then I saw that he was in fact very good-looking; a fine brown, clean young athlete. He never told me on what special contingency his decision depended; he only alluded familiarly to an expected telegram, and I perceived that he was probably not addicted to copious explanations. His mother's absence was an indication that when it was a question of gratifying him she had grown used to spare no pains, and I fancied her rummaging in some close storeroom, among old preserve-pots, while the dull maid-servant held the candle awry. I know not whether this same vision was in his own eyes; at all events it did not prevent him from saying suddenly, as he looked at his watch, that I must excuse him, as he had to go back to the club. He would return in half an hour—or in less. He walked away and I sat there alone, conscious, in the dark, dismantled, simplified room, in the deep silence that rests on American towns during the hot season (there was now and then a far cry or a plash in the water, and at intervals the tinkle of the bells of the horse-cars on the long bridge, slow in the suffocating night), of the strange influence, half sweet, half sad, that abides in houses uninhabited or about to become so—in places muffled and bereaved, where the unheeded sofas and patient belittered tables seem to know (like the disconcerted dogs) that it is the eve of a journey.

After a while I heard the sound of voices, of steps, the rustle of dresses, and I looked round, supposing these things to be the sign of the return of Mrs. Nettlepoint and her handmaiden, bearing the refreshment prepared for her son. What I saw however was two other female forms, visitors just admitted apparently, who were ushered into the room. They were not announced— the servant turned her back on them and rambled off to our hostess. They came forward in a wavering, tentative, unintroduced way—partly, I could see, because the place was dark and partly because their visit was in its nature experimental, a stretch of confidence. One of the ladies was stout and the other was slim, and I perceived in a moment that one was talkative and the other silent. I made out further that one was elderly and the other young and that the fact that they were so unlike did not prevent their being mother and daughter. Mrs. Nettlepoint reappeared in a very few minutes, but the interval had sufficed to establish a communication (really copious for the occasion) between the strangers and the unknown gentleman whom they found in possession, hat and stick in hand. This was not my doing (for what had I to go upon?) and still less was it the doing of the person whom I supposed and whom I indeed quickly and definitely learned to be the daughter. She spoke but once—when her companion informed me that she was going out to Europe the next day to be married. Then she said, 'Oh, mother!' protestingly, in a tone which struck me in the darkness as doubly strange, exciting my curiosity to see her face.

It had taken her mother but a moment to come to that and to other things besides, after I had explained that I myself was waiting for Mrs. Nettlepoint, who would doubtless soon come back.

'Well, she won't know me—I guess she hasn't ever heard much about me,' the good lady said; 'but I have come from Mrs. Allen and I guess that will make it all right. I presume you know Mrs. Allen?'

I was unacquainted with this influential personage, but I assented vaguely to the proposition. Mrs. Allen's emissary was good-humoured and familiar, but rather appealing than insistent (she remarked that if her friend *had* found time to come in the afternoon—she had so much to do, being just up for the day, that she couldn't be sure—it would be all right); and somehow even before she mentioned Merrimac Avenue (they had come all the way from there) my imagination had associated her with that indefinite social limbo known to the properly-constituted Boston mind as the South End—a nebulous region which condenses here and there into a pretty face, in which the daughters are an 'improvement' on the mothers and are sometimes acquainted with gentlemen resident in more distinguished districts of the New England capital—gentlemen whose wives and sisters in turn are not acquainted with them.

When at last Mrs. Nettlepoint came in, accompanied by candles and by a tray laden with glasses of coloured fluid which emitted a cool tinkling, I was in a position to officiate as master of the ceremonies, to introduce Mrs. Mavis and Miss Grace Mavis, to represent that Mrs. Allen had recommended them— nay, had urged them—to come that way, informally, and had been prevented only by the pressure of occupations so characteristic of her (especially when she was up from Mattapoisett just for a few hours' shopping) from herself calling in the course of the day to explain who they were and what was the favour they had to ask of Mrs. Nettlepoint. Good-natured women understand each other even when divided by the line of topographical fashion, and our hostess had quickly mastered the main facts: Mrs. Allen's visit in the morning in Merrimac Avenue to talk of Mrs. Amber's great idea, the classes at the public schools in vacation (she was interested with an equal charity to that of Mrs. Mavis—even in such weather!—in those of the South End) for games and exercises and music, to keep the poor unoccupied children out of the streets; then the revelation that it had suddenly been settled almost from one hour to the other that Grace should sail for Liverpool, Mr. Porterfield at last being ready. He was taking a little holiday; his mother was with him, they had come over from Paris to see some of the celebrated old buildings in England, and he had telegraphed to say that if Grace would start right off they would just finish it up and be married. It often happened that when things had dragged on that way for years they were all huddled up at the end. Of course in such a case she, Mrs. Mavis, had had to fly round. Her daughter's passage was taken, but it seemed too dreadful that she should make her journey all alone, the first time she had ever been at sea, without any companion or escort. *She* couldn't go—Mr. Mavis was too sick: she hadn't even been able to get him off to the seaside.

'Well, Mrs. Nettlepoint is going in that ship,' Mrs. Allen had said; and she had represented that nothing was simpler than to put the girl in her charge. When Mrs. Mavis had replied that that was all very well but that she didn't know the lady, Mrs. Allen had declared that that didn't make a speck of difference, for Mrs. Nettlepoint was kind enough for anything. It was easy enough to know her, if that was all the trouble. All Mrs. Mavis would have to do would be to go up to her the next morning when she took her daughter to the ship (she would see her there on the deck with her party) and tell her what she wanted. Mrs. Nettlepoint had daughters herself and she would easily understand. Very likely she would even look after Grace a little on the other side, in such a queer situation, going out alone to the gentleman she was engaged to; she would just help her to turn round before she was married. Mr. Porterfield seemed to think they wouldn't wait long, once she was there: they would have it right over at the American consul's. Mrs. Allen had said it would perhaps be better still to go and see Mrs. Nettlepoint beforehand, that day, to tell her what they wanted: then they wouldn't seem to spring it on her just as she was leaving. She herself (Mrs. Allen) would call and say a word for them if she could save ten minutes before catching her train. If she hadn't come it was because she hadn't saved her ten minutes; but she had made them feel that they must come all the same. Mrs. Mavis liked that better, because on the ship in the morning there would be such a confusion. She didn't think her daughter would be any trouble—conscientiously she didn't. It was just to have some one to speak to her and not sally forth like a servant-girl going to a situation.

'I see, I am to act as a sort of bridesmaid and to give her away,' said Mrs. Nettlepoint. She was in fact kind enough for anything and she showed on this occasion that it was easy enough to know her. There is nothing more tiresome than complications at sea, but she accepted without a protest the burden of the young lady's dependence and allowed her, as Mrs. Mavis said, to hook herself on. She evidently had the habit of patience, and her reception of her visitors' story reminded me afresh (I was reminded of it whenever I returned to my native land) that my dear compatriots are the people in the world who most freely take mutual accommodation for granted. They have always had to help themselves, and by a magnanimous extension they confound helping each other with that. In no country are there fewer forms and more reciprocities.

It was doubtless not singular that the ladies from Merrimac Avenue should not feel that they were importunate: what was striking was that Mrs. Nettlepoint did not appear to suspect it. However, she would in any case have thought it inhuman to show that—though I could see that under the surface she was amused at everything the lady from the South End took for granted. I know not whether the attitude of the younger visitor added or not to the merit of her good-nature. Mr. Porterfield's intended took no part in her mother's appeal, scarcely spoke, sat looking at the Back Bay and the lights on the long bridge. She declined the lemonade and the other mixtures which, at Mrs. Nettlepoint's request, I offered her, while her mother partook freely of everything and I reflected (for I as freely consumed the reviving liquid) that Mr. Jasper had better hurry back if he wished to profit by the refreshment prepared for him.

Was the effect of the young woman's reserve ungracious, or was it only natural that in her particular situation she should not have a flow of compliment at her command? I noticed that Mrs. Nettlepoint looked at her often, and certainly though she was undemonstrative Miss Mavis was interesting. The candle-light enabled me to see that if she was not in the very first flower of her youth she was still a handsome girl. Her eyes and hair were dark, her face was pale and she held up her head as if, with its thick braids, it were an appurtenance she was not ashamed of. If her mother was excellent and common she was not common (not flagrantly so) and perhaps not excellent. At all events she would not be, in appearance at least, a dreary appendage, and (in the case of a person 'hooking on') that was always something gained. Is it because something of a romantic or pathetic interest usually attaches to a good creature who has been the victim of a 'long engagement' that this young lady made an impression on me from the first—favoured as I had been so quickly with this glimpse of her history? Certainly she made no positive appeal; she only held her tongue and smiled, and her smile corrected whatever suggestion might have forced itself upon me that the spirit was dead—the spirit of that promise of which she found herself doomed to carry out the letter.

What corrected it less, I must add, was an odd recollection which gathered vividness as I listened to it—a mental association which the name of Mr. Porterfield had evoked. Surely I had a personal impression, over-smeared and confused, of the gentleman who was waiting at Liverpool, or who would be, for Mrs. Nettlepoint's *protégée*. I had met him, known him, some time, somewhere, somehow, in Europe. Was he not studying something— very hard—somewhere, probably in Paris, ten years before, and did he not make extraordinarily neat drawings, linear and architectural? Didn't he go to a *table d'hôte*, at two francs twenty-five, in the Rue Bonaparte, which I then frequented, and didn't he wear spectacles and a Scotch plaid arranged in a manner which seemed to say, 'I have trustworthy information that that is the way they do it in the Highlands'? Was he not exemplary and very poor, so that I supposed he had no overcoat and his tartan was what he slept under at night? Was he not working very hard still, and wouldn't he be in the natural course, not yet satisfied that he knew enough to launch out? He would be a man of long preparations—Miss Mavis's white face seemed to speak to one of that. It appeared to me that if I had been in love with her I should not have needed to lay such a train to marry her. Architecture was his line and he was a pupil of the École des Beaux Arts. This reminiscence grew so much more vivid with me that at the end of ten minutes I had a curious sense of knowing—by implication—a good deal about the young lady.

Even after it was settled that Mrs. Nettlepoint would do everything for her that she could her mother sat a little, sipping her syrup and telling how 'low' Mr. Mavis had been. At this period the girl's silence struck me as still more conscious, partly perhaps because she deprecated her mother's loquacity (she was enough of an 'improvement' to measure that) and partly because she was too full of pain at the idea of leaving her infirm, her perhaps dying father. I divined that they were poor and that she would take out a very small purse for her trousseau. Moreover for Mr. Porterfield to make up the sum his own case would have had to change. If he had enriched himself by the successful practice of his profession I had not encountered the buildings he had reared—his reputation had not come to my ears.

Mrs. Nettlepoint notified her new friends that she was a very inactive person at sea: she was prepared to suffer to the full with Miss Mavis, but she was not prepared to walk with her, to struggle with her, to accompany her to the table. To this the girl replied that she would trouble her little, she was sure: she had a belief that she should prove a wretched sailor and spend the voyage on her back. Her mother scoffed at this picture, prophesying perfect weather and a lovely time, and I said that if I might be trusted, as a tame old bachelor fairly sea-seasoned, I should be delighted to give the new member of our party an arm or any other countenance whenever she should require it. Both the ladies thanked me for this (taking my description only too literally), and the elder one declared that we were evidently going to be such a sociable group that it was too bad to have to stay at home. She inquired of Mrs. Nettlepoint if there were any one else—if she were to be accompanied by some of her family; and when our hostess mentioned her son—there was a chance of his embarking but (wasn't it absurd?) he had not decided yet, she rejoined with extraordinary candour—'Oh dear, I do hope he'll go: that would be so pleasant for Grace.'

Somehow the words made me think of poor Mr. Porterfield's tartan, especially as Jasper Nettlepoint strolled in again at that moment. His mother instantly challenged him: it was ten o'clock; had he by chance made up his great mind? Apparently he failed to hear her, being in the first place surprised at the strange ladies and then struck with the fact that one of them was not strange. The young man, after a slight hesitation, greeted Miss Mavis with a handshake and an 'Oh, good evening, how do you do?' He did not utter her name, and I could see that he had forgotten it; but she immediately pronounced his, availing herself of an American girl's discretion to introduce him to her mother.

'Well, you might have told me you knew him all this time!' Mrs. Mavis exclaimed. Then smiling at Mrs. Nettlepoint she added, 'It would have saved me a worry, an acquaintance already begun.'

'Ah, my son's acquaintances——!' Mrs. Nettlepoint murmured.

'Yes, and my daughter's too!' cried Mrs. Mavis, jovially. 'Mrs. Allen didn't tell us *you* were going,' she continued, to the young man.

'She would have been clever if she had been able to!' Mrs. Nettlepoint ejaculated.

'Dear mother, I have my telegram,' Jasper remarked, looking at Grace Mavis.

'I know you very little,' the girl said, returning his observation.

'I've danced with you at some ball—for some sufferers by something or other.'

'I think it was an inundation,' she replied, smiling. 'But it was a long time ago—and I haven't seen you since.'

'I have been in far countries—to my loss. I should have said it was for a big fire.'

'It was at the Horticultural Hall. I didn't remember your name,' said Grace Mavis.

'That is very unkind of you, when I recall vividly that you had a pink dress.'

'Oh, I remember that dress—you looked lovely in it!' Mrs. Mavis broke out. 'You must get another just like it—on the other side.'

'Yes, your daughter looked charming in it,' said Jasper Nettlepoint. Then he added, to the girl—'Yet you mentioned my name to your mother.'

'It came back to me—seeing you here. I had no idea this was your home.'

'Well, I confess it isn't, much. Oh, there are some drinks!' Jasper went on, approaching the tray and its glasses.

'Indeed there are and quite delicious,' Mrs. Mavis declared.

'Won't you have another then?—a pink one, like your daughter's gown.'

'With pleasure, sir. Oh, do see them over,' Mrs. Mavis continued, accepting from the young man's hand a third tumbler.

'My mother and that gentleman? Surely they can take care of themselves,' said Jasper Nettlepoint.

'But my daughter—she has a claim as an old friend.'

'Jasper, what does your telegram say?' his mother interposed.

He gave no heed to her question: he stood there with his glass in his hand, looking from Mrs. Mavis to Miss Grace.

'Ah, leave her to me, madam; I'm quite competent,' I said to Mrs. Mavis.

Then the young man looked at me. The next minute he asked of the young lady—'Do you mean you are going to Europe?'

'Yes, to-morrow; in the same ship as your mother.'

'That's what we've come here for, to see all about it,' said Mrs. Mavis.

'My son, take pity on me and tell me what light your telegram throws,' Mrs. Nettlepoint went on.

'I will, dearest, when I've quenched my thirst.' And Jasper slowly drained his glass.

'Well, you're worse than Gracie,' Mrs. Mavis commented. 'She was first one thing and then the other—but only about up to three o'clock yesterday.'

'Excuse me—won't you take something?' Jasper inquired of Gracie; who however declined, as if to make up for her mother's copious *consommation*.

I made privately the reflection that the two ladies ought to take leave, the question of Mrs. Nettlepoint's goodwill being so satisfactorily settled and the meeting of the morrow at the ship so near at hand; and I went so far as to judge that their protracted stay, with their hostess visibly in a fidget, was a sign of a want of breeding. Miss Grace after all then was not such an improvement on her mother, for she easily might have taken the initiative of departure, in spite of Mrs. Mavis's imbibing her glass of syrup in little interspaced sips, as if to make it last as long as possible. I watched the girl with an increasing curiosity; I could not help asking myself a question or two about her and even perceiving already (in a dim and general way) that there were some complications in her position. Was it not a complication that she should have wished to remain long enough to assuage a certain suspense, to learn whether or no Jasper were going to sail? Had not something particular passed between them on the occasion or at the period to which they had covertly alluded, and did she really not know that her mother was bringing her to *his* mother's, though she apparently had thought it well not to mention the circumstance? Such things were complications on the part of a young lady betrothed to that curious cross-barred phantom of a Mr. Porterfield. But I am bound to add that she gave me no further warrant for suspecting them than by the simple fact of her encouraging her mother, by her immobility, to linger. Somehow I had a sense that *she* knew better. I got up myself to go, but Mrs. Nettlepoint detained me after seeing that my movement would not be taken as a hint, and I perceived she wished me not to leave my fellow-visitors on her hands. Jasper complained of the closeness of the room, said that it was not a night to sit in a room—one ought to be out in the air, under the sky. He denounced the windows that overlooked the water for not opening upon a balcony or a terrace, until his mother, whom he had not yet satisfied about his telegram, reminded him that there was a beautiful balcony in front, with room for a dozen people. She assured him we would go and sit there if it would please him.

'It will be nice and cool to-morrow, when we steam into the great ocean,' said Miss Mavis, expressing with more vivacity than she had yet thrown into any of her utterances my own thought of half an hour before. Mrs. Nettlepoint replied that it would probably be freezing cold, and her son murmured that he would go and try the drawing-room balcony and report upon it. Just as he was turning away he said, smiling, to Miss Mavis—'Won't you come with me and see if it's pleasant?'

'Oh, well, we had better not stay all night!' her mother exclaimed, but without moving. The girl moved, after a moment's hesitation; she rose and accompanied Jasper into the other room. I observed that her slim tallness showed to advantage as she walked and that she looked well as she passed, with her head thrown back, into the darkness of the other part of the house. There was something rather marked, rather surprising (I scarcely knew why, for the act was simple enough) in her doing so, and perhaps it was our sense of this that held the rest of us somewhat stiffly silent as she remained away. I was waiting for Mrs. Mavis to go, so that I myself might go; and Mrs. Nettlepoint was waiting for her to go so that I might not. This doubtless made the young lady's absence appear to us longer than it really was—it was probably very brief. Her mother moreover, I think, had a vague consciousness of embarrassment. Jasper Nettlepoint presently returned to the back drawing-room to get a glass of syrup for his companion, and he took occasion to remark that it was lovely on the balcony: one really got some air, the breeze was from that quarter. I remembered, as he went away with his tinkling tumbler, that from *my* hand, a few minutes before, Miss Mavis had not been willing to accept this innocent offering. A little later Mrs. Nettlepoint said—'Well, if it's so pleasant there we had better go ourselves.' So we passed to the front and in the other room met the two young people coming in from the balcony. I wondered in the light of subsequent events exactly how long they had been sitting there together. (There were three or four cane chairs which had been placed there for the summer.) If it had been but five minutes, that only made subsequent events more curious. 'We must go, mother,' Miss Mavis immediately said; and a moment later, with a little renewal of chatter as to our general meeting on the ship, the visitors had taken leave. Jasper went down with them to the door and as soon as they had gone out Mrs. Nettlepoint exclaimed—'Ah, but she'll be a bore—she'll be a bore!'

'Not through talking too much—surely.'

'An affectation of silence is as bad. I hate that particular *pose*; it's coming up very much now; an imitation of the English, like everything else. A girl who tries to be statuesque at sea—that will act on one's nerves!'

'I don't know what she tries to be, but she succeeds in being very handsome.'

'So much the better for you. I'll leave her to you, for I shall be shut up. I like her being placed under my "care."'

'She will be under Jasper's,' I remarked.

'Ah, he won't go—I want it too much.'

'I have an idea he will go.'

'Why didn't he tell me so then—when he came in?'

'He was diverted by Miss Mavis—a beautiful unexpected girl sitting there.'

'Diverted from his mother—trembling for his decision?'

'She's an old friend; it was a meeting after a long separation.'

'Yes, such a lot of them as he knows!' said Mrs. Nettlepoint.

'Such a lot of them?'

'He has so many female friends—in the most varied circles.'

'Well, we can close round her then—for I on my side knew, or used to know, her young man.'

'Her young man?'

'The *fiancé*, the intended, the one she is going out to. He can't by the way be very young now.'

'How odd it sounds!' said Mrs. Nettlepoint.

I was going to reply that it was not odd if you knew Mr. Porterfield, but I reflected that that perhaps only made it odder. I told my companion briefly

141

who he was—that I had met him in the old days in Paris, when I believed for a fleeting hour that I could learn to paint, when I lived with the *jeunesse des écoles*, and her comment on this was simply—'Well, he had better have come out for her!'

'Perhaps so. She looked to me as she sat there as if she might change her mind at the last moment.'

'About her marriage?'

'About sailing. But she won't change now.'

Jasper came back, and his mother instantly challenged him. 'Well, *are* you going?'

'Yes, I shall go,' he said, smiling. 'I have got my telegram.'

'Oh, your telegram!' I ventured to exclaim. 'That charming girl is your telegram.'

He gave me a look, but in the dusk I could not make out very well what it conveyed. Then he bent over his mother, kissing her. 'My news isn't particularly satisfactory. I am going for *you*.'

'Oh, you humbug!' she rejoined. But of course she was delighted.

II

People usually spend the first hours of a voyage in squeezing themselves into their cabins, taking their little precautions, either so excessive or so inadequate, wondering how they can pass so many days in such a hole and asking idiotic questions of the stewards, who appear in comparison such men of the world. My own initiations were rapid, as became an old sailor, and so it seemed were Miss Mavis's, for when I mounted to the deck at the end of half an hour I found her there alone, in the stern of the ship, looking back at the dwindling continent. It dwindled very fast for so big a place. I accosted her, having had no conversation with her amid the crowd of leave-takers and the muddle of farewells before we put off; we talked a little about the boat, our fellow-passengers and our prospects, and then I said—'I think you mentioned last night a name I know—that of Mr. Porterfield.'

'Oh no, I never uttered it,' she replied, smiling at me through her closely-drawn veil.

'Then it was your mother.'

'Very likely it was my mother.' And she continued to smile, as if I ought to have known the difference.

'I venture to allude to him because I have an idea I used to know him,' I went on.

'Oh, I see.' Beyond this remark she manifested no interest in my having known him.

'That is if it's the same one.' It seemed to me it would be silly to say nothing more; so I added 'My Mr. Porterfield was called David.'

'Well, so is ours.' 'Ours' struck me as clever.

'I suppose I shall see him again if he is to meet you at Liverpool,' I continued.

'Well, it will be bad if he doesn't.'

It was too soon for me to have the idea that it would be bad if he did: that only came later. So I remarked that I had not seen him for so many years that it was very possible I should not know him.'

'Well, I have not seen him for a great many years, but I expect I shall know him all the same.'

'Oh, with you it's different,' I rejoined, smiling at her. 'Hasn't he been back since those days?'

'I don't know what days you mean.'

'When I knew him in Paris—ages ago. He was a pupil of the École des Beaux Arts. He was studying architecture.'

'Well, he is studying it still,' said Grace Mavis.

'Hasn't he learned it yet?'

'I don't know what he has learned. I shall see.' Then she added: 'Architecture is very difficult and he is tremendously thorough.'

'Oh, yes, I remember that. He was an admirable worker. But he must have become quite a foreigner, if it's so many years since he has been at home.'

'Oh, he is not changeable. If he were changeable———' But here my interlocutress paused. I suspect she had been going to say that if he were changeable he would have given her up long ago. After an instant she went on: 'He wouldn't have stuck so to his profession. You can't make much by it.'

'You can't make much?'

'It doesn't make you rich.'

'Oh, of course you have got to practise it—and to practise it long.'

'Yes—so Mr. Porterfield says.'

Something in the way she uttered these words made me laugh—they were so serene an implication that the gentleman in question did not live up

144

to his principles. But I checked myself, asking my companion if she expected to remain in Europe long—to live there.

'Well, it will be a good while if it takes me as long to come back as it has taken me to go out.'

'And I think your mother said last night that it was your first visit.'

Miss Mavis looked at me a moment. 'Didn't mother talk!'

'It was all very interesting.'

She continued to look at me. 'You don't think that.'

'What have I to gain by saying it if I don't?'

'Oh, men have always something to gain.'

'You make me feel a terrible failure, then! I hope at any rate that it gives you pleasure—the idea of seeing foreign lands.'

'Mercy—I should think so.'

'It's a pity our ship is not one of the fast ones, if you are impatient.'

She was silent a moment; then she exclaimed, 'Oh, I guess it will be fast enough!'

That evening I went in to see Mrs. Nettlepoint and sat on her sea-trunk, which was pulled out from under the berth to accommodate me. It was nine o'clock but not quite dark, as our northward course had already taken us into the latitude of the longer days. She had made her nest admirably and lay upon her sofa in a becoming dressing-gown and cap, resting from her labours. It was her regular practice to spend the voyage in her cabin, which smelt good (such was the refinement of her art), and she had a secret peculiar to herself for keeping her port open without shipping seas. She hated what she called the mess of the ship and the idea, if she should go above, of meeting stewards with plates of supererogatory food. She professed to be content with her situation (we promised to lend each other books and I assured her familiarly that I should be in and out of her room a dozen times a day), and pitied me for having to mingle in society. She judged this to be a limited privilege, for on the deck before we left the wharf she had taken a view of our fellow-passengers.

'Oh, I'm an inveterate, almost a professional observer,' I replied, 'and with that vice I am as well occupied as an old woman in the sun with her knitting. It puts it in my power, in any situation, to *see* things. I shall see them even here and I shall come down very often and tell you about them. You are not interested to-day, but you will be to-morrow, for a ship is a great school of gossip. You won't believe the number of researches and problems you will be engaged in by the middle of the voyage.'

'I? Never in the world—lying here with my nose in a book and never seeing anything.'

'You will participate at second hand. You will see through my eyes, hang upon my lips, take sides, feel passions, all sorts of sympathies and indignations. I have an idea that your young lady is the person on board who will interest me most.'

'Mine, indeed! She has not been near me since we left the dock.'

'Well, she is very curious.'

'You have such cold-blooded terms,' Mrs. Nettlepoint murmured. '*Elle ne sait pas se conduire*; she ought to have come to ask about me.'

'Yes, since you are under her care,' I said, smiling. 'As for her not knowing how to behave—well, that's exactly what we shall see.'

'You will, but not I! I wash my hands of her.'

'Don't say that—don't say that.'

Mrs. Nettlepoint looked at me a moment. 'Why do you speak so solemnly?'

In return I considered her. 'I will tell you before we land. And have you seen much of your son?'

'Oh yes, he has come in several times. He seems very much pleased. He has got a cabin to himself.'

'That's great luck,' I said, 'but I have an idea he is always in luck. I was sure I should have to offer him the second berth in my room.'

'And you wouldn't have enjoyed that, because you don't like him,' Mrs. Nettlepoint took upon herself to say.

'What put that into your head?'

'It isn't in my head—it's in my heart, my *cœur de mère*. We guess those things. You think he's selfish—I could see it last night.'

'Dear lady,' I said, 'I have no general ideas about him at all. He is just one of the phenomena I am going to observe. He seems to me a very fine young man. However,' I added, 'since you have mentioned last night I will admit that I thought he rather tantalised you. He played with your suspense.'

'Why, he came at the last just to please me,' said Mrs. Nettlepoint.

I was silent a moment. 'Are you sure it was for your sake?'

'Ah, perhaps it was for yours!'

'When he went out on the balcony with that girl perhaps she asked him to come,' I continued.

'Perhaps she did. But why should he do everything she asks him?'

'I don't know yet, but perhaps I shall know later. Not that he will tell me—for he will never tell me anything: he is not one of those who tell.'

'If she didn't ask him, what you say is a great wrong to her,' said Mrs. Nettlepoint.

'Yes, if she didn't. But you say that to protect Jasper, not to protect her,' I continued, smiling.

'You *are* cold-blooded—it's uncanny!' my companion exclaimed.

'Ah, this is nothing yet! Wait a while—you'll see. At sea in general I'm awful—I pass the limits. If I have outraged her in thought I will jump overboard. There are ways of asking (a man doesn't need to tell a woman that) without the crude words.'

'I don't know what you suppose between them,' said Mrs. Nettlepoint.

'Nothing but what was visible on the surface. It transpired, as the newspapers say, that they were old friends.'

'He met her at some promiscuous party—I asked him about it afterwards. She is not a person he could ever think of seriously.'

'That's exactly what I believe.'

'You don't observe—you imagine,' Mrs. Nettlepoint pursued.' How do you reconcile her laying a trap for Jasper with her going out to Liverpool on an errand of love?'

'I don't for an instant suppose she laid a trap; I believe she acted on the impulse of the moment. She is going out to Liverpool on an errand of marriage; that is not necessarily the same thing as an errand of love, especially for one who happens to have had a personal impression of the gentleman she is engaged to.'

'Well, there are certain decencies which in such a situation the most abandoned of her sex would still observe. You apparently judge her capable—on no evidence—of violating them.'

'Ah, you don't understand the shades of things,' I rejoined. 'Decencies and violations—there is no need for such heavy artillery! I can perfectly imagine that without the least immodesty she should have said to Jasper on the balcony, in fact if not in words—"I'm in dreadful spirits, but if you come I shall feel better, and that will be pleasant for you too."'

'And why is she in dreadful spirits?'

'She isn't!' I replied, laughing.

'What is she doing?'

'She is walking with your son.'

Mrs. Nettlepoint said nothing for a moment; then she broke out, inconsequently—'Ah, she's horrid!'

'No, she's charming!' I protested.

'You mean she's "curious"?'

'Well, for me it's the same thing!'

This led my friend of course to declare once more that I was cold-blooded. On the afternoon of the morrow we had another talk, and she told me that in the morning Miss Mavis had paid her a long visit. She knew nothing about anything, but her intentions were good and she was evidently in her own eyes conscientious and decorous. And Mrs. Nettlepoint concluded these remarks with the exclamation 'Poor young thing!'

'You think she is a good deal to be pitied, then?'

'Well, her story sounds dreary—she told me a great deal of it. She fell to talking little by little and went from one thing to another. She's in that situation when a girl *must* open herself—to some woman.'

'Hasn't she got Jasper?' I inquired.

'He isn't a woman. You strike me as jealous of him,' my companion added.

'I daresay *he* thinks so—or will before the end. Ah no—ah no!' And I asked Mrs. Nettlepoint if our young lady struck her as a flirt. She gave me no answer, but went on to remark that it was odd and interesting to her to see the way a girl like Grace Mavis resembled the girls of the kind she herself knew better, the girls of 'society,' at the same time that she differed from them; and the way the differences and resemblances were mixed up, so that on certain questions you couldn't tell where you would find her. You would think she would feel as you did because you had found her feeling so, and then suddenly, in regard to some other matter (which was yet quite the same) she would be terribly wanting. Mrs. Nettlepoint proceeded to observe (to such

149

idle speculations does the vanity of a sea-voyage give encouragement) that she wondered whether it were better to be an ordinary girl very well brought up or an extraordinary girl not brought up at all.

'Oh, I go in for the extraordinary girl under all circumstances.'

'It is true that if you are *very* well brought up you are not ordinary,' said Mrs. Nettlepoint, smelling her strong salts. 'You are a lady, at any rate. *C'est toujours ça.*'

'And Miss Mavis isn't one—is that what you mean?'

'Well—you have seen her mother.'

'Yes, but I think your contention would be that among such people the mother doesn't count.'

'Precisely; and that's bad.'

'I see what you mean. But isn't it rather hard? If your mother doesn't know anything it is better you should be independent of her, and yet if you are that constitutes a bad note.' I added that Mrs. Mavis had appeared to count sufficiently two nights before. She had said and done everything she wanted, while the girl sat silent and respectful. Grace's attitude (so far as her mother was concerned) had been eminently decent.

'Yes, but she couldn't bear it,' said Mrs. Nettlepoint.

'Ah, if you know it I may confess that she has told me as much.'

Mrs. Nettlepoint stared. 'Told you? There's one of the things they do!'

'Well, it was only a word. Won't you let me know whether you think she's a flirt?'

'Find out for yourself, since you pretend to study folks.'

'Oh, your judgment would probably not at all determine mine. It's in regard to yourself that I ask it.'

'In regard to myself?'

'To see the length of maternal immorality.'

Mrs. Nettlepoint continued to repeat my words. 'Maternal immorality?'

'You desire your son to have every possible distraction on his voyage, and if you can make up your mind in the sense I refer to that will make it all right. He will have no responsibility.'

'Heavens, how you analyse! I haven't in the least your passion for making up my mind.'

'Then if you chance it you'll be more immoral still.'

'Your reasoning is strange,' said the poor lady; 'when it was you who tried to put it into my head yesterday that she had asked him to come.'

'Yes, but in good faith.'

'How do you mean in good faith?'

'Why, as girls of that sort do. Their allowance and measure in such matters is much larger than that of young ladies who have been, as you say, *very* well brought up; and yet I am not sure that on the whole I don't think them the more innocent. Miss Mavis is engaged, and she's to be married next week, but it's an old, old story, and there's no more romance in it than if she were going to be photographed. So her usual life goes on, and her usual life consists (and that of ces demoiselles in general) in having plenty of gentlemen's society. Having it I mean without having any harm from it.'

'Well, if there is no harm from it what are you talking about and why am I immoral?'

I hesitated, laughing. 'I retract—you are sane and clear. I am sure she thinks there won't be any harm,' I added. 'That's the great point.'

'The great point?'

'I mean, to be settled.'

'Mercy, we are not trying them! How can *we* settle it?'

'I mean of course in our minds. There will be nothing more interesting for the next ten days for our minds to exercise themselves upon.'

'They will get very tired of it,' said Mrs. Nettlepoint.

'No, no, because the interest will increase and the plot will thicken. It can't help it.' She looked at me as if she thought me slightly Mephisthophelean, and I went on—'So she told you everything in her life was dreary?'

'Not everything but most things. And she didn't tell me so much as I guessed it. She'll tell me more the next time. She will behave properly now about coming in to see me; I told her she ought to.'

'I am glad of that,' I said. 'Keep her with you as much as possible.'

'I don't follow you much,' Mrs. Nettlepoint replied, 'but so far as I do I don't think your remarks are in very good taste.'

'I'm too excited, I lose my head, cold-blooded as you think me. Doesn't she like Mr. Porterfield?'

'Yes, that's the worst of it.'

'The worst of it?'

'He's so good—there's no fault to be found with him. Otherwise she would have thrown it all up. It has dragged on since she was eighteen: she became engaged to him before he went abroad to study. It was one of those childish muddles which parents in America might prevent so much more than they do. The thing is to insist on one's daughter's waiting, on the engagement's being long; and then after you have got that started to take it on every occasion as little seriously as possible—to make it die out. You can easily tire it out. However, Mr. Porterfield has taken it seriously for some years. He has done his part to keep it alive. She says he adores her.'

'His part? Surely his part would have been to marry her by this time.'

'He has absolutely no money.'

'He ought to have got some, in seven years.'

'So I think she thinks. There are some sorts of poverty that are contemptible. But he has a little more now. That's why he won't wait any longer. His mother has come out, she has something—a little—and she is able to help him. She will live with them and bear some of the expenses, and after her death the son will have what there is.'

'How old is she?' I asked, cynically.

'I haven't the least idea. But it doesn't sound very inspiring. He has not been to America since he first went out.'

'That's an odd way of adoring her.'

'I made that objection mentally, but I didn't express it to her. She met it indeed a little by telling me that he had had other chances to marry.'

'That surprises me,' I remarked. 'And did she say that *she* had had?'

'No, and that's one of the things I thought nice in her; for she must have had. She didn't try to make out that he had spoiled her life. She has three other sisters and there is very little money at home. She has tried to make money; she has written little things and painted little things, but her talent is apparently not in that direction. Her father has had a long illness and has lost his place—he was in receipt of a salary in connection with some waterworks—and one of her sisters has lately become a widow, with children and without means. And so as in fact she never has married any one else, whatever opportunities she may have encountered, she appears to have just made up her mind to go out to Mr. Porterfield as the least of her evils. But it isn't very amusing.'

'That only makes it the more honourable. She will go through with it, whatever it costs, rather than disappoint him after he has waited so long. It is true,' I continued, 'that when a woman acts from a sense of honour——'

'Well, when she does?' said Mrs. Nettlepoint, for I hesitated perceptibly.

'It is so extravagant a course that some one has to pay for it.'

'You are very impertinent. We all have to pay for each other, all the while; and for each other's virtues as well as vices.'

153

'That's precisely why I shall be sorry for Mr. Porterfield when she steps off the ship with her little bill. I mean with her teeth clenched.'

'Her teeth are not in the least clenched. She is in perfect good-humour.'

'Well, we must try and keep her so,' I said. 'You must take care that Jasper neglects nothing.'

I know not what reflection this innocent pleasantry of mine provoked on the good lady's part; the upshot of them at all events was to make her say—'Well, I never asked her to come; I'm very glad of that. It is all their own doing.'

'Their own—you mean Jasper's and hers?'

'No indeed. I mean her mother's and Mrs. Allen's; the girl's too of course. They put themselves upon us.'

'Oh yes, I can testify to that. Therefore I'm glad too. We should have missed it, I think.'

'How seriously you take it!' Mrs. Nettlepoint exclaimed.

'Ah, wait a few days!' I replied, getting up to leave her.

III

The *Patagonia* was slow, but she was spacious and comfortable, and
there was a kind of motherly decency in her long, nursing rock and her
rustling, old-fashioned gait. It was as if she wished not to present herself in
port with the splashed eagerness of a young creature. We were not numerous
enough to squeeze each other and yet we were not too few to entertain—with
that familiarity and relief which figures and objects acquire on the great bare
field of the ocean, beneath the great bright glass of the sky. I had never liked
the sea so much before, indeed I had never liked it at all; but now I had
a revelation of how, in a midsummer mood, it could please. It was darkly
and magnificently blue and imperturbably quiet—save for the great regular
swell of its heart-beats, the pulse of its life, and there grew to be something
so agreeable in the sense of floating there in infinite isolation and leisure
that it was a positive satisfaction the *Patagonia* was not a racer. One had
never thought of the sea as the great place of safety, but now it came over
one that there is no place so safe from the land. When it does not give you
trouble it takes it away—takes away letters and telegrams and newspapers and
visits and duties and efforts, all the complications, all the superfluities and
superstitions that we have stuffed into our terrene life. The simple absence
of the post, when the particular conditions enable you to enjoy the great fact
by which it is produced, becomes in itself a kind of bliss, and the clean stage
of the deck shows you a play that amuses, the personal drama of the voyage,
the movement and interaction, in the strong sea-light, of figures that end by
representing something—something moreover of which the interest is never,
even in its keenness, too great to suffer you to go to sleep. I, at any rate, dozed
a great deal, lying on my rug with a French novel, and when I opened my
eyes I generally saw Jasper Nettlepoint passing with his mother's *protégée* on
his arm. Somehow at these moments, between sleeping and waking, I had an
inconsequent sense that they were a part of the French novel. Perhaps this
was because I had fallen into the trick, at the start, of regarding Grace Mavis
almost as a married woman, which, as every one knows, is the necessary status

of the heroine of such a work. Every revolution of our engine at any rate would contribute to the effect of making her one.

In the saloon, at meals, my neighbour on the right was a certain little Mrs. Peck, a very short and very round person whose head was enveloped in a 'cloud' (a cloud of dirty white wool) and who promptly let me know that she was going to Europe for the education of her children. I had already perceived (an hour after we left the dock) that some energetic step was required in their interest, but as we were not in Europe yet the business could not be said to have begun. The four little Pecks, in the enjoyment of untrammelled leisure, swarmed about the ship as if they had been pirates boarding her, and their mother was as powerless to check their license as if she had been gagged and stowed away in the hold. They were especially to be trusted to run between the legs of the stewards when these attendants arrived with bowls of soup for the languid ladies. Their mother was too busy recounting to her fellow-passengers how many years Miss Mavis had been engaged. In the blank of a marine existence things that are nobody's business very soon become everybody's, and this was just one of those facts that are propagated with a mysterious and ridiculous rapidity. The whisper that carries them is very small, in the great scale of things, of air and space and progress, but it is also very safe, for there is no compression, no sounding-board, to make speakers responsible. And then repetition at sea is somehow not repetition; monotony is in the air, the mind is flat and everything recurs—the bells, the meals, the stewards' faces, the romp of children, the walk, the clothes, the very shoes and buttons of passengers taking their exercise. These things grow at last so insipid that, in comparison, revelations as to the personal history of one's companions have a taste, even when one cares little about the people.

Jasper Nettlepoint sat on my left hand when he was not upstairs seeing that Miss Mavis had her repast comfortably on deck. His mother's place would have been next mine had she shown herself, and then that of the young lady under her care. The two ladies, in other words, would have been between us, Jasper marking the limit of the party on that side. Miss Mavis was present at luncheon the first day, but dinner passed without her coming in, and when it was half over Jasper remarked that he would go up and look after her.

'Isn't that young lady coming—the one who was here to lunch?' Mrs. Peck asked of me as he left the saloon.

'Apparently not. My friend tells me she doesn't like the saloon.'

'You don't mean to say she's sick, do you?'

'Oh no, not in this weather. But she likes to be above.'

'And is that gentleman gone up to her?'

'Yes, she's under his mother's care.'

'And is his mother up there, too?' asked Mrs. Peck, whose processes were homely and direct.

'No, she remains in her cabin. People have different tastes. Perhaps that's one reason why Miss Mavis doesn't come to table,' I added—'her chaperon not being able to accompany her.'

'Her chaperon?'

'Mrs. Nettlepoint—the lady under whose protection she is.'

'Protection?' Mrs. Peck stared at me a moment, moving some valued morsel in her mouth; then she exclaimed, familiarly, 'Pshaw!' I was struck with this and I was on the point of asking her what she meant by it when she continued: 'Are we not going to see Mrs. Nettlepoint?'

'I am afraid not. She vows that she won't stir from her sofa.'

'Pshaw!' said Mrs. Peck again. 'That's quite a disappointment.'

'Do you know her then?'

'No, but I know all about her.' Then my companion added—'You don't meant to say she's any relation?'

'Do you mean to me?'

'No, to Grace Mavis.'

'None at all. They are very new friends, as I happen to know. Then you are acquainted with our young lady?' I had not noticed that any recognition passed between them at luncheon.

'Is she yours too?' asked Mrs. Peck, smiling at me.

'Ah, when people are in the same boat—literally—they belong a little to each other.'

'That's so,' said Mrs. Peck. 'I don't know Miss Mavis but I know all about her—I live opposite to her on Merrimac Avenue. I don't know whether you know that part.'

'Oh yes—it's very beautiful.'

The consequence of this remark was another 'Pshaw!' But Mrs. Peck went on—'When you've lived opposite to people like that for a long time you feel as if you were acquainted. But she didn't take it up to-day; she didn't speak to me. She knows who I am as well as she knows her own mother.'

'You had better speak to her first—she's shy,' I remarked.

'Shy? Why she's nearly thirty years old. I suppose you know where she's going.'

'Oh yes—we all take an interest in that.'

'That young man, I suppose, particularly.'

'That young man?'

'The handsome one, who sits there. Didn't you tell me he is Mrs. Nettlepoint's son?'

'Oh yes; he acts as her deputy. No doubt he does all he can to carry out her function.'

Mrs. Peck was silent a moment. I had spoken jocosely, but she received my pleasantry with a serious face. 'Well, she might let him eat his dinner in peace!' she presently exclaimed.

'Oh, he'll come back!' I said, glancing at his place. The repast continued and when it was finished I screwed my chair round to leave the table. Mrs. Peck performed the same movement and we quitted the saloon together. Outside of it was a kind of vestibule, with several seats, from which you could descend to the lower cabins or mount to the promenade-deck. Mrs. Peck appeared to hesitate as to her course and then solved the problem by going neither way. She dropped upon one of the benches and looked up at me.

'I thought you said he would come back.'

'Young Nettlepoint? I see he didn't. Miss Mavis then has given him half of her dinner.'

'It's very kind of her! She has been engaged for ages.'

'Yes, but that will soon be over.'

'So I suppose—as quick as we land. Every one knows it on Merrimac Avenue. Every one there takes a great interest in it.'

'Ah, of course, a girl like that: she has many friends.'

'I mean even people who don't know her.'

'I see,' I went on: 'she is so handsome that she attracts attention, people enter into her affairs.'

'She *used* to be pretty, but I can't say I think she's anything remarkable to-day. Anyhow, if she attracts attention she ought to be all the more careful what she does. You had better tell her that.'

'Oh, it's none of my business!' I replied, leaving Mrs. Peck and going above. The exclamation, I confess, was not perfectly in accordance with my feeling, or rather my feeling was not perfectly in harmony with the exclamation. The very first thing I did on reaching the deck was to notice that Miss Mavis was pacing it on Jasper Nettlepoint's arm and that whatever beauty she might have lost, according to Mrs. Peck's insinuation, she still kept enough to make one's eyes follow her. She had put on a sort of crimson hood, which was very becoming to her and which she wore for the rest of the voyage. She walked very well, with long steps, and I remember that at this moment the ocean had a gentle evening swell which made the great ship dip slowly, rhythmically, giving a movement that was graceful to graceful pedestrians and a more awkward one to the awkward. It was the loveliest hour of a fine day, the clear early evening, with the glow of the sunset in the air and a purple colour in the sea. I always thought that the waters ploughed by the Homeric heroes must have looked like that. I perceived on that particular occasion moreover that Grace Mavis would for the rest of the voyage be the most visible thing on the ship; the figure that would count most in the composition of groups. She couldn't help it, poor girl; nature had made her conspicuous—important, as the painters say. She paid for it by the exposure it brought with it—the danger that people would, as I had said to Mrs. Peck, enter into her affairs.

Jasper Nettlepoint went down at certain times to see his mother, and I watched for one of these occasions (on the third day out) and took advantage of it to go and sit by Miss Mavis. She wore a blue veil drawn tightly over her face, so that if the smile with which she greeted me was dim I could account for it partly by that.

'Well, we are getting on—we are getting on,' I said, cheerfully, looking at the friendly, twinkling sea.

'Are we going very fast?'

'Not fast, but steadily. *Ohne Hast, ohne Rast*—do you know German?'

'Well, I've studied it—some.'

'It will be useful to you over there when you travel.'

'Well yes, if we do. But I don't suppose we shall much. Mr. Nettlepoint says we ought,' my interlocutress added in a moment.

'Ah, of course *he* thinks so. He has been all over the world.'

'Yes, he has described some of the places. That's what I should like. I didn't know I should like it so much.'

160

'Like what so much?'

'Going on this way. I could go on for ever, for ever and ever.'

'Ah, you know it's not always like this,' I rejoined.

'Well, it's better than Boston.'

'It isn't so good as Paris,' I said, smiling.

'Oh, I know all about Paris. There is no freshness in that. I feel as if I had been there.'

'You mean you have heard so much about it?'

'Oh yes, nothing else for ten years.'

I had come to talk with Miss Mavis because she was attractive, but I had been rather conscious of the absence of a good topic, not feeling at liberty to revert to Mr. Porterfield. She had not encouraged me, when I spoke to her as we were leaving Boston, to go on with the history of my acquaintance with this gentleman; and yet now, unexpectedly, she appeared to imply (it was doubtless one of the disparities mentioned by Mrs. Nettlepoint) that he might be glanced at without indelicacy.

'I see, you mean by letters,' I remarked.

'I shan't live in a good part. I know enough to know that,' she went on.

'Dear young lady, there are no bad parts,' I answered, reassuringly.

'Why, Mr. Nettlepoint says it's horrid.'

'It's horrid?'

'Up there in the Batignolles. It's worse than Merrimac Avenue.'

'Worse—in what way?'

'Why, even less where the nice people live.'

'He oughtn't to say that,' I returned. 'Don't you call Mr. Porterfield a nice person?' I ventured to subjoin.

'Oh, it doesn't make any difference.' She rested her eyes on me a moment through her veil, the texture of which gave them a suffused prettiness. 'Do you know him very well?' she asked.

'Mr. Porterfield?'

'No, Mr. Nettlepoint.'

'Ah, very little. He's a good deal younger than I.'

She was silent a moment; after which she said: 'He's younger than me, too.' I know not what drollery there was in this but it was unexpected and it made me laugh. Neither do I know whether Miss Mavis took offence at my laughter, though I remember thinking at the moment with compunction that it had brought a certain colour to her cheek. At all events she got up, gathering her shawl and her books into her arm. 'I'm going down—I'm tired.'

'Tired of me, I'm afraid.'

'No, not yet.'

'I'm like you,' I pursued. 'I should like it to go on and on.'

She had begun to walk along the deck to the companion-way and I went with her. 'Oh, no, I shouldn't, after all!'

I had taken her shawl from her to carry it, but at the top of the steps that led down to the cabins I had to give it back. 'Your mother would be glad if she could know,' I observed as we parted.

'If she could know?'

'How well you are getting on. And that good Mrs. Allen.'

'Oh, mother, mother! She made me come, she pushed me off.' And almost as if not to say more she went quickly below.

I paid Mrs. Nettlepoint a morning visit after luncheon and another in the evening, before she 'turned in.' That same day, in the evening, she said to me suddenly, 'Do you know what I have done? I have asked Jasper.'

'Asked him what?'

'Why, if *she* asked him, you know.'

'I don't understand.'

'You do perfectly. If that girl really asked him—on the balcony—to sail with us.'

'My dear friend, do you suppose that if she did he would tell you?'

'That's just what he says. But he says she didn't.'

'And do you consider the statement valuable?' I asked, laughing out. 'You had better ask Miss Gracie herself.'

Mrs. Nettlepoint stared. 'I couldn't do that.'

'Incomparable friend, I am only joking. What does it signify now?'

'I thought you thought everything signified. You were so full of signification!'

'Yes, but we are farther out now, and somehow in mid-ocean everything becomes absolute.'

'What else *can* he do with decency?' Mrs. Nettlepoint went on. 'If, as my son, he were never to speak to her it would be very rude and you would think that stranger still. Then *you* would do what he does, and where would be the difference?'

'How do you know what he does? I haven't mentioned him for twenty-four hours.'

'Why, she told me herself: she came in this afternoon.'

'What an odd thing to tell you!' I exclaimed.

'Not as she says it. She says he's full of attention, perfectly devoted—looks after her all the while. She seems to want me to know it, so that I may commend him for it.'

'That's charming; it shows her good conscience.'

'Yes, or her great cleverness.'

Something in the tone in which Mrs. Nettlepoint said this caused me to exclaim in real surprise, 'Why, what do you suppose she has in her mind?'

'To get hold of him, to make him go so far that he can't retreat, to marry him, perhaps.'

'To marry him? And what will she do with Mr. Porterfield?'

'She'll ask me just to explain to him—or perhaps you.'

'Yes, as an old friend!' I replied, laughing. But I asked more seriously, 'Do you see Jasper caught like that?'

'Well, he's only a boy—he's younger at least than she.'

'Precisely; she regards him as a child.'

'As a child?'

'She remarked to me herself to-day that he is so much younger.'

Mrs. Nettlepoint stared. 'Does she talk of it with you? That shows she has a plan, that she has thought it over!'

I have sufficiently betrayed that I deemed Grace Mavis a singular girl, but I was far from judging her capable of laying a trap for our young companion. Moreover my reading of Jasper was not in the least that he was catchable—could be made to do a thing if he didn't want to do it. Of course it was not impossible that he might be inclined, that he might take it (or already have taken it) into his head to marry Miss Mavis; but to believe this I should require still more proof than his always being with her. He wanted at most to marry her for the voyage. 'If you have questioned him perhaps you have tried to make him feel responsible,' I said to his mother.

'A little, but it's very difficult. Interference makes him perverse. One has to go gently. Besides, it's too absurd—think of her age. If she can't take care of herself!' cried Mrs. Nettlepoint.

'Yes, let us keep thinking of her age, though it's not so prodigious. And if things get very bad you have one resource left,' I added.

'What is that?'

'You can go upstairs.'

'Ah, never, never! If it takes that to save her she must be lost. Besides, what good would it do? If I were to go up she could come down here.'

'Yes, but you could keep Jasper with you.'

'Could I?' Mrs. Nettlepoint demanded, in the manner of a woman who knew her son.

In the saloon the next day, after dinner, over the red cloth of the tables, beneath the swinging lamps and the racks of tumblers, decanters and wine-glasses, we sat down to whist, Mrs. Peck, among others, taking a hand in the game. She played very badly and talked too much, and when the rubber was over assuaged her discomfiture (though not mine—we had been partners) with a Welsh rabbit and a tumbler of something hot. We had done with the cards, but while she waited for this refreshment she sat with her elbows on the table shuffling a pack.

'She hasn't spoken to me yet—she won't do it,' she remarked in a moment.

'Is it possible there is any one on the ship who hasn't spoken to you?'

'Not that girl—she knows too well!' Mrs. Peck looked round our little circle with a smile of intelligence—she had familiar, communicative eyes. Several of our company had assembled, according to the wont, the last thing in the evening, of those who are cheerful at sea, for the consumption of grilled sardines and devilled bones.

'What then does she know?'

'Oh, she knows that I know.'

'Well, we know what Mrs. Peck knows,' one of the ladies of the group observed to me, with an air of privilege.

'Well, you wouldn't know if I hadn't told you—from the way she acts,' said Mrs. Peck, with a small laugh.

'She is going out to a gentleman who lives over there—he's waiting there to marry her,' the other lady went on, in the tone of authentic information. I remember that her name was Mrs. Gotch and that her mouth looked always as if she were whistling.

'Oh, he knows—I've told him,' said Mrs. Peck.

'Well, I presume every one knows,' Mrs. Gotch reflected.

'Dear madam, is it every one's business?' I asked.

'Why, don't you think it's a peculiar way to act?' Mrs. Gotch was evidently surprised at my little protest.

'Why, it's right there—straight in front of you, like a play at the theatre—as if you had paid to see it,' said Mrs. Peck. 'If you don't call it public——!'

'Aren't you mixing things up? What do you call public?'

'Why, the way they go on. They are up there now.'

'They cuddle up there half the night,' said Mrs. Gotch. 'I don't know when they come down. Any hour you like—when all the lights are out they are up there still.'

'Oh, you can't tire them out. They don't want relief—like the watch!' laughed one of the gentlemen.

'Well, if they enjoy each other's society what's the harm?' another asked. 'They'd do just the same on land.'

'They wouldn't do it on the public streets, I suppose,' said Mrs. Peck. 'And they wouldn't do it if Mr. Porterfield was round!'

'Isn't that just where your confusion comes in?' I inquired. 'It's public enough that Miss Mavis and Mr. Nettlepoint are always together, but it isn't in the least public that she is going to be married.'

'Why, how can you say—when the very sailors know it! The captain knows it and all the officers know it; they see them there—especially at night, when they're sailing the ship.'

'I thought there was some rule——' said Mrs. Gotch.

'Well, there is—that you've got to behave yourself,' Mrs. Peck rejoined. 'So the captain told me—he said they have some rule. He said they have to have, when people are too demonstrative.'

'Too demonstrative?'

'When they attract so much attention.'

'Ah, it's we who attract the attention—by talking about what doesn't concern us and about what we really don't know,' I ventured to declare.

'She said the captain said he would tell on her as soon as we arrive,' Mrs. Gotch interposed.

'*She* said——?' I repeated, bewildered.

'Well, he did say so, that he would think it his duty to inform Mr. Porterfield, when he comes on to meet her—if they keep it up in the same way,' said Mrs. Peck.

'Oh, they'll keep it up, don't you fear!' one of the gentlemen exclaimed.

'Dear madam, the captain is laughing at you.'

'No, he ain't—he's right down scandalised. He says he regards us all as a real family and wants the family to be properly behaved.' I could see Mrs. Peck was irritated by my controversial tone: she challenged me with considerable spirit. 'How can you say I don't know it when all the street knows it and has known it for years—for years and years?' She spoke as if the girl had been engaged at least for twenty. 'What is she going out for, if not to marry him?'

'Perhaps she is going to see how he looks,' suggested one of the gentlemen.

'He'd look queer—if he knew.'

167

'Well, I guess he'll know,' said Mrs. Gotch.

'She'd tell him herself—she wouldn't be afraid,' the gentleman went on.

'Well, she might as well kill him. He'll jump overboard.'

'Jump overboard?' cried Mrs. Gotch, as if she hoped then that Mr. Porterfield would be told.

'He has just been waiting for this—for years,' said Mrs. Peck.

'Do you happen to know him?' I inquired.

Mrs. Peck hesitated a moment. 'No, but I know a lady who does. Are you going up?'

I had risen from my place—I had not ordered supper. 'I'm going to take a turn before going to bed.'

'Well then, you'll see!'

Outside the saloon I hesitated, for Mrs. Peck's admonition made me feel for a moment that if I ascended to the deck I should have entered in a manner into her little conspiracy. But the night was so warm and splendid that I had been intending to smoke a cigar in the air before going below, and I did not see why I should deprive myself of this pleasure in order to seem not to mind Mrs. Peck. I went up and saw a few figures sitting or moving about in the darkness. The ocean looked black and small, as it is apt to do at night, and the long mass of the ship, with its vague dim wings, seemed to take up a great part of it. There were more stars than one saw on land and the heavens struck one more than ever as larger than the earth. Grace Mavis and her companion were not, so far as I perceived at first, among the few passengers who were lingering late, and I was glad, because I hated to hear her talked about in the manner of the gossips I had left at supper. I wished there had been some way to prevent it, but I could think of no way but to recommend her privately to change her habits. That would be a very delicate business, and perhaps it would be better to begin with Jasper, though that would be delicate too. At any rate one might let him know, in a friendly spirit, to how much remark he exposed the young lady—leaving this revelation to work its way upon him.

Unfortunately I could not altogether believe that the pair were unconscious of the observation and the opinion of the passengers. They were not a boy and a girl; they had a certain social perspective in their eye. I was not very clear as to the details of that behaviour which had made them (according to the version of my good friends in the saloon) a scandal to the ship, for though I looked at them a good deal I evidently had not looked at them so continuously and so hungrily as Mrs. Peck. Nevertheless the probability was that they knew what was thought of them—what naturally would be—and simply didn't care. That made Miss Mavis out rather cynical and even a little immodest; and yet, somehow, if she had such qualities I did not dislike her for them. I don't know what strange, secret excuses I found for her. I presently indeed encountered a need for them on the spot, for just as I was on the point of going below again, after several restless turns and (within the limit where smoking was allowed) as many puffs at a cigar as I cared for, I became aware that a couple of figures were seated behind one of the lifeboats that rested on the deck. They were so placed as to be visible only to a person going close to the rail and peering a little sidewise. I don't think I peered, but as I stood a moment beside the rail my eye was attracted by a dusky object which protruded beyond the boat and which, as I saw at a second glance, was the tail of a lady's dress. I bent forward an instant, but even then I saw very little more; that scarcely mattered, however, for I took for granted on the spot that the persons concealed in so snug a corner were Jasper Nettlepoint and Mr. Porterfield's intended. Concealed was the word, and I thought it a real pity; there was bad taste in it. I immediately turned away and the next moment I found myself face to face with the captain of the ship. I had already had some conversation with him (he had been so good as to invite me, as he had invited Mrs. Nettlepoint and her son and the young lady travelling with them, and also Mrs. Peck, to sit at his table) and had observed with pleasure that he had the art, not universal on the Atlantic liners, of mingling urbanity with seamanship.

'They don't waste much time—your friends in there,' he said, nodding in the direction in which he had seen me looking.

'Ah well, they haven't much to lose.'

'That's what I mean. I'm told *she* hasn't.'

I wanted to say something exculpatory but I scarcely knew what note to strike. I could only look vaguely about me at the starry darkness and the sea that seemed to sleep. 'Well, with these splendid nights, this perfection of weather, people are beguiled into late hours.'

'Yes. We want a nice little blow,' the captain said.

'A nice little blow?'

'That would clear the decks!'

The captain was rather dry and he went about his business. He had made me uneasy and instead of going below I walked a few steps more. The other walkers dropped off pair by pair (they were all men) till at last I was alone. Then, after a little, I quitted the field. Jasper and his companion were still behind their lifeboat. Personally I greatly preferred good weather, but as I went down I found myself vaguely wishing, in the interest of I scarcely knew what, unless of decorum, that we might have half a gale.

Miss Mavis turned out, in sea-phrase, early; for the next morning I saw her come up only a little while after I had finished my breakfast, a ceremony over which I contrived not to dawdle. She was alone and Jasper Nettlepoint, by a rare accident, was not on deck to help her. I went to meet her (she was encumbered as usual with her shawl, her sun-umbrella and a book) and laid my hands on her chair, placing it near the stern of the ship, where she liked best to be. But I proposed to her to walk a little before she sat down and she took my arm after I had put her accessories into the chair. The deck was clear at that hour and the morning light was gay; one got a sort of exhilarated impression of fair conditions and an absence of hindrance. I forget what we spoke of first, but it was because I felt these things pleasantly, and not to torment my companion nor to test her, that I could not help exclaiming cheerfully, after a moment, as I have mentioned having done the first day, 'Well, we are getting on, we are getting on!'

'Oh yes, I count every hour.'

'The last days always go quicker,' I said, 'and the last hours——'

'Well, the last hours?' she asked; for I had instinctively checked myself.

'Oh, one is so glad then that it is almost the same as if one had arrived. But we ought to be grateful when the elements have been so kind to us,' I added. 'I hope you will have enjoyed the voyage.'

She hesitated a moment, then she said, 'Yes, much more than I expected.'

'Did you think it would be very bad?'

'Horrible, horrible!'

The tone of these words was strange but I had not much time to reflect upon it, for turning round at that moment I saw Jasper Nettlepoint come towards us. He was separated from us by the expanse of the white deck and I could not help looking at him from head to foot as he drew nearer. I know not what rendered me on this occasion particularly sensitive to the impression, but it seemed to me that I saw him as I had never seen him before—saw him inside and out, in the intense sea-light, in his personal, his moral totality. It was a quick, vivid revelation; if it only lasted a moment it had a simplifying, certifying effect. He was intrinsically a pleasing apparition, with his handsome young face and a certain absence of compromise in his personal arrangements which, more than any one I have ever seen, he managed to exhibit on shipboard. He had none of the appearance of wearing out old clothes that usually prevails there, but dressed straight, as I heard some one say. This gave him a practical, successful air, as of a young man who would come best out of any predicament. I expected to feel my companion's hand loosen itself on my arm, as indication that now she must go to him, and was almost surprised she did not drop me. We stopped as we met and Jasper bade us a friendly good-morning. Of course the remark was not slow to be made that we had another lovely day, which led him to exclaim, in the manner of one to whom criticism came easily, 'Yes, but with this sort of thing consider what one of the others would do!'

'One of the other ships?'

'We should be there now, or at any rate to-morrow.'

'Well then, I'm glad it isn't one of the others,' I said, smiling at the young lady on my arm. My remark offered her a chance to say something appreciative and gave him one even more; but neither Jasper nor Grace Mavis took advantage of the opportunity. What they did do, I perceived, was to look at each other for an instant; after which Miss Mavis turned her eyes silently to the sea. She made no movement and uttered no word, contriving to give me the sense that she had all at once become perfectly passive, that she somehow declined responsibility. We remained standing there with Jasper in front of us, and if the touch of her arm did not suggest that I should give her up, neither did it intimate that we had better pass on. I had no idea of giving her up, albeit one of the things that I seemed to discover just then in Jasper's physiognomy was an imperturbable implication that she was his property. His eye met mine for a moment, and it was exactly as if he had said to me, 'I know what you think, but I don't care a rap.' What I really thought was that he was selfish beyond the limits: that was the substance of my little revelation. Youth is almost always selfish, just as it is almost always conceited, and, after all, when it is combined with health and good parts, good looks and good spirits, it has a right to be, and I easily forgive it if it be really youth. Still it is a question of degree, and what stuck out of Jasper Nettlepoint (if one felt that sort of thing) was that his egotism had a hardness, his love of his own way an avidity. These elements were jaunty and prosperous, they were accustomed to triumph. He was fond, very fond, of women; they were necessary to him and that was in his type; but he was not in the least in love with Grace Mavis. Among the reflections I quickly made this was the one that was most to the point. There was a degree of awkwardness, after a minute, in the way we were planted there, though the apprehension of it was doubtless not in the least with him.

'How is your mother this morning?' I asked.

'You had better go down and see.'

'Not till Miss Mavis is tired of me.'

She said nothing to this and I made her walk again. For some minutes she remained silent; then, rather unexpectedly, she began: 'I've seen you talking to that lady who sits at our table—the one who has so many children.'

'Mrs. Peck? Oh yes, I have talked with her.'

'Do you know her very well?'

'Only as one knows people at sea. An acquaintance makes itself. It doesn't mean very much.'

'She doesn't speak to me—she might if she wanted.'

'That's just what she says of you—that you might speak to her.'

'Oh, if she's waiting for that——!' said my companion, with a laugh. Then she added—'She lives in our street, nearly opposite.'

'Precisely. That's the reason why she thinks you might speak; she has seen you so often and seems to know so much about you.'

'What does she know about me?'

'Ah, you must ask her—I can't tell you!'

'I don't care what she knows,' said my young lady. After a moment she went on—'She must have seen that I'm not very sociable.' And then—'What are you laughing at?'

My laughter was for an instant irrepressible—there was something so droll in the way she had said that.

'Well, you are not sociable and yet you are. Mrs. Peck is, at any rate, and thought that ought to make it easy for you to enter into conversation with her.'

'Oh, I don't care for her conversation—I know what it amounts to.' I made no rejoinder—I scarcely knew what rejoinder to make—and the girl went on, 'I know what she thinks and I know what she says.' Still I was silent, but the next moment I saw that my delicacy had been wasted, for Miss Mavis asked, 'Does she make out that she knows Mr. Porterfield?'

'No, she only says that she knows a lady who knows him.'

'Yes, I know—Mrs. Jeremie. Mrs. Jeremie's an idiot!' I was not in a position to controvert this, and presently my young lady said she would sit down. I left her in her chair—I saw that she preferred it—and wandered to a distance. A few minutes later I met Jasper again, and he stopped of his own accord and said to me—

'We shall be in about six in the evening, on the eleventh day—they promise it.'

'If nothing happens, of course.'

'Well, what's going to happen?'

'That's just what I'm wondering!' And I turned away and went below with the foolish but innocent satisfaction of thinking that I had mystified him.

IV

'I don't know what to do, and you must help me,' Mrs. Nettlepoint said to me that evening, as soon as I went in to see her.

'I'll do what I can—but what's the matter?'

'She has been crying here and going on—she has quite upset me.'

'Crying? She doesn't look like that.'

'Exactly, and that's what startled me. She came in to see me this afternoon, as she has done before, and we talked about the weather and the run of the ship and the manners of the stewardess and little commonplaces like that, and then suddenly, in the midst of it, as she sat there, *à propos* of nothing, she burst into tears. I asked her what ailed her and tried to comfort her, but she didn't explain; she only said it was nothing, the effect of the sea, of leaving home. I asked her if it had anything to do with her prospects, with her marriage; whether she found as that drew near that her heart was not in it; I told her that she mustn't be nervous, that I could enter into that—in short I said what I could. All that she replied was that she *was* nervous, very nervous, but that it was already over; and then she jumped up and kissed me and went away. Does she look as if she had been crying?' Mrs. Nettlepoint asked.

'How can I tell, when she never quits that horrid veil? It's as if she were ashamed to show her face.'

'She's keeping it for Liverpool. But I don't like such incidents,' said Mrs. Nettlepoint. 'I shall go upstairs.'

'And is that where you want me to help you?'

'Oh, your arm and that sort of thing, yes. But something more. I feel as if something were going to happen.'

'That's exactly what I said to Jasper this morning.'

'And what did he say?'

'He only looked innocent, as if he thought I meant a fog or a storm.'

'Heaven forbid—it isn't that! I shall never be good-natured again,' Mrs. Nettlepoint went on; 'never have a girl put upon me that way. You always pay for it, there are always tiresome complications. What I am afraid of is after we get there. She'll throw up her engagement; there will be dreadful scenes; I shall be mixed up with them and have to look after her and keep her with me. I shall have to stay there with her till she can be sent back, or even take her up to London. *Voyez-vous ça?*

I listened respectfully to this and then I said: 'You are afraid of your son.'

'Afraid of him?'

'There are things you might say to him—and with your manner; because you have one when you choose.'

'Very likely, but what is my manner to his? Besides, I have said everything to him. That is I have said the great thing, that he is making her immensely talked about.'

'And of course in answer to that he has asked you how you know, and you have told him I have told you.'

'I had to; and he says it's none of your business.'

'I wish he would say that to my face.'

'He'll do so perfectly, if you give him a chance. That's where you can help me. Quarrel with him—he's rather good at a quarrel, and that will divert him and draw him off.'

'Then I'm ready to discuss the matter with him for the rest of the voyage.'

'Very well; I count on you. But he'll ask you, as he asks me, what the deuce you want him to do.'

'To go to bed,' I replied, laughing.

'Oh, it isn't a joke.'

'That's exactly what I told you at first.'

'Yes, but don't exult; I hate people who exult. Jasper wants to know why he should mind her being talked about if she doesn't mind it herself.'

'I'll tell him why,' I replied; and Mrs. Nettlepoint said she should be exceedingly obliged to me and repeated that she would come upstairs.

I looked for Jasper above that same evening, but circumstances did not favour my quest. I found him—that is I discovered that he was again ensconced behind the lifeboat with Miss Mavis; but there was a needless violence in breaking into their communion, and I put off our interview till the next day. Then I took the first opportunity, at breakfast, to make sure of it. He was in the saloon when I went in and was preparing to leave the table; but I stopped him and asked if he would give me a quarter of an hour on deck a little later—there was something particular I wanted to say to him. He said, 'Oh yes, if you like,' with just a visible surprise, but no look of an uncomfortable consciousness. When I had finished my breakfast I found him smoking on the forward-deck and I immediately began: 'I am going to say something that you won't at all like; to ask you a question that you will think impertinent.'

'Impertinent? that's bad.'

'I am a good deal older than you and I am a friend—of many years—of your mother. There's nothing I like less than to be meddlesome, but I think these things give me a certain right—a sort of privilege. For the rest, my inquiry will speak for itself.'

'Why so many preliminaries?' the young man asked, smiling.

We looked into each other's eyes a moment. What indeed was his mother's manner—her best manner—compared with his? 'Are you prepared to be responsible?'

'To you?'

'Dear no—to the young lady herself. I am speaking of course of Miss Mavis.'

'Ah yes, my mother tells me you have her greatly on your mind.'

'So has your mother herself—now.'

'She is so good as to say so—to oblige you.'

'She would oblige me a great deal more by reassuring me. I am aware that you know I have told her that Miss Mavis is greatly talked about.'

'Yes, but what on earth does it matter?'

'It matters as a sign.'

'A sign of what?'

'That she is in a false position.'

Jasper puffed his cigar, with his eyes on the horizon. 'I don't know whether it's *your* business, what you are attempting to discuss; but it really appears to me it is none of mine. What have I to do with the tattle with which a pack of old women console themselves for not being sea-sick?'

'Do you call it tattle that Miss Mavis is in love with you?'

'Drivelling.'

'Then you are very ungrateful. The tattle of a pack of old women has this importance, that she suspects or knows that it exists, and that nice girls are for the most part very sensitive to that sort of thing. To be prepared not to heed it in this case she must have a reason, and the reason must be the one I have taken the liberty to call your attention to.'

'In love with me in six days, just like that?' said Jasper, smoking.

'There is no accounting for tastes, and six days at sea are equivalent to sixty on land. I don't want to make you too proud. Of course if you recognise your responsibility it's all right and I have nothing to say.'

'I don't see what you mean,' Jasper went on.

'Surely you ought to have thought of that by this time. She's engaged to be married and the gentleman she is engaged to is to meet her at Liverpool.

The whole ship knows it (I didn't tell them!) and the whole ship is watching her. It's impertinent if you like, just as I am, but we make a little world here together and we can't blink its conditions. What I ask you is whether you are prepared to allow her to give up the gentleman I have just mentioned for your sake.'

'For my sake?'

'To marry her if she breaks with him.'

Jasper turned his eyes from the horizon to my own, and I found a strange expression in them. 'Has Miss Mavis commissioned you to make this inquiry?'

'Never in the world.'

'Well then, I don't understand it.'

'It isn't from another I make it. Let it come from yourself—*to* yourself.'

'Lord, you must think I lead myself a life! That's a question the young lady may put to me any moment that it pleases her.'

'Let me then express the hope that she will. But what will you answer?'

'My dear sir, it seems to me that in spite of all the titles you have enumerated you have no reason to expect I will tell you.' He turned away and I exclaimed, sincerely, 'Poor girl!' At this he faced me again and, looking at me from head to foot, demanded: 'What is it you want me to do?'

'I told your mother that you ought to go to bed.'

'You had better do that yourself!'

This time he walked off, and I reflected rather dolefully that the only clear result of my experiment would probably have been to make it vivid to him that she was in love with him. Mrs. Nettlepoint came up as she had announced, but the day was half over. it was nearly three o'clock. She was accompanied by her son, who established her on deck, arranged her chair and her shawls, saw that she was protected from sun and wind, and for an hour was very properly attentive. While this went on Grace Mavis was not visible, nor did she reappear during the whole afternoon. I had not observed that she had as yet been absent from the deck for so long a period. Jasper went away, but he came back at intervals to see how his mother got on, and when she asked him where Miss Mavis was he said he had not the least idea. I sat with Mrs. Nettlepoint at her particular request: she told me she knew that if I left her Mrs. Peck and Mrs. Gotch would come to speak to her. She was flurried and fatigued at having to make an effort, and I think that Grace Mavis's choosing this occasion for retirement suggested to her a little that she had been made a fool of. She remarked that the girl's not being there showed her complete want of breeding and that she was really very good to have put herself out for her so; she was a common creature and that was the end of it. I could see that Mrs. Nettlepoint's advent quickened the speculative activity of the other ladies; they watched her from the opposite side of the deck, keeping their eyes fixed on her very much as the man at the wheel kept his on the course of the ship. Mrs. Peck plainly meditated an approach, and it was from this danger that Mrs. Nettlepoint averted her face.

'It's just as we said,' she remarked to me as we sat there. 'It is like the bucket in the well. When I come up that girl goes down.'

'Yes, but you've succeeded, since Jasper remains here.'

'Remains? I don't see him.'

'He comes and goes—it's the same thing.'

'He goes more than he comes. But *n'en parlons plus*; I haven't gained anything. I don't admire the sea at all—what is it but a magnified water-tank? I shan't come up again.'

'I have an idea she'll stay in her cabin now,' I said. 'She tells me she has one to herself.' Mrs. Nettlepoint replied that she might do as she liked, and I repeated to her the little conversation I had had with Jasper.

She listened with interest, but 'Marry her? mercy!' she exclaimed. 'I like the manner in which you give my son away.'

'You wouldn't accept that.'

'Never in the world.'

'Then I don't understand your position.'

'Good heavens, I have none! It isn't a position to be bored to death.'

'You wouldn't accept it even in the case I put to him—that of her believing she had been encouraged to throw over poor Porterfield?'

'Not even—not even. Who knows what she believes?'

'Then you do exactly what I said you would—you show me a fine example of maternal immorality.'

'Maternal fiddlesticks! It was she began it.'

'Then why did you come up to-day?'

'To keep you quiet.'

Mrs. Nettlepoint's dinner was served on deck, but I went into the saloon. Jasper was there but not Grace Mavis, as I had half expected. I asked him what had become of her, if she were ill (he must have thought I had an ignoble pertinacity), and he replied that he knew nothing whatever about her. Mrs. Peck talked to me about Mrs. Nettlepoint and said it had been a great interest to her to see her; only it was a pity she didn't seem more sociable. To this I replied that she had to beg to be excused—she was not well.

'You don't mean to say she's sick, on this pond?'

'No, she's unwell in another way.'

'I guess I know the way!' Mrs. Peck laughed. And then she added, 'I suppose she came up to look after her charge.'

'Her charge?'

'Why, Miss Mavis. We've talked enough about that.'

'Quite enough. I don't know what that had to do with it. Miss Mavis hasn't been there to-day.'

'Oh, it goes on all the same.'

'It goes on?'

'Well, it's too late.'

'Too late?'

'Well, you'll see. There'll be a row.'

This was not comforting, but I did not repeat it above. Mrs. Nettlepoint returned early to her cabin, professing herself much tired. I know not what 'went on,' but Grace Mavis continued not to show. I went in late, to bid Mrs. Nettlepoint good-night, and learned from her that the girl had not been to her. She had sent the stewardess to her room for news, to see if she were ill and needed assistance, and the stewardess came back with the information that she was not there. I went above after this; the night was not quite so fair and the deck was almost empty. In a moment Jasper Nettlepoint and our young lady moved past me together. 'I hope you are better!' I called after her; and she replied, over her shoulder—

'Oh, yes, I had a headache; but the air now does me good!'

I went down again—I was the only person there but they, and I wished to not appear to be watching them—and returning to Mrs. Nettlepoint's room found (her door was open into the little passage) that she was still sitting up.

'She's all right!' I said. 'She's on the deck with Jasper.'

The old lady looked up at me from her book. 'I didn't know you called that all right.'

'Well, it's better than something else.'

'Something else?'

'Something I was a little afraid of.' Mrs. Nettlepoint continued to look at me; she asked me what that was. 'I'll tell you when we are ashore,' I said.

The next day I went to see her, at the usual hour of my morning visit, and found her in considerable agitation. 'The scenes have begun,' she said; 'you know I told you I shouldn't get through without them! You made me nervous last night—I haven't the least idea what you meant; but you made me nervous. She came in to see me an hour ago, and I had the courage to say to her, "I don't know why I shouldn't tell you frankly that I have been scolding my son about you." Of course she asked me what I meant by that, and I said—"It seems to me he drags you about the ship too much, for a girl in your position. He has the air of not remembering that you belong to some one else. There is a kind of want of taste and even of want of respect in it." That produced an explosion; she became very violent.'

'Do you mean angry?'

'Not exactly angry, but very hot and excited—at my presuming to think her relations with my son were not the simplest in the world. I might scold him as much as I liked—that was between ourselves; but she didn't see why I should tell her that I had done so. Did I think she allowed him to treat her with disrespect? That idea was not very complimentary to her! He had treated her better and been kinder to her than most other people—there were very few on the ship that hadn't been insulting. She should be glad enough when she got off it, to her own people, to some one whom no one would have a right to say anything about. What was there in her position that was not perfectly natural? What was the idea of making a fuss about her position? Did I mean that she took it too easily—that she didn't think as much as she ought about Mr. Porterfield? Didn't I believe she was attached to him—didn't I believe she was just counting the hours until she saw him? That would be the happiest moment of her life. It showed how little I knew her, if I thought anything else.'

'All that must have been rather fine—I should have liked to hear it,' I said. 'And what did you reply?'

'Oh, I grovelled; I told her that I accused her (as regards my son) of nothing worse than an excess of good nature. She helped him to pass his time—he ought to be immensely obliged. Also that it would be a very happy moment for me too when I should hand her over to Mr. Porterfield.'

'And will you come up to-day?'

'No indeed—she'll do very well now.'

I gave a sigh of relief. 'All's well that ends well!'

Jasper, that day, spent a great deal of time with his mother. She had told me that she really had had no proper opportunity to talk over with him their movements after disembarking. Everything changes a little, the last two or three days of a voyage; the spell is broken and new combinations take place. Grace Mavis was neither on deck nor at dinner, and I drew Mrs. Peck's attention to the extreme propriety with which she now conducted herself. She had spent the day in meditation and she judged it best to continue to meditate.

'Ah, she's afraid,' said my implacable neighbour.

'Afraid of what?'

'Well, that we'll tell tales when we get there.'

'Whom do you mean by "we"?'

'Well, there are plenty, on a ship like this.'

'Well then, we won't.'

'Maybe we won't have the chance,' said the dreadful little woman.

'Oh, at that moment a universal geniality reigns.'

'Well, she's afraid, all the same.'

'So much the better.'

'Yes, so much the better.'

All the next day, too, the girl remained invisible and Mrs. Nettlepoint told me that she had not been in to see her. She had inquired by the stewardess if she would receive her in her own cabin, and Grace Mavis had replied that it was littered up with things and unfit for visitors: she was packing a trunk over. Jasper made up for his devotion to his mother the day before by now

184

spending a great deal of his time in the smoking-room. I wanted to say to him 'This is much better,' but I thought it wiser to hold my tongue. Indeed I had begun to feel the emotion of prospective arrival (I was delighted to be almost back in my dear old Europe again) and had less to spare for other matters. It will doubtless appear to the critical reader that I had already devoted far too much to the little episode of which my story gives an account, but to this I can only reply that the event justified me. We sighted land, the dim yet rich coast of Ireland, about sunset and I leaned on the edge of the ship and looked at it. 'It doesn't look like much, does it?' I heard a voice say, beside me; and, turning, I found Grace Mavis was there. Almost for the first time she had her veil up, and I thought her very pale.

'It will be more to-morrow,' I said.

'Oh yes, a great deal more.'

'The first sight of land, at sea, changes everything,' I went on. 'I always think it's like waking up from a dream. It's a return to reality.'

For a moment she made no response to this; then she said, 'It doesn't look very real yet.'

'No, and meanwhile, this lovely evening, the dream is still present.'

She looked up at the sky, which had a brightness, though the light of the sun had left it and that of the stars had not come out. 'It *is* a lovely evening.'

'Oh yes, with this we shall do.'

She stood there a while longer, while the growing dusk effaced the line of the land more rapidly than our progress made it distinct. She said nothing more, she only looked in front of her; but her very quietness made me want to say something suggestive of sympathy and service. I was unable to think what to say—some things seemed too wide of the mark and others too importunate. At last, unexpectedly, she appeared to give me my chance. Irrelevantly, abruptly she broke out:

'Didn't you tell me that you knew Mr. Porterfield?'

185

'Dear me, yes—I used to see him. I have often wanted to talk to you about him.'

She turned her face upon me and in the deepened evening I fancied she looked whiter. 'What good would that do?'

'Why, it would be a pleasure,' I replied, rather foolishly.

'Do you mean for you?'

'Well, yes—call it that,' I said, smiling.

'Did you know him so well?'

My smile became a laugh and I said—'You are not easy to make speeches to.'

'I hate speeches!' The words came from her lips with a violence that surprised me; they were loud and hard. But before I had time to wonder at it she went on—'Shall you know him when you see him?'

'Perfectly, I think.' Her manner was so strange that one had to notice it in some way, and it appeared to me the best way was to notice it jocularly; so I added, 'Shan't you?'

'Oh, perhaps you'll point him out!' And she walked quickly away. As I looked after her I had a singular, a perverse and rather an embarrassed sense of having, during the previous days, and especially in speaking to Jasper Nettlepoint, interfered with her situation to her loss. I had a sort of pang in seeing her move about alone; I felt somehow responsible for it and asked myself why I could not have kept my hands off. I had seen Jasper in the smoking-room more than once that day, as I passed it, and half an hour before this I had observed, through the open door, that he was there. He had been with her so much that without him she had a bereaved, forsaken air. It was better, no doubt, but superficially it made her rather pitiable. Mrs. Peck would have told me that their separation was gammon; they didn't show together on deck and in the saloon, but they made it up elsewhere. The secret places on shipboard are not numerous; Mrs. Peck's 'elsewhere' would have been vague and I know not what license her imagination took. It was distinct that Jasper had fallen off, but of course what had passed between them on this subject was not so and could never be. Later, through his mother, I had *his* version of that, but I may remark that I didn't believe it. Poor Mrs. Nettlepoint did, of course. I was almost capable, after the girl had left me, of going to my young man and saying, 'After all, do return to her a little, just till we get in! It won't make any difference after we land.' And I don't think it was the fear he would tell me I was an idiot that prevented me. At any rate the next time I passed the door of the smoking-room I saw that he had left it. I paid my usual visit to Mrs. Nettlepoint that night, but I troubled her no further about Miss Mavis. She had made up her mind that everything was smooth and settled now, and it seemed to me that I had worried her and that she had worried herself enough. I left her to enjoy the foretaste of arrival, which had taken possession of her mind. Before turning in I went above and found more passengers on deck than I had ever seen so late. Jasper was walking about among them alone, but I forebore to join him. The coast of Ireland had disappeared, but the night and the sea were perfect. On the way to my cabin, when I came down, I met the stewardess in one of the passages and the idea entered my head to say to her—'Do you happen to know where Miss Mavis is?'

'Why, she's in her room, sir, at this hour.'

'Do you suppose I could speak to her?' It had come into my mind to ask her why she had inquired of me whether I should recognise Mr. Porterfield.

'No, sir,' said the stewardess; 'she has gone to bed.'

'That's all right.' And I followed the young lady's excellent example.

The next morning, while I was dressing, the steward of my side of the ship came to me as usual to see what I wanted. But the first thing he said to me was—'Rather a bad job, sir—a passenger missing.'

'A passenger—missing?'

'A lady, sir. I think you knew her. Miss Mavis, sir.'

'*Missing?*' I cried—staring at him, horror-stricken.

'She's not on the ship. They can't find her.'

'Then where to God is she?'

I remember his queer face. 'Well sir, I suppose you know that as well as I.'

'Do you mean she has jumped overboard?'

'Some time in the night, sir—on the quiet. But it's beyond every one, the way she escaped notice. They usually sees 'em, sir. It must have been about half-past two. Lord, but she was clever, sir. She didn't so much as make a splash. They say she *'ad* come against her will, sir.'

I had dropped upon my sofa—I felt faint. The man went on, liking to talk, as persons of his class do when they have something horrible to tell. She usually rang for the stewardess early, but this morning of course there had been no ring. The stewardess had gone in all the same about eight o'clock and found the cabin empty. That was about an hour ago. Her things were there in confusion—the things she usually wore when she went above. The stewardess thought she had been rather strange last night, but she waited a little and then went back. Miss Mavis hadn't turned up—and she didn't turn up. The stewardess began to look for her—she hadn't been seen on deck or in the saloon. Besides, she wasn't dressed—not to show herself; all her clothes were in her room. There was another lady, an old lady, Mrs. Nettlepoint—I would know her—that she was sometimes with, but the stewardess had been with *her* and she knew Miss Mavis had not come near her that morning. She had spoken to *him* and they had taken a quiet look—they had hunted everywhere. A ship's a big place, but you do come to the end of it, and if a person ain't there why they ain't. In short an hour had passed and the young lady was not accounted for: from which I might judge if she ever would be. The watch couldn't account for her, but no doubt the fishes in the sea could—poor miserable lady! The stewardess and he, they had of course thought it their duty very soon to speak to the doctor, and the doctor had spoken immediately to the captain. The captain didn't like it—they never did. But he would try to keep it quiet—they always did.

By the time I succeeded in pulling myself together and getting on, after a fashion, the rest of my clothes I had learned that Mrs. Nettlepoint had not yet been informed, unless the stewardess had broken it to her within the previous few minutes. Her son knew, the young gentleman on the other side of the ship (he had the other steward); my man had seen him come out of his cabin and rush above, just before he came in to me. He *had* gone above, my man was sure; he had not gone to the old lady's cabin. I remember a queer vision when the steward told me this—the wild flash of a picture of Jasper Nettlepoint leaping with a mad compunction in his young agility over the side of the ship. I hasten to add that no such incident was destined to contribute its horror to poor Grace Mavis's mysterious tragic act. What followed was miserable enough, but I can only glance at it. When I got to Mrs. Nettlepoint's door she was there in her dressing-gown; the stewardess had just told her and she was rushing out to come to me. I made her go back—I said I would go for Jasper. I went for him but I missed him, partly no doubt because it was really, at first, the captain I was after. I found this personage and found him highly scandalised, but he gave me no hope that we were in error, and his displeasure, expressed with seamanlike plainness, was a definite settlement of the question. From the deck, where I merely turned round and looked, I saw the light of another summer day, the coast of Ireland green and near and the sea a more charming colour than it had been at all. When I came below again Jasper had passed back; he had gone to his cabin and his mother had joined him there. He remained there till we reached Liverpool—I never saw him. His mother, after a little, at his request, left him alone. All the world went above to look at the land and chatter about our tragedy, but the poor lady spent the day, dismally enough, in her room. It seemed to me intolerably long; I was thinking so of vague Porterfield and of my prospect of having to face him on the morrow. Now of course I knew why she had asked me if I should recognise him; she had delegated to me mentally a certain pleasant office. I gave Mrs. Peck and Mrs. Gotch a wide berth—I couldn't talk to them. I could, or at least I did a little, to Mrs. Nettlepoint, but with too many reserves for comfort on either side, for I foresaw that it would not in the least do now to mention Jasper to her. I was obliged to assume by my silence that he had had nothing to do with what had happened; and of course I never really ascertained what he *had* had to do. The secret of what passed between him and the strange girl who would have sacrificed her marriage to him on so short an acquaintance remains shut up in his breast. His mother, I know, went to his door from time to time, but he refused her admission. That evening, to be human at a venture, I requested the steward to go in and ask him if he should care to see me, and the attendant returned with an answer which he candidly transmitted. 'Not in the least!' Jasper apparently was almost as scandalised as the captain.

At Liverpool, at the dock, when we had touched, twenty people came on board and I had already made out Mr. Porterfield at a distance. He was looking up at the side of the great vessel with disappointment written (to my eyes) in his face—disappointment at not seeing the woman he loved lean over it and wave her handkerchief to him. Every one was looking at him, every one but she (his identity flew about in a moment) and I wondered if he did not observe it. He used to be lean, he had grown almost fat. The interval between us diminished—he was on the plank and then on the deck with the jostling officers of the customs—all too soon for my equanimity. I met him instantly however, laid my hand on him and drew him away, though I perceived that he had no impression of having seen me before. It was not till afterwards that I thought this a little stupid of him. I drew him far away (I was conscious of Mrs. Peck and Mrs. Gotch looking at us as we passed) into the empty, stale smoking-room; he remained speechless, and that struck me as like him. I had to speak first, he could not even relieve me by saying 'Is anything the matter?' I told him first that she was ill. It was an odious moment.

THE LIAR

I

The train was half an hour late and the drive from the station longer than he had supposed, so that when he reached the house its inmates had dispersed to dress for dinner and he was conducted straight to his room. The curtains were drawn in this asylum, the candles were lighted, the fire was bright, and when the servant had quickly put out his clothes the comfortable little place became suggestive—seemed to promise a pleasant house, a various party, talks, acquaintances, affinities, to say nothing of very good cheer. He was too occupied with his profession to pay many country visits, but he had heard people who had more time for them speak of establishments where 'they do you very well.' He foresaw that the proprietors of Stayes would do him very well. In his bedroom at a country house he always looked first at the books on the shelf and the prints on the walls; he considered that these things gave a sort of measure of the culture and even of the character of his hosts. Though he had but little time to devote to them on this occasion a cursory inspection assured him that if the literature, as usual, was mainly American and humorous the art consisted neither of the water-colour studies of the children nor of 'goody' engravings. The walls were adorned with old-fashioned lithographs, principally portraits of country gentlemen with high collars and riding gloves: this suggested—and it was encouraging—that the tradition of portraiture was held in esteem. There was the customary novel of Mr. Le Fanu, for the bedside; the ideal reading in a country house for the hours after midnight. Oliver Lyon could scarcely forbear beginning it while he buttoned his shirt.

Perhaps that is why he not only found every one assembled in the hall when he went down, but perceived from the way the move to dinner was instantly made that they had been waiting for him. There was no delay, to introduce him to a lady, for he went out in a group of unmatched men, without this appendage. The men, straggling behind, sidled and edged as usual at the door of the dining-room, and the *dénouement* of this little comedy was that he came to his place last of all. This made him think that he was in a sufficiently distinguished company, for if he had been humiliated (which he was not), he could not have consoled himself with the reflection that such a fate was natural to an obscure, struggling young artist. He could no longer think of himself as very young, alas, and if his position was not so brilliant as it ought to be he could no longer justify it by calling it a struggle. He was something of a celebrity and he was apparently in a society of celebrities. This idea added to the curiosity with which he looked up and down the long table as he settled himself in his place.

It was a numerous party—five and twenty people; rather an odd occasion to have proposed to him, as he thought. He would not be surrounded by the quiet that ministers to good work; however, it had never interfered with his work to see the spectacle of human life before him in the intervals. And though he did not know it, it was never quiet at Stayes. When he was working well he found himself in that happy state—the happiest of all for an artist—in which things in general contribute to the particular idea and fall in with it, help it on and justify it, so that he feels for the hour as if nothing in the world can happen to him, even if it come in the guise of disaster or suffering, that will not be an enhancement of his subject. Moreover there was an exhilaration (he had felt it before) in the rapid change of scene—the jump, in the dusk of the afternoon, from foggy London and his familiar studio to a centre of festivity in the middle of Hertfordshire and a drama half acted, a drama of pretty women and noted men and wonderful orchids in silver jars. He observed as a not unimportant fact that one of the pretty women was beside him: a gentleman sat on his other hand. But he went into his neighbours little as yet: he was busy looking out for Sir David, whom he had never seen and about whom he naturally was curious.

Evidently, however, Sir David was not at dinner, a circumstance sufficiently explained by the other circumstance which constituted our friend's principal knowledge of him—his being ninety years of age. Oliver

Lyon had looked forward with great pleasure to the chance of painting a nonagenarian, and though the old man's absence from table was something of a disappointment (it was an opportunity the less to observe him before going to work), it seemed a sign that he was rather a sacred and perhaps therefore an impressive relic. Lyon looked at his son with the greater interest—wondered whether the glazed bloom of his cheek had been transmitted from Sir David. That would be jolly to paint, in the old man—the withered ruddiness of a winter apple, especially if the eye were still alive and the white hair carried out the frosty look. Arthur Ashmore's hair had a midsummer glow, but Lyon was glad his commission had been to delineate the father rather than the son, in spite of his never having seen the one and of the other being seated there before him now in the happy expansion of liberal hospitality.

Arthur Ashmore was a fresh-coloured, thick-necked English gentleman, but he was just not a subject; he might have been a farmer and he might have been a banker: you could scarcely paint him in characters. His wife did not make up the amount; she was a large, bright, negative woman, who had the same air as her husband of being somehow tremendously new; a sort of appearance of fresh varnish (Lyon could scarcely tell whether it came from her complexion or from her clothes), so that one felt she ought to sit in a gilt frame, suggesting reference to a catalogue or a price-list. It was as if she were already rather a bad though expensive portrait, knocked off by an eminent hand, and Lyon had no wish to copy that work. The pretty woman on his right was engaged with her neighbour and the gentleman on his other side looked shrinking and scared, so that he had time to lose himself in his favourite diversion of watching face after face. This amusement gave him the greatest pleasure he knew, and he often thought it a mercy that the human mask did interest him and that it was not less vivid than it was (sometimes it ran its success in this line very close), since he was to make his living by reproducing it. Even if Arthur Ashmore would not be inspiring to paint (a certain anxiety rose in him lest if he should make a hit with her father-in-law Mrs. Arthur should take it into her head that he had now proved himself worthy to *abander* her husband); even if he had looked a little less like a page (fine as to print and margin) without punctuation, he would still be a refreshing, iridescent surface. But the gentleman four persons off—what was he? Would he be a subject, or was his face only the legible door-plate of his identity, burnished with punctual washing and shaving—the least thing that was decent that you would know him by?

This face arrested Oliver Lyon: it struck him at first as very handsome. The gentleman might still be called young, and his features were regular: he had a plentiful, fair moustache that curled up at the ends, a brilliant, gallant, almost adventurous air, and a big shining breastpin in the middle of his shirt. He appeared a fine satisfied soul, and Lyon perceived that wherever he rested his friendly eye there fell an influence as pleasant as the September sun—as if he could make grapes and pears or even human affection ripen by looking at them. What was odd in him was a certain mixture of the correct and the extravagant: as if he were an adventurer imitating a gentleman with rare perfection or a gentleman who had taken a fancy to go about with hidden arms. He might have been a dethroned prince or the war-correspondent of a newspaper: he represented both enterprise and tradition, good manners and bad taste. Lyon at length fell into conversation with the lady beside him— they dispensed, as he had had to dispense at dinner-parties before, with an introduction—by asking who this personage might be.

'Oh, he's Colonel Capadose, don't you know?' Lyon didn't know and he asked for further information. His neighbour had a sociable manner and evidently was accustomed to quick transitions; she turned from her other interlocutor with a methodical air, as a good cook lifts the cover of the next saucepan. 'He has been a great deal in India—isn't he rather celebrated?' she inquired. Lyon confessed he had never heard of him, and she went on, 'Well, perhaps he isn't; but he says he is, and if you think it, that's just the same, isn't it?'

'If *you* think it?'

'I mean if he thinks it—that's just as good, I suppose.'

'Do you mean that he says that which is not?'

'Oh dear, no—because I never know. He is exceedingly clever and amusing—quite the cleverest person in the house, unless indeed you are more so. But that I can't tell yet, can I? I only know about the people I know; I think that's celebrity enough!'

'Enough for them?'

'Oh, I see you're clever. Enough for me! But I have heard of you,' the lady went on. 'I know your pictures; I admire them. But I don't think you look like them.'

'They are mostly portraits,' Lyon said; 'and what I usually try for is not my own resemblance.'

'I see what you mean. But they have much more colour. And now you are going to do some one here?'

'I have been invited to do Sir David. I'm rather disappointed at not seeing him this evening.'

'Oh, he goes to bed at some unnatural hour—eight o'clock or something of that sort. You know he's rather an old mummy.'

'An old mummy?' Oliver Lyon repeated.

'I mean he wears half a dozen waistcoats, and that sort of thing. He's always cold.'

'I have never seen him and never seen any portrait or photograph of him,' Lyon said. 'I'm surprised at his never having had anything done—at their waiting all these years.'

'Ah, that's because he was afraid, you know; it was a kind of superstition. He was sure that if anything were done he would die directly afterwards. He has only consented to-day.'

'He's ready to die then?'

'Oh, now he's so old he doesn't care.'

'Well, I hope I shan't kill him,' said Lyon. 'It was rather unnatural in his son to send for me.'

'Oh, they have nothing to gain—everything is theirs already!' his companion rejoined, as if she took this speech quite literally. Her talkativeness was systematic—she fraternised as seriously as she might have played whist. 'They do as they like—they fill the house with people—they have *carte blanche.*'

'I see—but there's still the title.'

'Yes, but what is it?'

Our artist broke into laughter at this, whereat his companion stared. Before he had recovered himself she was scouring the plain with her other neighbour. The gentleman on his left at last risked an observation, and they had some fragmentary talk. This personage played his part with difficulty: he uttered a remark as a lady fires a pistol, looking the other way. To catch the ball Lyon had to bend his ear, and this movement led to his observing a handsome creature who was seated on the same side, beyond his interlocutor. Her profile was presented to him and at first he was only struck with its beauty; then it produced an impression still more agreeable—a sense of undimmed remembrance and intimate association. He had not recognised her on the instant only because he had so little expected to see her there; he had not seen her anywhere for so long, and no news of her ever came to him. She was often in his thoughts, but she had passed out of his life. He thought of her twice a week; that may be called often in relation to a person one has not seen for twelve years. The moment after he recognised her he felt how true it was that it was only she who could look like that: of the most charming head in the world (and this lady had it) there could never be a replica. She was leaning forward a little; she remained in profile, apparently listening to some one on the other side of her. She was listening, but she was also looking, and after a moment Lyon followed the direction of her eyes. They rested upon the gentleman who had been described to him as Colonel Capadose—rested, as it appeared to him, with a kind of habitual, visible complacency. This was not strange, for the Colonel was unmistakably formed to attract the sympathetic gaze of woman; but Lyon was slightly disappointed that she could let *him* look at her so long without giving him a glance. There was nothing between them to-day and he had no rights, but she must have known he was coming (it was of course not such a tremendous event, but she could not have been staying in the house without hearing of it), and it was not natural that that should absolutely fail to affect her.

She was looking at Colonel Capadose as if she were in love with him—a queer accident for the proudest, most reserved of women. But doubtless it was all right, if her husband liked it or didn't notice it: he had heard indefinitely, years before, that she was married, and he took for granted (as he had not heard that she had become a widow) the presence of the happy man on whom she had conferred what she had refused to *him*, the poor art-student at Munich. Colonel Capadose appeared to be aware of nothing, and this circumstance, incongruously enough, rather irritated Lyon than gratified him. Suddenly the lady turned her head, showing her full face to our hero. He was so prepared with a greeting that he instantly smiled, as a shaken jug overflows; but she gave him no response, turned away again and sank back in her chair. All that her face said in that instant was, 'You see I'm as handsome as ever.' To which he mentally subjoined, 'Yes, and as much good it does me!' He asked the young man beside him if he knew who that beautiful being was—the fifth person beyond him. The young man leaned forward, considered and then said, 'I think she's Mrs. Capadose.'

'Do you mean his wife—that fellow's?' And Lyon indicated the subject of the information given him by his other neighbour.

'Oh, is *he* Mr. Capadose?' said the young man, who appeared very vague. He admitted his vagueness and explained it by saying that there were so many people and he had come only the day before. What was definite to Lyon was that Mrs. Capadose was in love with her husband; so that he wished more than ever that he had married her.

'She's very faithful,' he found himself saying three minutes later to the lady on his right. He added that he meant Mrs. Capadose.

'Ah, you know her then?'

'I knew her once upon a time—when I was living abroad.'

'Why then were you asking me about her husband?'

'Precisely for that reason. She married after that—I didn't even know her present name.'

'How then do you know it now?'

'This gentleman has just told me—he appears to know.'

'I didn't know he knew anything,' said the lady, glancing forward.

'I don't think he knows anything but that.'

'Then you have found out for yourself that she is faithful. What do you mean by that?'

'Ah, you mustn't question me—I want to question you,' Lyon said. 'How do you all like her here?'

'You ask too much! I can only speak for myself. I think she's hard.'

'That's only because she's honest and straightforward.'

'Do you mean I like people in proportion as they deceive?'

'I think we all do, so long as we don't find them out,' Lyon said. 'And then there's something in her face—a sort of Roman type, in spite of her having such an English eye. In fact she's English down to the ground; but her complexion, her low forehead and that beautiful close little wave in her dark hair make her look like a glorified *contadina*.'

'Yes, and she always sticks pins and daggers into her head, to increase that effect. I must say I like her husband better: he is so clever.'

'Well, when I knew her there was no comparison that could injure her. She was altogether the most delightful thing in Munich.'

'In Munich?'

'Her people lived there; they were not rich—in pursuit of economy in fact, and Munich was very cheap. Her father was the younger son of some noble house; he had married a second time and had a lot of little mouths to feed. She was the child of the first wife and she didn't like her stepmother, but she was charming to her little brothers and sisters. I once made a sketch of her as Werther's Charlotte, cutting bread and butter while they clustered all round her. All the artists in the place were in love with her but she wouldn't look at 'the likes' of us. She was too proud—I grant you that; but she wasn't stuck up nor young ladyish; she was simple and frank and kind about it. She used to remind me of Thackeray's Ethel Newcome. She told me she must marry well: it was the one thing she could do for her family. I suppose you would say that she *has* married well.'

'She told *you?*' smiled Lyon's neighbour.

'Oh, of course I proposed to her too. But she evidently thinks so herself!' he added.

When the ladies left the table the host as usual bade the gentlemen draw together, so that Lyon found himself opposite to Colonel Capadose. The conversation was mainly about the 'run,' for it had apparently been a great day in the hunting-field. Most of the gentlemen communicated their adventures and opinions, but Colonel Capadose's pleasant voice was the most audible in the chorus. It was a bright and fresh but masculine organ, just such a voice as, to Lyon's sense, such a 'fine man' ought to have had. It appeared from his remarks that he was a very straight rider, which was also very much what Lyon would have expected. Not that he swaggered, for his allusions were very quietly and casually made; but they were all too dangerous experiments and close shaves. Lyon perceived after a little that the attention paid by the company to the Colonel's remarks was not in direct relation to the interest they seemed to offer; the result of which was that the speaker, who noticed that *he* at least was listening, began to treat him as his particular auditor and to fix his eyes on him as he talked. Lyon had nothing to do but to look sympathetic and assent—Colonel Capadose appeared to take so much sympathy and assent for granted. A neighbouring squire had had an accident; he had come a cropper in an awkward place—just at the finish—with consequences that looked grave. He had struck his head; he remained insensible, up to the last accounts: there had evidently been concussion of the brain. There was some exchange of views as to his recovery—how soon it would take place or whether it would take place at all; which led the Colonel to confide to our artist across the table that *he* shouldn't despair of a fellow even if he didn't come round for weeks—for weeks and weeks and weeks—for months, almost for years. He leaned forward; Lyon leaned forward to listen, and Colonel Capadose mentioned that he knew from personal experience that there was really no limit to the time one might lie unconscious without being any the worse for it. It had happened to him in Ireland, years before; he had been pitched out of a dogcart, had turned a sheer somersault and landed on his head. They thought he was dead, but he wasn't; they carried him first to the nearest cabin, where he lay for some days with the pigs, and then to an inn in a neighbouring town—it was a near thing they didn't put him under ground. He had been completely insensible—without a ray of recognition of any human thing—for three whole months; had not a glimmer of consciousness of any blessed thing. It was touch and go to that degree that they couldn't come near him, they couldn't feed him, they could scarcely look at him. Then one day he had opened his eyes—as fit as a flea!

'I give you my honour it had done me good—it rested my brain.' He appeared to intimate that with an intelligence so active as his these periods of repose were providential. Lyon thought his story very striking, but he wanted to ask him whether he had not shammed a little—not in relating it, but in keeping so quiet. He hesitated however, in time, to imply a doubt—he was so impressed with the tone in which Colonel Capadose said that it was the turn of a hair that they hadn't buried him alive. That had happened to a friend of his in India—a fellow who was supposed to have died of jungle fever—they clapped him into a coffin. He was going on to recite the further fate of this unfortunate gentleman when Mr. Ashmore made a move and every one got up to adjourn to the drawing-room. Lyon noticed that by this time no one was heeding what his new friend said to him. They came round on either side of the table and met while the gentlemen dawdled before going out.

'And do you mean that your friend was literally buried alive?' asked Lyon, in some suspense.

Colonel Capadose looked at him a moment, as if he had already lost the thread of the conversation. Then his face brightened—and when it brightened it was doubly handsome. 'Upon my soul he was chucked into the ground!'

200

'And was he left there?'

'He was left there till I came and hauled him out.'

'*You* came?'

'I dreamed about him—it's the most extraordinary story: I heard him calling to me in the night. I took upon myself to dig him up. You know there are people in India—a kind of beastly race, the ghouls—who violate graves. I had a sort of presentiment that they would get at him first. I rode straight, I can tell you; and, by Jove, a couple of them had just broken ground! Crack—crack, from a couple of barrels, and they showed me their heels, as you may believe. Would you credit that I took him out myself? The air brought him to and he was none the worse. He has got his pension—he came home the other day; he would do anything for me.'

'He called to you in the night?' said Lyon, much startled.

'That's the interesting point. Now *what was it*? It wasn't his ghost, because he wasn't dead. It wasn't himself, because he couldn't. It was something or other! You see India's a strange country—there's an element of the mysterious: the air is full of things you can't explain.'

They passed out of the dining-room, and Colonel Capadose, who went among the first, was separated from Lyon; but a minute later, before they reached the drawing-room, he joined him again. 'Ashmore tells me who you are. Of course I have often heard of you—I'm very glad to make your acquaintance; my wife used to know you.'

'I'm glad she remembers me. I recognised her at dinner and I was afraid she didn't.'

'Ah, I daresay she was ashamed,' said the Colonel, with indulgent humour.

'Ashamed of me?' Lyon replied, in the same key.

'Wasn't there something about a picture? Yes; you painted her portrait.'

'Many times,' said the artist; 'and she may very well have been ashamed of what I made of her.'

'Well, I wasn't, my dear sir; it was the sight of that picture, which you were so good as to present to her, that made me first fall in love with her.'

'Do you mean that one with the children—cutting bread and butter?'

'Bread and butter? Bless me, no—vine leaves and a leopard skin—a kind of Bacchante.'

'Ah, yes,' said Lyon; 'I remember. It was the first decent portrait I painted. I should be curious to see it to-day.'

'Don't ask her to show it to you—she'll be mortified!' the Colonel exclaimed.

'Mortified?'

'We parted with it—in the most disinterested manner,' he laughed. 'An old friend of my wife's—her family had known him intimately when they lived in Germany—took the most extraordinary fancy to it: the Grand Duke of Silberstadt-Schreckenstein, don't you know? He came out to Bombay while we were there and he spotted your picture (you know he's one of the greatest collectors in Europe), and made such eyes at it that, upon my word— it happened to be his birthday—she told him he might have it, to get rid of him. He was perfectly enchanted—but we miss the picture.'

'It is very good of you,' Lyon said. 'If it's in a great collection—a work of my incompetent youth—I am infinitely honoured.'

'Oh, he has got it in one of his castles; I don't know which—you know he has so many. He sent us, before he left India—to return the compliment—a magnificent old vase.'

'That was more than the thing was worth,' Lyon remarked.

Colonel Capadose gave no heed to this observation; he seemed to be thinking of something. After a moment he said, 'If you'll come and see us in town she'll show you the vase.' And as they passed into the drawing-room he gave the artist a friendly propulsion. 'Go and speak to her; there she is—she'll be delighted.'

Oliver Lyon took but a few steps into the wide saloon; he stood there a moment looking at the bright composition of the lamplit group of fair women, the single figures, the great setting of white and gold, the panels of old damask, in the centre of each of which was a single celebrated picture. There was a subdued lustre in the scene and an air as of the shining trains of dresses tumbled over the carpet. At the furthest end of the room sat Mrs. Capadose, rather isolated; she was on a small sofa, with an empty place beside her. Lyon could not flatter himself she had been keeping it for him; her failure to respond to his recognition at table contradicted that, but he felt an extreme desire to go and occupy it. Moreover he had her husband's sanction; so he crossed the room, stepping over the tails of gowns, and stood before his old friend.

'I hope you don't mean to repudiate me,' he said.

She looked up at him with an expression of unalloyed pleasure. 'I am so glad to see you. I was delighted when I heard you were coming.'

'I tried to get a smile from you at dinner—but I couldn't.'

'I didn't see—I didn't understand. Besides, I hate smirking and telegraphing. Also I'm very shy—you won't have forgotten that. Now we can communicate comfortably.' And she made a better place for him on the little sofa. He sat down and they had a talk that he enjoyed, while the reason for which he used to like her so came back to him, as well as a good deal of the very same old liking. She was still the least spoiled beauty he had ever seen, with an absence of coquetry or any insinuating art that seemed almost like an omitted faculty; there were moments when she struck her interlocutor as some fine creature from an asylum—a surprising deaf-mute or one of the operative blind. Her noble pagan head gave her privileges that she neglected, and when people were admiring her brow she was wondering whether there were a good fire in her bedroom. She was simple, kind and good; inexpressive but not inhuman or stupid. Now and again she dropped something that had a sifted, selected air—the sound of an impression at first hand. She had no imagination, but she had added up her feelings, some of her reflections, about life. Lyon talked of the old days in Munich, reminded her of incidents, pleasures and pains, asked her about her father and the others; and she told him in return that she was so impressed with his own fame, his brilliant position in the world, that she had not felt very sure he would speak to her or that his little sign at table was meant for her. This was plainly a perfectly truthful speech—she was incapable of any other—and he was affected by such humility on the part of a woman whose grand line was unique. Her father was dead; one of her brothers was in the navy and the other on a ranch in America; two of her sisters were married and the youngest was just coming out and very pretty. She didn't mention her stepmother. She asked him about his own personal history and he said that the principal thing that had happened to him was that he had never married.

'Oh, you ought to,' she answered. 'It's the best thing.'

'I like that—from you!' he returned.

'Why not from me? I am very happy.'

'That's just why I can't be. It's cruel of you to praise your state. But I have had the pleasure of making the acquaintance of your husband. We had a good bit of talk in the other room.'

'You must know him better—you must know him really well,' said Mrs. Capadose.

'I am sure that the further you go the more you find. But he makes a fine show, too.'

She rested her good gray eyes on Lyon. 'Don't you think he's handsome?'

'Handsome and clever and entertaining. You see I'm generous.'

'Yes; you must know him well,' Mrs. Capadose repeated.

'He has seen a great deal of life,' said her companion.

'Yes, we have been in so many places. You must see my little girl. She is nine years old—she's too beautiful.'

'You must bring her to my studio some day—I should like to paint her.'

'Ah, don't speak of that,' said Mrs. Capadose. 'It reminds me of something so distressing.'

'I hope you don't mean when *you* used to sit to me—though that may well have bored you.'

'It's not what you did—it's what we have done. It's a confession I must make—it's a weight on my mind! I mean about that beautiful picture you gave me—it used to be so much admired. When you come to see me in London (I count on your doing that very soon) I shall see you looking all round. I can't tell you I keep it in my own room because I love it so, for the simple reason——' And she paused a moment.

'Because you can't tell wicked lies,' said Lyon.

'No, I can't. So before you ask for it——'

'Oh, I know you parted with it—the blow has already fallen,' Lyon interrupted.

'Ah then, you have heard? I was sure you would! But do you know what we got for it? Two hundred pounds.'

'You might have got much more,' said Lyon, smiling.

'That seemed a great deal at the time. We were in want of the money—it was a good while ago, when we first married. Our means were very small then, but fortunately that has changed rather for the better. We had the chance; it really seemed a big sum, and I am afraid we jumped at it. My husband had expectations which have partly come into effect, so that now we do well enough. But meanwhile the picture went.'

'Fortunately the original remained. But do you mean that two hundred was the value of the vase?' Lyon asked.

'Of the vase?'

'The beautiful old Indian vase—the Grand Duke's offering.'

'The Grand Duke?'

'What's his name?—Silberstadt-Schreckenstein. Your husband mentioned the transaction.'

'Oh, my husband,' said Mrs. Capadose; and Lyon saw that she coloured a little.

Not to add to her embarrassment, but to clear up the ambiguity, which he perceived the next moment he had better have left alone, he went on: 'He tells me it's now in his collection.'

'In the Grand Duke's? Ah, you know its reputation? I believe it contains treasures.' She was bewildered, but she recovered herself, and Lyon made the mental reflection that for some reason which would seem good when he knew it the husband and the wife had prepared different versions of the same incident. It was true that he did not exactly see Everina Brant preparing a version; that was not her line of old, and indeed it was not in her eyes to-day. At any rate they both had the matter too much on their conscience. He changed the subject, said Mrs. Capadose must really bring the little girl. He sat with her some time longer and thought—perhaps it was only a fancy—that she was rather absent, as if she were annoyed at their having been even for a moment at cross-purposes. This did not prevent him from saying to her at the last, just as the ladies began to gather themselves together to go to bed: 'You seem much impressed, from what you say, with my renown and my prosperity, and you are so good as greatly to exaggerate them. Would you have married me if you had known that I was destined to success?'

'I did know it.'

'Well, I didn't'

'You were too modest.'

'You didn't think so when I proposed to you.'

'Well, if I had married you I couldn't have married *him*—and he's so nice,' Mrs. Capadose said. Lyon knew she thought it—he had learned that at dinner—but it vexed him a little to hear her say it. The gentleman designated by the pronoun came up, amid the prolonged handshaking for good-night, and Mrs. Capadose remarked to her husband as she turned away, 'He wants to paint Amy.'

'Ah, she's a charming child, a most interesting little creature,' the Colonel said to Lyon. 'She does the most remarkable things.'

Mrs. Capadose stopped, in the rustling procession that followed the hostess out of the room. 'Don't tell him, please don't,' she said.

'Don't tell him what?'

'Why, what she does. Let him find out for himself.' And she passed on.

'She thinks I swagger about the child—that I bore people,' said the Colonel. 'I hope you smoke.' He appeared ten minutes later in the smoking-room, in a brilliant equipment, a suit of crimson foulard covered with little white spots. He gratified Lyon's eye, made him feel that the modern age has its splendour too and its opportunities for costume. If his wife was an antique he was a fine specimen of the period of colour: he might have passed for a Venetian of the sixteenth century. They were a remarkable couple, Lyon thought, and as he looked at the Colonel standing in bright erectness before the chimney-piece while he emitted great smoke-puffs he did not wonder that Everina could not regret she had not married *him*. All the gentlemen collected at Stayes were not smokers and some of them had gone to bed. Colonel Capadose remarked that there probably would be a smallish muster, they had had such a hard day's work. That was the worst of a hunting-house—the men were so sleepy after dinner; it was devilish stupid for the ladies, even for those who hunted themselves—for women were so extraordinary, they never showed it. But most fellows revived under the stimulating influences of the smoking-room, and some of them, in this confidence, would turn up yet. Some of the grounds of their confidence—not all of them—might have been seen in a cluster of glasses and bottles on a table near the fire, which made the great salver and its contents twinkle sociably. The others lurked as yet in various improper corners of the minds of the most loquacious. Lyon was alone with Colonel Capadose for some moments before their companions, in varied eccentricities of uniform, straggled in, and he perceived that this wonderful man had but little loss of vital tissue to repair.

They talked about the house, Lyon having noticed an oddity of construction in the smoking-room; and the Colonel explained that it consisted of two distinct parts, one of which was of very great antiquity. They were two complete houses in short, the old one and the new, each of great extent and each very fine in its way. The two formed together an enormous structure—Lyon must make a point of going all over it. The modern portion had been erected by the old man when he bought the property; oh yes, he had bought it, forty years before—it hadn't been in the family: there hadn't been any particular family for it to be in. He had had the good taste not to spoil the original house—he had not touched it beyond what was just necessary for joining it on. It was very curious indeed—a most irregular, rambling, mysterious pile, where they every now and then discovered a walled-up room or a secret staircase. To his mind it was essentially gloomy, however; even the modern additions, splendid as they were, failed to make it cheerful. There was some story about a skeleton having been found years before, during some repairs, under a stone slab of the floor of one of the passages; but the family were rather shy of its being talked about. The place they were in was of course in the old part, which contained after all some of the best rooms: he had an idea it had been the primitive kitchen, half modernised at some intermediate period.

'My room is in the old part too then—I'm very glad,' Lyon said. 'It's very comfortable and contains all the latest conveniences, but I observed the depth of the recess of the door and the evident antiquity of the corridor and staircase—the first short one—after I came out. That panelled corridor is admirable; it looks as if it stretched away, in its brown dimness (the lamps didn't seem to me to make much impression on it), for half a mile.'

'Oh, don't go to the end of it!' exclaimed the Colonel, smiling.

'Does it lead to the haunted room?' Lyon asked.

His companion looked at him a moment. 'Ah, you know about that?'

'No, I don't speak from knowledge, only from hope. I have never had any luck—I have never stayed in a dangerous house. The places I go to are always as safe as Charing Cross. I want to see—whatever there is, the regular thing. *Is* there a ghost here?'

'Of course there is—a rattling good one.'

'And have you seen him?'

'Oh, don't ask me what *I've* seen—I should tax your credulity. I don't like to talk of these things. But there are two or three as bad—that is, as good!—rooms as you'll find anywhere.'

'Do you mean in my corridor?' Lyon asked.

'I believe the worst is at the far end. But you would be ill-advised to sleep there.'

'Ill-advised?'

'Until you've finished your job. You'll get letters of importance the next morning, and you'll take the 10.20.'

'Do you mean I will invent a pretext for running away?'

'Unless you are braver than almost any one has ever been. They don't often put people to sleep there, but sometimes the house is so crowded that they have to. The same thing always happens—ill-concealed agitation at the breakfast-table and letters of the greatest importance. Of course it's a bachelor's room, and my wife and I are at the other end of the house. But we saw the comedy three days ago—the day after we got here. A young fellow had been put there—I forget his name—the house was so full; and the usual consequence followed. Letters at breakfast—an awfully queer face—an urgent call to town—so very sorry his visit was cut short. Ashmore and his wife looked at each other, and off the poor devil went.'

'Ah, that wouldn't suit me; I must paint my picture,' said Lyon. 'But do they mind your speaking of it? Some people who have a good ghost are very proud of it, you know.'

What answer Colonel Capadose was on the point of making to this inquiry our hero was not to learn, for at that moment their host had walked into the room accompanied by three or four gentlemen. Lyon was conscious that he was partly answered by the Colonel's not going on with the subject.

This however on the other hand was rendered natural by the fact that one of the gentlemen appealed to him for an opinion on a point under discussion, something to do with the everlasting history of the day's run. To Lyon himself Mr. Ashmore began to talk, expressing his regret at having had so little direct conversation with him as yet. The topic that suggested itself was naturally that most closely connected with the motive of the artist's visit. Lyon remarked that it was a great disadvantage to him not to have had some preliminary acquaintance with Sir David—in most cases he found that so important. But the present sitter was so far advanced in life that there was doubtless no time to lose. 'Oh, I can tell you all about him,' said Mr. Ashmore; and for half an hour he told him a good deal. It was very interesting as well as very eulogistic, and Lyon could see that he was a very nice old man, to have endeared himself so to a son who was evidently not a gusher. At last he got up—he said he must go to bed if he wished to be fresh for his work in the morning. To which his host replied, 'Then you must take your candle; the lights are out; I don't keep my servants up.'

In a moment Lyon had his glimmering taper in hand, and as he was leaving the room (he did not disturb the others with a good-night; they were absorbed in the lemon-squeezer and the soda-water cork) he remembered other occasions on which he had made his way to bed alone through a darkened country-house; such occasions had not been rare, for he was almost always the first to leave the smoking-room. If he had not stayed in houses conspicuously haunted he had, none the less (having the artistic temperament), sometimes found the great black halls and staircases rather 'creepy': there had been often a sinister effect, to his imagination, in the sound of his tread in the long passages or the way the winter moon peeped into tall windows on landings. It occurred to him that if houses without supernatural pretensions could look so wicked at night, the old corridors of Stayes would certainly give him a sensation. He didn't know whether the proprietors were sensitive; very often, as he had said to Colonel Capadose, people enjoyed the impeachment. What determined him to speak, with a certain sense of the risk, was the impression that the Colonel told queer stories. As he had his hand on the door he said to Arthur Ashmore, 'I hope I shan't meet any ghosts.'

'Any ghosts?'

'You ought to have some—in this fine old part.'

'We do our best, but *que voulez-vous?*' said Mr. Ashmore. 'I don't think they like the hot-water pipes.'

'They remind them too much of their own climate? But haven't you a haunted room—at the end of my passage?'

'Oh, there are stories—we try to keep them up.'

'I should like very much to sleep there,' Lyon said.

'Well, you can move there to-morrow if you like.'

'Perhaps I had better wait till I have done my work.'

'Very good; but you won't work there, you know. My father will sit to you in his own apartments.'

'Oh, it isn't that; it's the fear of running away, like that gentleman three days ago.'

'Three days ago? What gentleman?' Mr. Ashmore asked.

'The one who got urgent letters at breakfast and fled by the 10.20. Did he stand more than one night?'

'I don't know what you are talking about. There was no such gentleman—three days ago.'

'Ah, so much the better,' said Lyon, nodding good-night and departing. He took his course, as he remembered it, with his wavering candle, and, though he encountered a great many gruesome objects, safely reached the passage out of which his room opened. In the complete darkness it seemed to stretch away still further, but he followed it, for the curiosity of the thing, to the end. He passed several doors with the name of the room painted upon them, but he found nothing else. He was tempted to try the last door—to look into the room of evil fame; but he reflected that this would be indiscreet, since Colonel Capadose handled the brush—as a *raconteur*—with such freedom. There might be a ghost and there might not; but the Colonel himself, he inclined to think, was the most mystifying figure in the house.

II

Lyon found Sir David Ashmore a capital subject and a very comfortable sitter into the bargain. Moreover he was a very agreeable old man, tremendously puckered but not in the least dim; and he wore exactly the furred dressing-gown that Lyon would have chosen. He was proud of his age but ashamed of his infirmities, which however he greatly exaggerated and which did not prevent him from sitting there as submissive as if portraiture in oils had been a branch of surgery. He demolished the legend of his having feared the operation would be fatal, giving an explanation which pleased our friend much better. He held that a gentleman should be painted but once in his life—that it was eager and fatuous to be hung up all over the place. That was good for women, who made a pretty wall-pattern; but the male face didn't lend itself to decorative repetition. The proper time for the likeness was at the last, when the whole man was there—you got the totality of his experience. Lyon could not reply that that period was not a real compendium—you had to allow so for leakage; for there had been no crack in Sir David's crystallisation. He spoke of his portrait as a plain map of the country, to be consulted by his children in a case of uncertainty. A proper map could be drawn up only when the country had been travelled. He gave Lyon his mornings, till luncheon, and they talked of many things, not neglecting, as a stimulus to gossip, the people in the house. Now that he did not 'go out,' as he said, he saw much less of the visitors at Stayes: people came and went whom he knew nothing about, and he liked to hear Lyon describe them. The artist sketched with a fine point and did not caricature, and it usually befell that when Sir David did not know the sons and daughters he had known the fathers and mothers. He was one of those terrible old gentlemen who are a repository of antecedents. But in the case of the Capadose family, at whom they arrived by an easy stage, his knowledge embraced two, or even three, generations. General Capadose was an old crony, and he remembered his father before him. The general was rather a smart soldier, but in private life of too speculative a turn—always sneaking into the City to put his money into some rotten thing. He married a girl who brought him something and they had half a dozen children. He scarcely knew what had become of the rest of them, except that one was in the Church and had found preferment—wasn't he Dean of Rockingham? Clement, the fellow who was at Stayes, had some military talent; he had served in the East, he had married a pretty girl. He had been at Eton with his son, and he used to come to Stayes in his holidays. Lately, coming back to England, he had turned up with his wife again; that was before he—the old man—had been put to grass. He was a taking dog, but he had a monstrous foible.

'A monstrous foible?' said Lyon.

'He's a thumping liar.'

Lyon's brush stopped short, while he repeated, for somehow the formula startled him, 'A thumping liar?'

'You are very lucky not to have found it out.'

'Well, I confess I have noticed a romantic tinge——'

'Oh, it isn't always romantic. He'll lie about the time of day, about the name of his hatter. It appears there are people like that.'

'Well, they are precious scoundrels,' Lyon declared, his voice trembling a little with the thought of what Everina Brant had done with herself.

'Oh, not always,' said the old man. 'This fellow isn't in the least a scoundrel. There is no harm in him and no bad intention; he doesn't steal nor cheat nor gamble nor drink; he's very kind—he sticks to his wife, is fond of his children. He simply can't give you a straight answer.'

'Then everything he told me last night, I suppose, was mendacious: he delivered himself of a series of the stiffest statements. They stuck, when I tried to swallow them, but I never thought of so simple an explanation.'

'No doubt he was in the vein,' Sir David went on. 'It's a natural peculiarity—as you might limp or stutter or be left-handed. I believe it comes and goes, like intermittent fever. My son tells me that his friends usually understand it and don't haul him up—for the sake of his wife.'

'Oh, his wife—his wife!' Lyon murmured, painting fast.

'I daresay she's used to it.'

'Never in the world, Sir David. How can she be used to it?'

'Why, my dear sir, when a woman's fond!—And don't they mostly handle the long bow themselves? They are connoisseurs—they have a sympathy for a fellow-performer.'

Lyon was silent a moment; he had no ground for denying that Mrs. Capadose was attached to her husband. But after a little he rejoined: 'Oh, not this one! I knew her years ago—before her marriage; knew her well and admired her. She was as clear as a bell.'

'I like her very much,' Sir David said, 'but I have seen her back him up.'

Lyon considered Sir David for a moment, not in the light of a model. 'Are you very sure?'

The old man hesitated; then he answered, smiling, 'You're in love with her.'

'Very likely. God knows I used to be!'

'She must help him out—she can't expose him.'

'She can hold her tongue,' Lyon remarked.

'Well, before you probably she will.'

'That's what I am curious to see.' And Lyon added, privately, 'Mercy on us, what he must have made of her!' He kept this reflection to himself, for he considered that he had sufficiently betrayed his state of mind with regard to Mrs. Capadose. None the less it occupied him now immensely, the question of how such a woman would arrange herself in such a predicament. He watched her with an interest deeply quickened when he mingled with the company; he had had his own troubles in life, but he had rarely been so anxious about anything as he was now to see what the loyalty of a wife and the infection of an example would have made of an absolutely truthful mind. Oh, he held it as immutably established that whatever other women might be prone to do she, of old, had been perfectly incapable of a deviation. Even if she had not been too simple to deceive she would have been too proud; and if she had not had too much conscience she would have had too little eagerness. It was the last thing she would have endured or condoned—the particular thing she would not have forgiven. Did she sit in torment while her husband turned his somersaults, or was she now too so perverse that she thought it a fine thing to be striking at the expense of one's honour? It would have taken a wondrous alchemy—working backwards, as it were—to produce this latter result. Besides these two alternatives (that she suffered tortures in silence and that she was so much in love that her husband's humiliating idiosyncrasy seemed to her only an added richness—a proof of life and talent), there was still the possibility that she had not found him out, that she took his false pieces at his own valuation. A little reflection rendered this hypothesis untenable; it was too evident that the account he gave of things must repeatedly have contradicted her own knowledge. Within an hour or two of his meeting them Lyon had seen her confronted with that perfectly gratuitous invention about the profit they had made off his early picture. Even then indeed she had not, so far as he could see, smarted, and—but for the present he could only contemplate the case.

Even if it had not been interfused, through his uneradicated tenderness for Mrs. Capadose, with an element of suspense, the question would still have presented itself to him as a very curious problem, for he had not painted portraits during so many years without becoming something of a psychologist. His inquiry was limited for the moment to the opportunity that the following three days might yield, as the Colonel and his wife were going on to another house. It fixed itself largely of course upon the Colonel too—this gentleman was such a rare anomaly. Moreover it had to go on very quickly. Lyon was too scrupulous to ask other people what they thought of the business—he was too afraid of exposing the woman he once had loved. It was probable also that light would come to him from the talk of the rest of the company: the Colonel's queer habit, both as it affected his own situation and as it affected his wife, would be a familiar theme in any house in which he was in the habit of staying. Lyon had not observed in the circles in which he visited any marked abstention from comment on the singularities of their members. It interfered with his progress that the Colonel hunted all day, while he plied his brushes and chatted with Sir David; but a Sunday intervened and that partly made it up. Mrs. Capadose fortunately did not hunt, and when his work was over she was not inaccessible. He took a couple of longish walks with her (she was fond of that), and beguiled her at tea into a friendly nook in the hall. Regard her as he might he could not make out to himself that she was consumed by a hidden shame; the sense of being married to a man whose word had no worth was not, in her spirit, so far as he could guess, the canker within the rose. Her mind appeared to have nothing on it but its own placid frankness, and when he looked into her eyes (deeply, as he occasionally permitted himself to do), they had no uncomfortable consciousness. He talked to her again and still again of the dear old days—reminded her of things that he had not (before this reunion) the least idea that he remembered. Then he spoke to her of her husband, praised his appearance, his talent for conversation, professed to have felt a quick friendship for him and asked (with an inward audacity at which he trembled a little) what manner of man he was. 'What manner?' said Mrs. Capadose. 'Dear me, how can one describe one's husband? I like him very much.'

'Ah, you have told me that already!' Lyon exclaimed, with exaggerated ruefulness.

'Then why do you ask me again?' She added in a moment, as if she were so happy that she could afford to take pity on him, 'He is everything that's good and kind. He's a soldier—and a gentleman—and a dear! He hasn't a fault. And he has great ability.'

'Yes; he strikes one as having great ability. But of course I can't think him a dear.'

'I don't care what you think him!' said Mrs. Capadose, looking, it seemed to him, as she smiled, handsomer than he had ever seen her. She was either deeply cynical or still more deeply impenetrable, and he had little prospect of winning from her the intimation that he longed for—some hint that it had come over her that after all she had better have married a man

216

who was not a by-word for the most contemptible, the least heroic, of vices. Had she not seen—had she not felt—the smile go round when her husband executed some especially characteristic conversational caper? How could a woman of her quality endure that day after day, year after year, except by her quality's altering? But he would believe in the alteration only when he should have heard *her* lie. He was fascinated by his problem and yet half exasperated, and he asked himself all kinds of questions. Did she not lie, after all, when she let his falsehoods pass without a protest? Was not her life a perpetual complicity, and did she not aid and abet him by the simple fact that she was not disgusted with him? Then again perhaps she *was* disgusted and it was the mere desperation of her pride that had given her an inscrutable mask. Perhaps she protested in private, passionately; perhaps every night, in their own apartments, after the day's hideous performance, she made him the most scorching scene. But if such scenes were of no avail and he took no more trouble to cure himself, how could she regard him, and after so many years of marriage too, with the perfectly artless complacency that Lyon had surprised in her in the course of the first day's dinner? If our friend had not been in love with her he could have taken the diverting view of the Colonel's delinquencies; but as it was they turned to the tragical in his mind, even while he had a sense that his solicitude might also have been laughed at.

The observation of these three days showed him that if Capadose was an abundant he was not a malignant liar and that his fine faculty exercised itself mainly on subjects of small direct importance. 'He is the liar platonic,' he said to himself; 'he is disinterested, he doesn't operate with a hope of gain or with a desire to injure. It is art for art and he is prompted by the love of beauty. He has an inner vision of what might have been, of what ought to be, and he helps on the good cause by the simple substitution of a *nuance*. He paints, as it were, and so do I!' His manifestations had a considerable variety, but a family likeness ran through them, which consisted mainly of their singular futility. It was this that made them offensive; they encumbered the field of conversation, took up valuable space, converted it into a sort of brilliant sun-shot fog. For a fib told under pressure a convenient place can usually be found, as for a person who presents himself with an author's order at the first night of a play. But the supererogatory lie is the gentleman without a voucher or a ticket who accommodates himself with a stool in the passage.

In one particular Lyon acquitted his successful rival; it had puzzled him that irrepressible as he was he had not got into a mess in the service. But he perceived that he respected the service—that august institution was sacred from his depredations. Moreover though there was a great deal of swagger in his talk it was, oddly enough, rarely swagger about his military exploits. He had a passion for the chase, he had followed it in far countries and some of his finest flowers were reminiscences of lonely danger and escape. The more solitary the scene the bigger of course the flower. A new acquaintance, with the Colonel, always received the tribute of a bouquet: that generalisation Lyon very promptly made. And this extraordinary man had inconsistencies and unexpected lapses—lapses into flat veracity. Lyon recognised what Sir David had told him, that his aberrations came in fits or periods—that he would sometimes keep the truce of God for a month at a time. The muse breathed upon him at her pleasure; she often left him alone. He would neglect the finest openings and then set sail in the teeth of the breeze. As a general thing he affirmed the false rather than denied the true; yet this proportion was sometimes strikingly reversed. Very often he joined in the laugh against himself—he admitted that he was trying it on and that a good many of his anecdotes had an experimental character. Still he never completely retracted nor retreated—he dived and came up in another place. Lyon divined that he was capable at intervals of defending his position with violence, but only when it was a very bad one. Then he might easily be dangerous—then he would hit out and become calumnious. Such occasions would test his wife's equanimity—Lyon would have liked to see her there. In the smoking-room and elsewhere the company, so far as it was composed of his familiars, had an hilarious protest always at hand; but among the men who had known him long his rich tone was an old story, so old that they had ceased to talk about it, and Lyon did not care, as I have said, to elicit the judgment of those who might have shared his own surprise.

The oddest thing of all was that neither surprise nor familiarity prevented the Colonel's being liked; his largest drafts on a sceptical attention passed for an overflow of life and gaiety—almost of good looks. He was fond of portraying his bravery and used a very big brush, and yet he was unmistakably brave. He was a capital rider and shot, in spite of his fund of anecdote illustrating these accomplishments: in short he was very nearly as clever and his career had been very nearly as wonderful as he pretended. His best quality however remained that indiscriminate sociability which took interest and credulity for granted and about which he bragged least. It made him cheap, it made him even in a manner vulgar; but it was so contagious that his listener was more or less on his side as against the probabilities. It was a private reflection of Oliver Lyon's that he not only lied but made one feel one's self a bit of a liar, even (or especially) if one contradicted him. In the evening, at dinner and afterwards, our friend watched his wife's face to see if some faint shade or spasm never passed over it. But she showed nothing, and the wonder was that when he spoke she almost always listened. That was her pride: she wished not to be even suspected of not facing the music. Lyon had none the less an importunate vision of a veiled figure coming the next day in the dusk to certain places to repair the Colonel's ravages, as the relatives of kleptomaniacs punctually call at the shops that have suffered from their pilferings.

'I must apologise, of course it wasn't true, I hope no harm is done, it is only his incorrigible——' Oh, to hear that woman's voice in that deep abasement! Lyon had no nefarious plan, no conscious wish to practise upon her shame or her loyalty; but he did say to himself that he should like to bring her round to feel that there would have been more dignity in a union with a certain other person. He even dreamed of the hour when, with a burning face, she would ask *him* not to take it up. Then he should be almost consoled—he would be magnanimous.

Lyon finished his picture and took his departure, after having worked in a glow of interest which made him believe in his success, until he found he had pleased every one, especially Mr. and Mrs. Ashmore, when he began to be sceptical. The party at any rate changed: Colonel and Mrs. Capadose went their way. He was able to say to himself however that his separation from the lady was not so much an end as a beginning, and he called on her soon after his return to town. She had told him the hours she was at home— she seemed to like him. If she liked him why had she not married him or at any rate why was she not sorry she had not? If she was sorry she concealed it too well. Lyon's curiosity on this point may strike the reader as fatuous, but something must be allowed to a disappointed man. He did not ask much after all; not that she should love him to-day or that she should allow him to tell her that he loved her, but only that she should give him some sign she was sorry. Instead of this, for the present, she contented herself with exhibiting her little daughter to him. The child was beautiful and had the prettiest eyes of innocence he had ever seen: which did not prevent him from wondering whether she told horrid fibs. This idea gave him much entertainment—the picture of the anxiety with which her mother would watch as she grew older for the symptoms of heredity. That was a nice occupation for Everina Brant! Did she lie to the child herself, about her father—was that necessary, when she pressed her daughter to her bosom, to cover up his tracks? Did he control himself before the little girl—so that she might not hear him say things she knew to be other than he said? Lyon doubted this: his genius would be too strong for him, and the only safety for the child would be in her being too stupid to analyse. One couldn't judge yet—she was too young. If she should grow up clever she would be sure to tread in his steps—a delightful improvement in her mother's situation! Her little face was not shifty, but neither was her father's big one: so that proved nothing.

Lyon reminded his friends more than once of their promise that Amy should sit to him, and it was only a question of his leisure. The desire grew in him to paint the Colonel also—an operation from which he promised himself a rich private satisfaction. He would draw him out, he would set him up in that totality about which he had talked with Sir David, and none but the initiated would know. They, however, would rank the picture high, and it would be indeed six rows deep—a masterpiece of subtle characterisation, of legitimate treachery. He had dreamed for years of producing something which should bear the stamp of the psychologist as well as of the painter, and here at last was his subject. It was a pity it was not better, but that was not *his* fault. It was his impression that already no one drew the Colonel out more than he, and he did it not only by instinct but on a plan. There were moments when he was almost frightened at the success of his plan—the poor gentleman went so terribly far. He would pull up some day, look at Lyon between the eyes—guess he was being played upon—which would lead to his wife's guessing it also. Not that Lyon cared much for that however, so long as she failed to suppose (as she must) that she was a part of his joke. He formed such a habit now of going to see her of a Sunday afternoon that he was angry when she went out of town. This occurred often, as the couple were great visitors and the Colonel was always looking for sport, which he liked best when it could be had at other people's expense. Lyon would have supposed that this sort of life was particularly little to her taste, for he had an idea that it was in country-houses that her husband came out strongest. To let him go off without her, not to see him expose himself—that ought properly to have been a relief and a luxury to her. She told Lyon in fact that she preferred staying at home; but she neglected to say it was because in other people's houses she was on the rack: the reason she gave was that she liked so to be with the child. It was not perhaps criminal to draw such a bow, but it was vulgar: poor Lyon was delighted when he arrived at that formula. Certainly some day too he would cross the line—he would become a noxious animal. Yes, in the meantime he was vulgar, in spite of his talents, his fine person, his impunity. Twice, by exception, toward the end of the winter, when he left town for a few days' hunting, his wife remained at home. Lyon had not yet reached the point of asking himself whether the desire not to miss two of his visits had something to do with her immobility. That inquiry would perhaps have been more in place later, when he began to paint the child and she always came with her. But it was not in her to give the wrong name, to pretend, and Lyon could see that she had the maternal passion, in spite of the bad blood in the little girl's veins.

She came inveterately, though Lyon multiplied the sittings: Amy was never entrusted to the governess or the maid. He had knocked off poor old Sir David in ten days, but the portrait of the simple-faced child bade fair to stretch over into the following year. He asked for sitting after sitting, and it would have struck any one who might have witnessed the affair that he was wearing the little girl out. He knew better however and Mrs. Capadose also knew: they were present together at the long intermissions he gave her, when she left her pose and roamed about the great studio, amusing herself with its curiosities, playing with the old draperies and costumes, having unlimited leave to handle. Then her mother and Mr. Lyon sat and talked; he laid aside his brushes and leaned back in his chair; he always gave her tea. What Mrs. Capadose did not know was the way that during these weeks he neglected other orders: women have no faculty of imagination with regard to a man's work beyond a vague idea that it doesn't matter. In fact Lyon put off everything and made several celebrities wait. There were half-hours of silence, when he plied his brushes, during which he was mainly conscious that Everina was sitting there. She easily fell into that if he did not insist on talking, and she was not embarrassed nor bored by it. Sometimes she took up a book—there were plenty of them about; sometimes, a little way off, in her chair, she watched his progress (though without in the least advising or correcting), as if she cared for every stroke that represented her daughter. These strokes were occasionally a little wild; he was thinking so much more of his heart than of his hand. He was not more embarrassed than she was, but he was agitated: it was as if in the sittings (for the child, too, was beautifully quiet) something was growing between them or had already grown—a tacit confidence, an inexpressible secret. He felt it that way; but after all he could not be sure that she did. What he wanted her to do for him was very little; it was not even to confess that she was unhappy. He would be superabundantly gratified if she should simply let him know, even by a silent sign, that she recognised that with him her life would have been finer. Sometimes he guessed—his presumption went so far—that he might see this sign in her contentedly sitting there.

III

At last he broached the question of painting the Colonel: it was now very late in the season—there would be little time before the general dispersal. He said they must make the most of it; the great thing was to begin; then in the autumn, with the resumption of their London life, they could go forward. Mrs. Capadose objected to this that she really could not consent to accept another present of such value. Lyon had given her the portrait of herself of old, and he had seen what they had had the indelicacy to do with it. Now he had offered her this beautiful memorial of the child—beautiful it would evidently be when it was finished, if he could ever satisfy himself; a precious possession which they would cherish for ever. But his generosity must stop there—they couldn't be so tremendously 'beholden' to him. They couldn't order the picture—of course he would understand that, without her explaining: it was a luxury beyond their reach, for they knew the great prices he received. Besides, what had they ever done—what above all had *she* ever done, that he should overload them with benefits? No, he was too dreadfully good; it was really impossible that Clement should sit. Lyon listened to her without protest, without interruption, while he bent forward at his work, and at last he said: 'Well, if you won't take it why not let him sit for me for my own pleasure and profit? Let it be a favour, a service I ask of him. It will do me a lot of good to paint him and the picture will remain in my hands.'

'How will it do you a lot of good?' Mrs. Capadose asked.

'Why, he's such a rare model—such an interesting subject. He has such an expressive face. It will teach me no end of things.'

'Expressive of what?' said Mrs. Capadose.

'Why, of his nature.'

'And do you want to paint his nature?'

'Of course I do. That's what a great portrait gives you, and I shall make the Colonel's a great one. It will put me up high. So you see my request is eminently interested.'

'How can you be higher than you are?'

'Oh, I'm insatiable! Do consent,' said Lyon.

'Well, his nature is very noble,' Mrs. Capadose remarked.

'Ah, trust me, I shall bring it out!' Lyon exclaimed, feeling a little ashamed of himself.

Mrs. Capadose said before she went away that her husband would probably comply with his invitation, but she added, 'Nothing would induce me to let you pry into *me* that way!'

'Oh, you,' Lyon laughed—'I could do you in the dark!'

The Colonel shortly afterwards placed his leisure at the painter's disposal and by the end of July had paid him several visits. Lyon was disappointed neither in the quality of his sitter nor in the degree to which he himself rose to the occasion; he felt really confident that he should produce a fine thing. He was in the humour; he was charmed with his *motif* and deeply interested in his problem. The only point that troubled him was the idea that when he should send his picture to the Academy he should not be able to give the title, for the catalogue, simply as 'The Liar.' However, it little mattered, for he had now determined that this character should be perceptible even to the meanest intelligence—as overtopping as it had become to his own sense in the living man. As he saw nothing else in the Colonel to-day, so he gave himself up to the joy of painting nothing else. How he did it he could not have told you, but it seemed to him that the mystery of how to do it was revealed to him afresh every time he sat down to his work. It was in the eyes and it was in the mouth, it was in every line of the face and every fact of the attitude, in the indentation of the chin, in the way the hair was planted, the moustache was twisted, the smile came and went, the breath rose and fell. It was in the way he looked out at a bamboozled world in short—the way he would look out for ever. There were half a dozen portraits in Europe that Lyon rated as supreme; he regarded them as immortal, for they were as perfectly preserved as they were consummately painted. It was to this small exemplary group that he aspired to annex the canvas on which he was now engaged. One of the productions that helped to compose it was the magnificent Moroni of the National Gallery—the young tailor, in the white jacket, at his board with his shears. The Colonel was not a tailor, nor was Moroni's model, unlike many tailors, a liar; but as regards the masterly clearness with which the individual should be rendered his work would be on the same line as that. He had to a degree in which he had rarely had it before the satisfaction of feeling life grow and grow under his brush. The Colonel, as it turned out, liked to sit and he liked to talk while he was sitting: which was very fortunate, as his talk largely constituted Lyon's inspiration. Lyon put into practice that idea of drawing him out which he had been nursing for so many weeks: he could not possibly have been in a better relation to him for the purpose. He encouraged, beguiled, excited him, manifested an unfathomable credulity, and his only interruptions were when the Colonel did not respond to it. He had his intermissions, his hours of sterility, and then Lyon felt that the picture also languished. The higher his companion soared, the more gyrations he executed, in the blue, the better he painted; he couldn't make his flights long enough. He lashed him on when he flagged; his apprehension became great at moments that the Colonel would discover his game. But he never did, apparently; he basked and expanded in the fine steady light of the painter's attention. In this way the picture grew very fast; it was astonishing what a short business it was, compared with the little girl's. By the fifth of August it was pretty well finished: that was the date of the last sitting the Colonel was for the present able to give, as he was leaving town the next day with his wife. Lyon was amply content—he saw his way so clear: he should be able to do at his convenience what remained, with or without his friend's attendance. At any rate, as there was no hurry, he would let the thing stand over till his own return to London, in November, when he would come back to it with a fresh eye. On the Colonel's asking him if his wife might come and see it the next day, if she should find a minute—this was so greatly her desire—Lyon begged as a special favour that she would wait: he was so far from satisfied as yet. This was the repetition of a proposal Mrs. Capadose had made on the occasion of his last visit to her, and he had then asked for a delay—declared that he was by no means content. He was really delighted, and he was again a little ashamed of himself.

By the fifth of August the weather was very warm, and on that day, while the Colonel sat straight and gossiped, Lyon opened for the sake of ventilation a little subsidiary door which led directly from his studio into the garden and sometimes served as an entrance and an exit for models and for visitors of the humbler sort, and as a passage for canvases, frames, packing-boxes and other professional gear. The main entrance was through the house and his own apartments, and this approach had the charming effect of admitting you first to a high gallery, from which a crooked picturesque staircase enabled you to descend to the wide, decorated, encumbered room. The view of this room, beneath them, with all its artistic ingenuities and the objects of value that Lyon had collected, never failed to elicit exclamations of delight from persons stepping into the gallery. The way from the garden was plainer and at once more practicable and more private. Lyon's domain, in St. John's Wood, was not vast, but when the door stood open of a summer's day it offered a glimpse of flowers and trees, you smelt something sweet and you heard the birds. On this particular morning the side-door had been found convenient by an unannounced visitor, a youngish woman who stood in the room before the Colonel perceived her and whom he perceived before she was noticed by his friend. She was very quiet, and she looked from one of the men to the other. 'Oh, dear, here's another!' Lyon exclaimed, as soon as his eyes rested on her. She belonged, in fact, to a somewhat importunate class—the model in search of employment, and she explained that she had ventured to come straight in, that way, because very often when she went to call upon gentlemen the servants played her tricks, turned her off and wouldn't take in her name.

'But how did you get into the garden?' Lyon asked.

'The gate was open, sir—the servants' gate. The butcher's cart was there.'

'The butcher ought to have closed it,' said Lyon.

'Then you don't require me, sir?' the lady continued.

Lyon went on with his painting; he had given her a sharp look at first, but now his eyes lighted on her no more. The Colonel, however, examined her with interest. She was a person of whom you could scarcely say whether being young she looked old or old she looked young; she had at any rate evidently rounded several of the corners of life and had a face that was rosy but that somehow failed to suggest freshness. Nevertheless she was pretty and even looked as if at one time she might have sat for the complexion. She wore a hat with many feathers, a dress with many bugles, long black gloves, encircled with silver bracelets, and very bad shoes. There was something about her that was not exactly of the governess out of place nor completely of the actress seeking an engagement, but that savoured of an interrupted profession or even of a blighted career. She was rather soiled and tarnished, and after she had been in the room a few moments the air, or at any rate the nostril, became acquainted with a certain alcoholic waft. She was unpractised in the *h*, and when Lyon at last thanked her and said he didn't want her—he was doing nothing for which she could be useful—she replied with rather a wounded manner, 'Well, you know you *'ave* 'ad me!'

'I don't remember you,' Lyon answered.

'Well, I daresay the people that saw your pictures do! I haven't much time, but I thought I would look in.'

'I am much obliged to you.'

'If ever you should require me, if you just send me a postcard——'

'I never send postcards,' said Lyon.

'Oh well, I should value a private letter! Anything to Miss Geraldine, Mortimer Terrace Mews, Notting 'ill——'

'Very good; I'll remember,' said Lyon.

Miss Geraldine lingered. 'I thought I'd just stop, on the chance.'

'I'm afraid I can't hold out hopes, I'm so busy with portraits,' Lyon continued.

'Yes; I see you are. I wish I was in the gentleman's place.'

'I'm afraid in that case it wouldn't look like me,' said the Colonel, laughing.

'Oh, of course it couldn't compare—it wouldn't be so 'andsome! But I do hate them portraits!' Miss Geraldine declared. 'It's so much bread out of our mouths.'

'Well, there are many who can't paint them,' Lyon suggested, comfortingly.

'Oh, I've sat to the very first—and only to the first! There's many that couldn't do anything without me.'

'I'm glad you're in such demand.' Lyon was beginning to be bored and he added that he wouldn't detain her—he would send for her in case of need.

'Very well; remember it's the Mews—more's the pity! You don't sit so well as *us*!' Miss Geraldine pursued, looking at the Colonel. 'If *you* should require me, sir——'

'You put him out; you embarrass him,' said Lyon.

'Embarrass him, oh gracious!' the visitor cried, with a laugh which diffused a fragrance. 'Perhaps *you* send postcards, eh?' she went on to the Colonel; and then she retreated with a wavering step. She passed out into the garden as she had come.

'How very dreadful—she's drunk!' said Lyon. He was painting hard, but he looked up, checking himself: Miss Geraldine, in the open doorway, had thrust back her head.

'Yes, I do hate it—that sort of thing!' she cried with an explosion of mirth which confirmed Lyon's declaration. And then she disappeared.

'What sort of thing—what does she mean?' the Colonel asked.

'Oh, my painting you, when I might be painting her.'

'And have you ever painted her?'

'Never in the world; I have never seen her. She is quite mistaken.'

The Colonel was silent a moment; then he remarked, 'She was very pretty—ten years ago.'

'I daresay, but she's quite ruined. For me the least drop too much spoils them; I shouldn't care for her at all.'

'My dear fellow, she's not a model,' said the Colonel, laughing.

'To-day, no doubt, she's not worthy of the name; but she has been one.'

'*Jamais de la vie!* That's all a pretext.'

'A pretext?' Lyon pricked up his ears—he began to wonder what was coming now.

'She didn't want you—she wanted me.'

'I noticed she paid you some attention. What does she want of you?'

'Oh, to do me an ill turn. She hates me—lots of women do. She's watching me—she follows me.'

Lyon leaned back in his chair—he didn't believe a word of this. He was all the more delighted with it and with the Colonel's bright, candid manner. The story had bloomed, fragrant, on the spot. 'My dear Colonel!' he murmured, with friendly interest and commiseration.

'I was annoyed when she came in—but I wasn't startled,' his sitter continued.

'You concealed it very well, if you were.'

'Ah, when one has been through what I have! To-day however I confess I was half prepared. I have seen her hanging about—she knows my movements. She was near my house this morning—she must have followed me.'

'But who is she then—with such a *toupet*?'

'Yes, she has that,' said the Colonel; 'but as you observe she was primed. Still, there was a cheek, as they say, in her coming in. Oh, she's a bad one! She isn't a model and she never was; no doubt she has known some of those women and picked up their form. She had hold of a friend of mine ten years ago—a stupid young gander who might have been left to be plucked but whom I was obliged to take an interest in for family reasons. It's a long story—I had really forgotten all about it. She's thirty-seven if she's a day. I cut in and made him get rid of her—I sent her about her business. She knew it was me she had to thank. She has never forgiven me—I think she's off her head. Her name isn't Geraldine at all and I doubt very much if that's her address.'

'Ah, what is her name?' Lyon asked, most attentive. The details always began to multiply, to abound, when once his companion was well launched—they flowed forth in battalions.

'It's Pearson—Harriet Pearson; but she used to call herself Grenadine—wasn't that a rum appellation? Grenadine—Geraldine—the jump was easy.' Lyon was charmed with the promptitude of this response, and his interlocutor went on: 'I hadn't thought of her for years—I had quite lost sight of her. I don't know what her idea is, but practically she's harmless. As I came in I thought I saw her a little way up the road. She must have found out I come here and have arrived before me. I daresay—or rather I'm sure—she is waiting for me there now.'

'Hadn't you better have protection?' Lyon asked, laughing.

'The best protection is five shillings—I'm willing to go that length. Unless indeed she has a bottle of vitriol. But they only throw vitriol on the men who have deceived them, and I never deceived her—I told her the first time I saw her that it wouldn't do. Oh, if she's there we'll walk a little way together and talk it over and, as I say, I'll go as far as five shillings.'

'Well,' said Lyon, 'I'll contribute another five.' He felt that this was little to pay for his entertainment.

That entertainment was interrupted however for the time by the Colonel's departure. Lyon hoped for a letter recounting the fictive sequel; but apparently his brilliant sitter did not operate with the pen. At any rate he left town without writing; they had taken a rendezvous for three months later. Oliver Lyon always passed the holidays in the same way; during the first weeks he paid a visit to his elder brother, the happy possessor, in the south of England, of a rambling old house with formal gardens, in which he delighted, and then he went abroad—usually to Italy or Spain. This year he carried out his custom after taking a last look at his all but finished work and feeling as nearly pleased with it as he ever felt with the translation of the idea by the hand—always, as it seemed to him, a pitiful compromise. One yellow afternoon, in the country, as he was smoking his pipe on one of the old terraces he was seized with the desire to see it again and do two or three things more to it: he had thought of it so often while he lounged there. The impulse was too strong to be dismissed, and though he expected to return to town in the course of another week he was unable to face the delay. To look at the picture for five minutes would be enough—it would clear up certain questions which hummed in his brain; so that the next morning, to give himself this luxury, he took the train for London. He sent no word in advance; he would lunch at his club and probably return into Sussex by the 5.45.

In St. John's Wood the tide of human life flows at no time very fast, and in the first days of September Lyon found unmitigated emptiness in the straight sunny roads where the little plastered garden-walls, with their incommunicative doors, looked slightly Oriental. There was definite stillness in his own house, to which he admitted himself by his pass-key, having a theory that it was well sometimes to take servants unprepared. The good woman who was mainly in charge and who cumulated the functions of cook and housekeeper was, however, quickly summoned by his step, and (he cultivated frankness of intercourse with his domestics) received him without the confusion of surprise. He told her that she needn't mind the place being not quite straight, he had only come up for a few hours—he should be busy in the studio. To this she replied that he was just in time to see a lady and a gentleman who were there at the moment—they had arrived five minutes before. She had told them he was away from home but they said it was all right; they only wanted to look at a picture and would be very careful of everything. 'I hope it is all right, sir,' the housekeeper concluded. 'The gentleman says he's a sitter and he gave me his name—rather an odd name; I think it's military. The lady's a very fine lady, sir; at any rate there they are.'

'Oh, it's all right,' Lyon said, the identity of his visitors being clear. The good woman couldn't know, for she usually had little to do with the comings and goings; his man, who showed people in and out, had accompanied him to the country. He was a good deal surprised at Mrs. Capadose's having come to see her husband's portrait when she knew that the artist himself wished her to forbear; but it was a familiar truth to him that she was a woman of a high spirit. Besides, perhaps the lady was not Mrs. Capadose; the Colonel might have brought some inquisitive friend, a person who wanted a portrait of *her* husband. What were they doing in town, at any rate, at that moment? Lyon made his way to the studio with a certain curiosity; he wondered vaguely what his friends were 'up to.' He pushed aside the curtain that hung in the door of communication—the door opening upon the gallery which it had been found convenient to construct at the time the studio was added to the house. When I say he pushed it aside I should amend my phrase; he laid his hand upon it, but at that moment he was arrested by a very singular sound. It came from the floor of the room beneath him and it startled him extremely, consisting apparently as it did of a passionate wail—a sort of smothered shriek—accompanied by a violent burst of tears. Oliver Lyon listened intently a moment, and then he passed out upon the balcony, which was covered with an old thick Moorish rug. His step was noiseless, though he had not endeavoured to make it so, and after that first instant he found himself profiting irresistibly by the accident of his not having attracted the attention of the two persons in the studio, who were some twenty feet below him. In truth they were so deeply and so strangely engaged that their unconsciousness of observation was explained. The scene that took place before Lyon's eyes was one of the most extraordinary they had ever rested upon. Delicacy and the failure to comprehend kept him at first from interrupting it—for what he saw was a woman who had thrown herself in a flood of tears on her companion's bosom—and these influences were succeeded after a minute (the minutes were very few and very short) by a definite motive which presently had the force to make him step back behind the curtain. I may add that it also had the force to make him avail himself for further contemplation of a crevice formed by his gathering together the two halves of the *portière*. He was perfectly aware of what he was about—he was for the moment an eavesdropper, a spy; but he was also aware that a very odd business, in which his confidence had been trifled with, was going forward, and that if in a measure it didn't concern him, in a measure it very definitely did. His observation, his reflections, accomplished themselves in a flash.

His visitors were in the middle of the room; Mrs. Capadose clung to her husband, weeping, sobbing as if her heart would break. Her distress was horrible to Oliver Lyon but his astonishment was greater than his horror when he heard the Colonel respond to it by the words, vehemently uttered, 'Damn him, damn him, damn him!' What in the world had happened? Why was she sobbing and whom was he damning? What had happened, Lyon saw the next instant, was that the Colonel had finally rummaged out his unfinished portrait (he knew the corner where the artist usually placed it, out of the way, with its face to the wall) and had set it up before his wife on an empty easel. She had looked at it a few moments and then—apparently—what she saw in it had produced an explosion of dismay and resentment. She was too busy sobbing and the Colonel was too busy holding her and reiterating his objurgation, to look round or look up. The scene was so unexpected to Lyon that he could not take it, on the spot, as a proof of the triumph of his hand—of a tremendous hit: he could only wonder what on earth was the matter. The idea of the triumph came a little later. Yet he could see the portrait from where he stood; he was startled with its look of life—he had not thought it so masterly. Mrs. Capadose flung herself away from her husband—she dropped into the nearest chair, buried her face in her arms, leaning on a table. Her weeping suddenly ceased to be audible, but she shuddered there as if she were overwhelmed with anguish and shame. Her husband remained a moment staring at the picture; then he went to her, bent over her, took hold of her again, soothed her. 'What is it, darling, what the devil is it?' he demanded.

Lyon heard her answer. 'It's cruel—oh, it's too cruel!'

'Damn him—damn him—damn him!' the Colonel repeated.

'It's all there—it's all there!' Mrs. Capadose went on.

'Hang it, what's all there?'

'Everything there oughtn't to be—everything he has seen—it's too dreadful!'

'Everything he has seen? Why, ain't I a good-looking fellow? He has made me rather handsome.'

Mrs. Capadose had sprung up again; she had darted another glance at the painted betrayal. 'Handsome? Hideous, hideous! Not that—never, never!'

'Not *what*, in heaven's name?' the Colonel almost shouted. Lyon could see his flushed, bewildered face.

'What he has made of you—what you know! *He* knows—he has seen. Every one will know—every one will see. Fancy that thing in the Academy!'

'You're going wild, darling; but if you hate it so it needn't go.'

'Oh, he'll send it—it's so good! Come away—come away!' Mrs. Capadose wailed, seizing her husband.

'It's so good?' the poor man cried.

'Come away—come away,' she only repeated; and she turned toward the staircase that ascended to the gallery.

'Not that way—not through the house, in the state you're in,' Lyon heard the Colonel object. 'This way—we can pass,' he added; and he drew his wife to the small door that opened into the garden. It was bolted, but he pushed the bolt and opened the door. She passed out quickly, but he stood there looking back into the room. 'Wait for me a moment!' he cried out to her; and with an excited stride he re-entered the studio. He came up to the picture again, and again he stood looking at it. 'Damn him—damn him— damn him!' he broke out once more. It was not clear to Lyon whether this malediction had for its object the original or the painter of the portrait. The Colonel turned away and moved rapidly about the room, as if he were looking for something; Lyon was unable for the instant to guess his intention. Then the artist said to himself, below his breath, 'He's going to do it a harm!' His first impulse was to rush down and stop him; but he paused, with the sound of Everina Brant's sobs still in his ears. The Colonel found what he was looking for—found it among some odds and ends on a small table and rushed back with it to the easel. At one and the same moment Lyon perceived that

234

the object he had seized was a small Eastern dagger and that he had plunged it into the canvas. He seemed animated by a sudden fury, for with extreme vigour of hand he dragged the instrument down (Lyon knew it to have no very fine edge) making a long, abominable gash. Then he plucked it out and dashed it again several times into the face of the likeness, exactly as if he were stabbing a human victim: it had the oddest effect—that of a sort of figurative suicide. In a few seconds more the Colonel had tossed the dagger away—he looked at it as he did so, as if he expected it to reek with blood—and hurried out of the place, closing the door after him.

The strangest part of all was—as will doubtless appear—that Oliver Lyon made no movement to save his picture. But he did not feel as if he were losing it or cared not if he were, so much more did he feel that he was gaining a certitude. His old friend *was* ashamed of her husband, and he had made her so, and he had scored a great success, even though the picture had been reduced to rags. The revelation excited him so—as indeed the whole scene did—that when he came down the steps after the Colonel had gone he trembled with his happy agitation; he was dizzy and had to sit down a moment. The portrait had a dozen jagged wounds—the Colonel literally had hacked it to death. Lyon left it where it was, never touched it, scarcely looked at it; he only walked up and down his studio, still excited, for an hour. At the end of this time his good woman came to recommend that he should have some luncheon; there was a passage under the staircase from the offices.

'Ah, the lady and gentleman have gone, sir? I didn't hear them.'

'Yes; they went by the garden.'

But she had stopped, staring at the picture on the easel. 'Gracious, how you '*ave* served it, sir!'

Lyon imitated the Colonel. 'Yes, I cut it up—in a fit of disgust.'

'Mercy, after all your trouble! Because they weren't pleased, sir?'

'Yes; they weren't pleased.'

'Well, they must be very grand! Blessed if I would!'

'Have it chopped up; it will do to light fires,' Lyon said.

He returned to the country by the 3.30 and a few days later passed over to France. During the two months that he was absent from England he expected something—he could hardly have said what; a manifestation of some sort on the Colonel's part. Wouldn't he write, wouldn't he explain, wouldn't he take for granted Lyon had discovered the way he had, as the cook said, served him and deem it only decent to take pity in some fashion or other on his mystification? Would he plead guilty or would he repudiate suspicion? The latter course would be difficult and make a considerable draft upon his genius, in view of the certain testimony of Lyon's housekeeper, who had admitted the visitors and would establish the connection between their presence and the violence wrought. Would the Colonel proffer some apology or some amends, or would any word from him be only a further expression of that destructive petulance which our friend had seen his wife so suddenly and so potently communicate to him? He would have either to declare that he had not touched the picture or to admit that he had, and in either case he would have to tell a fine story. Lyon was impatient for the story and, as no letter came, disappointed that it was not produced. His impatience however was much greater in respect to Mrs. Capadose's version, if version there was to be; for certainly that would be the real test, would show how far she would go for her husband, on the one side, or for him, Oliver Lyon, on the other. He could scarcely wait to see what line she would take; whether she would simply adopt the Colonel's, whatever it might be. He wanted to draw her out without waiting, to get an idea in advance. He wrote to her, to this end, from Venice, in the tone of their established friendship, asking for news, narrating his wanderings, hoping they should soon meet in town and not saying a word about the picture. Day followed day, after the time, and he received no answer; upon which he reflected that she couldn't trust herself to write—was still too much under the influence of the emotion produced by his 'betrayal.' Her husband had espoused that emotion and she had espoused the action he had taken in consequence of it, and it was a complete rupture and everything was at an end. Lyon considered this prospect rather ruefully, at the same time that he thought it deplorable that such charming people should have put themselves so grossly in the wrong. He was at last cheered, though little further enlightened, by the arrival of a letter, brief but breathing good-humour and hinting neither at a grievance nor at a bad conscience. The most interesting part of it to Lyon was the postscript, which consisted of these words: 'I have a confession to make to you. We were in town for a couple of days, the 1st of September, and I took the occasion to defy your authority—it was very bad of me but I couldn't help it. I made Clement take me to your studio—I wanted so dreadfully to see what you had done with him, your wishes to the contrary notwithstanding. We made your servants let us in and I took a good look at the picture. It is really wonderful!' 'Wonderful' was non-committal, but at least with this letter there was no rupture.

The third day after Lyon's return to London was a Sunday, so that he could go and ask Mrs. Capadose for luncheon. She had given him in the spring a general invitation to do so and he had availed himself of it several times. These had been the occasions (before he sat to him) when he saw the Colonel most familiarly. Directly after the meal his host disappeared (he went out, as he said, to call on *his* women) and the second half-hour was the best, even when there were other people. Now, in the first days of December, Lyon had the luck to find the pair alone, without even Amy, who appeared but little in public. They were in the drawing-room, waiting for the repast to be announced, and as soon as he came in the Colonel broke out, 'My dear fellow, I'm delighted to see you! I'm so keen to begin again.'

'Oh, do go on, it's so beautiful,' Mrs. Capadose said, as she gave him her hand.

Lyon looked from one to the other; he didn't know what he had expected, but he had not expected this. 'Ah, then, you think I've got something?'

'You've got everything,' said Mrs. Capadose, smiling from her golden-brown eyes.

'She wrote you of our little crime?' her husband asked. 'She dragged me there—I had to go.' Lyon wondered for a moment whether he meant by their little crime the assault on the canvas; but the Colonel's next words didn't confirm this interpretation. 'You know I like to sit—it gives such a chance to my *bavardise*. And just now I have time.'

'You must remember I had almost finished,' Lyon remarked.

'So you had. More's the pity. I should like you to begin again.'

'My dear fellow, I shall have to begin again!' said Oliver Lyon with a laugh, looking at Mrs. Capadose. She did not meet his eyes—she had got up to ring for luncheon. 'The picture has been smashed,' Lyon continued.

'Smashed? Ah, what did you do that for?' Mrs. Capadose asked, standing there before him in all her clear, rich beauty. Now that she looked at him she was impenetrable.

'I didn't—I found it so—with a dozen holes punched in it!'

'I say!' cried the Colonel.

Lyon turned his eyes to him, smiling. 'I hope *you* didn't do it?'

'Is it ruined?' the Colonel inquired. He was as brightly true as his wife and he looked simply as if Lyon's question could not be serious. 'For the love of sitting to you? My dear fellow, if I had thought of it I would!'

'Nor you either?' the painter demanded of Mrs. Capadose.

Before she had time to reply her husband had seized her arm, as if a highly suggestive idea had come to him. 'I say, my dear, that woman—that woman!'

'That woman?' Mrs. Capadose repeated; and Lyon too wondered what woman he meant.

'Don't you remember when we came out, she was at the door—or a little way from it? I spoke to you of her—I told you about her. Geraldine—Grenadine—the one who burst in that day,' he explained to Lyon. 'We saw her hanging about—I called Everina's attention to her.'

'Do you mean she got at my picture?'

'Ah yes, I remember,' said Mrs. Capadose, with a sigh.

'She burst in again—she had learned the way—she was waiting for her chance,' the Colonel continued. 'Ah, the little brute!'

238

Lyon looked down; he felt himself colouring. This was what he had been waiting for—the day the Colonel should wantonly sacrifice some innocent person. And could his wife be a party to that final atrocity? Lyon had reminded himself repeatedly during the previous weeks that when the Colonel perpetrated his misdeed she had already quitted the room; but he had argued none the less—it was a virtual certainty—that he had on rejoining her immediately made his achievement plain to her. He was in the flush of performance; and even if he had not mentioned what he had done she would have guessed it. He did not for an instant believe that poor Miss Geraldine had been hovering about his door, nor had the account given by the Colonel the summer before of his relations with this lady deceived him in the slightest degree. Lyon had never seen her before the day she planted herself in his studio; but he knew her and classified her as if he had made her. He was acquainted with the London female model in all her varieties—in every phase of her development and every step of her decay. When he entered his house that September morning just after the arrival of his two friends there had been no symptoms whatever, up and down the road, of Miss Geraldine's reappearance. That fact had been fixed in his mind by his recollecting the vacancy of the prospect when his cook told him that a lady and a gentleman were in his studio: he had wondered there was not a carriage nor a cab at his door. Then he had reflected that they would have come by the underground railway; he was close to the Marlborough Road station and he knew the Colonel, coming to his sittings, more than once had availed himself of that convenience. 'How in the world did she get in?' He addressed the question to his companions indifferently.

'Let us go down to luncheon,' said Mrs. Capadose, passing out of the room.

'We went by the garden—without troubling your servant—I wanted to show my wife.' Lyon followed his hostess with her husband and the Colonel stopped him at the top of the stairs. 'My dear fellow, I *can't* have been guilty of the folly of not fastening the door?'

'I am sure I don't know, Colonel,' Lyon said as they went down. 'It was a very determined hand—a perfect wild-cat.'

'Well, she *is* a wild-cat—confound her! That's why I wanted to get him away from her.'

'But I don't understand her motive.'

'She's off her head—and she hates me; that was her motive.'

'But she doesn't hate me, my dear fellow!' Lyon said, laughing.

'She hated the picture—don't you remember she said so? The more portraits there are the less employment for such as her.'

'Yes; but if she is not really the model she pretends to be, how can that hurt her?' Lyon asked.

The inquiry baffled the Colonel an instant—but only an instant. 'Ah, she was in a vicious muddle! As I say, she's off her head.'

They went into the dining-room, where Mrs. Capadose was taking her place. 'It's too bad, it's too horrid!' she said. 'You see the fates are against you. Providence won't let you be so disinterested—painting masterpieces for nothing.'

'Did *you* see the woman?' Lyon demanded, with something like a sternness that he could not mitigate.

Mrs. Capadose appeared not to perceive it or not to heed it if she did. 'There was a person, not far from your door, whom Clement called my attention to. He told me something about her but we were going the other way.'

'And do you think she did it?'

'How can I tell? If she did she was mad, poor wretch.'

'I should like very much to get hold of her,' said Lyon. This was a false statement, for he had no desire for any further conversation with Miss Geraldine. He had exposed his friends to himself, but he had no desire to expose them to any one else, least of all to themselves.

'Oh, depend upon it she will never show again. You're safe!' the Colonel exclaimed.

'But I remember her address—Mortimer Terrace Mews, Notting Hill.'

'Oh, that's pure humbug; there isn't any such place.'

'Lord, what a deceiver!' said Lyon.

'Is there any one else you suspect?' the Colonel went on.

'Not a creature.'

'And what do your servants say?'

'They say it wasn't *them*, and I reply that I never said it was. That's about the substance of our conferences.'

'And when did they discover the havoc?'

'They never discovered it at all. I noticed it first—when I came back.'

'Well, she could easily have stepped in,' said the Colonel. 'Don't you remember how she turned up that day, like the clown in the ring?'

'Yes, yes; she could have done the job in three seconds, except that the picture wasn't out.'

'My dear fellow, don't curse me!—but of course I dragged it out.'

'You didn't put it back?' Lyon asked tragically.

'Ah, Clement, Clement, didn't I tell you to?' Mrs. Capadose exclaimed in a tone of exquisite reproach.

The Colonel groaned, dramatically; he covered his face with his hands. His wife's words were for Lyon the finishing touch; they made his whole vision crumble—his theory that she had secretly kept herself true. Even to her old lover she wouldn't be so! He was sick; he couldn't eat; he knew that he looked very strange. He murmured something about it being useless to cry over spilled milk—he tried to turn the conversation to other things. But it was a horrid effort and he wondered whether they felt it as much as he. He wondered all sorts of things: whether they guessed he disbelieved them (that he had seen them of course they would never guess); whether they had arranged their story in advance or it was only an inspiration of the moment; whether she had resisted, protested, when the Colonel proposed it to her, and then had been borne down by him; whether in short she didn't loathe herself as she sat there. The cruelty, the cowardice of fastening their unholy act upon the wretched woman struck him as monstrous—no less monstrous indeed than the levity that could make them run the risk of her giving them, in her righteous indignation, the lie. Of course that risk could only exculpate her and not inculpate them—the probabilities protected them so perfectly; and what the Colonel counted on (what he would have counted upon the day he delivered himself, after first seeing her, at the studio, if he had thought about the matter then at all and not spoken from the pure spontaneity of his genius) was simply that Miss Geraldine had really vanished for ever into her native unknown. Lyon wanted so much to quit the subject that when after a little Mrs. Capadose said to him, 'But can nothing be done, can't the picture be repaired? You know they do such wonders in that way now,' he only replied, 'I don't know, I don't care, it's all over, *n'en parlons plus!*' Her hypocrisy revolted him. And yet, by way of plucking off the last veil of her shame, he broke out to her again, shortly afterward, 'And you *did* like it, really?' To which she returned, looking him straight in his face, without a blush, a pallor, an evasion, 'Oh, I loved it!' Truly her husband had trained her well. After that Lyon said no more and his companions forbore temporarily to insist, like people of tact and sympathy aware that the odious accident had made him sore.

When they quitted the table the Colonel went away without coming upstairs; but Lyon returned to the drawing-room with his hostess, remarking to her however on the way that he could remain but a moment. He spent that moment—it prolonged itself a little—standing with her before the chimney-piece. She neither sat down nor asked him to; her manner denoted that she intended to go out. Yes, her husband had trained her well; yet Lyon dreamed for a moment that now he was alone with her she would perhaps break down, retract, apologise, confide, say to him, 'My dear old friend, forgive this hideous comedy—you understand!' And then how he would have loved her and pitied her, guarded her, helped her always! If she were not ready to do something of that sort why had she treated him as if he were a dear old friend; why had she let him for months suppose certain things—or almost; why had she come to his studio day after day to sit near him on the pretext of her child's portrait, as if she liked to think what might have been? Why had she come so near a tacit confession, in a word, if she was not willing to go an inch further? And she was not willing—she was not; he could see that as he lingered there. She moved about the room a little, rearranging two or three objects on the tables, but she did nothing more. Suddenly he said to her: 'Which way was she going, when you came out?'

'She—the woman we saw?'

'Yes, your husband's strange friend. It's a clew worth following.' He had no desire to frighten her; he only wanted to communicate the impulse which would make her say, 'Ah, spare me—and spare *him*! There was no such person.'

Instead of this Mrs. Capadose replied, 'She was going away from us—she crossed the road. We were coming towards the station.'

'And did she appear to recognise the Colonel—did she look round?'

'Yes; she looked round, but I didn't notice much. A hansom came along and we got into it. It was not till then that Clement told me who she was: I remember he said that she was there for no good. I suppose we ought to have gone back.'

'Yes; you would have saved the picture.'

For a moment she said nothing; then she smiled. 'For you, I am very sorry. But you must remember that I possess the original!'

At this Lyon turned away. 'Well, I must go,' he said; and he left her without any other farewell and made his way out of the house. As he went slowly up the street the sense came back to him of that first glimpse of her he had had at Stayes—the way he had seen her gaze across the table at her husband. Lyon stopped at the corner, looking vaguely up and down. He would never go back—he couldn't. She was still in love with the Colonel—he had trained her too well.

243

MRS. TEMPERLY

I

'Why, Cousin Raymond, how can you suppose? Why, she's only sixteen!'

'She told me she was seventeen,' said the young man, as if it made a great difference.

'Well, only *just*!' Mrs. Temperly replied, in the tone of graceful, reasonable concession.

'Well, that's a very good age for me. I'm very young.'

'You are old enough to know better,' the lady remarked, in her soft, pleasant voice, which always drew the sting from a reproach, and enabled you to swallow it as you would a cooked plum, without the stone. 'Why, she hasn't finished her education!'

'That's just what I mean,' said her interlocutor. 'It would finish it beautifully for her to marry me.'

'Have you finished yours, my dear?' Mrs. Temperly inquired. 'The way you young people talk about marrying!' she exclaimed, looking at the itinerant functionary with the long wand who touched into a flame the tall gas-lamp on the other side of the Fifth Avenue. The pair were standing, in the recess of a window, in one of the big public rooms of an immense hotel, and the October day was turning to dusk.

'Well, would you have us leave it to the old?' Raymond asked. 'That's just what I think—she would be such a help to me,' he continued. 'I want to go back to Paris to study more. I have come home too soon. I don't know half enough; they know more here than I thought. So it would be perfectly easy, and we should all be together.'

'Well, my dear, when you do come back to Paris we will talk about it,' said Mrs. Temperly, turning away from the window.

'I should like it better, Cousin Maria, if you trusted me a little more,' Raymond sighed, observing that she was not really giving her thoughts to what he said. She irritated him somehow; she was so full of her impending departure, of her arrangements, her last duties and memoranda. She was not exactly important, any more than she was humble; she was too conciliatory for the one and too positive for the other. But she bustled quietly and gave one the sense of being 'up to' everything; the successive steps of her enterprise were in advance perfectly clear to her, and he could see that her imagination (conventional as she was she had plenty of that faculty) had already taken up its abode on one of those fine *premiers* which she had never seen, but which by instinct she seemed to know all about, in the very best part of the quarter of the Champs Elysées. If she ruffled him envy had perhaps something to do with it: she was to set sail on the morrow for the city of his affection and he was to stop in New York, where the fact that he was but half pleased did not alter the fact that he had his studio on his hands and that it was a bad one (though perhaps as good as any use he should put it to), which no one would be in a hurry to relieve him of.

It was easy for him to talk to Mrs. Temperly in that airy way about going back, but he couldn't go back unless the old gentleman gave him the means. He had already given him a great many things in the past, and with the others coming on (Marian's marriage-outfit, within three months, had cost literally thousands), Raymond had not at present the face to ask for more. He must sell some pictures first, and to sell them he must first paint them. It was his misfortune that he saw what he wanted to do so much better than he could do it. But he must really try and please himself—an effort that appeared more possible now that the idea of following Dora across the ocean had become an incentive. In spite of secret aspirations and even intentions, however, it was not encouraging to feel that he made really no impression at all on Cousin Maria. This certitude was so far from agreeable to him that he almost found it in him to drop the endearing title by which he had hitherto addressed her. It was only that, after all, her husband had been distantly related to his mother. It was not as a cousin that he was interested in Dora, but as something very much more intimate. I know not whether it occurred to him that Mrs. Temperly herself would never give his displeasure the benefit of dropping the affectionate form. She might shut her door to him altogether, but he would always be her kinsman and her dear. She was much addicted to these little embellishments of human intercourse—the friendly apostrophe and even the caressing hand—and there was something homely and cosy, a rustic, motherly *bonhomie*, in her use of them. She was as lavish of them as she was really careful in the selection of her friends.

She stood there with her hand in her pocket, as if she were feeling for something; her little plain, pleasant face was presented to him with a musing smile, and he vaguely wondered whether she were fumbling for a piece of money to buy him off from wishing to marry her daughter. Such an idea would be quite in keeping with the disguised levity with which she treated his state of mind. If her levity was wrapped up in the air of tender solicitude for everything that related to the feelings of her child, that only made her failure to appreciate his suit more deliberate. She struck him almost as impertinent (at the same time that he knew this was never her intention) as she looked up at him—her tiny proportions always made her throw back her head and set something dancing in her cap—and inquired whether he had noticed if she gave two keys, tied together by a blue ribbon, to Susan Winkle, when that faithful but flurried domestic met them in the lobby. She was thinking only of questions of luggage, and the fact that he wished to marry Dora was the smallest incident in their getting off.

'I think you ask me that only to change the subject,' he said. 'I don't believe that ever in your life you have been unconscious of what you have done with your keys.'

'Not often, but you make me nervous,' she answered, with her patient, honest smile.

'Oh, Cousin Maria!' the young man exclaimed, ambiguously, while Mrs. Temperly looked humanely at some totally uninteresting people who came straggling into the great hot, frescoed, velvety drawing-room, where it

246

was as easy to see you were in an hotel as it was to see that, if you were, you were in one of the very best. Mrs. Temperly, since her husband's death, had passed much of her life at hotels, where she flattered herself that she preserved the tone of domestic life free from every taint and promoted the refined development of her children; but she selected them as well as she selected her friends. Somehow they became better from the very fact of her being there, and her children were smuggled in and out in the most extraordinary way; one never met them racing and whooping, as one did hundreds of others, in the lobbies. Her frequentation of hotels, where she paid enormous bills, was part of her expensive but practical way of living, and also of her theory that, from one week to another, she was going to Europe for a series of years as soon as she had wound up certain complicated affairs which had devolved upon her at her husband's death. If these affairs had dragged on it was owing to their inherent troublesomeness and implied no doubt of her capacity to bring them to a solution and to administer the very considerable fortune that Mr. Temperly had left. She used, in a superior, unprejudiced way, every convenience that the civilisation of her time offered her, and would have lived without hesitation in a lighthouse if this had contributed to her general scheme. She was now, in the interest of this scheme, preparing to use Europe, which she had not yet visited and with none of whose foreign tongues she was acquainted. This time she was certainly embarking.

She took no notice of the discredit which her young friend appeared to throw on the idea that she had nerves, and betrayed no suspicion that he believed her to have them in about the same degree as a sound, productive Alderney cow. She only moved toward one of the numerous doors of the room, as if to remind him of all she had still to do before night. They passed together into the long, wide corridor of the hotel—a vista of soft carpet, numbered doors, wandering women and perpetual gaslight—and approached the staircase by which she must ascend again to her domestic duties. She counted over, serenely, for his enlightenment, those that were still to be performed; but he could see that everything would be finished by nine o'clock—the time she had fixed in advance. The heavy luggage was then to go to the steamer; she herself was to be on board, with the children and the smaller things, at eleven o'clock the next morning. They had thirty pieces, but this was less than they had when they came from California five years before. She wouldn't have done that again. It was true that at that time she had had Mr. Temperly to help: he had died, Raymond remembered, six months after the settlement in New York. But, on the other hand, she knew more now. It was one of Mrs. Temperly's amiable qualities that she admitted herself so candidly to be still susceptible of development. She never professed to be in possession of all the knowledge requisite for her career; not only did she let her friends know that she was always learning, but she appealed to them to instruct her, in a manner which was in itself an example.

When Raymond said to her that he took for granted she would let him come down to the steamer for a last good-bye, she not only consented graciously but added that he was free to call again at the hotel in the evening, if he had nothing better to do. He must come between nine and ten; she expected several other friends—those who wished to see the last of them, yet didn't care to come to the ship. Then he would see all of them—she meant all of themselves, Dora and Effie and Tishy, and even Mademoiselle Bourde. She spoke exactly as if he had never approached her on the subject of Dora and as if Tishy, who was ten years of age, and Mademoiselle Bourde, who was the French governess and forty, were objects of no less an interest to him. He felt what a long pull he should have ever to get round her, and the sting of this knowledge was in his consciousness that Dora was really in her mother's hands. In Mrs. Temperly's composition there was not a hint of the bully; but none the less she held her children—she would hold them for ever. It was not simply by tenderness; but what it was by she knew best herself. Raymond appreciated the privilege of seeing Dora again that evening as well as on the morrow; yet he was so vexed with her mother that his vexation betrayed him into something that almost savoured of violence—a fact which I am ashamed to have to chronicle, as Mrs. Temperly's own urbanity deprived such breaches of every excuse. It may perhaps serve partly as an excuse for Raymond Bestwick that he was in love, or at least that he thought he was. Before she parted from him at the foot of the staircase he said to her, 'And of course, if things go as you like over there, Dora will marry some foreign prince.'

She gave no sign of resenting this speech, but she looked at him for the first time as if she were hesitating, as if it were not instantly clear to her what to say. It appeared to him, on his side, for a moment, that there was something strange in her hesitation, that abruptly, by an inspiration, she was almost making up her mind to reply that Dora's marriage to a prince was, considering Dora's peculiarities (he knew that her mother deemed her peculiar, and so did he, but that was precisely why he wished to marry her), so little probable that, after all, once such a union was out of the question, *he* might be no worse than another plain man. These, however, were not the words that fell from Mrs. Temperly's lips. Her embarrassment vanished in her clear smile. 'Do you know what Mr. Temperly used to say? He used to say that Dora was the pattern of an old maid—she would never make a choice.'

'I hope—because that would have been too foolish—that he didn't say she wouldn't have a chance.'

'Oh, a chance! what do you call by that fine name?' Cousin Maria exclaimed, laughing, as she ascended the stair.

II

When he came back, after dinner, she was again in one of the public rooms; she explained that a lot of the things for the ship were spread out in her own parlours: there was no space to sit down. Raymond was highly gratified by this fact; it offered an opportunity for strolling away a little with Dora, especially as, after he had been there ten minutes, other people began to come in. They were entertained by the rest, by Effie and Tishy, who was allowed to sit up a little, and by Mademoiselle Bourde, who besought every visitor to indicate her a remedy that was *really* effective against the sea—some charm, some philter, some potion or spell. 'Never mind, ma'm'selle, I've got a remedy,' said Cousin Maria, with her cheerful decision, each time; but the French instructress always began afresh.

As the young man was about to be parted for an indefinite period from the girl whom he was ready to swear that he adored, it is clear that he ought to have been equally ready to swear that she was the fairest of her species. In point of fact, however, it was no less vivid to him than it had been before that he loved Dora Temperly for qualities which had nothing to do with straightness of nose or pinkness of complexion. Her figure was straight, and so was her character, but her nose was not, and Philistines and other vulgar people would have committed themselves, without a blush on their own flat faces, to the assertion that she was decidedly plain. In his artistic imagination he had analogies for her, drawn from legend and literature; he was perfectly aware that she struck many persons as silent, shy and angular, while his own version of her peculiarities was that she was like a figure on the *predella* of an early Italian painting or a mediæval maiden wandering about a lonely castle, with her lover gone to the Crusades. To his sense, Dora had but one defect—her admiration for her mother was too undiscriminating. An ardent young man may well be slightly vexed when he finds that a young lady will probably never care for him so much as she cares for her parent; and Raymond Bestwick had this added ground for chagrin, that Dora had—if she chose to take it—so good a pretext for discriminating. For she had nothing whatever in common with the others; she was not of the same stuff as Mrs. Temperly and Effie and Tishy.

She was original and generous and uncalculating, besides being full of perception and taste in regard to the things *he* cared about. She knew nothing of conventional signs or estimates, but understood everything that might be said to her from an artistic point of view. She was formed to live in a studio, and not in a stiff drawing-room, amid upholstery horribly new; and moreover her eyes and her voice were both charming. It was only a pity she was so gentle; that is, he liked it for himself, but he deplored it for her mother. He considered that he had virtually given that lady his word that he would not make love to her; but his spirits had risen since his visit of three or four hours before. It seemed to him, after thinking things over more intently, that a way would be opened for him to return to Paris. It was not probable that in the interval Dora would be married off to a prince; for in the first place the foolish race of princes would be sure not to appreciate her, and in the second she would not, in this matter, simply do her mother's bidding— her gentleness would not go so far as that. She might remain single by the maternal decree, but she would not take a husband who was disagreeable to her. In this reasoning Raymond was obliged to shut his eyes very tight to the danger that some particular prince might not be disagreeable to her, as well as to the attraction proceeding from what her mother might announce that she would 'do.' He was perfectly aware that it was in Cousin Maria's power, and would probably be in her pleasure, to settle a handsome marriage-fee upon each of her daughters. He was equally certain that this had nothing to do with the nature of his own interest in the eldest, both because it was clear that Mrs. Temperly would do very little for *him*, and because he didn't care how little she did.

Effie and Tishy sat in the circle, on the edge of rather high chairs, while Mademoiselle Bourde surveyed in them with complacency the results of her own superiority. Tishy was a child, but Effie was fifteen, and they were both very nice little girls, arrayed in fresh travelling dresses and deriving a quaintness from the fact that Tishy was already armed, for foreign adventures, with a smart new reticule, from which she could not be induced to part, and that Effie had her finger in her 'place' in a fat red volume of *Murray*. Raymond knew that in a general way their mother would not have allowed them to appear in the drawing-room with these adjuncts, but something was to be allowed to the fever of anticipation. They were both pretty, with delicate features and blue eyes, and would grow up into worldly, conventional young ladies, just as Dora had not done. They looked at Mademoiselle Bourde for approval whenever they spoke, and, in addressing their mother alternately with that accomplished woman, kept their two languages neatly distinct.

Raymond had but a vague idea of who the people were who had come to bid Cousin Maria farewell, and he had no wish for a sharper one, though she introduced him, very definitely, to the whole group. She might make light of him in her secret soul, but she would never put herself in the wrong by omitting the smallest form. Fortunately, however, he was not obliged to like all her forms, and he foresaw the day when she would abandon this particular one. She was not so well made up in advance about Paris but that it would be in reserve for her to detest the period when she had thought it proper to 'introduce all round.' Raymond detested it already, and tried to make Dora understand that he wished her to take a walk with him in the corridors. There was a gentleman with a curl on his forehead who especially displeased him; he made childish jokes, at which the others laughed all at once, as if they had rehearsed for it—jokes *à la portée* of Effie and Tishy and mainly about them. These two joined in the merriment, as if they followed perfectly, as indeed they might, and gave a small sigh afterward, with a little factitious air. Dora remained grave, almost sad; it was when she was different, in this way, that he felt how much he liked her. He hated, in general, a large ring of people who had drawn up chairs in the public room of an hotel: some one was sure to undertake to be funny.

He succeeded at last in drawing Dora away; he endeavoured to give the movement a casual air. There was nothing peculiar, after all, in their walking a little in the passage; a dozen other persons were doing the same. The girl had the air of not suspecting in the least that he could have anything particular to say to her—of responding to his appeal simply out of her general gentleness. It was not in her companion's interest that her mind should be such a blank; nevertheless his conviction that in spite of the ministrations of Mademoiselle Bourde she was not falsely ingenuous made him repeat to himself that he would still make her his own. They took several turns in the hall, during which it might still have appeared to Dora Temperly that her cousin Raymond had nothing particular to say to her. He remarked several times that he should certainly turn up in Paris in the spring; but when once she had replied that she was very glad that subject seemed exhausted. The young man cared little, however; it was not a question now of making any declaration: he only wanted to be with her. Suddenly, when they were at the end of the corridor furthest removed from the room they had left, he said to her: 'Your mother is very strange. Why has she got such an idea about Paris?'

'How do you mean, such an idea?' He had stopped, making the girl stand there before him.

'Well, she thinks so much of it without having ever seen it, or really knowing anything. She appears to have planned out such a great life there.'

'She thinks it's the best place,' Dora rejoined, with the dim smile that always charmed our young man.

'The best place for what?'

'Well, to learn French.' The girl continued to smile.

'Do you mean for her? She'll never learn it; she can't.'

'No; for us. And other things.'

'You know it already. And *you* know other things,' said Raymond.

'She wants us to know them better—better than any girls know them.'

'I don't know what things you mean,' exclaimed the young man, rather impatiently.

'Well, we shall see,' Dora returned, laughing.

He said nothing for a minute, at the end of which he resumed: 'I hope you won't be offended if I say that it seems curious your mother should have such aspirations—such Napoleonic plans. I mean being just a quiet little lady from California, who has never seen any of the kind of thing that she has in her head.'

'That's just why she wants to see it, I suppose; and I don't know why her being from California should prevent. At any rate she wants us to have the best. Isn't the best taste in Paris?'

'Yes; and the worst.' It made him gloomy when she defended the old lady, and to change the subject he asked: 'Aren't you sorry, this last night, to leave your own country for such an indefinite time?'

It didn't cheer him up that the girl should answer: 'Oh, I would go anywhere with mother!'

'And with *her*?' Raymond demanded, sarcastically, as Mademoiselle Bourde came in sight, emerging from the drawing-room. She approached them; they met her in a moment, and she informed Dora that Mrs. Temperly wished her to come back and play a part of that composition of Saint-Saens—the last one she had been learning—for Mr. and Mrs. Parminter: they wanted to judge whether their daughter could manage it.

'I don't believe she can,' said Dora, smiling; but she was moving away to comply when her companion detained her a moment.

Are you going to bid me good-bye?'

'Won't you come back to the drawing-room?'

'I think not; I don't like it.'

'And to mamma—you'll say nothing?' the girl went on.

'Oh, we have made our farewell; we had a special interview this afternoon.'

'And you won't come to the ship in the morning?'

Raymond hesitated a moment. 'Will Mr. and Mrs. Parminter be there?'

'Oh, surely they will!' Mademoiselle Bourde declared, surveying the young couple with a certain tactful serenity, but standing very close to them, as if it might be her duty to interpose.

'Well then, I won't come.'

'Well, good-bye then,' said the girl gently, holding out her hand.

'Good-bye, Dora.' He took it, while she smiled at him, but he said nothing more—he was so annoyed at the way Mademoiselle Bourde watched them. He only looked at Dora; she seemed to him beautiful.

'My dear child—that poor Madame Parminter,' the governess murmured.

'I shall come over very soon,' said Raymond, as his companion turned away.

'That will be charming.' And she left him quickly, without looking back.

Mademoiselle Bourde lingered—he didn't know why, unless it was to make him feel, with her smooth, finished French assurance, which had the manner of extreme benignity, that she was following him up. He sometimes wondered whether she copied Mrs. Temperly or whether Mrs. Temperly tried to copy her. Presently she said, slowly rubbing her hands and smiling at him:

'You will have plenty of time. We shall be long in Paris.'

'Perhaps you will be disappointed,' Raymond suggested.

'How can we be—unless *you* disappoint us?' asked the governess, sweetly.

He left her without ceremony: the imitation was probably on the part of Cousin Maria.

III

'Only just ourselves,' her note had said; and he arrived, in his natural impatience, a few moments before the hour. He remembered his Cousin Maria's habitual punctuality, but when he entered the splendid *salon* in the quarter of the Parc Monceau—it was there that he had found her established—he saw that he should have it, for a little, to himself. This was pleasing, for he should be able to look round—there were admirable things to look at. Even to-day Raymond Bestwick was not sure that he had learned to paint, but he had no doubt of his judgment of the work of others, and a single glance showed him that Mrs. Temperly had 'known enough' to select, for the adornment of her walls, half a dozen immensely valuable specimens of contemporary French art. Her choice of other objects had been equally enlightened, and he remembered what Dora had said to him five years before—that her mother wished them to have the best. Evidently, now they had got it; if five years was a long time for him to have delayed (with his original plan of getting off so soon) to come to Paris, it was a very short one for Cousin Maria to have taken to arrive at the highest good.

Rather to his surprise the first person to come in was Effie, now so complete a young lady, and such a very pretty girl, that he scarcely would have known her. She was fair, she was graceful, she was lovely, and as she entered the room, blushing and smiling, with a little floating motion which suggested that she was in a liquid element, she brushed down the ribbons of a delicate Parisian *toilette de jeune fille*. She appeared to expect that he would be surprised, and as if to justify herself for being the first she said, 'Mamma told me to come; she knows you are here; she said I was not to wait.' More than once, while they conversed, during the next few moments, before any one else arrived, she repeated that she was acting by her mamma's directions. Raymond perceived that she had not only the costume but several other of the attributes of a *jeune fille*. They talked, I say, but with a certain difficulty, for Effie asked him no questions, and this made him feel a little stiff about thrusting information upon her. Then she was so pretty, so exquisite, that this by itself disconcerted him. It seemed to him almost that she had falsified a prophecy, instead of bringing one to pass. He had foretold that she would be like this; the only difference was that she was so much more like it. She made no inquiries about his arrival, his people in America, his plans; and they exchanged vague remarks about the pictures, quite as if they had met for the first time.

When Cousin Maria came in Effie was standing in front of the fire fastening a bracelet, and he was at a distance gazing in silence at a portrait of his hostess by Bastien-Lepage. One of his apprehensions had been that Cousin Maria would allude ironically to the difference there had been between his threat (because it had been really almost a threat) of following them speedily to Paris and what had in fact occurred; but he saw in a moment how superficial this calculation had been. Besides, when had Cousin Maria ever been ironical? She treated him as if she had seen him last week (which did not preclude kindness), and only expressed her regret at having missed his visit the day before, in consequence of which she had immediately written to him to come and dine. He might have come from round the corner, instead of from New York and across the wintry ocean. This was a part of her 'cosiness,' her friendly, motherly optimism, of which, even of old, the habit had been never to recognise nor allude to disagreeable things; so that to-day, in the midst of so much that was not disagreeable, the custom would of course be immensely confirmed.

Raymond was perfectly aware that it was not a pleasure, even for her, that, for several years past, things should have gone so ill in New York with his family and himself. His father's embarrassments, of which Marian's silly husband had been the cause and which had terminated in general ruin and humiliation, to say nothing of the old man's 'stroke' and the necessity, arising from it, for a renunciation on his own part of all present thoughts of leaving home again and even for a partial relinquishment of present work, the old man requiring so much of his personal attention—all this constituted an episode which could not fail to look sordid and dreary in the light of Mrs. Temperly's high success. The odour of success was in the warm, slightly heavy air, which seemed distilled from rare old fabrics, from brocades and tapestries, from the

257

deep, mingled tones of the pictures, the subdued radiance of cabinets and old porcelain and the jars of winter roses standing in soft circles of lamp-light. Raymond felt himself in the presence of an effect in regard to which he remained in ignorance of the cause—a mystery that required a key. Cousin Maria's success was unexplained so long as she simply stood there with her little familiar, comforting, upward gaze, talking in coaxing cadences, with exactly the same manner she had brought ten years ago from California, to a tall, bald, bending, smiling young man, evidently a foreigner, who had just come in and whose name Raymond had not caught from the lips of the *maître d'hôtel*. Was he just one of themselves—was he there for Effie, or perhaps even for Dora? The unexplained must preponderate till Dora came in; he found he counted upon her, even though in her letters (it was true that for the last couple of years they had come but at long intervals) she had told him so little about their life. She never spoke of people; she talked of the books she read, of the music she had heard or was studying (a whole page sometimes about the last concert at the Conservatoire), the new pictures and the manner of the different artists.

When she entered the room three or four minutes after the arrival of the young foreigner, with whom her mother conversed in just the accents Raymond had last heard at the hotel in the Fifth Avenue (he was obliged to admit that she gave herself no airs; it was clear that her success had not gone in the least to her head); when Dora at last appeared she was accompanied by Mademoiselle Bourde. The presence of this lady—he didn't know she was still in the house—Raymond took as a sign that they were really dining *en famille*, so that the young man was either an actual or a prospective intimate. Dora shook hands first with her cousin, but he watched the manner of her greeting with the other visitor and saw that it indicated extreme friendliness—on the part of the latter. If there was a charming flush in her cheek as he took her hand, that was the remainder of the colour that had risen there as she came toward Raymond. It will be seen that our young man still had an eye for the element of fascination, as he used to regard it, in this quiet, dimly-shining maiden.

He saw that Effie was the only one who had changed (Tishy remained yet to be judged), except that Dora really looked older, quite as much older as the number of years had given her a right to: there was as little difference in her as there was in her mother. Not that she was like her mother, but she was perfectly like herself. Her meeting with Raymond was bright, but very still; their phrases were awkward and commonplace, and the thing was mainly a contact of looks—conscious, embarrassed, indirect, but brightening every moment with old familiarities. Her mother appeared to pay no attention, and neither, to do her justice, did Mademoiselle Bourde, who, after an exchange of expressive salutations with Raymond began to scrutinise Effie with little admiring gestures and smiles. She surveyed her from head to foot; she pulled a ribbon straight; she was evidently a flattering governess. Cousin Maria explained to Cousin Raymond that they were waiting for one more friend—a very dear lady. 'But she lives near, and when people live near they are always late—haven't you noticed that?'

'Your hotel is far away, I know, and yet you were the first,' Dora said, smiling to Raymond.

'Oh, even if it were round the corner I should be the first—to come to *you!*' the young man answered, speaking loud and clear, so that his words might serve as a notification to Cousin Maria that his sentiments were unchanged.

'You are more French than the French,' Dora returned.

'You say that as if you didn't like them: I hope you don't,' said Raymond, still with intentions in regard to his hostess.

'We like them more and more, the more we see of them,' this lady interposed; but gently, impersonally, and with an air of not wishing to put Raymond in the wrong.

'*Mais j'espère bien!*' cried Mademoiselle Bourde, holding up her head and opening her eyes very wide. 'Such friendships as we form, and, I may say, as we inspire! *Je m'en rapporte à Effie*', the governess continued.

259

'We have received immense kindness; we have established relations that are so pleasant for us, Cousin Raymond. We have the *entrée* of so many charming homes,' Mrs. Temperly remarked.

'But ours is the most charming of all; that I will say,' exclaimed Mademoiselle Bourde. 'Isn't it so, Effie?'

'Oh yes, I think it is; especially when we are expecting the Marquise,' Effie responded. Then she added, 'But here she comes now; I hear her carriage in the court.'

The Marquise too was just one of themselves; she was a part of their charming home.

'She *is* such a love!' said Mrs. Temperly to the foreign gentleman, with an irrepressible movement of benevolence.

To which Raymond heard the gentleman reply that, Ah, she was the most distinguished woman in France.

'Do you know Madame de Brives?' Effie asked of Raymond, while they were waiting for her to come in.

She came in at that moment, and the girl turned away quickly without an answer.

'How in the world should I know her?' That was the answer he would have been tempted to give. He felt very much out of Cousin Maria's circle. The foreign gentleman fingered his moustache and looked at him sidewise. The Marquise was a very pretty woman, fair and slender, of middle age, with a smile, a complexion, a diamond necklace, of great splendour, and a charming manner. Her greeting to her friends was sweet and familiar, and was accompanied with much kissing, of a sisterly, motherly, daughterly kind; and yet with this expression of simple, almost homely sentiment there was something in her that astonished and dazzled. She might very well have been, as the foreign young man said, the most distinguished woman in France. Dora had not rushed forward to meet her with nearly so much *empressement* as Effie, and this gave him a chance to ask the former who she was. The girl replied that she was her mother's most intimate friend: to which he rejoined that that was not a description; what he wanted to know was her title to this exalted position.

'Why, can't you see it? She is beautiful and she is good.'

'I see that she is beautiful; but how can I see that she is good?'

'Good to mamma, I mean, and to Effie and Tishy.'

'And isn't she good to you?'

'Oh, I don't know her so well. But I delight to look at her.'

'Certainly, that must be a great pleasure,' said Raymond. He enjoyed it during dinner, which was now served, though his enjoyment was diminished by his not finding himself next to Dora. They sat at a small round table and he had at his right his Cousin Maria, whom he had taken in. On his left was Madame de Brives, who had the foreign gentleman for a neighbour. Then came Effie and Mademoiselle Bourde, and Dora was on the other side of her mother. Raymond regarded this as marked—a symbol of the fact that Cousin Maria would continue to separate them. He remained in ignorance of the other gentleman's identity, and remembered how he had prophesied at the hotel in New York that his hostess would give up introducing people. It was a friendly, easy little family repast, as she had said it would be, with just a marquise and a secretary of embassy—Raymond ended by guessing that the stranger was a secretary of embassy—thrown in. So far from interfering with the family tone Madame de Brives directly contributed to it. She eminently justified the affection in which she was held in the house; she was in the highest degree sociable and sympathetic, and at the same time witty (there was no insipidity in Madame de Brives), and was the cause of Raymond's making the reflection—as he had made it often in his earlier years—that an agreeable Frenchwoman is a triumph of civilisation. This did not prevent him from giving the Marquise no more than half of his attention; the rest was dedicated to Dora, who, on her side, though in common with Effie and Mademoiselle Bourde she bent a frequent, interested gaze on the splendid French lady, very often met our young man's eyes with mute, vague but, to his sense, none the less valuable intimations. It was as if she knew what was going on in his mind (it is true that he scarcely knew it himself), and might be trusted to clear things up at some convenient hour.

Madame de Brives talked across Raymond, in excellent English, to Cousin Maria, but this did not prevent her from being gracious, even encouraging, to the young man, who was a little afraid of her and thought her a delightful creature. She asked him more questions about himself than any of them had done. Her conversation with Mrs. Temperly was of an intimate, domestic order, and full of social, personal allusions, which Raymond was unable to follow. It appeared to be concerned considerably with the private affairs of the old French *noblesse*, into whose councils—to judge by the tone of the Marquise—Cousin Maria had been admitted by acclamation. Every now and then Madame de Brives broke into French, and it was in this tongue that she uttered an apostrophe to her hostess: 'Oh, you, *ma toute-bonne*, you who have the genius of good sense!' And she appealed to Raymond to know if his Cousin Maria had not the genius of good sense—the wisdom of the ages. The old lady did not defend herself from the compliment; she let it pass, with her motherly, tolerant smile; nor did Raymond attempt to defend her, for he felt the justice of his neighbour's description: Cousin Maria's good sense was incontestable, magnificent. She took an affectionate, indulgent view of most of the persons mentioned, and yet her tone was far from being vapid or vague. Madame de Brives usually remarked that they were coming very soon again to see her, she did them so much good. 'The freshness of your judgment— the freshness of your judgment!' she repeated, with a kind of glee, and she narrated that Eléonore (a personage unknown to Raymond) had said that she was a woman of Plutarch. Mrs. Temperly talked a great deal about the health of their friends; she seemed to keep the record of the influenzas and neuralgias of a numerous and susceptible circle. He did not find it in him quite to agree—the Marquise dropping the statement into his ear at a moment when their hostess was making some inquiry of Mademoiselle Bourde—that she was a nature absolutely marvellous; but he could easily see that to world-worn Parisians her quiet charities of speech and manner, with something quaint and rustic in their form, might be restorative and salutary. She allowed for everything, yet she was so good, and indeed Madame de Brives summed this up before they left the table in saying to her, 'Oh, you, my dear, your success, more than any other that has ever taken place, has been a *succès de bonté*!' Raymond was greatly amused at this idea of Cousin Maria's *succès de bonté*: it seemed to him delightfully Parisian.

Before dinner was over she inquired of him how he had got on 'in his profession' since they last met, and he was too proud, or so he thought, to tell her anything but the simple truth, that he had not got on very well. If he was to ask her again for Dora it would be just as he was, an honourable but not particularly successful man, making no show of lures and bribes. 'I am not a remarkably good painter,' he said. 'I judge myself perfectly. And then I have been handicapped at home. I have had a great many serious bothers and worries.'

'Ah, we were so sorry to hear about your dear father.'

The tone of these words was kind and sincere; still Raymond thought that in this case her *bonté* might have gone a little further. At any rate this was the only allusion that she made to his bothers and worries. Indeed, she always passed over such things lightly; she was an optimist for others as well as for herself, which doubtless had a great deal to do (Raymond indulged in the reflection) with the headway she made in a society tired of its own pessimism.

After dinner, when they went into the drawing-room, the young man noted with complacency that this apartment, vast in itself, communicated with two or three others into which it would be easy to pass without attracting attention, the doors being replaced by old tapestries, looped up and offering no barrier. With pictures and curiosities all over the place, there were plenty of pretexts for wandering away. He lost no time in asking Dora whether her mother would send Mademoiselle Bourde after them if she were to go with him into one of the other rooms, the same way she had done—didn't she remember?—that last night in New York, at the hotel. Dora didn't admit that she remembered (she was too loyal to her mother for that, and Raymond foresaw that this loyalty would be a source of irritation to him again, as it had been in the past), but he perceived, all the same, that she had not forgotten. She raised no difficulty, and a few moments later, while they stood in an adjacent *salon* (he had stopped to admire a bust of Effie, wonderfully living, slim and juvenile, the work of one of the sculptors who are the pride of contemporary French art), he said to her, looking about him, 'How has she done it so fast?'

'Done what, Raymond?'

'Why, done everything. Collected all these wonderful things; become intimate with Madame de Brives and every one else; organised her life—the life of all of you—so brilliantly.'

'I have never seen mamma in a hurry,' Dora replied.

'Perhaps she will be, now that I have come,' Raymond suggested, laughing.

The girl hesitated a moment 'Yes, she was, to invite you—the moment she knew you were here.'

'She has been most kind, and I talk like a brute. But I am liable to do worse—I give you notice. She won't like it any more than she did before, if she thinks I want to make up to you.'

'Don't, Raymond—don't!' the girl exclaimed, gently, but with a look of sudden pain.

'Don't what, Dora?—don't make up to you?'

'Don't begin to talk of those things. There is no need. We can go on being friends.'

'I will do exactly as you prescribe, and heaven forbid I should annoy you. But would you mind answering me a question? It is very particular, very intimate.' He stopped, and she only looked at him, saying nothing. So he went on: 'Is it an idea of your mother's that you should marry—some person here?' He gave her a chance to reply, but still she was silent, and he continued: 'Do you mind telling me this? Could it ever be an idea of your own?'

'Do you mean some Frenchman?'

Raymond smiled. 'Some protégé of Madame de Brives.'

Then the girl simply gave a slow, sad head-shake which struck him as the sweetest, proudest, most suggestive thing in the world. 'Well, well, that's all right,' he remarked, cheerfully, and looked again a while at the bust, which he thought extraordinarily clever. 'And haven't *you* been done by one of these great fellows?'

'Oh dear no; only mamma and Effie. But Tishy is going to be, in a month or two. The next time you come you must see her. She remembers you vividly.'

'And I remember her that last night, with her reticule. Is she always pretty?'

Dora hesitated a moment. 'She is a very sweet little creature, but she is not so pretty as Effie.'

'And have none of them wished to do you—none of the painters?'

'Oh, it's not a question of me. I only wish them to let me alone.'

'For me it would be a question of you, if you would sit for me. But I daresay your mother wouldn't allow that.'

'No, I think not,' said Dora, smiling.

She smiled, but her companion looked grave. However, not to pursue the subject, he asked, abruptly, 'Who is this Madame de Brives?'

'If you lived in Paris you would know. She is very celebrated.'

'Celebrated for what?'

'For everything.'

'And is she good—is she genuine?' Raymond asked. Then, seeing something in the girl's face, he added: 'I told you I should be brutal again. Has she undertaken to make a great marriage for Effie?'

'I don't know what she has undertaken,' said Dora, impatiently.

'And then for Tishy, when Effie has been disposed of?'

'Poor little Tishy!' the girl continued, rather inscrutably.

'And can she do nothing for you?' the young man inquired.

Her answer surprised him—after a moment. 'She has kindly offered to exert herself, but it's no use.'

'Well, that's good. And who is it the young man comes for—the secretary of embassy?'

'Oh, he comes for all of us,' said Dora, laughing.

'I suppose your mother would prefer a preference,' Raymond suggested.

To this she replied, irrelevantly, that she thought they had better go back; but as Raymond took no notice of the recommendation she mentioned that the secretary was no one in particular. At this moment Effie, looking very rosy and happy, pushed through the *portière* with the news that her sister must come and bid good-bye to the Marquise. She was taking her to the Duchess's—didn't Dora remember? To the *bal blanc*—the *sauterie de jeunes filles*.

'I thought we should be called,' said Raymond, as he followed Effie; and he remarked that perhaps Madame de Brives would find something suitable at the Duchess's.

'I don't know. Mamma would be very particular,' the girl rejoined; and this was said simply, sympathetically, without the least appearance of deflection from that loyalty which Raymond deplored.

IV

'You must come to us on the 17th; we expect to have a few people and some good music,' Cousin Maria said to him before he quitted the house; and he wondered whether, the 17th being still ten days off, this might not be an intimation that they could abstain from his society until then. He chose, at any rate, not to take it as such, and called several times in the interval, late in the afternoon, when the ladies would be sure to have come in.

They were always there, and Cousin Maria's welcome was, for each occasion, maternal, though when he took leave she made no allusion to future meetings—to his coming again; but there were always other visitors as well, collected at tea round the great fire of logs, in the friendly, brilliant drawing-room where the luxurious was no enemy to the casual and Mrs. Temperly's manner of dispensing hospitality recalled to our young man somehow certain memories of his youthful time: visits in New England, at old homesteads flanked with elms, where a talkative, democratic, delightful farmer's wife pressed upon her company rustic viands in which she herself had had a hand. Cousin Maria enjoyed the services of a distinguished *chef*, and delicious *petits fours* were served with her tea; but Raymond had a sense that to complete the impression hot home-made gingerbread should have been produced.

The atmosphere was suffused with the presence of Madame de Brives. She was either there or she was just coming or she was just gone; her name, her voice, her example and encouragement were in the air. Other ladies came and went—sometimes accompanied by gentlemen who looked worn out, had waxed moustaches and knew how to talk—and they were sometimes designated in the same manner as Madame de Brives; but she remained the Marquise *par excellence*, the incarnation of brilliancy and renown. The conversation moved among simple but civilised topics, was not dull and, considering that it consisted largely of personalities, was not ill-natured. Least of all was it scandalous, for the girls were always there, Cousin Maria not having thought it in the least necessary, in order to put herself in accord with French traditions, to relegate her daughters to the middle distance. They occupied a considerable part of the foreground, in the prettiest, most modest, most becoming attitudes.

It was Cousin Maria's theory of her own behaviour that she did in Paris simply as she had always done; and though this would not have been a complete account of the matter Raymond could not fail to notice the good sense and good taste with which she laid down her lines and the quiet *bonhomie* of the authority with which she caused the tone of the American home to be respected. Scandal stayed outside, not simply because Effie and Tishy were there, but because, even if Cousin Maria had received alone, she never would have received evil-speakers. Indeed, for Raymond, who had been accustomed to think that in a general way he knew pretty well what the French capital was, this was a strange, fresh Paris altogether, destitute of the salt that seasoned it for most palates, and yet not insipid nor innutritive. He marvelled at Cousin Maria's air, in such a city, of knowing, of recognising nothing bad: all the more that it represented an actual state of mind. He used to wonder sometimes what she would do and how she would feel if some day, in consequence of researches made by the Marquise in the *grand monde*, she should find herself in possession of a son-in-law formed according to one of the types of which *he* had impressions. However, it was not credible that Madame de Brives would play her a trick. There were moments when Raymond almost wished she might—to see how Cousin Maria would handle the gentleman.

Dora was almost always taken up by visitors, and he had scarcely any direct conversation with her. She was there, and he was glad she was there, and she knew he was glad (he knew that), but this was almost all the communion he had with her. She was mild, exquisitely mild—this was the term he mentally applied to her now—and it amply sufficed him, with the conviction he had that she was not stupid. She attended to the tea (for Mademoiselle Bourde was not always free), she handed the *petits fours*, she rang the bell when people went out; and it was in connection with these offices that the idea came to him once—he was rather ashamed of it afterward—that she was the Cinderella of the house, the domestic drudge, the one for whom there was no career, as it was useless for the Marquise to take up her case. He was ashamed of this fancy, I say, and yet it came back to him; he was even surprised that it had not occurred to him before. Her sisters were neither ugly nor proud (Tishy, indeed, was almost touchingly delicate and timid, with exceedingly pretty points, yet with a little appealing, old-womanish look, as if, small—very small—as she was, she was afraid she shouldn't grow any more); but her mother, like the mother in the fairy-tale, was a *femme forte*. Madame de Brives could do nothing for Dora, not absolutely because she was too plain, but because she would never lend herself, and that came to the same thing. Her mother accepted her as recalcitrant, but Cousin Maria's attitude, at the best, could only be resignation. She would respect her child's preferences, she would never put on the screw; but this would not make her love the child any more. So Raymond interpreted certain signs, which at the same time he felt to be very slight, while the conversation in Mrs. Temperly's *salon* (this was its preponderant tendency) rambled among questions of bric-à-brac, of where Tishy's portrait should be placed when it was finished, and the current prices of old Gobelins. *Ces dames* were not in the least above the discussion of prices.

On the 17th it was easy to see that more lamps than usual had been lighted. They streamed through all the windows of the charming hotel and mingled with the radiance of the carriage-lanterns, which followed each other slowly, in couples, in a close, long rank, into the fine sonorous court, where the high stepping of valuable horses was sharp on the stones, and up to the ruddy portico. The night was wet, not with a downpour, but with showers interspaced by starry patches, which only added to the glitter of the handsome, clean Parisian surfaces. The *sergents de ville* were about the place, and seemed to make the occasion important and official. These night aspects of Paris in the *beaux quartiers* had always for Raymond a particularly festive association, and as he passed from his cab under the wide permanent tin canopy, painted in stripes like an awning, which protected the low steps, it seemed to him odder than ever that all this established prosperity should be Cousin Maria's.

If the thought of how well she did it bore him company from the threshold, it deepened to admiration by the time he had been half an hour in the place. She stood near the entrance with her two elder daughters, distributing the most familiar, most encouraging smiles, together with hand-shakes which were in themselves a whole system of hospitality. If her party was grand Cousin Maria was not; she indulged in no assumption of stateliness and no attempt at graduated welcomes. It seemed to Raymond that it was only because it would have taken too much time that she didn't kiss every one. Effie looked lovely and just a little frightened, which was exactly what she ought to have done; and he noticed that among the arriving guests those who were not intimate (which he could not tell from Mrs. Temperly's manner, but could from their own) recognised her as a daughter much more quickly than they recognised Dora, who hung back disinterestedly, as if not to challenge their discernment, while the current passed her, keeping her little sister in position on its brink meanwhile by the tenderest small gesture.

'May I talk with you a little, later?' he asked of Dora, with only a few seconds for the question, as people were pressing behind him. She answered evasively that there would be very little talk—they would all have to listen—it was very serious; and the next moment he had received a programme from the hand of a monumental yet gracious personage who stood beyond and who had a silver chain round his neck.

The place was arranged for music, and how well arranged he saw later, when every one was seated, spaciously, luxuriously, without pushing or over-peeping, and the finest talents in Paris performed selections at which the best taste had presided. The singers and players were all stars of the first magnitude. Raymond was fond of music and he wondered whose taste it had been. He made up his mind it was Dora's—it was only she who could have conceived a combination so exquisite; and he said to himself: 'How they all pull together! She is not in it, she is not of it, and yet she too works for the common end.' And by 'all' he meant also Mademoiselle Bourde and the Marquise. This impression made him feel rather hopeless, as if, *en fin de compte*, Cousin Maria were too large an adversary. Great as was the pleasure of being present on an occasion so admirably organised, of sitting there in a beautiful room, in a still, attentive, brilliant company, with all the questions of temperature, space, light and decoration solved to the gratification of every

270

sense, and listening to the best artists doing their best—happily constituted as our young man was to enjoy such a privilege as this, the total effect was depressing: it made him feel as if the gods were not on his side.

'And does she do it so well without a man? There must be so many details a woman can't tackle,' he said to himself; for even counting in the Marquise and Mademoiselle Bourde this only made a multiplication of petticoats. Then it came over him that she *was* a man as well as a woman—the masculine element was included in her nature. He was sure that she bought her horses without being cheated, and very few men could do that. She had the American national quality—she had 'faculty' in a supreme degree. 'Faculty—faculty,' the voices of the quartette of singers seemed to repeat, in the quick movement of a composition they rendered beautifully, while they swelled and went faster, till the thing became a joyous chant of praise, a glorification of Cousin Maria's practical genius.

During the intermission, in the middle of the concert, people changed places more or less and circulated, so that, walking about at this time, he came upon the Marquise, who, in her sympathetic, demonstrative way, appeared to be on the point of clasping her hostess in her arms. 'Décidément, ma bonne, il n'y a que vous! C'est une perfection——' he heard her say. To which, gratified but unelated, Cousin Maria replied, according to her simple, sociable wont: 'Well, it *does* seem quite a successful occasion. If it will only keep on to the end!'

Raymond, wandering far, found himself in a world that was mainly quite new to him, and explained his ignorance of it by reflecting that the people were probably celebrated: so many of them had decorations and stars and a quiet of manner that could only be accounted for by renown. There were plenty of Americans with no badge but a certain fine negativeness, and *they* were quiet for a reason which by this time had become very familiar to Raymond: he had heard it so often mentioned that his country-people were supremely 'adaptable.' He tried to get hold of Dora, but he saw that her mother had arranged things beautifully to keep her occupied with other people; so at least he interpreted the fact—after all very natural—that she had half a dozen fluttered young girls on her mind, whom she was providing with programmes, seats, ices, occasional murmured remarks and general support and protection. When the concert was over she supplied them with further entertainment in the form of several young men who had pliable backs and flashing breastpins and whom she inarticulately introduced to them, which gave her still more to do, as after this serious step she had to stay and watch all parties. It was strange to Raymond to see her transformed by her mother into a precocious duenna. Him she introduced to no young girl, and he knew not whether to regard this as cold neglect or as high consideration. If he had liked he might have taken it as a sweet intimation that she knew he couldn't care for any girl but her.

On the whole he was glad, because it left him free—free to get hold of her mother, which by this time he had boldly determined to do. The conception was high, inasmuch as Cousin Maria's attention was obviously required by the ambassadors and other grandees who had flocked to do her homage. Nevertheless, while supper was going on (he wanted none, and neither apparently did she), he collared her, as he phrased it to himself, in just the right place—on the threshold of the conservatory. She was flanked on either side with a foreigner of distinction, but he didn't care for her foreigners now. Besides, a conservatory was meant only for couples; it was a sign of her comprehensive sociability that she should have been rambling among the palms and orchids with a double escort. Her friends would wish to quit her but would not wish to appear to give way to each other; and Raymond felt that he was relieving them both (though he didn't care) when he asked her to be so good as to give him a few minutes' conversation. He made her go back with him into the conservatory: it was the only thing he had ever made her do, or probably ever would. She began to talk about the great Gregorini—how it had been too sweet of her to repeat one of her songs, when it had really been understood in advance that repetitions were not expected. Raymond had no interest at present in the great Gregorini. He asked Cousin Maria vehemently if she remembered telling him in New York—that night at the hotel, five years before—that when he should have followed them to Paris he would be free to address her on the subject of Dora. She had given him a promise that she would listen to him in this case, and now he must keep her up to the mark. It was impossible to see her alone, but, at whatever inconvenience to herself, he must insist on her giving him his opportunity.

'About Dora, Cousin Raymond?' she asked, blandly and kindly—almost as if she didn't exactly know who Dora was.

'Surely you haven't forgotten what passed between us the evening before you left America. I was in love with her then and I have been in love with her ever since. I told you so then, and you stopped me off, but you gave me leave to make another appeal to you in the future. I make it now—this is the only way I have—and I think you ought to listen to it. Five years have passed, and I love her more than ever. I have behaved like a saint in the interval: I haven't attempted to practise upon her without your knowledge.'

'I am so glad; but she would have let me know,' said Cousin Maria, looking round the conservatory as if to see if the plants were all there.

'No doubt. I don't know what you do to her. But I trust that to-day your opposition falls—in face of the proof that we have given you of mutual fidelity.'

'Fidelity?' Cousin Maria repeated, smiling.

'Surely—unless you mean to imply that Dora has given me up. I have reason to believe that she hasn't.'

'I think she will like better to remain just as she is.'

'Just as she is?'

'I mean, not to make a choice,' Cousin Maria went on, smiling.

Raymond hesitated a moment. 'Do you mean that you have tried to make her make one?'

At this the good lady broke into a laugh. 'My dear Raymond, how little you must think I know my child!'

'Perhaps, if you haven't tried to make her, you have tried to prevent her. Haven't you told her I am unsuccessful, I am poor?'

She stopped him, laying her hand with unaffected solicitude on his arm. *Are* you poor, my dear? I should be so sorry!'

'Never mind; I can support a wife,' said the young man.

'It wouldn't matter, because I am happy to say that Dora has something of her own,' Cousin Maria went on, with her imperturbable candour. 'Her father thought that was the best way to arrange it. I had quite forgotten my opposition, as you call it; that was so long ago. Why, she was only a little girl. Wasn't that the ground I took? Well, dear, she's older now, and you can say anything to her you like. But I do think she wants to stay——' And she looked up at him, cheerily.

'Wants to stay?'

'With Effie and Tishy.'

'Ah, Cousin Maria,' the young man exclaimed, 'you are modest about yourself!'

'Well, we are all together. Now is that all? I *must* see if there is enough champagne. Certainly—you can say to her what you like. But twenty years hence she will be just as she is to-day; that's how I see her.'

'Lord, what is it you do to her?' Raymond groaned, as he accompanied his hostess back to the crowded rooms.

He knew exactly what she would have replied if she had been a Frenchwoman; she would have said to him, triumphantly, overwhelmingly: 'Que voulez-vous? Elle adore sa mère!' She was, however, only a Californian, unacquainted with the language of epigram, and her answer consisted simply of the words: 'I am sorry you have ideas that make you unhappy. I guess you are the only person here who hasn't enjoyed himself to-night.'

Raymond repeated to himself, gloomily, for the rest of the evening, 'Elle adore sa mère—elle adore sa mère!' He remained very late, and when but twenty people were left and he had observed that the Marquise, passing her hand into Mrs. Temperly's arm, led her aside as if for some important confabulation (some new light doubtless on what might be hoped for Effie), he persuaded Dora to let the rest of the guests depart in peace (apparently her mother had told her to look out for them to the very last), and come with him into some quiet corner. They found an empty sofa in the outlasting lamp-light, and there the girl sat down with him. Evidently she knew what he was going to say, or rather she thought she did; for in fact, after a little, after he had told her that he had spoken to her mother and she had told him he might speak to *her*, he said things that she could not very well have expected.

'Is it true that you wish to remain with Effie and Tishy? That's what your mother calls it when she means that you will give me up.'

'How can I give you up?' the girl demanded. 'Why can't we go on being friends, as I asked you the evening you dined here?'

'What do you mean by friends?'

'Well, not making everything impossible.'

'You didn't think anything impossible of old,' Raymond rejoined, bitterly. 'I thought you liked me then, and I have even thought so since.'

'I like you more than I like any one. I like you so much that it's my principal happiness.'

'Then why are there impossibilities?'

'Oh, some day I'll tell you!' said Dora, with a quick sigh. 'Perhaps after Tishy is married. And meanwhile, are you not going to remain in Paris, at any rate? Isn't your work here? You are not here for me only. You can come to the house often. That's what I mean by our being friends.'

Her companion sat looking at her with a gloomy stare, as if he were trying to make up the deficiencies in her logic.

'After Tishy is married? I don't see what that has to do with it. Tishy is little more than a baby; she may not be married for ten years.'

'That is very true.'

'And you dispose of the interval by a simple "meanwhile"? My dear Dora, your talk is strange,' Raymond continued, with his voice passionately lowered. 'And I may come to the house—often? How often do you mean—in ten years? Five times—or even twenty?' He saw that her eyes were filling with tears, but he went on: 'It has been coming over me little by little (I notice things very much if I have a reason), and now I think I understand your mother's system.'

'Don't say anything against my mother,' the girl broke in, beseechingly.

'I shall not say anything unjust. That is if I am unjust you must tell me. This is my idea, and your speaking of Tishy's marriage confirms it. To begin with she has had immense plans for you all; she wanted each of you to be a princess or a duchess—I mean a good one. But she has had to give *you* up.'

'No one has asked for me,' said Dora, with unexpected honesty.

'I don't believe it. Dozens of fellows have asked for you, and you have shaken your head in that divine way (divine for me, I mean) in which you shook it the other night.'

'My mother has never said an unkind word to me in her life,' the girl declared, in answer to this.

'I never said she had, and I don't know why you take the precaution of telling me so. But whatever you tell me or don't tell me,' Raymond pursued, 'there is one thing I see very well—that so long as you won't marry a duke Cousin Maria has found means to prevent you from marrying till your sisters have made rare alliances.'

'Has found means?' Dora repeated, as if she really wondered what was in his thought.

'Of course I mean only through your affection for her. How she works that, you know best yourself.'

'It's delightful to have a mother of whom every one is so fond,' said Dora, smiling.

'She is a most remarkable woman. Don't think for a moment that I don't appreciate her. You don't want to quarrel with her, and I daresay you are right.'

276

'Why, Raymond, of course I'm right!'

'It proves you are not madly in love with me. It seems to me that for you *I* would have quarrelled——'

'Raymond, Raymond!' she interrupted, with the tears again rising.

He sat looking at her, and then he said, 'Well, when they *are* married?'

'I don't know the future—I don't know what may happen.'

'You mean that Tishy is so small—she doesn't grow—and will therefore be difficult? Yes, she *is* small.' There was bitterness in his heart, but he laughed at his own words. 'However, Effie ought to go off easily,' he went on, as Dora said nothing. 'I really wonder that, with the Marquise and all, she hasn't gone off yet. This thing, to-night, ought to do a great deal for her.'

Dora listened to him with a fascinated gaze; it was as if he expressed things for her and relieved her spirit by making them clear and coherent. Her eyes managed, each time, to be dry again, and now a somewhat wan, ironical smile moved her lips. 'Mamma knows what she wants—she knows what she will take. And she will take only that.'

'Precisely—something tremendous. And she is willing to wait, eh? Well, Effie is very young, and she's charming. But she won't be charming if she has an ugly appendage in the shape of a poor unsuccessful American artist (not even a good one), whose father went bankrupt, for a brother-in-law. That won't smooth the way, of course; and if a prince is to come into the family, the family must be kept tidy to receive him.' Dora got up quickly, as if she could bear his lucidity no longer, but he kept close to her as she walked away. 'And she can sacrifice you like that, without a scruple, without a pang?'

'I might have escaped—if I would marry,' the girl replied.

'Do you call that escaping? She has succeeded with you, but is it a part of what the Marquise calls her *succès de bonté?*'

'Nothing that you can say (and it's far worse than the reality) can prevent her being delightful.'

'Yes, that's your loyalty, and I could shoot you for it!' he exclaimed, making her pause on the threshold of the adjoining room. 'So you think it will take about ten years, considering Tishy's size—or want of size?' He himself again was the only one to laugh at this. 'Your mother is closeted, as much as she can be closeted now, with Madame de Brives, and perhaps this time they are really settling something.'

'I have thought that before and nothing has come. Mamma wants something so good; not only every advantage and every grandeur, but every virtue under heaven, and every guarantee. Oh, she wouldn't expose them!'

'I see; that's where her goodness comes in and where the Marquise is impressed.' He took Dora's hand; he felt that he must go, for she exasperated him with her irony that stopped short and her patience that wouldn't stop. 'You simply propose that I should wait?' he said, as he held her hand.

'It seems to me that you might, if *I* can.' Then the girl remarked, 'Now that you are here, it's far better.'

There was a sweetness in this which made him, after glancing about a moment, raise her hand to his lips. He went away without taking leave of Cousin Maria, who was still out of sight, her conference with the Marquise apparently not having terminated. This looked (he reflected as he passed out) as if something might come of it. However, before he went home he fell again into a gloomy forecast. The weather had changed, the stars were all out, and he walked the empty streets for an hour. Tishy's perverse refusal to grow and Cousin Maria's conscientious exactions promised him a terrible probation. And in those intolerable years what further interference, what meddlesome, effective pressure, might not make itself felt? It may be added that Tishy is decidedly a dwarf and his probation is not yet over.

THE END

About Author

Henry James OM (15 April 1843 – 28 February 1916) was an American-British author regarded as a key transitional figure between literary realism and literary modernism, and is considered by many to be among the greatest novelists in the English language. He was the son of Henry James Sr. and the brother of renowned philosopher and psychologist William James and diarist Alice James.

He is best known for a number of novels dealing with the social and marital interplay between émigré Americans, English people, and continental Europeans. Examples of such novels include The Portrait of a Lady, The Ambassadors, and The Wings of the Dove. His later works were increasingly experimental. In describing the internal states of mind and social dynamics of his characters, James often made use of a style in which ambiguous or contradictory motives and impressions were overlaid or juxtaposed in the discussion of a character's psyche. For their unique ambiguity, as well as for other aspects of their composition, his late works have been compared to impressionist painting.

His novella The Turn of the Screw has garnered a reputation as the most analysed and ambiguous ghost story in the English language and remains his most widely adapted work in other media. He also wrote a number of other highly regarded ghost stories and is considered one of the greatest masters of the field.

James published articles and books of criticism, travel, biography, autobiography, and plays. Born in the United States, James largely relocated to Europe as a young man and eventually settled in England, becoming a British subject in 1915, one year before his death. James was nominated for the Nobel Prize in Literature in 1911, 1912 and 1916.

Life

Early years, 1843–1883

James was born at 2 Washington Place in New York City on 15 April 1843. His parents were Mary Walsh and Henry James Sr. His father was intelligent and steadfastly congenial. He was a lecturer and philosopher who had inherited independent means from his father, an Albany banker and investor. Mary came from a wealthy family long settled in New York City. Her sister Katherine lived with her adult family for an extended period of time. Henry Jr. had three brothers, William, who was one year his senior, and younger brothers Wilkinson (Wilkie) and Robertson. His younger sister was Alice. Both of his parents were of Irish and Scottish descent.

The family first lived in Albany, at 70 N. Pearl St., and then moved to Fourteenth Street in New York City when James was still a young boy. His education was calculated by his father to expose him to many influences, primarily scientific and philosophical; it was described by Percy Lubbock, the editor of his selected letters, as "extraordinarily haphazard and promiscuous." James did not share the usual education in Latin and Greek classics. Between 1855 and 1860, the James' household traveled to London, Paris, Geneva, Boulogne-sur-Mer and Newport, Rhode Island, according to the father's current interests and publishing ventures, retreating to the United States when funds were low. Henry studied primarily with tutors and briefly attended schools while the family traveled in Europe. Their longest stays were in France, where Henry began to feel at home and became fluent in French. He was afflicted with a stutter, which seems to have manifested itself only when he spoke English; in French, he did not stutter.

In 1860 the family returned to Newport. There Henry became a friend of the painter John La Farge, who introduced him to French literature, and in particular, to Balzac. James later called Balzac his "greatest master," and said that he had learned more about the craft of fiction from him than from anyone else.

In the autumn of 1861 Henry received an injury, probably to his back, while fighting a fire. This injury, which resurfaced at times throughout his life, made him unfit for military service in the American Civil War.

In 1864 the James family moved to Boston, Massachusetts to be near William, who had enrolled first in the Lawrence Scientific School at Harvard and then in the medical school. In 1862 Henry attended Harvard Law School, but realised that he was not interested in studying law. He pursued his interest in literature and associated with authors and critics William Dean Howells and Charles Eliot Norton in Boston and Cambridge, formed lifelong friendships with Oliver Wendell Holmes Jr., the future Supreme Court Justice, and with James and Annie Fields, his first professional mentors.

His first published work was a review of a stage performance, "Miss Maggie Mitchell in Fanchon the Cricket," published in 1863. About a year later, A Tragedy of Error, his first short story, was published anonymously. James's first payment was for an appreciation of Sir Walter Scott's novels, written for the North American Review. He wrote fiction and non-fiction pieces for The Nation and Atlantic Monthly, where Fields was editor. In 1871 he published his first novel, Watch and Ward, in serial form in the Atlantic Monthly. The novel was later published in book form in 1878.

During a 14-month trip through Europe in 1869–70 he met Ruskin, Dickens, Matthew Arnold, William Morris, and George Eliot. Rome impressed him profoundly. "Here I am then in the Eternal City," he wrote to his brother William. "At last—for the first time—I live!" He attempted to support himself as a freelance writer in Rome, then secured a position as Paris correspondent for the New York Tribune, through the influence of its editor John Hay. When these efforts failed he returned to New York City. During 1874 and 1875 he published Transatlantic Sketches, A Passionate Pilgrim, and Roderick Hudson. During this early period in his career he was influenced by Nathaniel Hawthorne.

In 1869 he settled in London. There he established relationships with Macmillan and other publishers, who paid for serial installments that they would later publish in book form. The audience for these serialized novels was largely made up of middle-class women, and James struggled to fashion serious literary work within the strictures imposed by editors' and publishers' notions of what was suitable for young women to read. He lived in rented rooms but was able to join gentlemen's clubs that had libraries and where he could entertain male friends. He was introduced to English society by Henry Adams and Charles Milnes Gaskell, the latter introducing him to the Travellers' and the Reform Clubs.

In the fall of 1875 he moved to the Latin Quarter of Paris. Aside from two trips to America, he spent the next three decades—the rest of his life—in Europe. In Paris he met Zola, Alphonse Daudet, Maupassant, Turgenev, and others. He stayed in Paris only a year before moving to London.

In England he met the leading figures of politics and culture. He continued to be a prolific writer, producing The American (1877), The Europeans (1878), a revision of Watch and Ward (1878), French Poets and Novelists (1878), Hawthorne (1879), and several shorter works of fiction. In 1878 Daisy Miller established his fame on both sides of the Atlantic. It drew notice perhaps mostly because it depicted a woman whose behavior is outside the social norms of Europe. He also began his first masterpiece, The Portrait of a Lady, which would appear in 1881.

In 1877 he first visited Wenlock Abbey in Shropshire, home of his friend Charles Milnes Gaskell whom he had met through Henry Adams. He was much inspired by the darkly romantic Abbey and the surrounding countryside, which features in his essay Abbeys and Castles. In particular the gloomy monastic fishponds behind the Abbey are said to have inspired the lake in The Turn of the Screw.

While living in London, James continued to follow the careers of the "French realists", Émile Zola in particular. Their stylistic methods influenced his own work in the years to come. Hawthorne's influence on him faded during this period, replaced by George Eliot and Ivan Turgenev. 1879–1882 saw the publication of The Europeans, Washington Square, Confidence, and The Portrait of a Lady. He visited America in 1882–1883, then returned to London.

The period from 1881 to 1883 was marked by several losses. His mother died in 1881, followed by his father a few months later, and then by his brother Wilkie. Emerson, an old family friend, died in 1882. His friend Turgenev died in 1883.

Middle years, 1884–1897

In 1884 James made another visit to Paris. There he met again with Zola, Daudet, and Goncourt. He had been following the careers of the French "realist" or "naturalist" writers, and was increasingly influenced by them. In 1886, he published The Bostonians and The Princess Casamassima, both influenced by the French writers he'd studied assiduously. Critical reaction and sales were poor. He wrote to Howells that the books had hurt his career rather than helped because they had "reduced the desire, and demand, for my productions to zero". During this time he became friends with Robert Louis Stevenson, John Singer Sargent, Edmund Gosse, George du Maurier, Paul Bourget, and Constance Fenimore Woolson. His third novel from the 1880s was The Tragic Muse. Although he was following the precepts of Zola in his novels of the '80s, their tone and attitude are closer to the fiction of Alphonse Daudet. The lack of critical and financial success for his novels during this period led him to try writing for the theatre. (His dramatic works and his experiences with theatre are discussed below.)

In the last quarter of 1889, he started translating "for pure and copious lucre" Port Tarascon, the third volume of Alphonse Daudet adventures of Tartarin de Tarascon. Serialized in Harper's Monthly Magazine from June 1890, this translation praised as "clever" by The Spectator was published in January 1891 by Sampson Low, Marston, Searle & Rivington.

After the stage failure of Guy Domville in 1895, James was near despair and thoughts of death plagued him. The years spent on dramatic works were not entirely a loss. As he moved into the last phase of his career he found ways to adapt dramatic techniques into the novel form.

In the late 1880s and throughout the 1890s James made several trips through Europe. He spent a long stay in Italy in 1887. In that year the short novel The Aspern Papers and The Reverberator were published.

Late years, 1898–1916

In 1897–1898 he moved to Rye, Sussex, and wrote The Turn of the Screw. 1899–1900 saw the publication of The Awkward Age and The Sacred

Fount. During 1902–1904 he wrote The Ambassadors, The Wings of the Dove, and The Golden Bowl.

In 1904 he revisited America and lectured on Balzac. In 1906–1910 he published The American Scene and edited the "New York Edition", a 24-volume collection of his works. In 1910 his brother William died; Henry had just joined William from an unsuccessful search for relief in Europe on what then turned out to be his (Henry's) last visit to the United States (from summer 1910 to July 1911), and was near him, according to a letter he wrote, when he died.

In 1913 he wrote his autobiographies, A Small Boy and Others, and Notes of a Son and Brother. After the outbreak of the First World War in 1914 he did war work. In 1915 he became a British subject and was awarded the Order of Merit the following year. He died on 28 February 1916, in Chelsea, London. As he requested, his ashes were buried in Cambridge Cemetery in Massachusetts.

Biographers

James regularly rejected suggestions that he should marry, and after settling in London proclaimed himself "a bachelor". F. W. Dupee, in several volumes on the James family, originated the theory that he had been in love with his cousin Mary ("Minnie") Temple, but that a neurotic fear of sex kept him from admitting such affections: "James's invalidism ... was itself the symptom of some fear of or scruple against sexual love on his part." Dupee used an episode from James's memoir A Small Boy and Others, recounting a dream of a Napoleonic image in the Louvre, to exemplify James's romanticism about Europe, a Napoleonic fantasy into which he fled.

Dupee had not had access to the James family papers and worked principally from James's published memoir of his older brother, William, and the limited collection of letters edited by Percy Lubbock, heavily weighted toward James's last years. His account therefore moved directly from James's childhood, when he trailed after his older brother, to elderly invalidism. As more material became available to scholars, including the diaries of contemporaries and hundreds of affectionate and sometimes erotic letters written by James to younger men, the picture of neurotic celibacy gave way to a portrait of a closeted homosexual.

Between 1953 and 1972, Leon Edel authored a major five-volume biography of James, which accessed unpublished letters and documents after Edel gained the permission of James's family. Edel's portrayal of James included the suggestion he was celibate. It was a view first propounded by critic Saul Rosenzweig in 1943. In 1996 Sheldon M. Novick published Henry James: The Young Master, followed by Henry James: The Mature Master (2007). The first book "caused something of an uproar in Jamesian circles" as it challenged the previous received notion of celibacy, a once-familiar paradigm in biographies of homosexuals when direct evidence was non-existent. Novick also criticised Edel for following the discounted Freudian interpretation of homosexuality "as a kind of failure." The difference of opinion erupted in a series of exchanges between Edel and Novick which were published by the online magazine Slate, with the latter arguing that even the suggestion of celibacy went against James's own injunction "live!"—not "fantasize!"

A letter James wrote in old age to Hugh Walpole has been cited as an explicit statement of this. Walpole confessed to him of indulging in "high jinks", and James wrote a reply endorsing it: "We must know, as much as possible, in our beautiful art, yours & mine, what we are talking about — & the only way to know it is to have lived & loved & cursed & floundered & enjoyed & suffered — I don't think I regret a single 'excess' of my responsive youth".

The interpretation of James as living a less austere emotional life has been subsequently explored by other scholars. The often intense politics of Jamesian scholarship has also been the subject of studies. Author Colm Tóibín has said that Eve Kosofsky Sedgwick's Epistemology of the Closet made a landmark difference to Jamesian scholarship by arguing that he be read as a homosexual writer whose desire to keep his sexuality a secret shaped his layered style and dramatic artistry. According to Tóibín such a reading "removed James from the realm of dead white males who wrote about posh people. He became our contemporary."

James's letters to expatriate American sculptor Hendrik Christian Andersen have attracted particular attention. James met the 27-year-old Andersen in Rome in 1899, when James was 56, and wrote letters to Andersen that are intensely emotional: "I hold you, dearest boy, in my innermost love, & count on your feeling me—in every throb of your soul". In a letter of 6 May 1904, to his brother William, James referred to himself as "always your hopelessly celibate even though sexagenarian Henry". How accurate that description might have been is the subject of contention among James's biographers,   but the letters to Andersen were occasionally quasi-erotic: "I put, my dear boy, my arm around you, & feel the pulsation, thereby, as it were, of our excellent future & your admirable endowment." To his homosexual friend Howard Sturgis, James could write: "I repeat, almost to indiscretion, that I could live with you. Meanwhile I can only try to live without you."

His numerous letters to the many young gay men among his close male friends are more forthcoming. In a letter to Howard Sturgis, following a long visit, James refers jocularly to their "happy little congress of two" and in letters to Hugh Walpole he pursues convoluted jokes and puns about their relationship, referring to himself as an elephant who "paws you oh so benevolently" and winds about Walpole his "well meaning old trunk". His letters to Walter Berry printed by the Black Sun Press have long been celebrated for their lightly veiled eroticism.

He corresponded in almost equally extravagant language with his many female friends, writing, for example, to fellow novelist Lucy Clifford: "Dearest Lucy! What shall I say? when I love you so very, very much, and see you nine times for once that I see Others! Therefore I think that—if you want it made clear to the meanest intelligence—I love you more than I love Others." To his New York friend Mary Cadwalader Jones: "Dearest Mary Cadwalader. I yearn over you, but I yearn in vain; & your long silence really breaks my heart, mystifies, depresses, almost alarms me, to the point even of making me wonder if poor unconscious & doting old Célimare [Jones's pet name for James] has 'done' anything, in some dark somnambulism of the spirit, which has ... given you a bad moment, or a wrong impression, or a 'colourable pretext' ... However these things may be, he loves you as tenderly as ever;

nothing, to the end of time, will ever detach him from you, & he remembers those Eleventh St. matutinal intimes hours, those telephonic matinées, as the most romantic of his life ..." His long friendship with American novelist Constance Fenimore Woolson, in whose house he lived for a number of weeks in Italy in 1887, and his shock and grief over her suicide in 1894, are discussed in detail in Edel's biography and play a central role in a study by Lyndall Gordon. (Edel conjectured that Woolson was in love with James and killed herself in part because of his coldness, but Woolson's biographers have objected to Edel's account.)

Works

Style and themes

James is one of the major figures of trans-Atlantic literature. His works frequently juxtapose characters from the Old World (Europe), embodying a feudal civilisation that is beautiful, often corrupt, and alluring, and from the New World (United States), where people are often brash, open, and assertive and embody the virtues—freedom and a more highly evolved moral character—of the new American society. James explores this clash of personalities and cultures, in stories of personal relationships in which power is exercised well or badly. His protagonists were often young American women facing oppression or abuse, and as his secretary Theodora Bosanquet remarked in her monograph Henry James at Work:

> When he walked out of the refuge of his study and into the world and looked around him, he saw a place of torment, where creatures of prey perpetually thrust their claws into the quivering flesh of doomed, defenseless children of light ... His novels are a repeated exposure of this wickedness, a reiterated and passionate plea for the fullest freedom of development, unimperiled by reckless and barbarous stupidity.

Critics have jokingly described three phases in the development of James's prose: "James I, James II, and The Old Pretender." He wrote short stories and plays. Finally, in his third and last period he returned to the long, serialised novel. Beginning in the second period, but most noticeably in the third, he increasingly abandoned direct statement in favour of frequent

289

double negatives, and complex descriptive imagery. Single paragraphs began to run for page after page, in which an initial noun would be succeeded by pronouns surrounded by clouds of adjectives and prepositional clauses, far from their original referents, and verbs would be deferred and then preceded by a series of adverbs. The overall effect could be a vivid evocation of a scene as perceived by a sensitive observer. It has been debated whether this change of style was engendered by James's shifting from writing to dictating to a typist, a change made during the composition of What Maisie Knew.

In its intense focus on the consciousness of his major characters, James's later work foreshadows extensive developments in 20th century fiction. Indeed, he might have influenced stream-of-consciousness writers such as Virginia Woolf, who not only read some of his novels but also wrote essays about them. Both contemporary and modern readers have found the late style difficult and unnecessary; his friend Edith Wharton, who admired him greatly, said that there were passages in his work that were all but incomprehensible. James was harshly portrayed by H. G. Wells as a hippopotamus laboriously attempting to pick up a pea that had got into a corner of its cage. The "late James" style was ably parodied by Max Beerbohm in "The Mote in the Middle Distance".

More important for his work overall may have been his position as an expatriate, and in other ways an outsider, living in Europe. While he came from middle-class and provincial beginnings (seen from the perspective of European polite society) he worked very hard to gain access to all levels of society, and the settings of his fiction range from working class to aristocratic, and often describe the efforts of middle-class Americans to make their way in European capitals. He confessed he got some of his best story ideas from gossip at the dinner table or at country house weekends. He worked for a living, however, and lacked the experiences of select schools, university, and army service, the common bonds of masculine society. He was furthermore a man whose tastes and interests were, according to the prevailing standards of Victorian era Anglo-American culture, rather feminine, and who was shadowed by the cloud of prejudice that then and later accompanied suspicions of his homosexuality. Edmund Wilson famously compared James's objectivity to Shakespeare's:

One would be in a position to appreciate James better if one compared him with the dramatists of the seventeenth century—Racine and Molière, whom he resembles in form as well as in point of view, and even Shakespeare, when allowances are made for the most extreme differences in subject and form. These poets are not, like Dickens and Hardy, writers of melodrama—either humorous or pessimistic, nor secretaries of society like Balzac, nor prophets like Tolstoy: they are occupied simply with the presentation of conflicts of moral character, which they do not concern themselves about softening or averting. They do not indict society for these situations: they regard them as universal and inevitable. They do not even blame God for allowing them: they accept them as the conditions of life.

It is also possible to see many of James's stories as psychological thought-experiments. In his preface to the New York edition of The American he describes the development of the story in his mind as exactly such: the "situation" of an American, "some robust but insidiously beguiled and betrayed, some cruelly wronged, compatriot..." with the focus of the story being on the response of this wronged man. The Portrait of a Lady may be an experiment to see what happens when an idealistic young woman suddenly becomes very rich. In many of his tales, characters seem to exemplify alternative futures and possibilities, as most markedly in "The Jolly Corner", in which the protagonist and a ghost-doppelganger live alternative American and European lives; and in others, like The Ambassadors, an older James seems fondly to regard his own younger self facing a crucial moment.

Major novels

The first period of James's fiction, usually considered to have culminated in The Portrait of a Lady, concentrated on the contrast between Europe and America. The style of these novels is generally straightforward and, though personally characteristic, well within the norms of 19th-century fiction. Roderick Hudson (1875) is a Künstlerroman that traces the development of the title character, an extremely talented sculptor. Although the book shows some signs of immaturity—this was James's first serious attempt at a full-length novel—it has attracted favourable comment due to the vivid realisation of the three major characters: Roderick Hudson, superbly gifted but unstable and unreliable; Rowland Mallet, Roderick's limited but much more mature friend and patron; and Christina Light, one of James's most enchanting and maddening femmes fatales. The pair of Hudson and Mallet has been seen as representing the two sides of James's own nature: the wildly imaginative artist and the brooding conscientious mentor.

In The Portrait of a Lady (1881) James concluded the first phase of his career with a novel that remains his most popular piece of long fiction. The story is of a spirited young American woman, Isabel Archer, who "affronts her destiny" and finds it overwhelming. She inherits a large amount of money and subsequently becomes the victim of Machiavellian scheming by two American expatriates. The narrative is set mainly in Europe, especially in England and Italy. Generally regarded as the masterpiece of his early phase, The Portrait of a Lady is described as a psychological novel, exploring the minds of his characters, and almost a work of social science, exploring the differences between Europeans and Americans, the old and the new worlds.

The second period of James's career, which extends from the publication of The Portrait of a Lady through the end of the nineteenth century, features less popular novels including The Princess Casamassima, published serially in The Atlantic Monthly in 1885–1886, and The Bostonians, published serially in The Century Magazine during the same period. This period also featured James's celebrated Gothic novella, The Turn of the Screw.

The third period of James's career reached its most significant achievement in three novels published just around the start of the 20th century: The Wings of the Dove (1902), The Ambassadors (1903), and The Golden Bowl (1904). Critic F. O. Matthiessen called this "trilogy" James's major phase, and these novels have certainly received intense critical study. It was the second-written of the books, The Wings of the Dove (1902) that was the first published because it attracted no serialization. This novel tells the story of Milly Theale, an American heiress stricken with a serious disease, and her impact on the people around her. Some of these people befriend Milly with honourable motives, while others are more self-interested. James stated in his autobiographical books that Milly was based on Minny Temple, his beloved cousin who died at an early age of tuberculosis. He said that he attempted in the novel to wrap her memory in the "beauty and dignity of art".

Shorter narratives

James was particularly interested in what he called the "beautiful and blest nouvelle", or the longer form of short narrative. Still, he produced a number of very short stories in which he achieved notable compression of sometimes complex subjects. The following narratives are representative of James's achievement in the shorter forms of fiction.

- "A Tragedy of Error" (1864), short story
- "The Story of a Year" (1865), short story
- A Passionate Pilgrim (1871), novella
- Madame de Mauves (1874), novella
- Daisy Miller (1878), novella
- The Aspern Papers (1888), novella
- The Lesson of the Master (1888), novella
- The Pupil (1891), short story
- "The Figure in the Carpet" (1896), short story
- The Beast in the Jungle (1903), novella
- An International Episode (1878)
- Picture and Text
- Four Meetings (1885)
- A London Life, and Other Tales (1889)
- The Spoils of Poynton (1896)

- Embarrassments (1896)

- The Two Magics: The Turn of the Screw, Covering End (1898)

- A Little Tour of France (1900)

- The Sacred Fount (1901)

- Views and Reviews (1908)

- The Wings of the Dove, Volume I (1902)

- The Wings of the Dove, Volume II (1909)

- The Finer Grain (1910)

- The Outcry (1911)

- Lady Barbarina: The Siege of London, An International Episode and Other Tales (1922)

- The Birthplace (1922)

Plays

At several points in his career James wrote plays, beginning with one-act plays written for periodicals in 1869 and 1871 and a dramatisation of his popular novella Daisy Miller in 1882. From 1890 to 1892, having received a bequest that freed him from magazine publication, he made a strenuous effort to succeed on the London stage, writing a half-dozen plays of which only one, a dramatisation of his novel The American, was produced. This play was performed for several years by a touring repertory company and had a respectable run in London, but did not earn very much money for James. His other plays written at this time were not produced.

In 1893, however, he responded to a request from actor-manager George Alexander for a serious play for the opening of his renovated St. James's Theatre, and wrote a long drama, Guy Domville, which Alexander produced. There was a noisy uproar on the opening night, 5 January 1895, with hissing from the gallery when James took his bow after the final curtain, and the author was upset. The play received moderately good reviews and had a modest run of four weeks before being taken off to make way for Oscar Wilde's The Importance of Being Earnest, which Alexander thought would have better prospects for the coming season.

After the stresses and disappointment of these efforts James insisted that he would write no more for the theatre, but within weeks had agreed to write a curtain-raiser for Ellen Terry. This became the one-act "Summersoft", which he later rewrote into a short story, "Covering End", and then expanded into a full-length play, The High Bid, which had a brief run in London in 1907, when James made another concerted effort to write for the stage. He wrote three new plays, two of which were in production when the death of Edward VII on 6 May 1910 plunged London into mourning and theatres closed. Discouraged by failing health and the stresses of theatrical work, James did not renew his efforts in the theatre, but recycled his plays as successful novels. The Outcry was a best-seller in the United States when it was published in 1911. During the years 1890–1893 when he was most engaged with the theatre, James wrote a good deal of theatrical criticism and assisted Elizabeth Robins and others in translating and producing Henrik Ibsen for the first time in London.

Leon Edel argued in his psychoanalytic biography that James was traumatised by the opening night uproar that greeted Guy Domville, and that it plunged him into a prolonged depression. The successful later novels, in Edel's view, were the result of a kind of self-analysis, expressed in fiction, which partly freed him from his fears. Other biographers and scholars have not accepted this account, however; the more common view being that of F.O. Matthiessen, who wrote: "Instead of being crushed by the collapse of his hopes [for the theatre]... he felt a resurgence of new energy."

Non-fiction

Beyond his fiction, James was one of the more important literary critics in the history of the novel. In his classic essay The Art of Fiction (1884), he argued against rigid prescriptions on the novelist's choice of subject and method of treatment. He maintained that the widest possible freedom in content and approach would help ensure narrative fiction's continued vitality.

James wrote many valuable critical articles on other novelists; typical is his book-length study of Nathaniel Hawthorne, which has been the subject of critical debate. Richard Brodhead has suggested that the study was emblematic of James's struggle with Hawthorne's influence, and constituted an effort to place the elder writer "at a disadvantage." Gordon Fraser, meanwhile, has suggested that the study was part of a more commercial effort by James to introduce himself to British readers as Hawthorne's natural successor.

When James assembled the New York Edition of his fiction in his final years, he wrote a series of prefaces that subjected his own work to searching, occasionally harsh criticism.

At 22 James wrote The Noble School of Fiction for The Nation's first issue in 1865. He would write, in all, over 200 essays and book, art, and theatre reviews for the magazine.

For most of his life James harboured ambitions for success as a playwright. He converted his novel The American into a play that enjoyed modest returns in the early 1890s. In all he wrote about a dozen plays, most of which went unproduced. His costume drama Guy Domville failed disastrously on its opening night in 1895. James then largely abandoned his efforts to conquer the stage and returned to his fiction. In his Notebooks he maintained that his theatrical experiment benefited his novels and tales by helping him dramatise his characters' thoughts and emotions. James produced a small but valuable amount of theatrical criticism, including perceptive appreciations of Henrik Ibsen.

With his wide-ranging artistic interests, James occasionally wrote on the visual arts. Perhaps his most valuable contribution was his favourable assessment of fellow expatriate John Singer Sargent, a painter whose critical status has improved markedly in recent decades. James also wrote sometimes charming, sometimes brooding articles about various places he visited and lived in. His most famous books of travel writing include Italian Hours (an example of the charming approach) and The American Scene (most definitely on the brooding side).

James was one of the great letter-writers of any era. More than ten thousand of his personal letters are extant, and over three thousand have been published in a large number of collections. A complete edition of James's letters began publication in 2006, edited by Pierre Walker and Greg Zacharias. As of 2014, eight volumes have been published, covering the period from 1855 to 1880. James's correspondents included celebrated contemporaries like Robert Louis Stevenson, Edith Wharton and Joseph Conrad, along with many others in his wide circle of friends and acquaintances. The letters range from the "mere twaddle of graciousness" to serious discussions of artistic, social and personal issues.

Very late in life James began a series of autobiographical works: A Small Boy and Others, Notes of a Son and Brother, and the unfinished The Middle Years. These books portray the development of a classic observer who was passionately interested in artistic creation but was somewhat reticent about participating fully in the life around him.

Reception

Criticism, biographies and fictional treatments

James's work has remained steadily popular with the limited audience of educated readers to whom he spoke during his lifetime, and has remained firmly in the canon, but, after his death, some American critics, such as Van Wyck Brooks, expressed hostility towards James for his long expatriation and eventual naturalisation as a British subject. Other critics such as E. M. Forster complained about what they saw as James's squeamishness in the treatment of sex and other possibly controversial material, or dismissed his late style as difficult and obscure, relying heavily on extremely long sentences and excessively latinate language. Similarly Oscar Wilde criticised him for writing "fiction as if it were a painful duty". Vernon Parrington, composing a canon of American literature, condemned James for having cut himself off from America. Jorge Luis Borges wrote about him, "Despite the scruples and delicate complexities of James, his work suffers from a major defect: the absence of life." And Virginia Woolf, writing to Lytton Strachey, asked, "Please tell me what you find in Henry James. ... we have his works here, and

I read, and I can't find anything but faintly tinged rose water, urbane and sleek, but vulgar and pale as Walter Lamb. Is there really any sense in it?" The novelist W. Somerset Maugham wrote, "He did not know the English as an Englishman instinctively knows them and so his English characters never to my mind quite ring true," and argued "The great novelists, even in seclusion, have lived life passionately. Henry James was content to observe it from a window." Maugham nevertheless wrote, "The fact remains that those last novels of his, notwithstanding their unreality, make all other novels, except the very best, unreadable." Colm Tóibín observed that James "never really wrote about the English very well. His English characters don't work for me."

Despite these criticisms, James is now valued for his psychological and moral realism, his masterful creation of character, his low-key but playful humour, and his assured command of the language. In his 1983 book, The Novels of Henry James, Edward Wagenknecht offers an assessment that echoes Theodora Bosanquet's:

> "To be completely great," Henry James wrote in an early review, "a work of art must lift up the heart," and his own novels do this to an outstanding degree ... More than sixty years after his death, the great novelist who sometimes professed to have no opinions stands foursquare in the great Christian humanistic and democratic tradition. The men and women who, at the height of World War II, raided the secondhand shops for his out-of-print books knew what they were about. For no writer ever raised a braver banner to which all who love freedom might adhere.

William Dean Howells saw James as a representative of a new realist school of literary art which broke with the English romantic tradition epitomised by the works of Charles Dickens and William Makepeace Thackeray. Howells wrote that realism found "its chief exemplar in Mr. James... A novelist he is not, after the old fashion, or after any fashion but his own." F.R. Leavis championed Henry James as a novelist of "established pre-eminence" in The Great Tradition (1948), asserting that The Portrait of a Lady and The Bostonians were "the two most brilliant novels in the language." James is now prized as a master of point of view who moved literary fiction forward by insisting in showing, not telling, his stories to the reader. (Source: Wikipedia)

NOTABLE WORKS

NOVELS

Watch and Ward (1871)

Roderick Hudson (1875)

The American (1877)

The Europeans (1878)

Confidence (1879)

Washington Square (1880)

The Portrait of a Lady (1881)

The Bostonians (1886)

The Princess Casamassima (1886)

The Reverberator (1888)

The Tragic Muse (1890)

The Other House (1896)

The Spoils of Poynton (1897)

What Maisie Knew (1897)

The Awkward Age (1899)

The Sacred Fount (1901)

The Wings of the Dove (1902)

The Ambassadors (1903)

The Golden Bowl (1904)

The Whole Family (collaborative novel with eleven other authors, 1908)

The Outcry (1911)

The Ivory Tower (unfinished, published posthumously 1917)

The Sense of the Past (unfinished, published posthumously 1917)

SHORT STORIES AND NOVELLAS

A Tragedy of Error (1864)

The Story of a Year (1865)

A Landscape Painter (1866)

A Day of Days (1866)

My Friend Bingham (1867)

Poor Richard (1867)

The Story of a Masterpiece (1868)

A Most Extraordinary Case (1868)

A Problem (1868)

De Grey: A Romance (1868)

Osborne's Revenge (1868)

The Romance of Certain Old Clothes (1868)

A Light Man (1869)

Gabrielle de Bergerac (1869)

Travelling Companions (1870)

A Passionate Pilgrim (1871)

At Isella (1871)

Master Eustace (1871)

Guest's Confession (1872)

The Madonna of the Future (1873)

The Sweetheart of M. Briseux (1873)

The Last of the Valerii (1874)

Madame de Mauves (1874)

Adina (1874)

Professor Fargo (1874)

Eugene Pickering (1874)

Benvolio (1875)

Crawford's Consistency (1876)

The Ghostly Rental (1876)

Four Meetings (1877)

Rose-Agathe (1878, as Théodolinde)

Daisy Miller (1878)

Longstaff's Marriage (1878)

An International Episode (1878)

The Pension Beaurepas (1879)

A Diary of a Man of Fifty (1879)

A Bundle of Letters (1879)

The Point of View (1882)

The Siege of London (1883)

Impressions of a Cousin (1883)

Lady Barberina (1884)

Pandora (1884)

The Author of Beltraffio (1884)

Georgina's Reasons (1884)

A New England Winter (1884)

The Path of Duty (1884)

Mrs. Temperly (1887)

Louisa Pallant (1888)

The Aspern Papers (1888)

The Liar (1888)

The Modern Warning (1888, originally published as The Two Countries)

A London Life (1888)

The Patagonia (1888)

The Lesson of the Master (1888)

The Solution (1888)

The Pupil (1891)

Brooksmith (1891)

The Marriages (1891)

The Chaperon (1891)

Sir Edmund Orme (1891)

Nona Vincent (1892)

The Real Thing (1892)

The Private Life (1892)

Lord Beaupré (1892)

The Visits (1892)

Sir Dominick Ferrand (1892)

Greville Fane (1892)

Collaboration (1892)

Owen Wingrave (1892)

The Wheel of Time (1892)

The Middle Years (1893)

The Death of the Lion (1894)

The Coxon Fund (1894)

The Next Time (1895)

Glasses (1896)

The Altar of the Dead (1895)

The Figure in the Carpet (1896)

The Way It Came (1896, also published as The Friends of the Friends)

The Turn of the Screw (1898)

Covering End (1898)

In the Cage (1898)

John Delavoy (1898)

The Given Case (1898)

Europe (1899)

The Great Condition (1899)

The Real Right Thing (1899)

Paste (1899)

The Great Good Place (1900)

Maud-Evelyn (1900)

Miss Gunton of Poughkeepsie (1900)

The Tree of Knowledge (1900)

The Abasement of the Northmores (1900)

The Third Person (1900)

The Special Type (1900)

The Tone of Time (1900)

Broken Wings (1900)

The Two Faces (1900)

Mrs. Medwin (1901)

The Beldonald Holbein (1901)

The Story in It (1902)

Flickerbridge (1902)

The Birthplace (1903)

The Beast in the Jungle (1903)

The Papers (1903)

Fordham Castle (1904)

Julia Bride (1908)

The Jolly Corner (1908)

The Velvet Glove (1909)

Mora Montravers (1909)

Crapy Cornelia (1909)

The Bench of Desolation (1909)

A Round of Visits (1910)

OTHER

Transatlantic Sketches (1875)

French Poets and Novelists (1878)

Hawthorne (1879)

Portraits of Places (1883)

A Little Tour in France (1884)

Partial Portraits (1888)

Essays in London and Elsewhere (1893)

Picture and Text (1893)

Terminations (1893)

Theatricals (1894)

Theatricals: Second Series (1895)

Guy Domville (1895)

The Soft Side (1900)

William Wetmore Story and His Friends (1903)

The Better Sort (1903)

English Hours (1905)

The Question of our Speech; The Lesson of Balzac. Two Lectures (1905)

The American Scene (1907)

Views and Reviews (1908)

Italian Hours (1909)

A Small Boy and Others (1913)

Notes on Novelists (1914)

Notes of a Son and Brother (1914)

Within the Rim (1918)

Travelling Companions (1919)

Notebooks (various, published posthumously)

The Middle Years (unfinished, published posthumously 1917)

A Most Unholy Trade (1925, published posthumously)

The Art of the Novel : Critical Prefaces (1934)

CPSIA information can be obtained
at www.ICGtesting.com
Printed in the USA
LVHW042300050920
665177LV00005B/668